RANDOM HOUSE

LARGE PRINT

Little
Big
Love

Little Big Love

Katy Regan

R A N D O M   H O U S E
LARGE PRINT

Copyright © 2018 by Katy Regan

All rights reserved.

Published in the United States of America by Random House Large Print in association with Berkley, an imprint of Penguin Random House LLC, New York.

Cover design and illustration by Allison Colpoys
Title page art: watercolor waves © Shizayats/
Shutterstock

The Library of Congress has established a Cataloging-in-Publication record for this title.

ISBN: 978-0-5256-3189-7

www.penguinrandomhouse.com/large-print-format-books

FIRST LARGE PRINT EDITION

Printed in the United States of America

10 9 8 7 6 5 4 3 2 1

This Large Print edition published in accord with the standards of the N.A.V.H.

For Yoshi Sato,
who will always be in my thoughts

Little
Big
Love

New Year's Eve 2015

**Dear Liam
(maybe one day I will call you Dad but
not yet),**

**This is your son, Zac. I am writing
this letter to give you an opportunity. I
know you did a runner just before I was
born and weren't interested in being my
dad, but how could you decide if we'd
never met? I didn't know I wanted to be
Teagan's friend until she moved onto the
same estate as me. Luckily she was nice,
but she could have been really annoying.
I don't want to be offensive, but I have
been really angry with you since the day
my mum and me went on the promenade
train in Cleethorpes when I was three
and my mum told me you existed. I don't**

know why you didn't want to see me or even phone me if I was your child. You have never even sent me a birthday card. (In case you don't know, my birthday is May 25th.) What kind of dad doesn't send their kid a birthday card?

So I am giving you the opportunity to come to my party when I'm eleven. It's five months away so lots of time to organize it. If you have any more children, you could bring them, as long as they like Toby Carvery because that's where I'm going.

BE WARNED: my mum is really mad with you and my nan says you make her sick, but I am willing to give you a chance.

My grandad says, "Don't knock it till you've tried it," and I agree. For example, I never used to like mushrooms, but now I would have them on my death row dinner. I think if you met me you'd change your mind too.

Please write back.

From Zac

P.S. Just so you know, you can only get two slices of meat at Toby Carvery, but you can have as many vegetables and Yorkshire puddings as you want.

1

Zac

**Fact: There are only three animals
in the world that have a blue tongue:
a chow chow dog, a blue-tongued
lizard, and a black bear.**

So I'd already written to my dad on New Year's
Eve, but deciding to look for him only started,
really, the night of my mum's Date from Hell. She
kicked everything off that spring; she made everything start happening that would change our lives
for the better and make them brilliant. She says it
was me that did it, but it wasn't, it was her. (Even
though she was drunk, it was still her.) That's the
only good thing about wine, I suppose. It can
sometimes help you to tell the truth.

Grimsby, early February 2016

Sam Bale's dad was walking across our estate in
the snow. It was just him with his big furry hood

up. He could have been trekking across the North Pole.

"How many points would you give him, then?" I said.

"What, Sam's dad?" said Teagan. "None. No way. He's been in prison for fighting people, he has."

"He's rich, though," I said.

"How do you know?"

"He's got a bath that's a Jacuzzi—and he's got a gold car. Imagine how much that would cost. A gold car!"

Me and Teagan were high up, leaning out of her bedroom window playing the dad game. Teagan's my best friend. She lives on our estate but in one of the high blocks on the seventh floor, where you can see the whole of Grimsby, even to the sea. We live in a boring old maisonette with only two floors, but it's nicer than Teagan's inside because my mum can work, whereas Teagan's mum's got this disease where she's tired all the time, so if you weigh everything up, it comes out equal.

I was round at hers for a sleepover because my mum was on a date. I don't usually go round to people's houses for sleepovers on a school night, but then, my mum doesn't usually go on dates. This was her first in a year and a half. Before that, she was going out with Jason, but they split up because there was no chemistry.

The dad game is something me and Teagan

made up after Teagan's dad left her mum—and Teagan, and her sister, Tia—for Gayle from Ladbrokes. Since then, she hasn't seen her dad much. Teagan's dead angry with her dad and thinks she'll have to get a new one eventually. My dad did a runner just before I was born, but Mum's always said we had a lucky escape because he was a waste of space. So I'd like to get a proper dad too someday, and me and Teagan thought it would be good to work out what sort of dad would be best.

Our game's called Top Trumps for Dads. It's just like normal Top Trumps, except we give scores based on how good a dad we think someone would be: how kind, strict, or funny they are; if they're rich and could take us on adventures; if they'd be able to stick up for us in a fight—and not a fight like Sam Bale's dad's been in, but a proper one, where you're fighting for something worth it, not just for the sake of it.

Teagan writes down scores for the dads in our special file. So far, Jacob Wilmore's dad scores the highest. He's got a six-pack and a Porsche and he's just a really nice man. He used to play football professionally and now he sometimes coaches the under-elevens. I wish I was good at football, just so I could see him more. We've finished doing all the dads at school now, though, so we're scoring others we know, like Sam Bale's.

"He might be rich, Zac, but he's still been in prison," said Teagan. "There's no point having a dad in prison all the time; you'd never get to see him."

"Yeah, and when you went to visit him, you wouldn't be able to touch him and you'd have to be careful because he might be in with all the murderers."

"And he'd have to wear an orange suit," said Teagan. "I've seen it on **Coronation Street**."

As well as living on the Harlequin Estate with me, Teagan's at the same school as me but in a different class, so on Mondays and Thursdays, when I'm not at Nan and Grandad's, we sometimes play together after tea. We like playing "the Olympics," where Teagan does her gymnastics on the bars (three metal bars, basically, all of different heights, in the middle of our estate) and I do the commentary like on the Olympics. **This is Teagan O'Brien on the bars, for the United Kingdom!** When it's cold or rainy, though, we like stopping in and leaning out of Teagan's bedroom window and looking at all of Grimsby like we own it. Our estate is at the edge of the town near the sea (it's not actually the sea, it's the Humber estuary, but it goes into the North Sea). But don't go thinking there's a beach like there is at Cleethorpes—it's not like that. If you look at where the sea meets the town in Grimsby, from high up here in Teagan's flat, you can just see loads of cranes and boat masts, with the Dock Tower in the middle, poking out like a red rocket. The line where the water meets the town goes in and out where all the different trawlers have their parking spots. Our town is a fishing port. It used to be the greatest fishing port in the world back when my great-grandad was a fisherman, in the glory days. But then there were the Cod Wars, where Iceland and our country rowed about who was allowed to fish where, and that ruined everything basically.

"Hey, if you squint your eyes and look at all the snow," I said, closing one eye, the way Mr. Singh from Costcutter does when you go in there and he pretends to be asleep, "you could be in Canada."

"Jacob Wilmore's been to Canada. He told me it was boring," said Teagan.

"I bet it's not. I bet it's amazing." The snow was amazing here too, if you looked closely. It wasn't white; it was loads of different colors. That's because it's actually frozen droplets of water reflecting the light. I told Teagan this. "It's the same for polar bears," I said. "Their fur's not white either, it's transparent; it just reflects the light so it looks all dazzling. Underneath, their skin is black and under that are eleven centimeters of fat."

"No way. **Eleven** centimeters?"

"Well, you'd need eleven centimeters of fat if you lived in the Arctic."

"It's like living in the Arctic in this house," said Teagan. "And where's my eleven centimeters?"

She leaned farther out of the window. She makes me nervous when she does that, because she's so light, she could flutter away like a crisp packet. Teagan might be the smallest in our year but she's not scared of anything, ever. I'm scared most of the time. Sometimes it feels like our bodies have been swapped around.

I leaned a little bit farther out too. The cold was lovely, it crept right through your clothes, and the moon was orange, with this sad, kind face.

"I wonder what my mum's doing now," I said.

"Why, where is she?" asked Teagan, flicking her hair round. Teagan's hair is her best feature, like mine is my eyes. It's chocolate colored and wavy.

"On a date," I said.

"What, with a man?"

"No, a chimpanzee," I said and Teagan laughed. She's got this mad, crazy laugh; you can't help joining in. I hadn't said anything to Teagan because I didn't want to jinx it, but I was really worried about my mum's date. I wanted it to go well so badly that I'd prayed on **Factblaster** before I came out. Grandad always gets me a present just from him at Christmas, and last Christmas it was **Factblaster. Every fact you've ever wanted to know, answered!**, it says on the front. It's totally awesome. I think it's got lucky powers. I love my facts like I love my cooking. Out of my class, I'm probably second best at facts after Jacob, who knows literally everything, but that's because his dad works on the rigs so can afford to take him all over.

My mum's date was with a man called Dom. He

knows my aunty Laura (she's not my real aunty; she's my mum's best friend—I just call her aunty) and he's got a sports car. My mum really needs a boyfriend. She loves me to bits, but we need a man in the house and, also, I liked it better when she was going out with Jason. I kind of miss him. Maybe I even loved him.

Teagan sighed. "Rather her than me," she said.

"What do you mean?"

"I mean, rather your mum than me going on a date. I'm not going on any dates when I'm older. I'm not going to have a husband or even a boyfriend."

"Why not?" I said.

"'Cause men are stupid idiots, that's why. You won't be, obviously. But that's because you're different."

I wondered what she meant by different. People don't like different, in my experience. They don't like fat, or really thin; they don't like people who are poor. But then, they don't like too rich either, or big noses, ADHD, smelliness, sticky-out ears, funny teeth, glasses, people with one arm, weird names, or weird parents. They don't like anyone who stands out, basically. I don't think any of these things matter—it's the person inside that counts. But not everyone thinks like that, do they? That's just not real life.

The windows in the flats across the way were glowing orange. The way they were lit up, it made the flats look so cozy and I thought, that's how Teagan's flat must look from there too, but also how it was a trick, because you couldn't see how scruffy her bedroom was on the inside, you couldn't see the black damp in the corners, like you can't see the black skin underneath a polar bear's fur. You couldn't see there was no dad there or that her mum was in bed because she'd got the tired disease. You can't see the truth just by looking on the surface. That's something else I'd worked out.

I was thinking about all this when, all of a sudden, Teagan took a huge lungful of air. **"Bogeys!"** she shouted, so loud I bet it hurt her throat. I just saw Sam Bale's dad look up before she tugged at my arm and yanked me down and then we were sitting with our backs against the wall, cracking up for ages. I laugh loads when I'm with Teagan; it makes me forget the bad stuff.

"Do you want some sweets?" she said, suddenly sliding onto her belly and under her bed. Teagan's so little you could slide her anywhere. You could hide her like Anne Frank if you had to. She wriggled under her bed and brought out a plastic orange bucket. It was full of sweets from Halloween. "Have what you want."

"Really?"

"Yeah, 'course."

I couldn't believe she'd saved them. Halloween had been four months ago!

I chose a mini Mars Bar, a Drumstick lolly, and a Maoam.

"Is that all?" she said. She couldn't talk properly due to the humongous gobstopper in her mouth. "You can have more. Go on, take more."

Teagan's the only person my age in the world I can eat in front of without going red. She's the only person my age I can talk to about food too— about what I baked with my nan or what recipe I made up. She's the only person my age who knows I want to be a chef like my uncle Jamie too. She never looks at me funny. Not like that. Not like most people look at me. When she talks to me, she just looks in my eyes. Sometimes I wonder if she's even noticed.

We sat on the bed. It was quiet except for the rustling of our sweet wrappers and the room was full of the moon, making Teagan's tongue look blue from the gobstopper. Then suddenly, there was shouting.

"Why?" a lady was going. "Why? Why? **Why?**" Teagan looked at me and we burst out laughing. "Wanker!" the woman shouted and we cracked up even more. We couldn't get to the window fast enough to see what was going on, which was that there were two people, a man and a woman, having an actual scrap in the snow! The man was skidding around trying to duck from the lady, who was hitting him over the head with her handbag.

She was shouting but crying at the same time. She had blondish/brownish hair the same style as my mum's and she was wearing a turquoise coat.

I recognized that coat.

"Oh. My. God," Teagan said slowly. She wasn't laughing anymore and neither was I. "Isn't that your . . . ?"

I can tell you now, no ten-year-old kid wants to see their mum having a scrap in the snow, whacking someone over the head with her handbag. It makes the mum look mental and it's not very ladylike. But that was exactly what was happening. I watched as my mum stomped off back home in the snow, and then I sat on Teagan's bed for a bit, deciding what to do. I went home in the end. Teagan understood because she knows what it's like to be worried about your mum.

The back door was open when I got there, so I just walked in. Mum was frying sausages in the kitchen. She'd got changed into her PJs, but she still had her makeup on, plus the dangly earrings she'd bought from Matalan especially for the date. I wished she hadn't bothered.

"Zac! Jesus . . . Bloody hell . . ." She jumped out of her skin when she saw me. It might have been funny, but it wasn't, if you know what I mean. "Why aren't you at Teagan's?" she said, wiping under her eyes with her fingers. Her eyes weren't looking at me straight and she had black tears down her cheeks.

"She felt sick," I said. Lying makes me nervous, but I didn't have a choice. She asked me for a cuddle and I gave her one. She smelled really strong of the pub.

"What's wrong?" I asked as she hugged me, really tight. It hurt a bit, but I didn't want to say. "What happened on the date—it went wrong, didn't it?"

But she ignored me. She just started putting the sausages on the slices of bread she had on the side. They had big clumps of butter on and even bigger holes. "Do you want one of these, darlin'? Mummy's special sausage sandwich?"

Her voice was funny—I didn't like it—and she wasn't cutting the sandwich all neat like she normally does; she was making a mess.

"Why're you acting strange?"

"Strange? I'm not acting strange," she said, but she was walking toward the cupboard to get some plates out and even her walk was weird. The way she was talking. I hated it. All of it.

"Are you drunk?" I said. "Because I don't like it. Just act normal, Mum. You're freaking me out."

She reached up to get the plates, but when she turned around and looked at me, I saw that she was crying again, horrible crying with all her face crumpled up. "How can I be normal, Zac, when I'm not?" she said, doing this horrible sob, so big that a little snot bubble came out of her nose. "When I'm this disgusting fat pig? This big fat mess of a person? I'm not surprised Dom didn't want to kiss me or that your dad never—" That was when a plate slid out of the cupboard and smashed first on her head, then all over the floor, and then Mum was shouting and crying and I was too, and I was trying to pick up the pieces of the plate as well as hugging her at the same time and I just wanted this whole stupid date, this whole night, never to have happened.

I DIDN'T WANT Mum to be on her own, so I got into her bed and we ate our sausage sandwiches— Mum was dropping ketchup everywhere because she was still drunk, you could tell.

Afterward, I lay on her boobs. I love doing that 'cause they're so soft, like pillows. I even have names for them. One's Larry (he's a bit bigger) and one's Gary. Nobody but my mum and me know.

"What am I going to do, Zac?" Mum said suddenly. Her voice was all funny like she had a bad cold, because she'd been crying so much. "I'm never going to get myself a man like this, am I? Never going to get you a dad. And then you'll leave me and marry a gorgeous girl, because you deserve a gorgeous girl, and I'll just be a lonely old woman with cats."

"But you wouldn't be lonely if you had cats, would you?" I said. "Plus, you can get really friendly cats. And anyway, I'm not moving out—

ever. Even if I do get married, I always want to live with you."

Mum laughed. "You won't always feel like that," she said, kissing my head. "I promise you."

"Anyway, you will meet someone. Nan says Liam ruined all your confidence but you'll get it back when you get a new boyfriend. You're dead pretty. I think you are."

That was when Mum said the thing that made me glad this night had happened after all. "But that's the problem, Zac." She was stroking my hair; it felt dead relaxing. "I only ever loved Liam. I don't think I even want a boyfriend if it's not him."

My heart was going boom. I didn't dare speak in case she stopped talking.

"I loved him and he loved me—so much. He did, I know he did. And I just can't imagine finding that again."

She was quiet for a bit then, and I thought she'd fallen asleep. Then she did a big sigh.

"Bastard," she said.

2

Juliet

"Right," I say, holding my head at both sides as if it might explode or topple off if I don't—I'm at the limit of human headaches; nothing would surprise me. "What would you like for your main breakfast, Mr. Zac? You can have anything you want."

Zac's eyebrows shoot up. "What, anything?"

"Yeah, if we've got it. Come on, what's your death row breakfast? Bacon, eggs, Uncle Jamie's pancakes . . . ?"

Hangovers always make me emotionally wobbly, and an image pops up, bringing a lump to my throat, with no warning whatsoever: my little brother, cooking his special pancakes in our childhood kitchen, all big, curly bed-hair and purple hooded dressing gown. He used to make us pancakes every Sunday morning, showing off his culinary skills with how high he could toss them, and every single Sunday morning Dad would joke, "That's my boy—a professional tosser!" And every single Sunday morning Mum would snap, "Michael, please, it is **not** funny. What would people think if you said that in public?"

And Jamie and I would snigger to ourselves—more at the fact that Mum got cross every time than at Dad making the same rubbish joke.

"You have to say your death row breakfast first." Zac grins at me, bringing my attention back to him, to now, making the tears that were threatening to leak retreat to where they belong at seven fifteen on a Friday morning. He seems cheerful enough after last night, which is unnerving, to be honest. What promises did I make? What did I say? I used to trust myself, even under the influence, not to say anything I might regret, especially about his father. But now, worn down by ten years of single parenthood, I don't so much.

"Oooh, Crunchy Nut Corn Flakes followed by two boiled eggs and a gigantic mug of coffee," I say, still holding my poor, throbbing head. **That's if I don't die of natural causes before my execution.** (Imagining the Last Suppers of soon-to-be-executed serial killers might not be everyone's idea of fun, but it seems to be ours.)

Zac inspects me suspiciously with his gorgeous aqua eyes. (He gets those from his dad, worst luck.) He can smell overcompensation all right, but he's all for exploitation and I don't blame him.

"Okaaay, pancakes then," he says, his face lighting up. I briefly wonder how long we have left of his face brightening at the mere mention of his favorite food or TV program; how long it will be before simple pleasures don't cut it anymore. Will I be able to keep up? Will I be enough?

"But can I make them and you toss them?" he says. "And can I have syrup and bacon with them like Uncle Jamie says in his recipe?"

"You can, darling."

"Really?!"

Normally the chances of me letting him cook before school are basically zero. I'm definitely still drunk.

Zac slides off the breakfast-bar stool. "Yes! Uncle Jamie's pancakes for breakfast!" he sing-songs, padding to the fridge to get the ingredients.

My son has the look of my brother—the coarse, fair hair that tends to grow out rather than down; something about the openness of his face, the wide-set eyes. But even now, ten years on, when I hear my brother's name, the shock that he will never again be on this earth occasionally—like now—hits me the way it did the day I found out. And then I get a pang of hate for Liam for his part in what happened that night. And I'm glad of that feeling, because you know where you are with hating someone, don't you? It's safer. Cut and dried.

A FEW YEARS ago, when Zac was about seven, we went on a day trip to London. It was absolutely brilliant. I'd saved up my Tesco vouchers to go to the London Aquarium. Zac still talks about touching the stingrays and eating a crepe (you can imagine the hilarity), but for me, the main thing I'll remember about that day is what happened on the train home, which is that I went to the loo, closed the door, but forgot to press "lock"—only for someone to come and press "open" seconds later and the door to open as slowly as it's surely possible for a door **to** open, revealing yours truly with her knickers round her ankles to a packed rush-hour train. The walk of shame back to my seat was torture; teenage boys applauded me: "What happened? Get your arse stuck in the toilet seat, did you, love?"

If anyone ever asked me, "What's the most embarrassing thing that's happened to you?" I used to tell them this story; but now I fear what happened last night has surpassed it.

OBVIOUSLY I DON'T normally go to school with Zac on the bus (Zac makes me get the early-bird one, it just not being acceptable to get the bus with your mum when you're in Year 6, apparently), but, as luck would have it, what with me being unable to string a sentence together and stinking of wine, I've been called in for a meeting today with his teachers.

We sit at the top at the back, Zac nearest the window, me in the aisle seat. The snow has turned to gray sludge, making this part of Grimsby look grimmer than ever as we pass the tired, low-roofed offices and shops of Freeman Street: Poundstretcher and Iceland, Khan's Fashions and the Carpet Warehouse. A cold wind's blowing a gale just to add to matters, and a trolley has made a break for it from the queue of them in front of Iceland. It's alone and desolate, turning slowly and almost elegantly like a big fat silver fairy.

"Mum, how much did you have to drink last night?" says Zac suddenly, and my stomach flips.

"Why?"

"I just want to know."

Now, how do you answer that? Because either way you're screwed, if you ask me.

"Only half a lager, son." **Really, and that was the state you were in? I think you should give up drinking, Mum.**

"A bottle and a half of white wine." (That is the truth.) **Really?**—rings AA or Childline—**I think you should give up drinking, Mum.**

Actually, in my defense, I don't normally drink like I did last night. Booze isn't my drug of choice—you only need to look at me to figure out what is—but I was a bag of nerves and I made two basic errors: going out on an empty stomach and drinking white wine. There's only one way that ever goes.

I put my hand into Zac's chubby, tanned one—

I still love to hold his hand—and say, "A little bit too much, I think, Zac."

I shouldn't be allowed on dates—I'm a liability. When I look at my dating history over the past ten years, it's a car crash. I should do everyone a favor and just forget it. After Liam and the awful events of that June weekend in 2005, I didn't dare go near another man for seven years—not surprising considering what happened the last time I got involved with one. Then, in August 2012, Jason popped up—literally, from behind the bar at the Pavilion nightclub in Cleethorpes. He was working two jobs back then, fitness training by day and bar work at night. I, meanwhile, was on a rare evening out with my best friend, Laura, who—worried I was depressed (I wasn't arguing) and beginning to take on a deathly pallor because I was in the flat so much—had insisted on paying for me. I hadn't been out in months and I went a bit off the rails, although to the outside eye it probably looked like I was having the time of my life. But even if no one else could spot it, I knew that when I pounded that dance floor till I was pouring with sweat, when I downed those shots of tequila and banged the empty glass on the bar, it was with a rage I kept suppressed the rest of the time. **Fuck you, Liam. Fuck you.** And when Jason accepted my very slurred request for a date, which I only remembered doing when he called me the next day, he had unknowingly been handed an exploding bomb.

The bus rounds a corner and we pass Your Fitness, where Jason works. I pass it every single morning, just to add salt to the wound, and every single morning I feel a pang of regret about that messy year I put him through. If there had to be a messy rebound boyfriend, after all, I would really have liked it to be someone less lovely and more deserving than Jase. Just to give you some indication of what I passed up (besides the most beautiful biceps you've ever seen in your life), when I finally stopped running hot and cold, and admitted I was in no state for a relationship, Jason still wanted to be friends. Zac was delighted, because he adored Jase, but I'm just not one of those girls who thinks that being mates with exes is a good idea, so I'm trying to cool the whole friendship thing off. I think we both need to move on.

"Mum?" Zac says, nudging me suddenly, making me jump.

I have a moment's worry he's noticed Your Fitness too and is about to start asking when we can next see Jason.

"I said, you do remember, don't you?"

"Remember what?" I ask warily.

"What you said last night? You know, about Dad?"

I freeze. My stomach rolls horribly. So I did say something—but what and how much? Did I just blab everything when I was pissed? Deliver the news that would blow his whole world apart and I can't even remember? **Oh yeah, so, you know you're upset about your dad abandoning you? Well, actually, that's the least of your problems, because the whole truth is about a thousand times worse.**

My hangover suddenly intensifies and my heart starts going like the clappers, but then I look at Zac's smiling, inquisitive face. Surely if I'd told him everything, he'd be upset this morning? I study his expression for a few panicky moments, and only when I'm completely satisfied it isn't one of horror do I allow myself to exhale.

"Of course I remember, Zac," I say, like, **What do you take me for?**

He leans his head on my shoulder. "The last bit, Mum," he says, chuckling to himself. "That was well funny. When you just sat up and swore . . ."

Oh God.

We pass the park and the pebble-dashed sprawl of the Goode Estate, with me frantically trying to piece together last night. But there are huge gaps in my memory. I can't even remember what Dom and I talked about; I just remember the feelings: the flutter when I fancied him the moment I saw him, and the excitement as we seemed to click—or, at least, I thought we did; the giddiness when he gave me a lift home in his sports car and I gushed drunkenly about how flash it was, splaying myself all over it, stroking the seats. **Jesus** . . . Us walking arm in arm across the estate, everything so white and perfect in the snow. (That was how I saw it, anyway; he probably only had his arm in mine to hold me up.) I remember lifting my face up to kiss him, closing my eyes—and then the rejection, like a slap in the face when he turned his cheek.

There was just this rage then—like there was that night I first met Jason—that rose up in me like a . . . like a bottle and a half of white wine, let's face it, and suddenly I was shouting, "Why? Why? Why?" even though I knew why; it was obvious why. But I can't help thinking, why did he go on a date with me then? He'd seen a picture (albeit head and shoulders only, but the absence of any visible bone—collar, cheek, or otherwise—is clear as day).

There are fat-girl brush-offs, however, and Dom went for the classic "Look, you've got a really pretty face"—after he'd as good as recoiled from it. I would have laughed if I hadn't already been crying.

I close my eyes and rest my pounding head on the cool window. **Christ, Juliet,** I think. **You love your boy so much, but it didn't stop you last night, did it? It wasn't enough to make you rein in the wine and the general self-loathing?**

Mercifully, back home is also patchy. I just remember tears—from me, and possibly Zac because he absolutely hates it when I cry—and that when I stepped out of bed this morning, I went flying on the remains of a sausage sandwich that I'd obviously made when I got home, pissed. Because not only does white wine bore huge holes in your memory, it also makes you crave lard like there's no tomorrow, and before you know it, you've knocked up an extra five hundred calories inhaling a sausage sandwich that you can't even remember eating.

THERE ARE THREE of them waiting for me after I drop Zac off at his classroom: Miss Kendall, Zac's teacher—pretty, young, slim (naturally, Zac's in love with her); Mrs. Bond, the headmistress; and Brenda—a school counselor.

"Brenda will just be someone to emotionally support him at school," they said when they brought her in at the beginning of November last year. Zac was struggling a bit—he'd even bunked off one day, which was most unlike him—and they said Brenda was someone he'd be able to talk to, who was **totally on his side**. (I wondered who I was, then—the enemy?)

"Nice to see you, Juliet. How are you?" says Mrs. Bond as I take off what feels like never-ending scarves and jumpers, revealing a slightly smaller me each time, like a Russian doll. Except, of course, even without all the layers, I'm not exactly **small**.

I'm sweating like a pig from the hangover, and the chair is much lower than I anticipate, meaning a little yelp slips out when I eventually land.

Three pairs of eyes then, all staring at me. I can feel the sheen of toxic sweat pooling on my top lip.

"Well, this looks serious," I say cheerily, realizing it might be precisely that. "Oh God, what's he done?"

He hasn't **done** anything, they say. He just seems like a different boy to the one they knew in Year 5; he's not fulfilling his academic potential; he seems angry sometimes and upset, anxious.

"But he's a kid," I say, "not a robot. Surely he's allowed off days like anyone else?"

"Of course," says Brenda soothingly. "Of course he's allowed off days. But it doesn't feel like it is the odd 'off day,' it feels like he's fundamentally . . ." She tilts her head to the side, searching for the right word. I'm dreading what it might be. "Struggling at the moment."

My throat constricts. I know that feeling.

"Obviously, I only met him in November, but even I can tell that this is a child who's got a lot on his shoulders. And maybe nothing has changed since Year 5, but for whatever reason, he's not coping as well as he was."

"Can we also just chat about his issues with food?" interjects Mrs. Bond, and I actually laugh.

"Sorry, issues with food? I don't think so. Zac'll eat anything."

You can practically hear the tumbleweed.

Brenda leans forward, as if she's a cancer doctor about to impart bad news. That's how it feels, like she's telling me he has a disease, that my perfect boy is somehow defective. "We're just a little concerned about Zac's weight. He does seem to have put on quite a lot more since starting Year 6, and we just wanted to raise that with you."

The alcohol has as good as worn off now, the postdrinking paranoia is setting in, and I'm suddenly aware of how my thighs are spilling over this ludicrously small chair, like a Pizza Hut cheesy crust. I even start to feel like they might have given me this chair on purpose, to make a point. I wonder about the possibility of it breaking, right now, into two, and how I'd never survive the humiliation, how I'd have to make Zac change schools . . .

"Has anything happened at home that might have triggered the sudden weight gain?" she asks.

Sudden weight gain? What is she on about? I live with him; surely I'd have noticed.

"Is he perhaps eating in secret, you know, taking food you're not aware of?" suggests Brenda. "Some children do that if they're upset in any way."

I feel my cheeks flushing, tears threatening. **How do** you **know?** I think. **You who can probably eat anything you want and still stay skinny?** I hold the words—just—behind gritted teeth.

"He was found in a corner of the playground— almost as if he was hiding—eating a doughnut on his own," she says and at first I laugh, partly because I'm nervous and partly because she'd have looked less serious if he'd been caught with a four-pack of Special Brew.

"Well, I never gave him a doughnut. If anyone's having a doughnut, it's me!" I say. Then I burst into tears.

"It's the hangover," I say. "Hangovers . . . they always make me emotional." Which unsurprisingly is met with icy stares.

Brenda passes me a tissue. "I'm sorry," I say, dabbing under my eyes. "I really don't know what's wrong with me."

"Don't worry, it's a very emotive issue," says Brenda, which only makes me feel worse.

"Look, he must have bought the doughnut on the way to school, because I always just put an apple in his bag." God knows we've had enough letters go home saying they can only have fruit or vegetables for their snack.

"Well, perhaps we need to help Zac," says Miss Kendall gently. Everything about her is gentle: her voice, her face, her fluffy blond hair; she looks like a nymph, an angel. "By making sure he doesn't have access to money to spend on the way to school, or access to those kinds of foods."

Those kinds of foods? I start to feel resentful, like they're telling me what I can and can't feed my kid.

"If I can just butt in," adds Brenda. "Having

seen Zac now for half a term, I think we've got to know one another pretty well and I see a child for whom things feel out of control at the moment."

He feels out of control? I'm failing miserably to stem my tears with a tissue.

"Everything's related for him, and it's a vicious cycle: the overeating, the weight gain, and consequently the bullying, which then leads to struggling generally at school, and on and on it—"

"Hang on a minute, bullying?" My stomach drops as if beginning the plunge from the highest dip of a roller coaster. "What kind of bullying? I know Zac's big for his age, but I can tell you now, he's the gentlest boy in the world. He wouldn't hurt a fly."

Brenda reaches over and lightly touches my hand. "Oh no, we know that. Zac is a lovely boy. No, what we're concerned about is him being a victim of bullying, and one of the reasons for getting you here today is because we want you to know we have a zero-tolerance bullying policy at this school and that these incidents have not escaped our attention—especially what happened at swimming last Thursday."

Swimming? Thursday?

"I'm presuming you noticed he came home in a different shirt and jumper?"

I think back.

"Well, no, to be honest, because I sometimes work late on a Thursday, so Zac lets himself in.

By the time I get back, it's gone ten p.m. and he's asleep . . ." Those looks again; I feel so judged. "I have no choice. I work in a sandwich shop, but we do catering events—you know, birthdays, business meetings, work parties—and I have to work shifts. That includes evenings."

It transpires that on Thursday, after Zac's swimming lesson, some little shit stole his school shirt and jumper. Nobody would confess and time was running out before the next lesson, so he was forced to wear clothes from the lost-property box, none of which fitted him. And there's worse: a fortnight or so ago, all the Year 6s had to be weighed—some government policy or something; I know because I stupidly signed the consent form—and Zac apparently freaked.

"He just did not—would not—take off his school jumper," says Brenda. "And he got himself into a bit of a state."

"What sort of a state?"

"Well, tears. Lots of tears," she says. "And protesting, locking himself in the cupboard. I did manage to calm him down in the end, but he was very upset."

"But why?" I ask, a sob escaping. I can't stand to think of my usually calm and happy Zac so upset that he locks himself in a room; that doesn't sound like him at all. But then, I'm beginning to wonder if I know him as well as I think I do.

"I suspect his size really bothers him," says

Mrs. Bond. "In fact, I think it's really getting him down."

Or is he desperately unhappy and I just haven't noticed because I'm far too eaten up with my own issues? The thought sinks to the pit of my stomach, like a stone to the bottom of the sea.

"I know he's a bit on the chubby side, but he's not, you know . . ." The room seems to be getting smaller. "I do not feed him rubbish."

Mrs. Bond looks at Brenda and then at me. It's momentary—but it's there all right. The one-second once-over that says, **Well, you're clearly doing something wrong**.

"Actually, Zac is one of the children who was found to be medically above a normal weight for his age," says Mrs. Bond. "You should have received a letter by now."

"What letter? I haven't got any letter." The tears have all but stopped. I'm just starting to feel angry. "And what do you mean, **above a normal weight**? Who decides what's normal anyway?"

OBESE, THEY SAID.

"Obese?" I repeated, dumbfounded. "He's ten. I know he's on the chunky side, but it's puppy fat. It'll go when he shoots up."

Also, what am I meant to do about him eating doughnuts when I'm not there? I can't watch him every minute of every day, I told them; I work. What did they want me to do? Tell shops not to serve him? Put locks on the cupboard doors? Deny him anything nice? Life is hard enough for Zac what with his shithead absent father.

There's also his love of cooking. He's a foodie! And how many telly chefs could they think of who are skin and bone? I said. Jamie Oliver is chubby . . . And James Martin, who used to present **Saturday Kitchen**, isn't exactly svelte.

"I mean, he just loves cooking and baking. He takes after my brother, you see, although unfortunately my brother's not with us anymore. And he loves mashed potato; mashed potato is his absolute favorite. He'd have mash for breakfast, dinner, and tea if you let him. He likes to experiment with all sorts of mashed potato. **What do you want me to do? Stop buying potatoes?!**"

Like I say, hangovers always make me emotional.

COSTCUTTER IS OPPOSITE the bus stop in the middle of the little parade of shops on our estate, and after I get off the bus—where I spent the entire journey sobbing like someone had died—I go in there to get a few bits. The hangover and whole apocalyptic feel of the world now the snow's melted to sludge isn't doing anything to lift my mood, but I feel helpless and so angry. Angry toward whichever little shit stole my boy's clothes, angry toward the school for having the audacity to call my son fat in the first place and somehow suggesting (in my mind, at any rate) that this makes him a valid target, and angry at Zac for not telling me about any of this. But most of all I'm angry at myself, because I feel this is **my** fault—that, fundamentally, none of this would be happening if I was a better person, a better mother; if he didn't have to make do with just me. And then I'm back in that spiral of thought: Liam left Grimsby and us, and, yes, perhaps he felt he had no option at the time. But that was ten years ago and I wonder what I hate him for more these days—what he did that night or the fact that he's never come back. Does he not want our forgiveness? Does he never miss Zac and me? What does it say about me that he never, ever fought for us? That he basically left one life and started another, without so much as a backward glance?

Often I wonder what he's doing and where he is, but when I try to picture it, my mind is completely blank; as if, after that night, he walked out of our lives and out of this world; as if he just jumped off its curve into fathomless black. I try but I can't conceive of him existing without us.

THERE'S A HOT counter in Costcutter where they do sausage rolls and pasties, and the hot pastry smell hits you from about a mile away. I knew resistance was futile as soon as I stepped off the bus, and anyway, I deserve one. I deserve a week's supply of pasties after the twenty-four hours I've had. So I go over there, get a sausage roll, and put it in one of the white takeaway bags with the silver lining (every cloud and all that). And then I get a few other bits, bread and some toilet roll, and I hit the aisle where all the biscuits and cereals are with every intention of going straight to the till. Who am I kidding? I've decided already. I probably decided before I even set foot in the shop, no doubt back when Mrs. Bond was delivering the news that my baby was being terrorized, and once the seed is planted in my mind and the adrenaline is rushing through my veins in anticipation, that's it, game over—and before I know it, my hand has stretched out, taken something, and slipped it into my bag. It's so easy I do it again. I don't even know what I've taken; I just know that something glints gold at the bottom of my bag and it's giving me a thrill. That I feel like I've got one up, not on Mr. Singh, the shop owner—I feel eternally guilty about Mr. Singh—but on the universe. Because otherwise I feel like it will swallow me whole.

I walk across the estate to our block, the wintry sun low in the sky. There's a bunch of girls smoking on the corner and Eunice cruising across to Costcutter on her mobility scooter as she does every single day at this time.

I wave at her.

"Snow's all gone!" she says. "Be spring before you know it."

"Can't wait, I've had enough of this gray sludge!" I call back, but inside I feel a tiny pang of dread. Nearly spring means June is just around the corner with the anniversary of Jamie's death; the anniversary of Liam leaving. It never seems to get any easier.

I walk the half flight of stairs to our front door and let myself in. I don't relish coming home to an empty flat, never have. You'd think I'd be used to it after ten years, wouldn't you? But I can't seem to let go of the feeling it wasn't meant to be like this. I put the shopping on the table, take the sausage roll out of its silver lining, and open the cupboard above me to get out a plate. It's as I'm doing this that I spot the brown envelope on the doormat, in between the **Evening Telegraph** and a pizza delivery leaflet. It has **North East Lincolnshire Health Authority** stamped on it, and even from here I can see the words **Parent or Guardian of Zachary Hutchinson** through the little plastic window. I stare at it for a moment, frozen, like it's a mouse I've just spotted. I feel as resentful, as invaded, as if it **were**. I imagine some jobsworth civil servant typing it out—probably twenty stone themselves—condemning my child to being fat and lazy. What gives anyone the right?

I'm about to pick it up and chuck it in the bin, but something stops me; something to do with a vision of my boy, standing in the middle of the swimming changing rooms with no top on, feeling ashamed and scared. I know how that feels, and I'm all grown-up. I feel like I owe it to him to at least open the stupid letter. I lean down and pick it up before I change my mind.

3

Zac

**Fact: Doctors in medieval times used
to treat the plague with cow dung,
because they thought the bad smell
drove out disease.**

After what happened at swimming, Brenda
called me and Aidan into her office. Brenda
asked him how he'd feel if I pinched his clothes
and he said sad. We shook hands. We're not friends
now, but we're not enemies either, and this week
he and his disciples have mainly left me alone.

Anyway, after what Mum told me about my
dad, I felt like I could deal with anything. I felt
like my happiness could equal out any badness,
like, if someone nicked my clothes in swimming
now, I'd be, like, "Take 'em! I don't care!" Like, I
might even do a lap of the swimming pool in the
nuddy. (Okay, maybe not that, but I wouldn't care
as much, no way.) I've thought about what Mum
said all week. I even wrote it down so I didn't for-

get it. **I only ever loved Liam.** That was what she said. **I don't think I even want a boyfriend if it's not him.** I came to the conclusion that the thing I need to know now is: If my parents did love each other and my dad wasn't a loser after all, then why did he run away? Did he not want to be my dad that much? I could ask my mum, I suppose, but detectives don't work like that. They don't go for the obvious; they work out what they think first and then they try and prove it. And I wanted to do this properly. I decided I was going to start by asking Nan and Grandad when I went there next.

I go to Nan and Grandad's after school on Tuesdays (after I've been to after-school club, that is) and on Wednesdays, when we always go to see Uncle Jamie's grave. Uncle Jamie was my mum's brother, but he died soon after I was born. His grave is in the bit with all the little children's and the babies' graves, even though he didn't die until he was eighteen so he was lucky in a way. The babies' graves are the saddest. You can't believe that a baby could die, but it's true. You can tell how much people loved the people who died by what their grave looks like. My uncle Jamie's is smooth and white like a white chocolate Magnum and it's made of marble with gold letters on. Some of the other graves are scruffy with moss all over them so you can't even read their names. Even if they died a hundred years ago from the plague, there's no excuse because they're our ancestors, and the people down the family tree who are alive now should still keep on making the grave look nice. We've been doing family trees at school in history, which has been good. (History is my favorite subject because there are loads of good facts.) Except, my one's lopsided—it's got half the tree missing where my dad's side of the family should be. But Miss Kendall said it's okay, because families come in all shapes and sizes, and anyway, after what Mum told me, I feel like I know my dad a bit. I feel like I could put him on my family tree now and it wouldn't even be a lie.

MY NAN GOES every day but Saturday to Uncle Jamie's grave. I always go on Wednesdays with both her and Grandad because it's one of my days when I'm at their house anyway. I love going to Nan and Grandad's. We always do the same thing, which is to go up to the grave then get fish and chips. Sometimes I do baking with my nan after that or watch telly with Grandad. We watch football (me and my grandad are both Manchester United fans, but I'm not just a fan because he is; I loved them from the start) or nature programs with David Attenborough. You can learn loads of facts by watching telly.

You should never come empty-handed to the cemetery, my nan says, and every Wednesday we bring Uncle Jamie something. Today we brought some snowdrops with foil wrapped around them and I'd written down the recipe for Marmite pasta. My uncle Jamie was a really good chef and everyone says I'm going to take after him. Nan says if he was still alive, he'd be really proud of me and how I'm into my cooking, so sometimes, if I've come up with a new recipe, I write it down, then bring it to the grave so he can read it from heaven.

Marmite pasta is dead easy: you just cook some normal spaghetti, put loads of butter in so it goes all shiny, then put a big spoonful of Marmite in and sprinkle cheese on top. Trust me, it's an epic tea.

Nan and Grandad were arguing over the flowers. This always happens because the flower holder doesn't work.

Nan (snapping like a dog): "Mick"—that's my grandad's name—"for Christ's sake. You don't put the flowers in like that; they're just going to topple over."

Grandad (giving me the "look"): "All right, Lynda"—and that's my nan's—"calm down. It's not the end of the world." Once, my nan burst out crying when he said that and shouted, "Actually, it is!"

It's my job to look around the graveyard for some stones to help weigh the flowerpot down. I like sneaking a look at the gravestones when I go past. I've seen one Zachary—that was one of the poor dead babies—but I've never seen a Teagan. If she died, she'd be the first Teagan in this whole graveyard, probably the first Teagan ever to die in Grimsby. I went back with the stones, being careful not to tread on the graves because if you do that, you could make the dead person angry and their spirit could go bad and start haunting you. Grandad put the stones in the bottom of the flowerpot. It worked and the snowdrops stood up.

"Thank you, Zac," said Nan. "At least someone here has got some sense."

Then I slipped my Marmite pasta recipe under the flowerpot where it wouldn't blow away. Even if it did, it wouldn't matter, because it would just float straight up to heaven.

The words on my uncle Jamie's gravestone read: **James Hutchinson. Beloved son, brother, and uncle. Taken from us aged 18 on June 12th 2005. Gone but never forgotten.**

I'm glad it says "uncle" because it proves I had one. I was only two and a half weeks old when he died, so I don't remember ever meeting him, even though he bought me a little suit with tiger ears. There's a massive picture of him holding me in it in Nan and Grandad's lounge.

After we've made Uncle Jamie's grave look nice, we sit on the bench for a bit and be peaceful. Sometimes Nan and Grandad tell me stories about Uncle Jamie. Sometimes me and Grandad go and look at the old graves and imagine what lives the people lived. Grandad knows some of them because they were fishermen like him and they died at sea. My grandad was a fisherman for twenty-five years, just like his dad before that, and his dad before that. It used to take three days just to get to Iceland and my grandad would be gone for three whole weeks. It's why my nan's so good at baking: because all the wives had to keep themselves busy.

Fishing is one of the most dangerous jobs in the world for dying—it's why there's even a special church in Grimsby, just for the dead fishermen. You can get tangled up in the nets and wires or go overboard, and that's it, you're a goner. Sometimes they don't even find the bodies.

One of our favorite things to talk about on the bench is what Uncle Jamie might be doing up in heaven.

"Nan, what do you think he's doing today?" I said.

"Oh," said Nan. "I don't know, love."

"Watching the match and having a pint," said Grandad, looking up to the sky.

"Give over," said Nan. "He is not. I think he's on a beautiful walk in one of the many gardens of heaven or cooking a fantastic dinner for all his new friends up there. What do you think, Zac?"

"I think he's playing football for Man U—the match of his life!" (I stood up to demonstrate.) "He passes to Carrick, who passes to Rooney, who nutmegs the center half, volleys it up, then slots it into the top corner and oh! What a goal! Absolutely beautiful!"

It always makes Nan and Grandad laugh when I do the commentary.

Me and Teagan have got this theory that heaven is one big corridor, with loads of different doors for every day of your life. Written on the door on a golden plaque is what happened every day—like a diary but in door form—and if you want to re-live that day, you can just knock on the door and you'll get let in. If you'd rather never see that day again, say if it was really bad like the day Aidan Turner nicked my clothes, you can just walk past. We've already picked the day we want to live over and over again when we're in heaven. Teagan's is the day we found a ten-pound note in the lift and spent it all on pick-a-mix, and mine's the day me and Grandad caught a trout.

Nan and Grandad know about my theory and sometimes I ask them what door Uncle Jamie might be choosing today. I like it when they say, "The day you were born," and tell how he came to see me in hospital, to make up for the fact that Dad had already gone off. "And he was so proud to be an uncle and he put you in that tiger suit, and you were so cute with so much hair!" Nan's told me that story loads of times, but I still like it and the door game cheers my nan up because it means she only remembers the good days of her son's life. I never ask her what doors he'd walk straight past.

———

MY UNCLE JAMIE died jumping off a bridge. The bit of water he jumped into wasn't deep enough and his spinal cord broke. If your spinal cord breaks, you can die, easily, because the blood and messages can't get to your brain, which means it stops working, which means your body dies but not your soul. I know this because Teagan told me, whereas nobody in my family likes talking about what happened to my uncle Jamie. Nan always says, "All you need to know is that he was taken—he didn't just die, Zac—and he should be here."

Mum used to say that too, but now she just says she'd rather talk about the good memories than him dying off a bridge.

When Grandad and I go fishing that's when we have our best chats. Grandad tells me stories about the glory days in Grimsby when the fishermen used to get drunk all the way to Iceland! Now he has to work in an office in a factory and he misses fishing; that's why he likes going with me.

One day last summer—the day we caught the trout—I asked him to tell me how Uncle Jamie died and after he went quiet for a long time, he told me about the bridge and how Uncle Jamie's spinal cord broke. Then I asked him some more questions: "Did he just jump?" "Why did he jump if there wasn't enough water? Could he not see?" "Was he murdered?"

Grandad said it was just a terrible accident but that I must never tell Nan he said that. I swore on our trout that I wouldn't, but I still didn't understand why, if that was the truth. That was when he told me how truth can be different for different people. Say, when me and Teagan found the ten-pound note in the lift and we spent it on sweets, if she told the story back to people in a way that I thought had all the facts wrong and wasn't what had happened at all, that would make me mad and upset and that's how Nan would feel if she heard Grandad's version.

AFTER WE'D BEEN to the cemetery, we got fish and chips. Then we went back to Nan and Grandad's but called in to the shop on the way, because I wanted to make Uncle Jamie's lemon drizzle cake after tea. Nan's got a whole book of his recipes at her house and Mum's got one at ours. You might think lemon drizzle cake is easy, but it's actually one of the hardest cakes you can make. You have to not bake it too hard, otherwise it's crumbly instead of squidgy, and you have to put the drizzle on at just the right time.

"Your uncle Jamie used to make a fine lemon drizzle," Nan said, pushing the greaseproof paper into the cake tin. That's the hardest bit. She always has to do that for me. "Lemon drizzle and coffee and walnut—those were his best cakes. But then obviously he was an absolute whiz at fish too. He could make fabulous sauces, Zac, better than you'd pay for in a restaurant."

Nan put the cake in the oven and I got to lick the bowl (that's my favorite bit). I was thinking this might be a good time to ask my questions; I'd even decided how I could start. You see, as well as the heaven corridor, me and Teagan believe that how long you cry when someone dies shows how much you loved them.

"Nan, how long did you cry when Uncle Jamie died?" I asked when she'd started washing up.

"Oh, a long, long time, Zac. I still cry, even now."

"Do you think my dad would cry if my mum died?"

I blurted it out because I was worried about saying it.

Nan looked down at the soapy water for ages. "What an odd question," she said eventually.

"Would he, though?"

"I do not know."

"Do you think Mum would cry if Dad died, then?" I asked and she looked a bit mad then.

"Like I said, I don't know, Zac." She took the bowl off me to wash up, even though there was still loads of cake mixture left and I hadn't finished. "And to be perfectly honest, I don't care either. I have no interest in that man or what he thinks or feels about anything and neither should you—he's not worth it."

Nan doesn't like my dad because he abandoned us. She says he's a waste of space. But I think he can't have been, not if my mum loved him so much, because she's got good taste, my mum; she knows what a good person is.

"But why did he even leave," I said, "if he still loved my mum?"

"Zac, please, that's enough," snapped Nan, turning off the taps. "What's with all the questions all of a sudden?"

But I'd started now and so I had to finish.

"But, like, even if he didn't want to be my dad, he still loved my mum and she loved him, didn't she? So why did he leave us all?" I wanted so bad to tell her what Mum had said, but I didn't dare—I didn't even dare tell Mum what she'd said yet, in case she took it back.

"How do you know, Zac, if . . ." Nan's eyes had gone all teary and I really did not want to make Nan cry. "Your mum and your father were very young; they didn't know what they felt."

I didn't really understand or believe it. It felt like Nan was trying to palm me off. I was only ten, but I knew what I felt. I knew I loved Mum, Nan, and Grandad—even Teagan in a best-friend-who's-a-girl kind of way—so why would my parents not know? They were miles older than me. The question I was thinking now, though, was, never mind him doing a runner, why did Mum let him if she loved him so much?

And if they loved each other then, why couldn't they now?

After I'd finished baking with Nan, I went and watched telly with Grandad. It was a history program all about the First World War. It showed all the soldiers in the trenches—they had to sleep there, even when it had been raining and it was so muddy that the mud came up to their thighs. Some soldiers saw their friends' legs being blown off right in front of their eyes, or even half their face. I like history at school and watching **Horrible Histories** and learning all the facts, but sometimes I find it hard to believe that what they say happened actually did; that they **are** actually facts. It's the same with everything that happens that you're not there to see. It's like a parallel universe—but if you're not there, how can you be sure it exists? What if it's all a lie, just to make a good story?

Grandad says it's important to remember that we could all just be a speck on someone's shoe. We think we're these important people living on earth, the most important place in the universe— but what if we've got it wrong? And what if Nan, Grandad, and my mum had got my dad wrong too? What if Dad was somewhere, knowing the real reason he just left, and nobody had bothered to ask him?

Nan came into the lounge then and saw what me and Grandad were watching. "Mick, is this really suitable for Zac?"

It was showing a soldier being blown up—but it was only actors, you could tell. Grandad started to explain this to her, but I wasn't really listening because I was thinking about my dad. I was thinking how the only way I was going to find out the truth—and not just have to trust what everyone was telling me—was to find him myself and ask him in person. The letter was one thing, but I only really wrote that because I'd wanted him to come and help us. Now it was almost like I wanted to help him; to give him a chance to explain himself. I started to get dead excited when I thought about it. The feeling grew in my belly and bubbled right up to my smile. If I found my dad, then maybe him and Mum could be in love again and Mum wouldn't have to go on any more crap dates and maybe he'd even change his mind about being my dad.

"Zac," said Nan. "What are you grinning at?"

Maybe Nan would even change her mind about him too.

4

Mick

"Find a place where you can be on your own," Carol had said at our session last week. "Somewhere you can think. And make it a regular thing to go there—a regular meeting with yourself."

Carol's my counselor. (Now, that's something I never thought I'd say.) But I like her; I liked her the moment we met, at my very first session back at the beginning of January.

I'd originally gone to the doctor in November. Juliet and Zac were struggling; Zac in particular was low and just not himself. The feeling this was all my fault seemed to have reached crescendo levels, which I could no longer get even the shortest respite from. "I've lost the plot" was the phrase I used in the doctor's surgery, and he, unperturbed, suggested "talking therapy."

I must have looked like a rabbit in headlights that first time, but Carol put me at ease immediately. She was not how I imagined a "therapist" to be. She's no-nonsense, she gives great advice, and already, I must admit, I feel a sense of release sitting here in the Jubilee Café, my old greasy spoon down the docks where I'd have a fry-up before we went to sea. Today seems as good as any to start going over everything, and I mean **really** going through everything that's happened. Putting the events in some order and holding them up to examine them.

I need to understand how we got to this point; how our son isn't here anymore and why I couldn't protect him. How I let both our kids down. Sixty years old may not sound old, after all, but when you've hammered your body like I have, when your own dad dropped dead at sixty-two and you've used up as many lives as I have after twenty-five years at sea, it begins to feel it, believe me. And I need to understand what happened before it's too late. Zac's already asking questions and he deserves the truth. I love that kid more than life itself. It scares me how much.

I think I'll start with Lynda since, as I say, she's a big part of everything.

I met her in the summer of '76—the "hottest summer on record," as it will be known for evermore. Cleethorpes was like the Costa del Sol. The fishing industry in Grimsby had begun to decline at that point—it was way past its heyday of the fifties, my old man's era when Grimsby was the center of the world. But there were still two hundred or so trawlers and work to be got if you knew people, and the pubs of Freeman Street were always rammed. I'd just got back from a really good trip. We'd made three hundred boxes and I had fourteen hundred pounds burning a hole in my back pocket. They used to call us the "three-day millionaires," because we'd be away fishing for three weeks, only to come back for three days, spending most of it (the time and the money) in the pub.

They say you meet someone when you're least expecting it, and I couldn't have been expecting it less, still in my ducksuit, the only shower I'd had in a fortnight being a saltwater one, but there she was, my future wife, standing outside the White Knight in a sheer cream blouse, hair a halo of blond. I thought Farrah Fawcett had landed in Grimsby. I thought I stood no chance too, but I was much cockier in those days before life and booze had knocked the bravado out of me. I think my opening line was "What's a classy girl like you doing hanging around a place like this?" Not very original. She was called Lynda Cruickshank, she told me—Lynda with a "y," the "posh" way—and she was a "meggie"; that is, she was from Cleethorpes not Grimsby. Her dad did something in tax investigation—clearly she was a cut above—but she told me she "liked a bit of rough," and there was "something romantic about sailors."

By some miracle we ended up kissing that night

and I walked her home—still in the ducksuit. She said she was likely to fancy me even more if I cared to have a bath before our "next date" and I remember grinning at that phrase: "**next** date." 'Course, two dates turned into ten, turned into a wedding and two kids, but I suppose I've always thought it was a miracle that it did—I've never felt I was good enough for her. I've always believed that one day she'd wake up, smell the coffee, and be off.

I told Lynda right from the start that I didn't want kids. I said I didn't like the snotty-nosed little rug rats, when nothing could be further from the truth because anyone will tell you, I'm a big kid myself. But I didn't want to tell her that it was the responsibility that scared the living daylights out of me, the fear I'd turn out like my ol' man: a drunk, a waste of space . . . that I just wasn't up to the job. Turned out I was right on that front. Like father, like son.

Anyway, she talked me round, or rather beat me down as she does with everything, and I went along with it because it was easier—and I loved her. She's a difficult woman, but I still love her.

They say there are only two emotions in life, two reasons we do anything: fear and love; and it felt like a perfect storm of the two when Jamie and Juliet were born. I was in no way prepared for this explosion of the heart, and it was instant—with both my kids. It wasn't a choice I made or anything I was in control of. It knocked me sideways, like sliding off the deck in a force-ten gale (and believe me, I've been there too and there's sweet FA you can do about that either).

Lynda always said she couldn't describe the pain of childbirth; that it was unlike anything she'd ever known as pain. But that was how I felt about the love: that it wasn't anything like love as I knew it. That it deserved a new word. It was the best feeling I'd ever had—and the most frightening.

Obviously I was in the pub when our Jamie was born—you just were back in those days. It was 1987. Plus, it was a Saturday, and I was dead on my feet most of the time, working ten hours in the kipper factory skinning salmon, waiting for a new job to start, so I was damned if I wasn't making the most of my weekends. I was down the Smokers with Vaughan Jones when my mum called the pub phone to tell me that my son was here and to get down the hospital. It's mad, dark, poetic even, to think now that the moment I heard my son had entered the world, I was having a pint with the man whose son would, eighteen years later, be the one to blame for him leaving it far too early. Lynda always said, "Like father, like son"—though, funnily enough, never when it came to me, only when it came to Liam—and she despised Vaughan for his drinking and his brawling and, more importantly, his leading **me** astray, toward the bottle and away from her. He'd spent time inside for assault in the past, and their family, as far as she was concerned, gave fishing families a bad name. "Nobody in their right mind would want to keep up with those Joneses," she used to say. She blamed Vaughan for corrupting me, but I never needed any encouragement.

The first time I held my boy in my arms, I bloody cried like a baby myself. "Why is Daddy crying?" Juliet, who was two and a half at the time, said. Lynda laughed—she was still laughing back then. "Because he's drunk!" she said. Then, more to me than Juliet, "And happy, and scared out of his wits."

How it's changed, down here at the docks in the thirty years or so since my kids were born. What a crying shame. All the factories and the smokehouses closed down, the ice factory derelict. It only reminds you how much time you've let slip through your fingers and it's all coming into focus now, now I don't have the crutch of the booze, and enough time has passed that I can think of other things except Jamie for longer than five minutes. I feel like I fell underground, only to wake up several years later, crawl to the top, and find everything gone.

I'm thinking of my relationship with our Jamie now and shaking my head, because I realize most of it was conducted in the pub. Either he was hanging around outside the White Knight eating endless crisps while I got rat-arsed inside or, when he was older, he was getting rat-arsed with me. We were close, best mates, Jamie and I—more than father and son. It's only in the past few years that I've realized he needed me to be his father, not his drinking buddy.

They used to serve you a pint with your breakfast at six a.m. on landing day at the TC's Club, straight off the boat, and I remember once, when Jamie was about seven, Lynda bringing him down around eight a.m. because he couldn't wait to see me, and the look of rage on her face when she saw I was half-cut. But then there were later times, when he was a teenager; underage but nobody gave a toss back then. And those were good, fun times. Maybe we shouldn't have been doing it, but they were still good times.

The relationship with your son is completely different from that with your daughter. As I said, Jamie was my mate, my buddy. Juliet was, from the minute she was born, someone to be looked after. I knew a different Jamie from the one his mother knew: lovely, baby-faced Jamie, who'd take his mum breakfast in bed (he knew which side his bread was buttered on). But he was different in the pub with the lads. He did stupid, irresponsible shit, the same as any lad his age. When he died, aged eighteen, he was already well on his way to becoming a chip off the old block, and I think Lynda was always in denial about that. So quick to see it with Liam and yet incapable of seeing it with Jamie.

What else? It was different with each of them right from the beginning. When I first held Juliet in my arms, there was just this surge of protectiveness. She was tiny—I couldn't say what weight— but I just remember this need to keep her safe, and most of all to make sure that whichever man she ended up with, he'd love and protect her too. But that's the difference with a daughter: you know one day she'll love someone else more passionately than she loves you, and so right from the start you're already letting go. But with a boy, it's different. They're more an extension of you, more for keeps—at least I thought so. Turned out I took that for granted. And all I see when I close my eyes at night is our boy, lying dying with all those tubes in him on that hospital bed, the piston-puff of the ventilator; all I can hear is Liam pacing up and down outside and Lynda shouting, "I know you're there. You're not wanted here. Go! Get out!"

5

Juliet

Zac looks at his plate and then up at me. "What's that for?" he says.

"What's it for? It's fruit," I say. "It's nice. Look, I put it in a smiley face and everything."

I had too: a banana for the smile, grapes for the eyes and the nose, and tangerine segments for the eyebrows.

Zac just stares at it.

"Hey, it looks a bit like Raymond," I say, trying to lift the wall of doom that's descended with the appearance of fruit at the breakfast table. Raymond is the deliveryman at work. Zac loves him, because if he's got time, he lets him help carry the boxes of sandwich supplies from the van to the kitchen, then unpack them, Zac imagining all the different filling combinations, completely in his element.

"No offense, Mum, but the thought of eating Raymond's face for breakfast . . ." Zac shakes his head then pretends to gag (so that went well). "I think I'll just have the usual, please."

The usual is cereal and toast, which I've always thought was a perfectly healthy breakfast, but since the Letter of Condemnation, almost two weeks ago now, I've begun to wonder. I must be doing something wrong, after all. I sit down opposite him.

"Zac, sweetheart," I say, looking straight into his lovely light blue eyes. "I'd really like you to eat the fruit, please."

"But why?" he says, folding his arms sulkily. "I hate fruit."

"You do not."

"I do, it's disgusting."

"Don't be ridiculous. You'll never make it as a chef if you discard a whole food group, and you love strawberry jam, don't you? And that's just strawberries, Zac, that's all it is."

"But why do I have to eat it?"

"Because it's good for you, and also, it's delicious." I pick up one of the tangerine eyebrows and put it in my mouth just to demonstrate how delicious it really is. It's a bit tart, so I have to try not to wince. This is the problem with fruit for breakfast, if you ask me: your mouth's just not ready for it.

Zac leans his cheeks on his fists and looks down at my smiley fruit face forlornly.

"But I'll be starving in five minutes. That's not

going to fill me up. I'll only eat it if I can have toast too. Or pancakes! Hey, I could make Uncle Jamie's pancakes but put fruit on them!" He's asked to make pancakes every morning since the morning after the doomed date with Dom, and on most of them, I've been too knackered to argue. (Plus, Zac makes **the best** pancakes.) I'm too tired to argue now too, and he has to start getting ready for school and me for work.

The "fruity pancake" seems like a good compromise.

FOR THE WEEK after it arrived, the Letter of Condemnation sat on top of the microwave staring at me. I couldn't bring myself to read it again. I found the whole thing totally overwhelming. That letter was a can of worms as far as I was concerned, and I felt like I had enough on my plate, if you'll excuse the pun. But then I was called into a follow-up meeting with the school nurse and Brenda about easy changes Zac could make— things like having oatmeal and fruit for breakfast, rather than Honey Cheerios and butter with toast (that way around), and I had to admit, they were nice, they were human. Most of all, like me, all they wanted was to help Zac. I thought I should at least show myself willing.

I felt the same could not be said of the tone of the letter:

**Your child is above a healthy weight
for his height, with a BMI of 30, which
places him medically in the "obese"
category.**

Along with the letter, there were leaflets for
things like "weight management classes" and
"walking clubs," where he'd meet other chubby
kids to walk around People's Park with or do hula-
hooping with. As if they didn't feel bad enough
about themselves already to then have to hula-
hoop en masse in public. It felt like throwing him
to the wolves. Since getting the letter, I've swung
from anger at how a stranger has the right to brand
my son "too fat," to frustration because, to be honest, I can't understand why he is the "f" word—if
he even is. He doesn't eat anything different from
other kids—I mean, they'll all go for a burger over
a salad, won't they? I guess he's on the chubby
side, but I've always thought kids were sort of self-
regulating like babies, that they only ate what they
needed to grow. "Too fat" seems like such a damn-
ing label to give a ten-year-old, and I'm terrified of
harming his self-esteem, which has already taken
a colossal blow, let's face it, since as far as he's concerned, his father doesn't want him. You want to
know what hurts the most about getting that letter, though? The feeling that something beautiful
and sacred has been soiled. Because to me, Zac

has always been perfect—the only thing in my
life that is—and yet here's this letter telling me in
black and white that he isn't; that the only thing
I'm proud of in my life isn't even good enough.

"SO REMEMBER." ZAC stands on the doorstep,
his school rucksack on, while I make him look
at me. We've been through this rigmarole every
day since the arrival of the letter. "You are beautiful as you are and anyone who thinks otherwise,
well . . ."

"That is their failing as a human being," parrots
Zac. "Mum, you're hurting my cheeks."

"I love you."

"Me too," he says.

I watch as my boy and his Man U rucksack
become a smudge in the distance, and then I go
inside to make myself a bacon sarnie and have a
little sob.

There's no denying it—although obviously I'm
having a good go at doing just that—worrying
about Zac at school is making me eat more. Which
is perverse, I know, even while stuffing down my
sixth chocolate Hobnob, like taking up smoking
when your kid's been diagnosed with asthma. But
it's the only thing that eases the gnawing anxiety I
have from the moment he leaves in the morning to
the moment he comes home. Is he all right? Is he
being picked on? As a single parent, there's always

that niggle in your head, after all: no matter that I do my best, is my best good enough?

I have about half an hour before I have to leave for work, so I make the bacon sandwich, but then find myself wandering from room to room. This happens a lot these days. When Zac was really little, I used to crave time on my own. As much as I adored him, I used to live for the moment he went to bed so I could watch something other than Mr. Tumble and trough my way through several rounds of cheese on toast—my equivalent of cracking open the wine, I suppose, which I'd never have afforded even if I'd wanted it. Now, though, I hate it when Zac's not here. It makes me feel edgy. I feel safer when he's around, basically, which worries me, because what sort of parent does that make me? Sometimes it feels like he's the man of the house and my child, all rolled into one: my little big man.

I go into his room and sit on the bed to eat my sandwich. It's Man U–tastic in here; has been since we moved here when he was six, and as he had his own room (and bed) for the first time in his life, I let him choose the theme. Obviously Mum and Dad helped with the cost, but we went the whole hog: Man Utd duvet cover, lampshade, and curtains. We could have got Man U wallpaper too, but it's nice he has the walls blank, so you can actually see the pictures he has up there

without them being lost in a sea of red. I like looking at them. They're thumbprints of Zac and who
he is. There's a poster about Arctic animals—the
orca being his favorite animal "of all time"; a map
of the world, which makes me feel like crying,
since besides that one day in London, he's barely
been out of Grimsby; and a framed photo of my
brother. He's in his chef whites on his graduation
day from catering college, looking mighty chuffed
with himself: **Look at me, I've achieved something off my own back, not just followed Dad
into fishing.** He was the first to break the chain
in four generations.

I wander over to the picture. I like to get right
up close to it, look into Jamie's eyes, and see if
I can reach my brother somehow, whichever universe he's in; meet him at a time and place before
everything happened. I've always thought it was
so lovely how Zac looks up to his uncle Jamie even
though he never knew him. I just wish I could tell
him more about him, like I wish I could tell him
about his dad. I fantasize about us being a normal family with stories, rather than secrets. You
know, the "how Mum and Dad met" story and
the "what it was like when I was born" story. But
for us, for Zac, those conversations are off-limits,
like a boarded-up house with **Danger** plastered
across it, because you never know what questions
they're going to lead to.

It doesn't stop me imagining what I'd say if things were different, though, and I like to lie, when he's asleep next to me sometimes, and pretend I'm telling him the story of our first kiss: **So, when your daddy and I kissed for the first time, it was outside the Fiddler in Cleethorpes— classy—and a dodgy local band was playing "Living on a Prayer" inside, but I could hardly hear it, because I was too busy concentrating on the feel of your dad's lips on mine—because he had the softest lips in the world, just like yours. And the sky was pink with clouds that looked like they were racing away from us, and the seagulls that crisscrossed between the buildings above us were in silhouette. It was a beautiful night and your dad stopped kissing me for a moment. "Look, it's a mackerel sky," he said. "Which means we're about four hundred kilometers ahead of the rain . . ." And even though I'd heard stuff like that a hundred times before, being a skipper's daughter (and even though it was only our first kiss and your daddy was just a deckhand), it was the most romantic thing anyone had ever said to me. I was already praying I'd become a fisherman's wife . . .**

Yeah, that's what I'd tell him. But the problem is, when I think about them, those stories don't seem real to me anymore. They seem like ghosts of stories that once existed. They feel dead because they feature another man, a different hero—a man who'd never dream of abandoning his son.

FOR THE FIRST few months after Liam left, it was the night Jamie died I used to obsess over, and how if Liam hadn't behaved as he did, my brother would still be here. I was worried sick about Mum and could not get out of my head the memory of her climbing onto the hospital bed with Jamie after they'd taken out all of his tubes, to cuddle him for one last time. She was broken—she still is—and that was the worst night of my life. But in some ways, where my feelings toward Liam were concerned, it was easier back then. While my grief was so raw, I couldn't feel anything more complicated than anger toward him. I only needed to look at the state of my parents to know there was no way I could be with him.

But then, as time went on, my feelings changed. It wasn't like I actually ever blamed Liam for "killing" my brother, but whereas my anger had initially been directed toward his recklessness and I'd joined Mum and Dad in shunning him from Grimsby, now my anger was directed at the fact that he hadn't come back. Wasn't he going to fight for us? Couldn't he see that it was up to him to seek us out, because for me to do that would be to betray my parents? Especially Mum. Her grief was like a burning lump of coal. Too hot to handle; it had to be passed on. Blame was the thing holding her together. How could I trample on that?

Even before Jamie died, Mum always said Liam was no good. "He'll go the same way as his dad," she used to say. "Drinking, fighting, prison . . ." And I always blew up in anger, always defended him, because all I cared about was the heart inside this man, which I knew was as big as the ocean. And then Jamie died, and that changed everything. For a while, I thought he'd proved Mum right. I still do sometimes. The difference is that now it's not because of what happened to Jamie; it's because he never bothered to come back for me and his son.

ZAC'S PAJAMAS AND dressing gown (Man Utd, naturally) lie in a red heap in the middle of his bedroom floor where he obviously stepped out of them in a rush this morning. I lean down and pick up the dressing gown, thinking how there can't possibly be a more football-mad kid who never plays football, and hold it to my face. It smells of Zac—washing powder, cooking from this morning's pancakes, and his hair, his skin— and I inhale deeply, almost as if to bottle up inside of me this essence of my ten-year-old forever, so that later, when he falls in love with a woman and leaves me, I can open it up and remember how we were.

For so long it's been Zac and me and he's taken

my word for everything. But in less than three months he'll be eleven; his innocence won't last forever. Then there'll be the questions, the sadness and rejection . . . I resent Liam for leaving me to deal with all this—all this worry and fear, all this terrifying love—on my own.

IT'S POSSIBLY IRONIC that I work in the food industry, since that was always our Jamie's calling—I had no interest in food other than eating it. But Gino, my boss at Sandwich King, knows my dad (everyone in this town knows my dad), so he lets me work cash in hand so I can still claim benefits, and I can do extra hours at evening catering events if I need, which I always do. And I know some people might judge me for leaving my kid to let himself in and put himself to bed once a week, but to those people I say this: try living off £110 a week all in. Because it's doable—just—when nothing goes wrong and there's nothing extra to pay for, save for surviving. But if you want to live at all—and I'm not talking restaurants and holidays here, I mean the odd ice cream, putting a bit by for birthdays—you have to work extra.

Sometimes, like today when I'm walking into town to work and I pass the shiny high-rise offices near Victoria Wharf, I fantasize about having a proper job. I wonder where I'd be working if I hadn't reached the dizzy heights of Sandwich

King, but then, generally, draw a blank. Grimsby isn't famed for being a "going places" sort of town. "There's one road in and one road out of this town," my nan used to say, like this was a good thing. "Which means everyone here is Grimsby pedigree." Famous bands? People? Famous anything from Grimsby? Nope, me neither. When you drive into Grim, the welcome sign says, **Welcome to Grimsby, Home to Young's Fish**. Manchester gets Brit Pop and we get frozen prawns. But despite this handicap I did have ambitions when I was a teenager; I did intend to get out and get a good job—maybe even go to university. I used to think I'd like to be a teacher, because I've always loved kids and people say I'm patient. Or maybe I'd have worked in an office doing one of those exciting-sounding glossy jobs I don't even fully understand: events organizer, copywriter . . . The point is, I never got to explore any of these things, since in the space of three weeks, in that June of 2005, I had a baby, lost my brother and my boyfriend, and my life went on a whole different path to the one I'd imagined; one that led to the Harlequin Estate.

It's funny that I ended up on the Quin, as it's known round here, because Mum used to be snotty about the estate when we were growing up; she still is. It's one of the key points of conflict between her and Dad, because Dad was born and bred on the Harlequin; pretty much all the fishing families were. "They're my people, Jules, the salt of the earth," he'd say. There were only actually two roads that separated where we lived on Queens Road, which boasted pebble-dashed semis and which was where many skippers like Dad lived, and the Quin, where deckhands (and now me and Zac) roughed it out in the high-rises and blocks of maisonettes. But those two roads were everything in my mother's mind, who, as much as she loves Dad, has always felt she "married down." Mum wanted bigger, better things for us, and I suppose I'm a disappointment.

I'M ON THE nine a.m. till five p.m. shift at work and Laura and I are doing the first job of the day, which is to make the sandwich mixes to go in the trays at the front. It's an art form, no doubt about it. You've got to get the sizes of the egg or the chicken pieces even and just the right amount of mayo or else people get very upset—especially Gino. He's protective over his sandwich fillings, which are gourmet, don't you know?: Hawaiian mix, coronation chicken mix, coming to you in a subway roll, a seeded bagel, a Danish bloomer . . . We've had the same ones for four years now. Try and suggest change at your peril. If it were just Gino and I, there would probably have been a murder by now, but there's also Laura, and it's her and my regulars that make this job bearable. Laura's dad's an ex-fisherman too. I've known her since I was knee-high and we used to go down the docks and wave off our daddies on sailing day, competing as to who could do the most dramatic show of emotion. (I always won.)

"So what's up with you?" says Laura, as we stand side by side, her chopping chicken, me the eggs. That's one of the drawbacks of working with your best friend: you can't go to work as an escape from the crap happening in your daily life. Especially if your BFF has got Russell Grant–level skills of perception and you've got a face like mine, that wears it all.

"Me? There's nothing wrong with me," I say, but actually, I'm worrying about Zac. It's nearly ten a.m.—he'll have break time soon, but will he have a friend to play with? Is he okay?

"Why the face like a dropped pie, then?" says Laura.

I sigh. Nothing gets past her. "I'm just a bit worried about Zac," I say, trying to sound breezy, for me as much as her. "He's being picked on."

"Picked on?" Laura stops, wielding her butter knife. "Who by? Who's picking on my Zac?" Laura is Zac's godmother, not that I'm remotely a God-type person, but since he didn't have his father or his uncle on the scene I felt he needed as many guardians as possible, so I had him christened. Just the two of us never seemed safe; what if something happened to me, like it all just got too much one day and I threw myself off the roof of Garibaldi House, the high-rise where we used to live? I'd be lying if I hadn't thought about it—especially in the early days, after everything happened.

"Come on, who's bullying him? I want to know," says Laura again. "Because I'm from the East Marsh Estate, I'll have you know, and I'm hard as nails—much harder than you Harlequin pussies—and whoever's bullying my Zac will need to answer to me."

"Right you are, Laurs . . ." She knows as well as I do how well vigilantism would go down round here. I go back to my chopping.

"What's he being picked on for anyway?" she says, when I still don't say anything. "His weird mother?"

"Funny, but no. His size," I say, chopping just ever so slightly harder. "I mean, can you believe it? He's **ten** and I know he's a bit chubby, but no more than other kids and it's just puppy fat, anyone can see that. To make out he's actually **fat** . . . I mean, 'obese' was the word they used. Obese! Can you believe it?" Why isn't Laura saying anything? "It's ridiculous, don't you think?"

Laura stops chopping the chicken and looks away, knife poised.

"Well, you know who else was the fat kid, don't you?" she says after a way-too-long pause, and I shake my head blankly. "Me! Don't you remember?"

Laura and I were at school together in the same group. (The one that actually wanted to get out of Grimsby and make something of our lives. There have been many lunchtimes at the sandwich shop devoted to working out how four of that six-strong group are now working in London in flashy PR jobs while we're wearing hairnets and buttering baps . . .)

"Well, I was, wasn't I?" she says. "Even though you wouldn't know it now, obviously." She puts her hands on her hips to accentuate her thin waist. Laura's skinny, probably a size ten. Whereas I've got wider since school, she's got narrower. I didn't see her for a year or two when Zac was between the ages of about four and six—some stupid falling-out that's not even worth going into—during which she dropped about five stone and I put on three. It was funny in a way, how we both stood in the street chatting, and nobody mentioned the other person's complete body transformation.

"I was a right old porker," continues Laura. "A total heifer. I had a forty-two-inch back at fourteen! Don't you remember? The boys were merciless. I messed up my exams over my weight . . ."

"You did not. You're totally exaggerating," I say, but there's a feeling, a sense of dread I can't rationalize, something ominous on the horizon like an incoming typhoon.

———

IT'S WHAT LAURA and I call a seesaw shift: up
one minute and down the other. We have a last-
minute buffet to do in the morning for a business
meeting down at the fish market, Gino breathing
down our necks like his life depends on it, and
then after that, nothing. The afternoon drags, the
sky darkening by three p.m. Gino is out at a sup-
plier's and so Laura and I pass the time by creating
and sampling new potential sandwich fillings—
vital for business progression, if Gino ever sees
sense—and her reminiscing darkly about her days
as a fat child. For some reason, I keep pushing her
for details. And how was it then, being morbidly
obese? Shit, she tells me, utterly humiliating—
and, as her best friend, I hadn't even given it a
second thought.

Zac knows to come straight here after school
on a Monday so he's always here by three forty-
five p.m. By four, however, there's no sign of him.
I check my phone, but it's dead. It would kind of
be typical, wouldn't it, that the day my son needs
me the most is the day my phone has run out of
battery at precisely the time he's probably enter-
ing his own version of a living hell? So the first I
know of it is when he eventually walks through
the door at four fifteen, with brown stuff smeared
all over him, and I start shaking. I stand behind
the counter, up to my eyes in coronation chicken,
shaking like a leaf because I think it's shit he's got
pasted all over his school shirt, in his lovely gold

hair, all over his face, and I think, **I swear to God, whoever's done this to him, I am going to kill them.**

Then he drops his Man Utd rucksack and, dragging his feet, comes around to my side of the counter and I realize it's not shit because it doesn't smell like shit. A quick sniff confirms this. He has chocolate cake or muffin all over him. Crumby clumps of it in his hair like grains of instant coffee.

Laura starts to shout. **"Who did this, Zac?"**

But I can't do or say anything except, "Oh God, oh God . . ."

"Mum, I need some trousers," says Zac.

I've got my hand to my mouth. I'm still wearing my plastic food-handling glove, and it stinks of coronation chicken, but it's so I don't scream. "What do you mean you need some trousers?"

Then he turns around and I see that the whole seat of his school trousers has been ripped out, so all you can see are his bright red Angry Bird boxers.

Well, I'm an angry bird now. Oh yeah, I'm a bloody livid bird, I am.

"Who did this to you?"

"Dunno, some kids. Mum . . ." His eyes dart to the door. "Have you got any trousers here? Some spares?" He has his hands over his bum. "Have you got a coat I can wear? Everyone can see my pants."

"I can see that, but I don't care about your pants

right now, Zac. I want to know who did this to you."

"I don't know!" He says it like he's annoyed with me. "Some kids on the bus."

"What, and the bus driver did **nothing**?"

"Mum, don't shout. He didn't see."

"You're telling me some kids throw choco-late cake all over you, then tear your trousers to shreds, and the driver doesn't even see?"

"They were giving me a wedgie—it started as a joke."

"Joke? Zac, sweetheart . . ." Honestly, my boy, he sees the best in people. It's the thing I love most about him, but it is also his downfall. "Was it Aidan Turner?"

"No."

"It was, wasn't it?" I don't know why I'm even asking because I can tell by his face. Zac may be able to see the best in people, but he can't lie to save his life. "Zac, tell me the truth."

"Look, it started off as a joke; he was giving me a wedgie. He's my friend normally, honestly; he's . . ." His voice fades. "It all went too far. He didn't mean to."

"I'll kill him," says Laura from where she's standing.

"Laura, leave it," I say. "I'll deal with this."

I can feel the anger building in me now, fizzing like a firework, but Zac's big blue eyes are welling up and I feel bad for shouting, so I give him a hug, curry-covered gloves and all—well, it doesn't matter now, does it? We're in a right sodding mess. Then Gino comes out from round the back of the shop, arms in the air, all Mediterranean and dramatic, which is all we need. Gino's all right when you're on the right side of him, but he can also be a real twat sometimes—like a lot of men, in my experience.

"Juliet, Jesus, what's the fucking racket?" He's leaning against the door frame in his kitchen whites like Gordon bloody Ramsay. "What's going on?"

"Someone's attacked my son, Gino, that's what's going on."

I'm holding Zac's head next to my chest, like I'll never let him go. Gino steps forward, almost like he doesn't dare, peers at Zac, swears under his breath, and walks off, hands on his head. I shout after him, "Calm down, it's **chocolate**!"

Just then the bell goes and a customer walks in. You can see Gino's whole body tense and he comes over and speaks in Zac's ear. "I'm sorry, my friend. I'm sorry, this is horrible, but can you go in the back, get yourself cleaned up?"

Zac does as he's told—my good boy—but I'm already taking my apron off. I am a woman on a mission.

"I'm going down to the school."

The way Gino looks at me, it's like I'm abandoning him at the foot of Everest.

"You've seen the state of him, haven't you? I'm

his mother," I say. Gino's not quite grasped yet that Zac comes first, but he will.

"And we have customers. You clock off at five, can't you wait till then?"

"No, I can't." I'm careful to keep my voice down. I don't want to scare off customers, but Gino isn't making this easy for me. "The head-mistress will be gone by then and I need to know why this has been allowed to happen **now**." And damn it, I'm crying now. "Make Zac a sandwich," I say to Laura. "He doesn't like crusts and he likes the chicken and sweet corn." Then I pick up my bag and coat and walk out the door, telling Gino I'll make up the time tomorrow.

It's freezing out; the trees are angry stick men. The sun is just setting and the sky is on fire. I walk quickly to the bus stop, my arms wrapped tight around me. There's a siren wailing, getting louder and louder. I think about that feeling I had in my chest when I thought it was shit he had all over him, that feeling like an earthquake was building, about to create havoc. Murderous—that was the word. In that moment, I would have murdered whoever did that to him. The moment passed, but it scared me to death, because what would happen if I actually did kill someone? We'd be in an even bigger mess than we were now, that's for sure.

An ambulance careens around the corner, its wail deafening, and I cover my ears. It feels like it's coming for me. Like the emergency is coming from inside me. And it hits me, then, that feeling I had when Laura was talking, that feeling like the incoming tornado. He's the Fat Kid. My son, he's **the** Fat Kid, the one everyone will remember as such, like they remember Laura, and I have to do something. I have to help him.

6

Zac

**Fact: Inside the womb, touch is the
first of the five senses to form.**

Miss Kendall's real name is the same as my
mum's except for one letter. It's Julie whereas
my mum's is Juliet. I really like Miss Kendall. She
can be strict, but she's really kind too. Since what
happened on the bus last week, she says I can go
and talk to her anytime I want, and every day, just
before home time, we have our special thing where
she goes, "Zac, out of five?" And I have to put up
the number of fingers I think the day has been
worth. If it's below three, then we can have a chat,
but if I don't want to, she doesn't make me. It's just
our code so she can keep an eye on me.

It was Monday—one of my worst days usually because we have PE in the afternoon—and
we were about to start guided reading, but Miss
Kendall was standing at the front, clapping to get

our attention. We have to clap back to show we're listening.

"So, children," she said, "before we start with our reading today, I've got a little announcement. A bit of good news."

Connor, who sits next to me, was singing. I nudged him to be quiet so we could hear the good news.

"Some of you may have noticed that I've been getting a bit bigger, especially around the tummy area. And in case you thought I'd just eaten a lot of cakes, I wanted to tell you my news, which is that if everything goes well, around the end of May, I'll become a mum!"

There were some gasps—mostly from the girls. I was smiling. I felt dead happy. The baby could even have the same birthday as me!

"What you smiling for?" said Connor.

"It's 'cause he's pregnant too," said Luke Shallcross behind us—Luke is one of Aidan's sheep. "That's why his belly's massive, 'cause he can't stop eating cakes either."

All the people at Luke's table laughed, but I just ignored them like Brenda says I should, then Jack went, "So are you actually pregnant, miss?"

"I am," said Miss Kendall. She had a smile as wide as a character from a cartoon. I'd never seen anyone look so happy.

"And do you know if it's a boy or a girl?"

"I do know. Would you like to guess?"

It was mad then, because nearly all the boys guessed it would be a boy and all the girls guessed it would be a girl. When she said it was a girl (I was right!) a couple of boys moaned and Connor pretended to be sick. Miss Kendall was just laughing, though; she said we were all crackers.

Some people wanted to know if Miss Kendall had thought of a name for it yet. She said she hadn't but was open to ideas and Connor suggested Mango. Everyone started laughing, including me. It was really, really funny. Connor has ADHD and Tourette's but only mild. Sometimes he gets angry and tells you to fuck off, but also he likes the word "mango"—nobody knows why. Sometimes he calls me a fat mango, but he's still my really good friend.

Courtney put her hand up. "But, miss, you're not married. I thought you had to be married to have a baby."

"Uh, no. That's not actually true, Courtney. Some people are; some people aren't."

Certain kids started calling out then, saying their parents weren't married and yet they'd still been born. I wondered how many of those didn't even know who their dads were. I did a scan of everyone in the class and decided I was the only one.

Miss Kendall started clapping again then, to get us to pay attention.

"So, children, I think Courtney has raised a

very important question. There isn't one right way
to have a baby and there isn't one type of family,
is there? As we touched on when we did our family trees, families come with married parents, non-
married parents, and sometimes only one parent.
Yes, Lauren?"

"I've got two dads, miss. My real one lives in
Hull, but my stepdad acts like my real dad and
lives in our house."

"Well, there we are. All sorts of family shapes."

"They used to be best friends, but now because
Alan's with my mum, my dad's not allowed to
come anymore."

"Oh." Miss Kendall frowned. "Well, that is
sad. I think the most important thing in a family,
though, is love. Love is all you need."

Then Joe Hilditch went, "Do you have to love
someone then to have a baby, miss?"

"Yes, I think so," she said, after considering this
for a bit. "I think it certainly helps."

"So are you in love?" Joe said and suddenly everyone was killing themselves laughing again.

"Yes," Miss Kendall said. (She was going red
and everything!) "Yes, Joe, I am in love."

It was definitely more proof that what my mum
said was true—she must have been in love with
my dad, because you have to be in love with the
other person to even have a baby; Miss Kendall
said so. I decided I'd put it in my Find Dad mission folder as soon as I got home.

Normally I tell Teagan absolutely everything—well, not about the bad stuff at school, but everything else. I haven't told her my idea about finding my dad yet, though, and that I want to give him a chance. I don't want to hurt her feelings since her own dad left not that long ago, and also, if I was going to ask her to help me (which I am), I wanted to have a few ideas before I did. I wanted to have done some groundwork, like a proper detective. It's my mission, after all, and before you start any mission, you've got to have an MO. That stands for **modus operandi**. It's Latin—I looked it up on Wikipedia—but in English it means "method of operation." Serial killers have MOs, like how Jack the Ripper slashed his victims' throats and took out all their hearts and stomachs—that's how you knew he'd done it.

MOs can also be used for investigations, though, which is what I'm doing.

In my folder so far, my MO says:

- **I WILL NOT tell Mum, Nan, Grandad, or anyone except Teagan what I'm doing. I want it to be a surprise. I know my mum will be dead happy when it actually happens. Whereas if I tell her beforehand, I think she'll just go mad.**

- **I WILL find out which Liam Jones is my dad because there are loads. When**

I put it in Google ages ago there was
a famous jockey and a photographer
called Liam Jones. What if my dad is
actually famous?!

- I WILL find out his address so I can
  actually send him my letter inviting
  him to my eleventh birthday, even
  though I wrote the letter before the
  Find Dad mission officially existed.
  (What if he doesn't even live in
  Grimsby anymore, though? He might
  have emigrated to Australia like Ellie
  Moran did in Year 3. I hope not. I'd
  have to abort my mission then, because
  it would take probably seventy years
  to save up to fly to Australia, by which
  point he'd be dead.)

- I WILL have to do my research and
  ask Mum, Nan, and Grandad lots of
  questions about my dad, but without
  making them suspicious. If you're
  trying to find a person—like when they
  were trying to find Jack the Ripper—
  you have to find out as much as possible
  about them.

- I WILL write down all my progress in
  my mission folder. It's what you have to
  do to keep track.

I MET UP with Teagan in the dinner queue as I normally do. She gets free dinners like me so we always go together. It was pork patties and mashed potato, and Dean, who is one of the dinner ladies, except he's a dinner man, was working in the canteen. It's brilliant when Dean's working because he always gives us extra. He's got a tattoo of a Smurf on one arm and the birth dates of his children next to his heart. He must really love his kids to have gone through that pain. When me and Teagan found out, he went up in rank on the Top Trumps for Dads chart from fifth to second, just under Jacob Wilmore's dad.

"Hey, it's ma homies!" said Dean when he saw us. Dean has to wear an orange beard net when he's serving us food; it's very, very funny. "How's my favorite twosome?"

He went to give us a massive extra dollop of mash as usual, but as he was putting it on Teagan's plate, she stopped him. "No, thanks, Dean, we don't want extra mash today." His spoon was hovering; you could tell he was surprised. "Or Zac," she said. "He doesn't want any either."

"Why'd you do that?" I said, when we were sitting down.

"I'm just not into mash that much anymore."

"But I am," I said. "What about me?"

"Shh," she said, "let's not talk about mash anymore. Let's talk about something good."

That was when I told her what Mum had said when she was drunk about loving my dad.

Teagan was staring at me and frowning at the same time.

"But I thought you said he was an idiot," she said, and I felt bad then for all the times I'd said that. I used to think my dad would look like a messed-up person, like Sam Bale's dad, with some teeth missing and scars from fighting, but now I knew he wouldn't. I knew he'd look like a proper dad.

"I thought he was. But now I think, how can he be? If she really loved him and he loved her?"

"But hang on," said Teagan. "Why, if he loved her, did he even do a runner then?"

"That's what I want to find out!" I said, thinking it was awesome that we thought the same thing. "I want to give him a chance to explain and tell the truth and maybe then he'll be my dad and maybe even get together with my mum again. But I can only find out if I find him, can't I? I need to speak to him face-to-face."

That was when I asked Teagan if she'd help me and she said yes. That was when she officially became my deputy on the Find Dad mission.

GRANDAD SAYS THAT most days are rhubarb and custard days, like rhubarb and custard sweets, but that it's about sucking on the sweet custard bits so hard that you don't taste the sour rhubarb.

That Thursday was a good example of a rhubarb and custard day, because there was the happy bit about Miss Kendall's baby and then there was the journey home on the bus . . .

I've got a technique now. I sit on the top deck, but in one of the seats right at the front. If I'm lucky, when Aidan Turner or any of his lot get on, they don't even notice I'm there. This works extra well if I remember to take a hoodie because they can't recognize me from the back of my head, and the fact that it could be me doesn't even come into their brains.

Today, however, there was already someone on the front seat and too many people downstairs, otherwise I'd have stood by the driver where they don't harass me as much. In the end, the only seat was two rows in front of Aidan Turner. At first they were just whispering, but as the journey went on, it got louder.

"Hey, Jabba the Hutch, I'm talking to you. When's your baby due? Did you have sex with Miss Kendall? I hope you didn't go on top of her 'cause you would have squashed her."

My heart was pounding so hard I could hear it, but I just looked out of the window. It didn't even make sense because a man can't have a baby.

Sometimes in one day you can get a rhubarb and custard bit several times over—that's the good thing about it: just because you've had a rhubarb bit doesn't mean you can't get a nice sweet custard bit after, even if you've already had one.

When I got off the bus, I decided to walk the long way home, past Your Fitness—just in case Jason was there.

I stopped outside and ate my Hula Hoops. The sun had come out—it felt like eons since it had— and it was warm and lovely on my face, like when I lie in the bath with a hot flannel over my head; everyone should try it, it's really relaxing.

I can fit five Hula Hoops on my little finger and one on the next finger, but no more. When I was nine, I could fit a Hula Hoop up to my middle finger so I know I've grown. You have to bite down just the right amount so that it cracks the Hula Hoop but not your finger and each time I was doing this, I was secretly making a wish that Jason would just magically come out and see me and then . . . it came true! It was sick! It was the cus-tard bit happening, like magic because Jason came walking straight out of the Your Fitness center.

He seemed proper pleased and surprised to see me. "Zac, my man, what are you doing here?"

"I was just walking past."

"It's good to see you," said Jason and he put his hand on my shoulder; it felt nice. Jason's got dead big muscles and he's six feet, three inches tall. The tallest man in England is Neil Fingleton, who is seven feet, seven inches, so he's not that far off. I come up to Jason's chest, but I bet if I stood next to Neil Fingleton, I'd only come up to his knees. "So are you looking into joining our boxing club?" Jason teaches boxing as well as aikido and karate. He can do twenty pull-ups on our kitchen door frame.

"Um, no, not really."

"Come on!" he said, pushing me away, but I knew he was just teasing. "Footie?"

"Nah."

"Come on, you're a good little goalie."

"I'm not."

"You are!"

"That was ages ago."

"Once a good goalie, always a good goalie," Jason said, and then he hugged me but just with one arm. I felt a bit embarrassed but only because I haven't seen him for ages.

"And how's life?"

"Good." I felt guilty about not telling him about my Find Dad mission—I don't know why.

"And how's your mum?"

"She's all right, she's fine."

"Been out in Cleethorpes recently, has she? Strutting her stuff on the dance floor again?" He helped himself to three of my Hula Hoops, but I didn't mind. "She's a great dancer, your mum," he said and I felt sad because I knew he was probably thinking of the good times when he was her boyfriend, like his mum's fiftieth birthday party down the Casablanca Club when we all danced all night. I didn't know anyone there, I'd only just met Jason's family that night, but they were so nice and friendly and I danced nonstop and at the end I was so hot I poured a glass of freezing-cold water over my head. Nobody could believe it. It was the best night of my life.

In case Jason was thinking of the good times, I said, "No, she's not been anywhere," but then, before I could stop it, "except on a date . . . She didn't like him, though!" I said it quickly, even though it was too late. I've got this problem: I can't lie or even leave stuff out that's true. It's like there's this Devil voice going, **You have to say it**, talking in my ear.

"Didn't she?" said Jason.

"Nah. She hit him."

"She **hit** him?" His eyes popped out of his head then, and he laughed and so did I, I don't know why.

"Yeah, over the head with her handbag; in the snow in the middle of our estate. I saw her! It was absolutely hilarious."

"Who was this guy?"

"Dunno. Dom someone?" My heart was beating. I wished I could stop talking.

"Dom Parish?" said Jason.

"I . . . I'm not sure."

"Why did she hit him? Had he done something to her?" Jason's smile completely went then and he looked dead worried.

"No!" I didn't want him to worry about my mum, because he loves her. "She just wanted to kiss him and he didn't want to kiss her . . . and . . ." I wanted to go, badly. "I wasn't really looking."

I used to think Mum and Jason might get back together. I once went in the Christian Center and prayed for it to happen. It has **Ask Jesus and He Will Answer** painted on the side of the building so I did, but it didn't come true; not that I blame Jesus because I bet he gets asked loads of stuff and there's only so many hours in the day. And anyway, now I knew they definitely wouldn't be being boyfriend and girlfriend again, not because of Dom but because of my dad being the only man my mum's ever loved.

There was a pause then. It went on quite long. I was beginning to think Mum was right about not seeing Jason so much anymore—it felt a bit weird.

"Well, listen, tell your mum I said hello, won't you?" Jason said eventually, putting his hand on my shoulder again. "Tell her it'd be nice to come round for a coffee again soon, or me and you could hang out?"

"Deffo."

"Have a kick around up in the field?" he said, and I smiled to be polite, but I wasn't sure I wanted to—it'd been ages and I was probably crap again by now.

"All right, well, take it easy and make sure you give your mum my love, won't you?"

"All right then," I said. "See ya." But I'd already started to walk away. I didn't want to say, **She sends her love back**, because I knew she didn't, not now. I knew she only had romantic feelings for my dad.

EVER SINCE WE had the letter going home saying I'm above the normal weight for my age, Mum's started trying to get me to eat more healthy stuff. We still have Chinese on a Friday, but she's been trying to encourage me to eat fruit for breakfast (it's all right if you put it on a pancake) and she put all the crisps and biscuits in the secret cupboard, so I have to ask if I want anything.

Mum doesn't know this, but I know where the secret cupboard is, so when she's at work I can just help myself. I try and resist but it's really hard. If they wanted children not to eat so much, they shouldn't make stuff that's bad for you so nice. That's what I would do if I was the prime minister: I'd tell the people who make the chocolate biscuits and the crisps not to make them so nice so people like me wouldn't want to eat them all the time.

I know I'm big for my age and I hate getting

teased about it, but I'm only ten and it's puppy fat. Nan says I've got my whole life to go on a diet. Mind you, my nan's been on a diet her whole life and it hasn't made any difference. I just think I'm like my uncle Jamie. It's what chefs are like; they just love their food. The main problem is when I come home from school on my own. It's a really long time from dinner break to home time, so by the time I get back, I'm starvin' marvin. Tonight, for example, I tried for ages to resist the Call of the Stomach (that's what me and Mum call it when we're hungry), and to wait till tea, but I was starving by half past four, so I got a packet of Nik Naks and a caramel wafer from the secret cupboard— then I waited till the six o'clock fridge. We get most of our food from the six o'clock fridge at the Tesco at the bottom of the road. It's where they sell off food from that day, but for really cheap. You can get steak for £1, then just put it in the freezer. It's great for junior chefs like me, because you can't choose what's there; you just have to see then make something good from it. Today there were only some Aunt Bessie's Yorkshire puddings and some carrots, but together they only cost me 70p! So I got them, then I went home and I made my tea (Yorkshire pudding, gravy, carrots, and mash). But today I had cheesy mash. (It's lovely, you should definitely try it.)

I go to bed about nine p.m. when my mum's at work and I take my **Factblaster** book with me. It's totally boss. It's got a picture of someone's brain on the front with everything coming out of it: dinosaurs and robots and planets; machines, a volcano, and a Greek temple—with its roof blown off so you can see the inside. It's meant to show how when you read it, you'll know about all this stuff too. My favorite bit is the flags of all the different countries at the back. I like learning them off by heart and then testing myself.

One of my other favorite bits of the book is the index, because you can just go down it with your finger and there are so many subjects to choose from. I looked up about sex, but it wasn't under a section called "sex"—it was like it was trying to fool you—it was under a section called "life cycle." There was a picture of a sperm going into an egg. It told you about how the egg is fertilized, and then how the baby grows. **Touch is the first of the five senses to form in the womb,** it said. So I've touched the inside of my mum's womb! I thought. The blood and skin and everything—it felt mad. I turned back to the index then. The book's really heavy so you have to be careful that it doesn't slide off your knee, and I got my bedside lamp so the light was shining right on the index. Then I looked under "D." It does say **Every fact you've ever wanted to know** on the front, after all, and so I thought it was worth a try; it was even exciting. There was "dams," there was even "death," but, worst luck, there was nothing about dads. That was when I decided to add what Mum had said about loving my dad to the end of the letter I'd written before all this started, because you wouldn't ignore a letter with that on it, would you? And what if my dad didn't even know that she had ever loved him? What if that was why he left in the first place?

I've got a secret: when I wrote the letter this New Year's Eve, even though I said everyone was mad with Liam except me, I was mad too—a little bit. The year 2015 had been rubbish. I felt scared and sad all the time. Since my birthday when I was ten in May, Mum seemed to have got sadder too. She was crying a lot and saying she was fat and disgusting, even though I told her I thought she looked fine and, anyway, it's the person inside that counts. But then, on Halloween last year, she got caught in Morrisons with a Halloween cake and a packet of KitKat Chunkys in her bag. She said it was a mistake and that she'd done the scanning machine wrong, but she had to go into a room with a policeman while another lady policeman stayed with me outside and Mum cried so much she couldn't breathe. We weren't allowed to shop in Morrisons after that, and I started to worry a lot about what would happen to us: like, what if she got caught with something in her bag in Tesco or Costcutter? Where would we get our food then? I got so worried that one day, I didn't even go to school. I just wandered around town and bought whatever I wanted to eat with my money I'd got for my birthday, until Jacob Wilmore's mum saw me and told my mum. That was when they got me Brenda to talk to. So while it was true that I wanted to give Dad a chance and for him to come to my party, I mainly just wanted him to come and help us, help me. And that was what I was thinking when I wrote the letter. Now, though, things had changed. I still wanted him to come and help us, but I also wanted him to see my mum again and realize he loves her as much as she loves him, and then we can **all** be happy.

I OPENED MY bedside table drawer where I had the letter and got my pen out. Then I wrote the extra bit at the end about my mum loving my dad. Now I just had to get his address or, better still, find him and give it to him in person, because there was no way he'd be able to ignore that bit.

7

Mick

"Are you the father of James Hutchinson?" I'll
never forget those words. It was just after
midnight on June 12, 2005, and I'd opened the
door to find two policemen in neon jackets standing on my doorstep, a swirl of blue lights behind
them.

"Yes," I said. I'd been passed out on the settee
and I was disorientated. I thought I might still be
dreaming.

They glanced to the side of me, through the
house.

"Are you in alone or is your wife in too?" That
was the point at which I knew something was seriously wrong and my heart began to bang in my
mouth.

"No, she's at work—she works at a care home.
She's on a night shift."

"Can we come in and sit down?" they said.

I felt my bowels disintegrate; utter fear swept through me like an icy wind.

"What the hell's he done now?" I said it with a smile on my face, but I already knew something terrible had happened.

"I think it's best if we come in and sit down."

They ducked their heads; they seemed to take up our whole lounge with their neon jackets and their walkie-talkies that bleeped and spluttered. They both looked barely out of their teens and almost as scared as me, and I've often wondered, in the years that followed, if this was the first time they'd done this: knock on some poor bastard's door in the small hours and open up a great hole in his life.

They came in and sat down, but I didn't. There was a barely touched cup of coffee and a half-eaten sandwich on the arm of the sofa. I took it and moved it into the kitchen, perhaps to delay whatever bad news I knew they were here to tell me. They explained there'd been an incident down by the wharf on Victoria Street. Jamie and Liam Jones, who they believed to be the partner of my daughter, which I confirmed, had been involved in a serious fight down there with another individual. They couldn't tell me his name because it was part of their ongoing investigation, but I had a good idea it was Chris Hynd, a local I'd known for a long time and just a well-known wind-up merchant. The fight had resulted in Jamie being knocked to the ground, cracking his head on the corner of the pavement, and being knocked unconscious.

My stomach capsized. A picture flashed up of him being thrown backward in slow motion, cheeks reverberating with the force, spit flying, bone splintering.

"But he's okay?"

"It's serious, I'm afraid."

"How bad?"

"He's been taken to A&E. The doctors are doing everything they can."

They asked me if I wanted them to drive me to the care home where Lynda was working and come with me to tell her, or if I'd prefer they radioed for another officer to go, and we meet at the hospital. I said let's go straight to the hospital. They must have thought how strange it was that I didn't want to immediately be with my wife, the mother of my son, at a time like this, but even then I knew I didn't want to look her square in the eye, that I couldn't. Sometimes I feel like I've not been able to look Lynda in the eye since. I can't bear to see her pain and to know, to know . . .

We walked toward the police car. The flashing light was blinding me and my legs were shaking so much one of the officers had to help me in. I wasn't crying, not at this point; the crying was to come later when the scale of it all hit me. Right then, I was numb with shock.

I was holding my head in my hands in the backseat and rambling. How long was he down on the floor? Was he knocked unconscious immediately? Who else was involved in the fight? I wanted to hear names. I wanted to punish myself. Meanwhile Saturday night rolled on outside, and soon it would be light. How would I face this new day, this new world, if my son wasn't in it?

"At the moment this is an investigation, Mr. Hutchinson. We have to take statements, but we can't do that until everyone who was involved has sobered up." I tried to swallow, but I had no spit, my throat was so dry.

"How pissed were they?"

"They were heavily intoxicated. Please try and stay as calm as possible," the older one in the passenger seat said. "We'll get you some sugary tea as soon as we get to the hospital."

I don't want fucking tea, I thought. **I want my boy.** And I wanted, oh, how I wanted, to be somebody else.

Liam was already in reception when we got to A&E. He was sitting on a red plastic chair, clutching a polystyrene cup, and his hands were trembling so much you could see the hot liquid quivering inside, and when he looked up, his eyes were wet with tears.

I walked over to him, but he couldn't look at me and he was shaking his head as if to escape it. "I'm sorry, I'm so sorry" was all he could say. He was jigging his knees up and down, in a total state, and I could smell the alcohol on him, even though he'd no doubt sobered up by now.

I sat down on the chair opposite him and leaned forward, my hands clasped together as if in prayer.

"It's not your fault," I said, but he just shook his head.

"But it is. It is my fault. I started it, Mick," he said, looking me square in the eye then. "I punched Hynd, and if I hadn't, then Jamie wouldn't have tried to intervene . . . the rest would never have happened . . . Oh God." He was looking up at the ceiling, almost rocking; he couldn't bear this. "But I was so angry, **so** worked up."

"By what?" I said, even though I knew what.

"If I'd have just walked away, if I'd have just kept my cool, not been so fucking **drunk**," he said, and the blood rushed to my face. "I've never thrown a punch at someone, ever."

"Look, Liam," I said. I felt compassion for him at that point—after all, Jamie wasn't dead yet, was he? And there was still the hope that everything would be okay, my family would get back to normal, and we'd get another chance. "You can't think like that. And anyway, I . . ." I started, but I couldn't finish the sentence. I couldn't say the words, even then. But I told myself I couldn't think about me then, anyway; or Liam. All I could think of was Jamie and how much I needed him to be okay.

A&E WAS PACKED. It was Saturday night, after all, and it was bedlam in there: babies crying, phones ringing, nurses dashing, queues growing, and my son lying, clinging to life, somewhere in the middle of all this. Liam sat there, thighs jiggling, biting his fingernails down like a scared little boy. Suddenly he sat up straight and I knew, just by the look in his eyes, it was because Lynda had walked in.

I stood up and turned around. She was making her way toward us, wild-eyed and white as a sheet. I could tell she'd seen Liam, but she didn't speak to him; she didn't even look at him. Of course, she already had her ideas about the man our daughter was in love with, and right then it must have seemed that her worst fears were about to be confirmed. They were, but she didn't know that yet.

We barely said a word to each other—there were no words. A nurse came and said she was taking us to the relatives' room. And so we began down various corridors, past cubicles—some with curtains closed, some without. There were tubes and machines; relatives in coats on plastic chairs, speaking in hushed voices, holding hands. It was stark and quiet inside the relatives' room—lamp-lit, rather than the bright strip lights of the A&E

reception, as if they were trying to cocoon you from the horror. It didn't work. My heart just seemed to bang harder, my panic growing in intensity in the fake calm of that room.

The doctor—he didn't call himself "Dr.," he was "Mr." Lazarus, and he said he was a neuro-surgeon. Just the word made me go cold all over. He explained that Jamie had come round in the ambulance and arrived conscious at the hospital, but that as sometimes happened with the sort of head injury he had, he'd deteriorated rapidly. They'd already scanned him and found a "signifi-cant" bleed to the head. He was unconscious now and we weren't to be "alarmed" by the sound and sight of the tubes and machines, but he was on a ventilator, to help him breathe. These words, these facts he was telling me, I couldn't take them in. It was like he was talking about somebody else's son.

He'd been taken to intensive care and they were doing everything they could, but there was a strong possibility that he wouldn't recover, he told us.

Silence hung then.

"But he will, won't he?" Lynda said eventually. I couldn't look at her. I was staring at a coaster on the table in front of us, which advertised some drug or other.

"Like I say, I'm afraid there's a high possibility

he won't. The prognosis with a head injury like this is poor."

"But there's still a possibility he will, isn't there?" I said. My teeth had begun to chatter.

"There is a small possibility," said Mr. Lazarus. "But the bleed on his brain is, as I say, significant, and there's a strong chance it could get bigger."

Lynda started to sob then and I knew I should hold her hand, but somehow my hand wouldn't move from my thigh. I was wondering what the doctor must be thinking of me, when Lynda placed her hand on top of mine and took a big breath as if to ready herself for the onslaught of angry questions and accusations that followed: "How on earth could he arrive at the hospital conscious, talking, and then be close to death? **Explain that to me.**" What had they done to him? What had they **not** done? Not tried? How long did it take for the ambulance to get to him?

"My Jamie is not the fighting type," she said. "He would never, ever have started a fight. Whereas Liam, **Liam**, sitting outside perfectly fine . . . **How is that?**" She was raising her voice and I tried to shush her, but she threw me a look.

We were allowed in to see him. He was a big lad, was Jamie: chunky, with big feet, a loud voice—we used to joke that even his hair was big. But he looked like a little boy lying there, under all this equipment keeping him alive, and it felt like the first time in so long, maybe the first time ever, that I'd seen him like that: my lad, to protect. I'd failed.

Lynda was stroking Jamie's hair and talking to him: "Hello, baby, it's Mummy. You're going to be fine, okay? You're going to be absolutely fine. I love you."

It was then that I told her about Liam. I don't know why I told her then. I suppose I felt she ought to know and I wanted her to have the truth, or some of it, anyway, rather than throwing around accusations—even if those accusations were true. And most importantly, let's face it, this was the **only** truth I could give her.

She didn't utter a word as I was telling her. There was just a mother's love in her eyes, the grim, tight set of her mouth the only indication of her fury.

At first I didn't notice Liam standing by the gap in the cubicle curtains, but when our eyes met, he flinched. He knew he shouldn't be there. I glared at him, wanting him to go, for his own sake. At that stage, I still felt for him, I understood this must be terrible for him too, but also that Lynda wouldn't see that, nor care.

I had no idea she knew he was there until she started to speak to him. She must have seen him too—if only the shape of him behind the privacy curtain.

"You did this," she said. "You started it. Why the hell were you fighting, Liam, when this was meant to be a night out to celebrate becoming a father? What sort of father are you now? Tell me that. What sort of man?"

She was shaking all over, and I'll never forget the downturn set of her mouth. It was like it set that night, and it has remained like that. The wind had changed, after all; a cold front had moved in permanently.

"I want you to know that I blame you for this. You're just like your father!" she added, her voice rising. Liam stood there, out of Lynda's eyeshot, but I could still see him. I tried to calm Lynda down. Like I say, Jamie wasn't dead yet.

But then at 3:34 a.m. on June 12, 2005, my only son died from a cardiac arrest. They took the tubes out; he didn't need them now after all.

As he slipped away the nurse told us, "Take as much time as you need with him," which was the emptiest of statements, the most heartbreaking, because no length of time is as much as you need. When do you decide you've had enough time with your child to last you a lifetime? After an hour? Two hours? When rigor mortis has set in?

Lynda climbed up on the bed and cuddled him, like she did when he was little and he'd had a nightmare. But me, I was too panicked, too wretched. I literally couldn't stand myself. Everything had changed, and I left the cubicle and pursued Liam like a wild animal then, like a man possessed. I didn't have to go far to find him, walking slowly, sadly, toward the exit, and I grabbed him by the shoulder and I swung him around.

"Yeah, that figures. Leave just as he dies, you coward."

His eyes were unblinking with disbelief. "He's dead?" It was a whisper. "No, he isn't. He can't be."

"He's dead," I said, and he actually staggered with the shock. I thought his legs might give way beneath him.

I got right in Liam's face. I couldn't help myself—the words flew out of my mouth, spit spraying everywhere. I was white with rage, but it was fear, mostly; total fear. "I want you to know I blame you too," I said. "I don't know why I didn't listen to Lynda. She was right. You're just like your father, Liam. You're no better than him. You've got it in your blood; you can't help it. You say you've never started fights before, but this is just the first of many, I assure you. This is where it all begins."

"No, no. Jesus, Mick." Liam was crying, tears running down his face. "Please, I—"

But I told him he needed to go, to leave this family and this town. "You will never survive here," I said. "I promise you that."

Our eyes met then. I remember my teeth were still chattering. And I knew what he was thinking. **I fucked up, but I'm not the only one and you know it.**

"You're just like your father," I said again, as if to stop him saying the thought out loud, and he seemed to dissolve right in front of my eyes. "Never forget it."

He held my gaze, as if imploring me to say something, to soften, but I was merciless, and when he realized I was standing my ground, he turned, and he left. I watched him walk down the corridor, went back in to see my dead son, and broke down.

"I didn't protect him, Lynda." I was holding his lifeless body, sobbing, rocking him in my arms. "I told you I shouldn't have kids, that I wasn't capable of protecting them."

Lynda reached across Jamie and took my hand. "It's not your fault," she said. That's all I keep going back to in my head. **It's not your fault.**

Juliet

"So this here is our selection of notebooks."
The woman helping me in Gifts Galore looks like the sort of person who uses a notebook. She's wearing a silky scarf and dangly silver earrings. "As you can see, there's everything from your hardback decorative ones to your bog-standard ring-bound, or what about a Moleskine?" she says, picking up a plain black one with a bit of elastic around it. "Now, they're lovely notebooks. Hemingway used a Moleskine, apparently."

"How much is that?" I say, taking it from her.

"Ten pounds."

I swiftly put it back on the stand, feeling my cheeks burn. Ten pounds? For a plain black notebook? You must be joking. I don't care if Barack Obama uses them, you could buy a week's food for that in Aldi if you were clever.

"But as I say, Moleskines are a special type of

notebook," she says, clearly noting the look of horror on my face. "Is it for something or someone in particular?"

"Oh no, no," I say, running my fingers up and down the stand over the other ones, but then I think about it. "Well, yeah, actually, I suppose it is. It's for a sort of project I'm starting."

I HAVE A project, a plan to help Zac, and it feels good. More than good. It feels amazing. I'm buzzing. The idea to get a new notebook for it came to me this morning while I was lying in bed. I've been making notes on my phone so far, but Zac is always playing Clash of Clans or Plants vs. Zombies on it, which means the chances of him seeing them is high and the last thing I want is for him to think I'm up to something, that he's officially on "a diet." That would make him run a mile (if he could even run a mile—I'm pretty sure I couldn't) and I don't need that right now; I have to get him on board.

I decided I'd get the notebook on my way to work, so I've already been to Tesco and looked at the no-frills £1.50 jobs there, but I even hemmed and hawed about those. (Actually, I even considered you-know-whatting one because, as I say, every penny I have is accounted for.) But then I thought, no, no, this is sacred—this is my boy's future we're talking about here. If I can't afford to give him a new life, then I sure as hell can afford to buy a notebook in which to record ways to make the one he has better. And so I've come here to Gifts Galore to get a nice one. I never come into shops like this ordinarily, though, because they sell nothing you need and everything you don't: tin boxes with **Beer Money** written on them that cost ten quid themselves. I'd been wandering around, looking a bit lost, until this sales assistant took pity on me.

"I think I'll take that one," I say, picking up a purple hardback with pictures of old-fashioned bikes all over it. I think it might, you know, in-spire me—and also £3.50, although still an unprecedented amount for me to spend on some-thing as frivolous as a notebook, seems almost sen-sible compared to a tenner. I pay for it and leave the shop, taking the shortcut through Freshney Place as I always do. But then I can't even wait till I get to work; I sit down on a bench in the middle of the precinct and I get the notebook out of the posh paper bag. It feels lovely and solid in my hands and smells of newness. I rummage in my handbag—I only have a red felt-tip on me—and I write in the inside cover **THE GET ZAC FIT CAMPAIGN**. Then I think about it, cross it out, and write **THE GET ZAC HAPPY CAMPAIGN**.

I WALK MY normal route to work, a route I've taken every day for the last three years. It's nine forty-five a.m. on an ordinary Monday in February and yet I feel different, I feel alive; I notice things. Like, how the shaft of sunshine jutting from a fat gray cloud, which is no doubt about to unleash its torrent any moment, is just now turning the canal into liquid gold. I notice how there are buds on the trees, and snowdrops everywhere, clusters of them around the churchyard and in the town square, little spotlights of nature and beauty, in among the mangy pigeons pecking at litter dropped on the damp pavements of this town, with one road in and one road out.

How long has it been since I've had a plan? Besides getting through this day and living to see the next? (And losing weight. But then, this is about Zac now, not me and my endless, idle threats to myself.)

I used to have plans all the time when I was little—before real life didn't so much take over but career into me, sending me off the edge. If I wasn't building my business empire from peddling bottles of rancid homemade "rose" perfume, I was making badges and selling them at school, or thinking of ways to save the drunkards and homeless of this world—"this world" being the East Marsh of Grimsby, where there were plenty of those to keep me going. Me and my brother used to hatch schemes all the time. We used to play this game called, cunningly, Murder, We Wrote, which basically consisted of making up a murder then trying to solve it. We'd trawl the streets looking for "evidence": a broken beer bottle wasn't just a bottle, it was a murder weapon; that glove found in a bush was one our victim had had to surrender when they fled . . . I remember going to bed so excited to get up the next day and carry on with our project, and this is how I've felt for the last week since hatching my new plan. I've felt like a proper mum looking after her child. I've felt like a good mum, and I haven't felt like that for a very long time.

I decided I needed a Plan with a capital "P" the night of the hideous chocolate incident, two weeks ago. The snow had delayed the buses, so the school was shut, everyone gone home, by the time I got there, which I'm glad about now. I'd calmed down by then anyway, and as I peered inside the window of Mrs. Bond's office, all I could see staring back at me was Zac, back at Sandwich King, covered in chocolate, going, "Mum, please don't go to school, you'll just make it worse!" So, while if it were up to me, I'd have Aidan Turner receive the wedgie of his life, hauled up to the rafters by his underpants in front of the whole school, I agreed I wouldn't call this time. There's a "bully box" at school where the kids can post names of bullies anonymously, which means staff can deal with them in a way that doesn't point the finger at their victim, exacerbating things, so as a compromise Zac promised me he'd put Aidan's name in there and we left it at that. That evening all he wanted to do was go to bed early, me cuddled up next to him, and do a quiz from his **Factblaster** book.

I've never known a kid with a hunger for facts like Zac. It's like he needs his daily dose, like they make him feel safe. And when I see him with my dad watching one of those nature programs they both like so much, Zac firing a gazillion questions at Dad and Dad talking to him, explaining everything like Zac is the most important person in the world, I worry about my inquisitive boy and all his unanswered questions. I imagine all those questions he must have about his dad and me floating around in his mind, like driftwood on the sea, questions he knows he can't ask. Where do they go? I wonder. And what is that doing to him?

Zac slept in my bed the night after the chocolate bullying incident and went out like a light while I tossed and turned, looking at my boy's freckled, sleeping face in the moonlight; his mouth open, his body slack—it felt like the ultimate show of trust. And I wracked my brains for ways to help him lose weight and be accepted in a way that wouldn't affect his confidence. (Even though I felt resentful that that was what we'd have to do to get the bullies off his back. Why couldn't the world love and accept him as he was?)

I'VE STARTED TO use my breaks at work to think about ways I can help Zac—to lose weight and get fitter, be less of a target for bullies; to be happier, basically. It was the obvious stuff at first: stop buying chocolate biscuits and multipacks of crisps and pizzas and sausage rolls and those bloody gorgeous chocolate champagne truffles for a quid (a quid!) from Aldi; encourage him to exercise. But there was a stumbling block right away, because you won't find a more exercise-shy kid than Zac: he balks at the mere mention of "walk." I'd always thought it was lucky he wasn't sporty because sport costs, clubs cost. It's £3.50 to take him swimming, £7 a week to do football or cricket, and, frankly, that's £10.50 a week I need for other things. But if I wanted to help him lose weight, then I knew we'd have to confront his exercise phobia. Not to mention mine.

"So what about running? Running's free," says Laura now, sitting across from me and my new notebook. (Laura's delighted I have a plan—a little too delighted, if you ask me. She has the air of someone who thinks this should have happened ages ago.)

"I said, I'm more than happy to come running with you, Juliet," she adds, when I'm clearly not listening. "Seriously, it'll be fun."

I look at her. "With all due respect to Zac," I say, "does my son look like a runner? And do I look to you like I could run anything but a bath?"

"Oh, Juliet, who I'd love if she were twenty-six stone or six, if I can just state the obvious," says Laura witheringly, "the only way you're going to look more like a runner, or feel like one, is if you start actually running, and I'll help. I'll take Zac running. I'll take both of you! We can go running along Cleethorpes Prom, up over the sand dunes—it's glorious out there. Seriously, you're missing out."

"Okay, now you're scaring me," I say, passing a hand nervously around the back of my neck. "Because you've gone and put 'running' and 'glorious' in the same sentence." I say it with humor, but in no way am I being humorous. I know how defeatist I sound; pathetic, really. It's just the thought of going for a run with Laura, gazelle-like in her tiny Lycra things, me hippo-like in a billowing T-shirt . . . ?

"Okay." Laura shrugs, defeated. "I'm just saying, I think you should get other people on board who he'll listen to, who he likes. And also to help **you**, Juliet, because you always do everything on your own when it comes to Zac and you do amazingly, but it's hard making all the decisions."

I smile, while feeling like a complete fraud. **You've not a clue,** I think, **how crap I am, how I don't cope, how weak my so-called coping mechanisms are, including eating entire cheesecakes at four a.m., and nicking food, telling myself it's okay because I'm broke. You've no**

**idea that I have such little self-respect I attack
people when they reject me and get so wasted I
can't remember what I said to my ten-year-old.**

It's strange, but these truths, my dirty little secrets, they're hidden most of the time in far-flung
parts of my consciousness because that's the only
way I can face myself, but this past week, since deciding I have to do something, I've become aware
of them suddenly leaping out in front of me, like
ghouls on a ghost train, giving me no choice but to
stare them right in their ugly little faces. Not that
I am ready to admit any of this to Laura.

"You're right," I say. "I do make all the decisions
and it's tough, but what are you suggesting? That
Zac wouldn't listen to me?"

"No offense, darlin'"—Laura gets up and carries both our lunch plates to the sink—"but when
did you ever listen to your mum?"

Damn it, she's right.

"Just think about the other people in his life,
that's all; the people he loves and respects—get
them on board. Make it a team effort."

I SPEND THE following few days trying to do
just that. I don't have to worry about Teagan, having already spoken to her when I bumped into her
hanging off the bars as usual, on my day off. She
was wearing a giant fake red flower in her hair, but
no coat—in early March—and I asked her why
she wasn't at school.

"I had an asthma attack last night. We had to go to hospital in an ambulance. The doctor said if we'd left it any later then it could have been a different story. He meant, I could have been dead," she added darkly, just to clarify things.

"So what on earth are you doing playing outside with no coat?" I said, which was when she told me how she was "never cold" when practicing her gymnastics and that her mum said it was better for her chest to be outside instead of inside with all the damp. I swear, if I ever win the lottery, I'll buy Teagan a new house, not to mention gymnastics lessons. I've never been inside Teagan's house, but Zac says that there's black up the walls and green fur on her bedroom blinds; and he's not one to exaggerate. Her mum, Nicky, is catatonically depressed. No wonder Teagan likes coming round ours so much.

"They keep saying they're going to move us, but there's no spare houses at the moment so we have to stay here. Is Zac playing after school?" She changed the subject as if to save my embarrassment and sense of helplessness at the wretched state of her life. This I saw as my opening to talk to her about him.

Part of me wished I hadn't.

"So let me get this right: they prick his bum with a **compass**?" I said in total disbelief.

"Yep, then they pretend like his bum bursts like a balloon and they call him Jabba the Hutch—

because his surname's Hutchinson—and they say that there'll be no water left in the swimming pool if he gets in, and whisper horrible things when he walks down the corridor."

That murderous feeling again, rearing up like a tidal wave.

"And does he not fight back?"

"Nope, and he says it doesn't bother him that much, but I know it does because I then get his funny mood." The way she said it, hand on her chest like she was his long-suffering wife, made me laugh through the tears that had begun to threaten. "If it was me, I'd punch them in the face," she added before launching into a revenge fantasy involving locking the bullies in the paint cupboard at school for days, feeding them only gruel . . .

We talked until our shadows were so long we looked like giants, looming over the estate, and it was so cold that I shared half my coat with Teagan.

"In your opinion," I said, before I left, "as Zac's best friend, do you think helping him lose weight will help stop the bullying?"

"Yes. But I know what would help more."

"What would help him more, Teagan?"

"Not being scared; at least a lot less scared than he is, because bullies can smell fear, you know, like dogs, and I should know because they used to pick on me. They used to call me a pauper and say I smelled funny because of the damp and I used to put up with it, until one day, I just went mad. I'm not kidding. I was like the Incredible Hulk! My mum had to go and see Mrs. Bond and I had to stay in at break time for a whole week. But it was worth it," she said, with considerable relish. "Because they left me alone after that."

"Okay, so besides encouraging him to lamp them one, do you think you might be able to help Zac be less scared for me?" I said. "Maybe lose a bit of weight, get fitter, just to feel better about himself? I'm not sure I can do this on my own, Teagan."

"Yeah, but I can't just tell him what to do," she said. "He has to do some work too."

"Yep." I felt more determined. "Yes, I know that."

It was only when I got home that I realized the saddest thing about the whole conversation was that Teagan hadn't even mentioned the chocolate incident, which told me she didn't know about it. And this broke my heart all over again, because I realized Zac didn't even tell his best friend the truth about all that went on. But then, I was one to talk.

GET ON BOARD those he loves and respects, Laura said, so I decide I should talk to Mum, because if there's anyone in this world Zac loves and respects, it's his nan. Not forgetting his grandad, of course; his grandad's his hero. It's just, where the food issue is concerned, it's Mum I need to talk to. It's how to broach the subject without an argument or the cold shoulder for days, though. Things are complex and fragile with me and Mum. If I was to say that to her, she'd say it was ridiculous, but I think that's only because the reasons it's true are so big, and so deeply rooted, she literally cannot speak of them.

Then again, the moment you walk into my parents' house, there's my brother, right there. Mum and Dad live in one of those terraces where you walk straight into the lounge, and on the facing wall (and it takes up half the wall) is a photo of Jamie. I often wonder if the fact that she can't talk about these things is the reason her displays of them are so big, and all over the house, as if she's saying, **Here. Here is my pain.**

Liam, Zac, and I all lived with Mum and Dad when Zac was born—although we were due to move into our own place if everything that happened hadn't. But when it **did** happen, I moved out into my own place as soon as I could, no matter how shit it was, because this house was like a shrine: everywhere you looked was my brother's face and my mother's pain.

In the picture that's in the lounge as you walk in, Jamie is holding Zac, when he was about four days old. Zac's wearing the tiger suit Jamie bought for him and Jamie's wearing an expression that is a mix of joy, pride, and the thought **Holy shit! My sister just had a baby.** You know what I see when I look at that picture, however? I see the person who links my son and my brother. I see the deep-rooted reason things are fragile between me and Mum.

I see Liam.

In all these years of her spouting vitriol about him, she's never once blamed me for being with him in the first place, for bringing him into the family. But the blame is definitely there, in the undercurrent. I feel the coldness of its fingers, pointing at me.

BAKING: THE SMELL wafts straight up my nostrils, making my mouth water as soon as I'm inside. "Mum, I've made an Oreo cake!" Zac shouts from the kitchen at the back of the house, and I think, **Brilliant**. I'm not quite sure which sort of brilliant: the sarcastic one or the one that could murder that whole cake right now. In order to give Zac moral support, I'm trying to be good and I've done really well today, but now I'm ravenous. Mum comes out wearing her **Keep Calm and Keep Baking** apron, icing sugar down it.

"Oh, hello, love, you're early," she says, running a hand through her gray-blond hair. "As you can see we've been very busy this afternoon. Absolute chip off his uncle's block, this one—came up with the recipe himself."

Zac comes from the kitchen into the lounge holding his cake so proudly on a plate, smiling my brother's cheeky, dimpled smile, and the most awful thing happens. In those steps—of which there are a few, because my parents' kitchen stretches quite far back since their extension—I see how big Zac is. No less beautiful to me, but still big. I see for the first time that it's hard for him to walk very fast, because his thighs rub together, and it absolutely floors me.

"Do you want a piece, Mum?" He's looking up at me so expectantly, so proud to be offering me something he's made himself, and I have to look away because my eyes have filled with tears. I also know I must decline, even though I want a slice so bad it hurts. "I've just eaten, darlin'," I say when I've composed myself. "But save me some for later."

Zac goes into the lounge to watch telly and eat cake with Dad, so once I know the coast is clear, I take my chance.

"Mum, can we have a little chat? About Zac?"

"Oh, what about Zac?" says Mum, backing against the worktop, as if bracing herself for attack.

I take a breath and look out at the backyard, which is shrouded in darkness now. You can just make out the pebble-dash of the wall, the washing line, and, beyond all that, the twinkly lights of the docks. It's the same backyard Liam and I sat in, marveling at Zac, the day we brought him home from hospital, unable to believe how lucky we were. I don't want to have this conversation. I guess I'm just so glad Mum and Zac have a close relationship, because it could so easily have gone the other way, that I'm very wary of saying anything that might jeopardize that. Grief and anger have made Mum brittle boned. She snaps easily; I tread lightly.

I explain everything—his weight, the bullying, how I need her to help me, to help him—with more than a little eye rolling and glowering on her part.

"Look, I'm not saying don't give him anything to eat when he comes round to yours. I just think maybe not a big meal, and can we reduce the baking?" The look of horror on her face! "I know he loves it, Mum . . ."

"Honestly, that poor child. As if life isn't hard enough with no father figure around, and now he can't do the one thing he's passionate about. He's so like your brother, you know. It was always when he was happiest too, when he had his hands in a bowl of flour . . ."

Part of me feels like saying, **But Zac isn't Jamie, Mum. He's his own person and he's my son, not yours**, while the other part of me thinks, how can I take that away from her? That small pleasure she gets from watching Zac bake, and remembering lovely times.

I sigh at the ceiling. "Look, Mum, I'm not suggesting stopping altogether. Just maybe not a cake every week. It's hard," I say with more resolve. "But I just think we're going to have to start saying no to him; not always give in."

Mum folds her arms, lips pursed accusingly. "Well, that's you, that is."

"I beg your pardon?"

"That's you who gives in to him, Juliet, and I know it's all out of love . . ."

You sneak, I think, **wrapping it up in a backhanded compliment.**

"But it's basically comfort feeding, that's what it is. You say yes to him because you feel bad."

"Hang on." Tears immediately spring into my eyes. "You were the one who just called him 'poor Zac with no father.'"

"Well, I just mean any father—not **him**, he's no father; it's not a shame he hasn't got **him**."

"I just thought you'd be pleased I was doing something productive," I say. "Something to help Zac."

"I am!" Her eyes fill with tears too then, and I feel bad. "Just, I like to bake with him, Juliet. It's our thing. It was mine and Jamie's thing too. Can't you just let me have that?"

IF IT WAS up to me, and this was about me, the last person I would ask for help from was Jason. Not because he wouldn't help—because I know he definitely would—but because I feel like, after that year I put him through, I owe him, not the other way round.

Still, I remind myself as I walk through the revolving doors of Your Fitness on the Saturday morning after the Wednesday I spoke to Mum, this isn't about me, it's about Zac, so I can leave my pride and rampant self-sabotage at home.

"Can I help you?" asks the girl on reception. Her name badge says **Hayley**. She has a spray tan and eyelashes like dustpan brushes.

"Is Jason Stone around? I'd like to have a word with him if possible."

"Ooh, sounds ominous. I hope he's not in trouble," she says, turning to consult a rota on a whiteboard behind her. She's wearing a polo shirt in the uniform turquoise, and black leggings, and she's so thin she has an actual gap from the tops of her thighs right the way down. How do people get so thin? I wonder. How do they not want to eat, like, all the time?

"He's in the gym," she says, swinging round before I am expecting it so I have to quickly avert my gaze, stop gawping at her thigh gap. "But you can go down if you like. It's fine, I don't think he's with a client."

I make my way through the labyrinth of passages and various swing doors, past herds of gazelles, with their tiny Lycra and taut brown midriffs. How do you actually get a stomach like that? It seems humanly impossible. You'd have to devote your whole life to it like some people devote their lives to the poor, or climate change. You wouldn't be able to have a job.

Eventually I find the gymnasium. There's a crushing (literally) moment when I try to get in the door as a gym-goer is trying to get out, but we've both gone at exactly the same time—it's merely unfortunate—which means for a few seconds we are actually wedged, until I turn my body in such a way as to unwedge myself and therefore him. I'm sweating already, just trying to get into a gym. Also, Jason **is** with a client; he has this guy "sitting" against the wall—the only catch being there is no seat—sweat pouring down his face, legs shaking, as he (Jason) paces forward and backward, perfectly calm, almost like he's goading him!

"One, two, three," Jason is counting. "Keep holding, keep holding. Four"—pause—"five"—even longer pause, while client blows air out of his mouth, in desperation, spraying bits of sweat everywhere—"six . . ." I can't bear to stand back and watch this any longer.

"Hey, that's not fair. You're doing even longer pauses between each count."

Jason does an about-turn. "Jules? Hello. What are you doing here?"

"I'm asking myself that very same question," I

say, looking around the place. "But you can have a rest now," I joke, calling over at the poor guy sitting against the wall with no seat. "I've saved you from yourself!"

He stands up and mops his brow with a towel. "Actually, I pay him to do this," he says flatly. He looks extremely unimpressed with me interrupting his personal training session. He's also so toned and pumped up I'm half expecting to see a valve on him somewhere, like a pool float.

Jason wants to laugh, you can tell, but he is nothing if not professional. "I'll be one second, Pete. Do you want to stretch out?" he says and, like an obedient dog, Pete is down on that floor.

Jason turns to me, one thick black eyebrow raised. "So what's this all about?" he says, a smile playing on his lips. "Trying to make sure I've got no job, as well as no girlfriend?"

"I'm thinking of joining," I deadpan, ignoring his dig. We're at that stage now, over two years since we both finally accepted I was in no state for a relationship, where we can joke about it. He knows when I said "it's not you, it's me" that I wasn't just trying to flatter him. "I've signed up for a triathlon."

Jason rolls his eyes and glances behind me.

"Is Zac here?" The way his face lights up at the mention of his name touches me unexpectedly, and I remember with a pang of nostalgia how nice it was, me, Zac, and Jase hanging out as a threesome. At least when I wasn't being nuts, turfing Jason out in the middle of the night due to a sudden body image crisis. (I never could get over the fact that he fancied me even though he was a fitness trainer and spent all day with size-ten model types.)

"No, he's at home," I say, "but it is about Zac, actually."

Jason's face falls. "Is he all right?"

"Yeah, sort of . . . Sorry, I didn't know you had a client." I suddenly feel very conspicuous, aware of a line of runners facing me on treadmills, and I begin to feel like a baby elephant being pursued by a pride of cheetahs.

"It's all right, we finish in five minutes," Jason says, glancing back at Pete, his knee up by his chin on the floor. "Shall I see you upstairs in the café?"

As I leave I hear Pete say, "Is that one of your clients?"

It's not often you can read the thoughts of perfect strangers, I think, but this time I can.

WE SIT OPPOSITE each other in the gym café—a far-too-bright room, if you ask me, surrounded by floor-length windows that make you feel like you're in a goldfish bowl, being watched. There are only three other people in here, but, again, I feel exposed.

"Bullied? What about?" says Jason, taking a

swig of his fat Coke (doesn't even have to think about his body weight, he lifts so many of the iron kind), and for a fleeting second I wonder if I've been making a huge mountain out of a molehill, that I've somehow let the school brainwash me, because if not, wasn't it obvious?

"Have a guess?" I say, but Jason looks stumped.

Then I see the realization darken his face. "Jesus, really? But that's like picking on kids 'cause they wear glasses or they're ginger—that's so passé."

"Nope, fat shaming is alive and well, I'm afraid. His life at school is hell, Jase . . ." Oh, here we go with the wobbly bottom lip. I really have to stop the crying; it's not helping anyone. "And I never realized, and I'm his mum. They stole his clothes the other day, at his swimming class. They stab him in the bum with a compass, for fuck's sake."

Jason passes a hand across his beard—it's a recent thing, but it suits him, makes him look more manly, because although Jason is very tall (six foot three to my five foot four—another reason we always looked slightly odd together) he's got a real baby face: a gummy smile and rosy cheeks; dark, tufty hair; and boyishly wide green eyes. He looks like the friendliest guy on the planet and then you see him in action, putting his clients through what appears to be torture, and you think, he's got more grit than he possibly looks like on the outside. He's not just Mr. Nice.

"So what do you want me to do, come and sort the little bastards out?" he says, mirroring my thoughts exactly. "Take them down in one karate move?"

I laugh into my tea, even though I know, in that moment, he means it—that he has that same murderous feeling I had. I look at his biceps, flexed now and covered in fine dark hair; huge, strong arms that, for as many nights as I let him, held me. Part of me would love it if he'd walk into the playground, pick up Aidan Turner with one hand, and deliver an **if you ever fucking touch Zac Hutchinson again** speech before throwing him down on the floor, like Hulk Hogan—but I also know this will have to remain a fantasy.

"I'm not sure vigilantism is the way forward. Plus, Aidan's mum is well hard. No, I was thinking more along the lines of you helping Zac to, you know, feel better about himself."

Jason frowns.

"Like, do some exercise with him, get him interested in something physical. Anything!" I say, slightly desperately. "I mean, I know he's, like, the least sporty kid you ever want to meet, that he's massively exercise averse . . ."

Jason tuts and looks out of the window, where some kids are going up and down on scooters.

"Jules, how do you know he hates sport if he's never had the chance to do it?" he says. "How do you know he hates gyms, if he's never been in one? He's played footie with me a few times and he liked it. He was a good little goalie."

"You played football with him?" This is news to me.

"Yeah, just a kick about, when he dropped in here on his way home from school sometimes."

"He never told me," I say, wondering why not, and Jason looks surprised. "Look, obviously I'll pay you," I say, and Jason laughs.

"Juliet, you can't pay me, you have no money."

"I'll find some."

"Don't be stupid."

"It's important—I'll find it from somewhere."

Jason leans forward, clasping his hands. "I'll help," he says. "Obviously I'll help."

I have a sudden idea. "Okay, sandwiches then."

"What?"

"I'll pay you in sandwiches—since that seems to be all I have to offer people in this world."

Jason frowns and shakes his head, despairing of me. "Look, if it makes you feel better, then pay me in sandwiches by all means, but I want gourmet, healthy stuff, mind. None of your bog-standard cheese on white."

I smile, feeling a sudden wave of gratitude.

"Thank you," I say. "And I really mean that."

We chat for a bit, about nothing in particular, and it's nice, without Zac, being somewhere that's neutral, and I realize I've missed this, just having a chat with Jase, with another adult human being who is not in my family or Laura, then he says, "So, can I ask you a question? How come you went on a date with Dom?"

I am so shocked that a loud "ha!" escapes. "What? How do you . . . ?" The penny drops. "Oh, Zac, you little bugger." Here I am, asking Jason for a pretty huge favor, and here is Jason . . . "Do you know him?"

"Yeah, he's a client of mine."

"Oh God. Look." Could you keep anything a secret in this town? "It was nothing, it was a date, it was a car crash, actually—and don't"—I flash him a look—"say why that does not surprise you."

Jason's mouth is curling at one side; whether in faint amusement or hurt, I can't tell. He leans back in his chair.

"If I was a different kind of man," he says, "I could be quite hurt, you know, that you're apparently, in your words, 'too mental for a relationship' but not, it seems, with somebody else." He raises his eyebrows questioningly at me.

He's right, of course. I was too all over the place for a relationship with him, but I still am—for a relationship with anyone! I mean, what sort of grown woman attacks a guy for simply not wanting to kiss her?

The room feels suddenly very hot, our voices loud. I lean across the table.

"Look, Jase," I say. "I went out with you for a year. You were the first person since . . . since, you know, everything happened."

"Well, that makes me feel better."

I look at him while he picks a bit of laminate off the table.

This seems like a very bad idea all of a sudden. I get up to go. "God, look, sorry, I should never have come here asking you to help us. I'm sure you just want to see the back of me after the way I've been." I pick up my keys and bag, but Jason makes a groaning, irritated noise.

"Juliet, stop," he says, and when I look at him I realize he actually looks quite cross. "Just stop, will you? Just stop reacting all the time. I'm curious, that's all. I know it's you, not me, that you're off your rocker not to snap me up." He grins mischievously.

"It meant nothing."

"Zac said you were upset."

"Oh, great, so you know everything. You know about me hitting him over the head with my handbag?"

"Erm . . ."

"Oh! Bloody marvelous!"

"Look, Juliet." Jason rubs his face. I'm exhausting him. I always exhausted him. "I said I'd do it, all right? I think you should do it with him too, though."

"What? Why? What do you mean?"

"I think you should do the exercise with Zac—
or on your own, with me—but just support him
either way. I've got a free pass for the whole center.
We can do swimming, badminton, table tennis,
anything you like . . . I think it'll do the both of
you good."

I have a sudden flash of panic. I'm not sure exactly what about: him seeing me in a swimming
cozzie, perhaps. Do I even possess one?

"Look, Jason, that's really nice of you, but no,
basically." What am I even doing here? Aren't I
trying to cool off this whole friendship thing? But
then, he could help Zac, I know that. He could
really help him.

"Why not?"

"Because this isn't about me. It's about Zac,"
I say.

"Is it, Jules?" says Jason, picking at the laminate
again. "Really, is it?"

9

Zac

**Fact: The heaviest man ever recorded
weighed a hundred stone.**

The Fisherman's Chapel was built in 1966; it says so at the top of the door.

To the Glory of God and in solemn remembrance of those who died at sea, it says. "Solemn" means sad and serious. I always feel solemn when I come here. It's automatic; it just happens when you walk in. It's sad, but it's also really interesting. There are boards with all the names of the seafarers who've died since 1920 ("seafarers" is just another name for fishermen, but I like it better because it sounds dead adventurous). It even tells you what boats they went down on. One time, I'm going to come and spend the whole day memorizing the historical facts; I'm going to bring a packed lunch and memorize the names of the trawlers—it's my all-time ambition. On January 28, 1932, for example, a trawler called the **S. T. Leicester** sank and the whole crew was lost at sea. Their bones are probably still floating around.

I don't just come to the chapel to read the dead men's stories, though; I come because I've got the sea in my veins (not the actual sea—I've got blood like everyone else—it's just a saying, it means I'm from a fishing family). So when I'm here, I feel like I'm with them, like my family's bigger than just my mum, nan, and grandad. I can't describe it, but it's a nice feeling. Also, I come and pray. When I say my prayers, I don't kneel down; I just sit on the bench and say them in my head. That's the good thing about praying, nobody needs to know you're doing it.

Today my prayer went like this:

Dear Jesus (my prayer was to God too, but I feel like I've got more in common with Jesus because his dad wasn't around either, and his friends were all fishermen), **I hope you're listening because I've got a confession. I never put Aidan Turner's name in the bully box. I told my mum I did to make her happy, but I didn't. I'm sorry. It's because if I did, he'd know it was me, he just would, and then I'd be scared of what he might do and Teagan says bullies can smell fear like dogs can. Jesus, I don't want to be scared anymore. I hate it. It makes my belly hurt. I feel really bad about the lying, but I'm going to have to get used to it and you are too, just for a bit, till I get the big prize at the end. That's all**

I'm doing this for, to give my dad a chance and also to find the only man my mum ever loved. I can't let the bullies take all my energy because I need it for my mission, and that's also why I didn't put Aidan's name in the box. The good thing is, just knowing my mum loved my dad is already making me less scared, so can you forgive me for a bit longer, Jesus? You know I don't normally lie, and it'll be worth it. P.S. If you are not too angry with me, could I put in an extra request for you to help me find my dad sooner rather than later?

Just then—it was mad—the chapel doors swung open, letting the sunshine in, and the blue glass window was suddenly lit up like a giant sapphire. Maybe this was Jesus come to answer my prayer? But it wasn't Jesus. It was an old man; he was tall and wearing one of those caps that all old men wear. He stopped in front of me. I smiled at him, but he didn't smile back, he just walked, really slowly, around the chapel in silence. You could only hear his shoes going **clip-clop** on the floor. It was proper spooky. I didn't know whether I should go or stay, so I stayed. My bum felt like it was stuck to the chair, anyway. Suddenly the man turned around.

Him: "Can I ask you what you're doing?"

Me: "Nothin', just looking." (I didn't want to tell him I'd been praying; it's private and a bit embarrassing.) "Are you the owner?"

Him: "No, I'm a trustee of the chapel. Now, what are you doing on your own in here? Because I'll tell you something, I wasn't born yesterday. I know how you boys have been coming in here recently, using it as a drop-in center, disrespecting this place."

Why do some adults think all children are bad? I started walking out in protest.

Him (calling after me, probably feeling guilty now): "Well, shouldn't you be with someone? Your mum or dad? Your family, if you're going to come in here and just sit there?"

Me (turning back from the door, pointing at the memorial boards): "They are my family, actually. Every person on that board is like my family. My grandad was a fisherman for twenty-five years! I've got the sea in my veins." (He looked very surprised.)

I walked home. I felt angry and sad for the fishermen because I bet they wouldn't have wanted a bossy trustee like that and they don't get a say now they're dead. But most of all, I felt good. I felt big, but inside me. I looked at myself in the shop window and laughed, because I was smiling my head off, even though nobody else was there.

TEAGAN AND I decided that Mondays would be our Find Dad mission day. Everyone knows that Mondays are the most boring day of the week, but now Mondays were the day I looked

forward to the most. Mum said I didn't have to go
and meet her from work on Mondays now either.
I could just go straight home, which gave me and
Teagan more time to have our Find Dad mission
club. That Monday, however, had been a bad day
at school. Someone had put a letter on my chair
so that when we came in from break I found it.
It said: **Dear Jabba the Hutch, will you go out
with me? I find fat boys so sexy!!!** Aidan Turner
and that lot laughed when I read it. It was stupid.
I threw it in the bin, but it made me feel horrible
inside—sick but starving, both at the same time—
like when I realized they'd stolen my clothes at the
swimming pool or when I was just about to go on
stage at last year's Christmas play.

We'd already had one meeting so far, but that
was at our headquarters on the merry-go-round
on our estate. The merry-go-round is all rotted so
your foot goes through the wood; it's the perfect
headquarters for a secret mission: because it's so
rubbish, nobody would suspect you were planning
something as important as finding your dad on it.
Today it was raining, though, so we were having
the meeting in my room. Teagan was on my bed
and I was on my beanbag. Beanbags are definitely
the comfiest things in the world; when you sit in
them, they give you a big hug.

"So what have you found out so far?" Teagan
had our folder on her lap and was clicking my
Man Utd pen on and off. "I'll take notes."

Our first meeting was just about the rules, like, you're not allowed to talk when the other person's talking and we're sworn to secrecy: if anyone tells anyone anything, they'll get thrown out of the Find Dad mission club (and since there's only two of us in it, that would be a disaster), and if you want to talk about it when outside of meetings you have to say "mango" before you start. We got it from Connor. It's our secret password.

This was our first proper meeting, though. It felt exciting and scary, like a real investigation.

"I told you what I know," I said. I was embarrassed it wasn't much after a week. I thought it was going to be easy asking Mum about Dad now I knew she didn't hate him, but it wasn't, it was harder, because it felt like it mattered more. And whenever I mention my dad to Nan, all she says is, "The only thing you need to know about him is that you're better off knowing nothing." So that just leaves Grandad and he'll only talk about Dad when Nan's not around. But then on Wednesday, we went to get fish and chips, so I asked him some questions (and I got some answers!).

"I know you told me, but just tell me again," said Teagan. "So I can write in the file." Sometimes I think Teagan just likes writing things down in different pens, it doesn't matter what it is.

"His name's Liam Jones, he grew up in Grimsby, and he was a deckhand when he was with my mum—which meant he did all the cooking for the crew on the boats, as well as doing the fishing, obviously. He was probably going to be a fisherman like my grandad."

"Did you find out anything about what he looked like?" asked Teagan.

"He's got dark hair and he's normal sized."

"What do you mean, normal sized?" When Teagan speaks, the giant red flower in her hair wobbles. It's her favorite thing—she wears it all the time since she found it outside Domino's—and I like it too because I can see her from miles off. "Like, what's normal? Everything that exists is normal—that's why it's normal, because it exists. Only things that you never see aren't normal."

"What like?"

"Like people with horns or three eyes. You never see that, do you?"

I shook my head.

"That's because it's not normal."

She was definitely right.

"I mean, not really fat and not really thin," I said. "In-between sized, that's what I mean."

"In-between sized," said Teagan, changing from my Man Utd pen to a green felt-tip. "I'm going to write that in green, because it's in the description part, okay?"

She sat back on my bed, leaning against the radiator—it's the coziest place to sit after my beanbag—and looked at the information in our file. Then she did a great big sigh. "There's no way we're going to find him with this information. There's loads of people in Grimsby with dark hair who are in-between sized."

"Not loads of people called Liam Jones, though. Also, I know!" I said, clicking my fingers (I'd had a brain wave). "We could go and ask people down the docks. If he was a deckhand, they might know him."

Teagan screwed her face up. Her nose looks even smaller when she does that, and she's already got the smallest nose you've ever seen. It's no wonder she finds it hard to breathe sometimes.

"But we don't know if your dad is in fishing now. Just because he's from Grimsby and was in fishing when you were born doesn't mean he has to be in it now—my dad's from Grimsby, and he didn't even have a job. He might have run away and changed jobs after you were born and then we'll have wasted loads of time in the investigation. I think we should find out some facts about him first and where he lives. We could always look around town for people who look like you too."

"But he doesn't look like me."

"How do you know?"

Because he's normal sized, for a start.

"I just do."

I wish I had a picture of my dad to help us, but I haven't. I've never seen what he looks like because before I was born, he ran away; he never even saw me or cuddled me, he just went. But now I know he must have had a really good reason if my mum loved him so much. And I'm going to find out what it is.

We both sat in silence, thinking. I could hear Mum in the kitchen cooking our tea. Then I had another brain wave. "I've got an idea," I said, getting up. It's quite hard to get up out of a beanbag, that's the only bad thing about them. "Just wait here."

I tiptoed downstairs. "Y' all right, Zac?" Mum called from the kitchen. I should have sent Teagan instead of me. She can go anywhere and you'd never hear her. It's really very useful.

"Yeah," I called back.

"What're you doing?"

"Just getting something to show Teagan."

"Okay, but it's tea very soon. Tuna pasta bake all right?"

Since the letter, Mum's been looking up healthy recipes on the iPad and doing some cooking herself. "Oh, nice."

"Ten minutes, okay?"

"Yeah, we'll be down."

I crept into the front room, took the iPad from the arm of the settee where Mum had been looking up recipes, and stuffed it up my jumper. I didn't feel guilty. Nan and Grandad got us the iPad for a joint Christmas present, and, anyway, all this was for a good cause. When I found my dad and Mum had the love of her life back and we even had more money, they'd thank me. I put in the code (my birthday), then I went back upstairs and sat down next to Teagan.

"Watch this," I said, then I typed "how to find your dad" into Google.

Loads of stuff came up straightaway! The Internet is epic, after all; it can tell you facts about anything you want to know—you just have to ask it a question. You can even put "10 facts about bananas" and it will tell you fifteen. Did you know, for example, that bananas are radioactive?

The website that appeared at the top was called www.findergenie.com. We liked the name, so we clicked on it. **Need to find your dad?** it said. **We can help you find your dad.** There was a picture of a lady with her dad looking happy, to show you what would happen, and there was also a video. "Click on it!" said Teagan, clapping her hands. It was a lady with blond hair talking to you: **"They found full contact details and an address in twenty-four hours."** Teagan was squealing like a baby pig. But the woman didn't even look that happy. She was talking like they'd found a shoe she'd lost. **If I find my dad, I'll be much more excited, then they can have me on their video.**

We looked at the Finder Genie website. All you had to do to start looking for your dad was to fill in a form, but the form asked for an e-mail address and we didn't have one.

"But there's a phone number," said Teagan. "Call them up!"

"I daren't."

"Why not?"

"I just daren't."

It was probably Jesus answering my prayer, but it felt too soon; I wasn't prepared. What if they found my dad in twenty-four hours? That would be tomorrow and I didn't want our investigation to be over that soon. Also, I was suddenly a bit scared of meeting my dad, but I didn't want to tell Teagan that.

So, I went into Mum's bedroom—she has a phone next to her bed—and I picked up the phone. But then I just stood with it in my hand.

What if he didn't like me? What if he didn't support Man U or do cooking? What if he already had a son he could play football with? Proper good football, where the son doesn't always have to be the goalie?

I could hear Teagan calling me, but I didn't want to go back in there yet. From my mum's room you can see across to where we used to live in Garibaldi House, where I had to share a bedroom with Mum, and a bed that sank in the middle. The lights were all on in the flat windows, so they were shining orange. They reminded me of the lozenges Mum gives me if I have a cough or sore throat.

If we found my dad in twenty-four hours, then my life could change before the end of the week. I'd have a dad and Mum would have a boyfriend and it wouldn't be just me and her anymore.

Just then, Teagan came running in, her big red flower wobbling. "What are you doing?"

I held the phone out to her. "Please can you do it? I don't want to."

Teagan sat down next to me and pushed my hand away, but only gently. "No, you have to do it, Zac," she said. Her eyelashes are so long, they nearly reach right up to her eyebrows. "It's your dad you want to find."

My heart was banging. There was the sick-but-starving feeling again. I punched in the number. Someone answered!

"Hello and welcome to Finder Genie!"

She was American and sounded really friendly.

"Hello," I said. "My name's Zac Hutchinson and I go to Thornby Academy in Grimsby and I need to find my dad, please . . ."

But she just kept on talking. "We are so pleased you have chosen us to find the people who matter to you and we are very proud to tell you that your search ends here, because results are guaranteed. As one of the most successful finder companies in the world, however . . ."

"Hello?" I said again. "Can you hear me?"

"What's up?" whispered Teagan.

"She's just talking over me. She says we're in a queue."

"Tell her we need to do it fast. Because if your mum finds out, she's gonna go mental."

"Er, excuse me, do you think we might be able to go to the beginning of the queue?"

But then there was music playing. It was Ellie Goulding, "Anything Could Happen." Me and Teagan were laughing; it was really funny. She'd just put music on and ignored us!

"Zac? What are you doing in my bedroom?"

Then all of a sudden, Mum was at the door, looking cross.

"Nothing."

"Who are you on the phone to?"

"Nobody."

"Well, I hope you've got the money to pay for talking to that nobody because I certainly haven't."

Then Teagan saved the day. "I just needed to call my mum, actually, Juliet, to check she's all right because my sister's not in till later and she's on her own." Her eyes slid across to me. I had to suck my cheeks in so I didn't smile.

Mum looked at me, then Teagan. You could tell she didn't believe it, but she was choosing her battles. "Right, well, can you come downstairs now, please? Your tea's ready."

After tea, me and Teagan called up Finder Genie again, and this time we got through. But that was when we found out it was a paid-for service. At first I thought she meant they pay me, but no, worst luck, she meant we had to pay them! It was £400 to start off with and we only had £146 in both our bank accounts and that's even putting them together. Also, you had to be sixteen to use Finder Genie—or have a parent come and help you.

So that was that. We didn't have £400, we didn't have an e-mail address, and we couldn't get my mum to come on the phone and help us. We decided that Finder Genie was not the way to do it.

I walked Teagan home. It was still raining really hard and we put our tongues out to drink it straight from the sky. It's totally safe to drink rain as long as you don't live near radioactive places like Chernobyl, and it tastes really nice. Like, if you were to make a drink called "The World," that's what it would taste like: rivers and sky and forests and mountains.

"I think we should just go back to our original plan of asking local people for information," Teagan said, when we got to her block. "We can't just rely on your mum or nan, because in proper investigations they ask around."

"I don't know who I'd dare ask, though."

"Just anyone who has any information."

"What if they get mad with us?"

"They're not going to get mad. Also, Zac?" She

looked away, like she was nervous of saying the next bit. "I just want to say, it might not be enough just to want to meet your dad."

"What do you mean?" The light outside her block made her eyes shine, like a tiger's.

"I just mean, I want to see my dad, but he doesn't want to see me, and he even lived with me until a year ago."

"I know," I said, looking at the floor. I didn't know what else to say.

"I'm not saying the same thing will happen to you, and I really hope it doesn't. But it might, so I want you to be prepared."

"All right," I said, even though I didn't know what the point of all this was if we weren't even going to find him.

"Anyway, let's just make the most of the mission," she said, smiling then. "Let's make from now till your birthday the best days of our lives. I think you should try and have the best time and be the best you can be, whether or not we find your dad."

"All right," I repeated. Again, I didn't know what else to say. "See you tomorrow."

As I walked home, I had a secret rain drink all on my own. I wondered where my dad was. Was he even in the same country? Was he under the same rain as me? Did he ever think about me? There was so much I wanted to know.

"Zac, come here, I want to talk to you," Mum

called when I got back, and I thought I might be in trouble after the phone call in her room. "So, you're going to be pleased about this," she said, when we were both sitting down on the settee. "On Mondays now, instead of coming home and having to wait for me to get back from work, I've arranged for you to go and meet Jason instead."

My heart dropped like it does in the lift when it goes down too fast.

"What for?"

"To do fun stuff," said Mum. "At the fitness center. He might take you to play football, or swimming. You could even have a go in his gym, Zac. He can use any of the facilities for free. It's such a good opportunity."

"I can't do Mondays," I said, thinking about the Find Dad mission club—how was I going to explain that?

But Mum laughed. "Zac, you're ten, what do you mean you **can't do** Mondays? What have you got on? Darts? Night out with the lads?"

"I just can't, I don't want to," I said. Then Mum looked upset, and I felt bad.

"Zac," said Mum. She shifted back on the settee and looked at me as if she didn't really know me. "This isn't like you. I thought you'd be really pleased. I thought you missed Jason—you're always asking when we're going to see him. Just because we didn't work out, I don't see why you should have to never see him again."

I felt stressed and just wanted to go. "I do like Jason. I do miss him. But he'll probably just run off anyway, won't he? Like my real dad did. Like all men do, except my grandad. He's the only one I trust."

I stood up to go then. I did think all the things I said, but not as bad as they came out. I said them so I could have an excuse to stand up and walk away. But Mum got hold of my hand and pulled me back on the settee.

"Zac, sit down. Now you have to tell me what's going on. Why all this talk about your dad all of a sudden? Why all the questions? I'm sorry he never got in touch, darling, but there's nothing I can do about it. I've told you, he doesn't deserve you and you're better off without him—why can't you just accept that?" Her eyes had gone all teary and her hands were shaking. It was sort of annoying. Why was she lying, saying I was better off without him, when I knew how she really felt about him? "And we're okay, aren't we, Zac?" she said, stroking my back—but that was because she was upset, not me. "Aren't we? Just you and me?"

"Yeah," I said, but I didn't know, not really. I didn't know what to think or believe anymore.

"So can I tell Jason you said yes then?"

I didn't want Mum to start crying, so I nodded and she smiled and went to leave the room, but I had a lot of questions still.

"I'll go, but why don't you just tell me the

truth?" I called after her, and Mum stopped, just before the door.

"About what?" she asked, turning around.

"About my dad. Why do you keep saying he was a horrid person and a waste of space, when you loved him? I don't get it."

Mum put both her hands over her mouth and took a deep breath like Brenda tells me to do when I'm stressed or upset. "What do you mean, I loved him, Zac?"

"You said it," I said. I couldn't hold it in anymore; I was sick of holding it in. "That night when you were drunk, you said you loved him and he loved you, and you only wanted a boyfriend if it could be him. If you loved him that much then he **must** be a nice person and I want to know the truth about him, Mum. I want you to tell me about him."

Mum wasn't saying anything, she was just staring at me, like she couldn't believe I was saying all this.

"Zac, sweetheart," she said quietly, and when my heart started pounding, I realized how long it had been since it had, as hard as this anyway, because I'd been holding my breath. "I don't love your dad." And I could feel the sick and starving feeling creeping into my belly, taking over the happy one, like waking up from a nice dream. "I did love him once, a long time ago, but not anymore. How could I after he left us—left you, the most important thing in my life? Zac, sometimes you think you know someone, but you don't. I thought he was a good person that I could trust, but it turned out not to be the case."

And then I burst into tears. I tried to hold it in, but I couldn't help it.

10

Juliet

After Zac goes up to bed it starts with the toast. Filling that anxious space in my stomach **always** starts with the toast. Especially at nine o'clock at night. Toast seems benign somehow, more benign than chocolate truffles or Viennetta, or sausage sarnies, bacon and melted cheese . . . until the entire loaf is gone. Thing is, I know as soon as I put a single slice in the toaster, when I'm in this state, that the only thing that will ease it will be a shitload more toast.

How long did I think I'd have? Until he was thirteen? Sixteen? Did I think I'd somehow be able to get to the end of my life without ever having to tell him the truth about his dad? I put two more slices of bread into the toaster, wondering when my denial got this bad. And I said I loved him! Apparently, although the jury is out as to whether Zac misheard that one. Why did I say that? How could I love him after everything?

As far as Zac is concerned, however, I've always told him the same thing, and he's always bought it—at least I've been consistent in that. **Your dad never wanted to know, he left before you were even born. He never met you. He's a waste of space.** It was only to protect him, and it was all fine until recently when the questions started trickling through. But I thought it was just a bit of healthy curiosity and I could handle that. I guess he wouldn't be normal, I thought, if he didn't ask the odd question. But tonight, it went up a whole new level for me. Those were big questions, big claims—and what was I meant to say? The truth would devastate him.

The first-ever time he asked me about the whereabouts of his father, he was three. It was August and we were on the little train that goes around Cleethorpes Prom. There was a little girl about the same age as Zac in the carriage in front of us with her dad, and every time we went past something of interest—the boating lake, or a donkey on the beach—she shouted at the top of her voice, "Daddy! Daddy! Look!"

Zac was transfixed. He sat there in silence, gawping, absolutely mesmerized by this little girl, out with her daddy, until suddenly he went, "Where's my daddy?" He said it while looking out at the sea, as if asking the sea the biggest question of his life so far, and when I didn't answer (because I was too busy panicking) he started to shout instead:

"Where's my daddy? Where's my daddy?" The little girl thought this was hilarious, and so she joined
in and the pair of them then carried on shouting,
"Where's my daddy?" for the whole train journey
until the little girl's dad turned around and said,
over their racket, jokingly, "Probably doing something more relaxing than this if he's more sensible
than me."

I thought I'd got away with it, save for the general humiliation on that little train. But that night
when I was putting Zac to bed, he asked me about
his dad again, in a way that was much more difficult to brush off.

"Where's my daddy?" he said, those big, glacier-
blue eyes looking straight at me, so trusting. I got
into bed with him, which was my bed at the time
anyway and which sank in the middle like a ham-
mock so we rolled together, like two fish in a net,
and I said, "Darling, everyone's got a daddy, but
not everyone's daddy lives with them and not everyone's daddy is a good daddy, unfortunately."

"Is mine a good daddy?"

"No, not really, sweetheart."

"Why?"

"Because he didn't want to even try and be your
daddy, and that isn't your fault; it's because he's
very stupid." The language changed as he grew
older, so "didn't want to try" became "did a runner," and "he was very stupid" became "he was a
waste of space." But the message was the same: **he**

didn't want to know you and you're better off without him.

The toast pops up, making me jump, and I smear it with so much butter that it gathers in a pool on top like a flooded field. I eat both slices quickly, the butter deliciously salty, running down my chin; the toast soggy and golden just as I like it. But the anxiety is still there, making it stick in my throat. Zac's sleeping upstairs; I know that tomorrow I'm probably going to have to answer more questions about his father and I don't know what I'll say. Was he a waste of space? I didn't used to think so—I used to think he was fucking magnificent! I couldn't believe he was mine. But what am I supposed to think, Liam Jones, when you're not here to answer for yourself? To answer the millions of questions I have carried around with me for a decade: What really happened that night—why did you start a fight? Were you always like your father and I was just too blind with love to see it? Why did you never contact us or fight for us? Did you ever really love me? Most of all, did you not wonder how your son was? You spent two loved-up weeks with him. Has there not been a gaping hole in your life without him—like there has for me, without you?

It's nine thirty. I put the telly on to distract me, but nothing holds my attention; there's still this horrible clenched-stomach feeling and I know resistance is futile. This is what worry, heartache, whatever you want to call it, does to me—it tricks me into believing that I'll die from it if I don't extinguish it, like a blanket over a fire; numb it with food. So I go into the kitchen intending to make one more slice of toast, only to emerge, half an hour or so later, having eaten three more, and almost a whole garlic baguette that I cannot, for the life of me, even remember putting in the oven. I've really gone and done it now, so I may as well go all the way, is my thinking. So then it's a massive piece of Viennetta with truffles on top and it's like I've eaten that in a trance too, because by the time I'm licking the bowl clean with my finger, I'm so appalled with myself, I consider making myself sick. The thought passes, however; clearly I'm not quite appalled enough with myself. So I switch the telly back on to try to distract myself again. But there's nothing on, and there's at least an hour before I can really call it bedtime, and I feel this chasm of misery and loneliness open up inside of me, like some huge realization has taken place, a devastating one, that I can't pinpoint and don't really understand—perhaps like the first few seconds you wake up the morning after someone you love has died: it hasn't hit you yet, but you know it's coming.

I remember there are two cans of lager in the fridge, and so I drink them, sitting by the table, by the glow of the fridge, not even bothering to put the kitchen light on. So then I suppose I'm a tiny bit drunk, which may be why I do what I do next, which is go upstairs. I've no full-lengths in the house, but I've got a medium-sized mirror that shows you up to your middle, and another similar-sized one in the bathroom. And so I lean one against the radiator in my bedroom and the other so that it balances on top, leaning against the woodchip. If I stand back far enough, I can just about see the whole of me. I want a fat-shaming party, all on my own. So I take off my sweatshirt first and stand in my bra. It's not too bad from the front, and I still go in and out where I'm meant to, I suppose. I still look like a woman, albeit a soft and rounded one, wider than the picture I'd had in my mind but nothing worse than I suspected. But then I take off my jeans so I'm standing just in my underwear and I turn to the side and take off my bra. I gaze at my reflection, forcing my- self to really look. It goes in and out all right, but those are the rolls of back fat, two or three of them hanging over the back of my ribs, like extra fabric I've slung over my shoulder. My stomach is blue- white, not having seen the sun for several years, and hangs over my knickers like an apron. I try pulling it in with my so-called stomach muscles, but still it hangs, like a big, fat apology, and I lean forward, just to offend myself more, really, letting it all hang out, like a giant udder that doesn't even look like it belongs to me. If I gather it with my hands, I have enough skin and fat to cover a small child.

Sometimes I wonder whether Liam has ever looked me up on Facebook, like I have him (he's not on there; he obviously does not want to be found), seen the size I am now, and thought he's the one to have had the lucky escape, not me. Then again, I was never slim and I wonder if all that time he was going out with me he never fancied me anyway. All that time he said I looked beautiful pregnant and even before then, when he always said he loved my curves, was he bullshitting me? It would make sense. He left with so much ease.

After I had Zac, even though I loved him from the word go, physically things were hard, especially in that first week. I got mastitis, and Zac wouldn't feed, then my stitches (from the second-degree tear—Zac was a ten-pound baby) got infected. But Liam was so tender to me, so loving. I've never felt as secure as I did during that time. I thought nobody could ever love me that much. But now I wonder, when he laid warm flannels on my sore, hard breasts, when he held me as I cried and half laughed, with that awful dragging pain below, and said, "So, Liam Jones, do you still fancy me now?" and he answered, "More. I fancy you more," did he out-and-out lie to me? Did he go off that night they were meant to be just "wetting the baby's head," get so drunk and start a

fight **because** he felt trapped and frustrated all of a
sudden? A dad, at twenty-one, when all his mates
were still free and single.

He had a wobble when I found out I was pregnant. We were so young—me twenty, him twenty-
one—and it was such a shock that we didn't see
each other for a week and Mum said, "I told you,
Juliet, that he wasn't up to the job. If you want to
know the measure of a man, just look at his father.
Liam's the same as Vaughan." Liam was always so
honest, though, and when we met up again he admitted he was scared he wouldn't do a good job
as a father—he never lied about that fear. But he
said he loved me, and he was standing by me, and
that he'd do everything in his power not to re-
peat history. And we hugged and I was reassured
rather than put off by his honesty, because that
was Liam—he never put on a front. He wore his
heart on his sleeve. But now I wonder if Mum was
right: he was simply never up to the job. Or, more
to the point, it was a job he didn't want.

"Jules, don't you think we better take the washing in before we light the barbecue?"

It still, ten years on, makes me smile when I
think of Liam saying that. It was hardly a memo-
rable line—it wasn't a declaration of undying love,
or particularly funny—but it's the line I play over
and over, that rolls around my mind, flooding it
with long-lost love, because it epitomizes Liam at
that time, in those weeks. It encapsulates the man

and the father he'd become immediately when Zac was born.

He was standing in my parents' kitchen when he said it, Zac in a sling on his chest, chopping cabbage for his homemade coleslaw. Zac was ten days old, and friends and family were coming round for a barbecue.

I laughed at him. "Who are you?" I said, wedging myself between the worktop and Zac, putting my arms around the both of them. "Mrs. Tiggy-Winkle?" He drew back to look at me, pushing my hair from my face, like he always used to, with his big, soft hands. His dark hair hung over one eye, and the sun that bounced off the shiny metal of the barbecue we'd bought that morning from B&Q—a gift to Mum and Dad and a show of our official adult status—was shining straight into his eyes, showcasing the yellow around his pupils, and I remember thinking how happy I felt. And how handsome he looked. Even more so with our baby strapped to his chest.

"What?" he said, half laughing, half affronted I was taking the piss out of his show of domesticity. "I don't want his onesies to get smoky. I'm just being sensible. Someone's got to be." And he was right, that's the thing. He had become the sensible one, the homebody who seemed to have taken to this parenting lark like a duck to water, while I was still finding my feet. At that time, it felt like Liam had waited his whole life to say lines like "we'd better take the washing in." That he'd grown up not knowing that sort of cozy domesticity, ever, and that he was reveling in it.

But now, even ten years on, I just can't marry these two men: the one that talked about bringing in his baby's clothes in case they got smoky, and who stood chopping cabbage on a Saturday afternoon, and the one that started a fight so bad it ended with my brother dead and him disappearing off the face of the earth—never to see his son again.

Feeling masochistic now, I take the mirror on top and turn around and hold it in front of me so I can get a view of my back, the whole of the back of me, massive arse and all, in the mirror that remains on top of the radiator. That's when the tears come, because it isn't necessarily the size of me or even the spare flesh. It's the condition of everything: the cellulite that puckers my buttocks so that they look like two sacks of porridge; the sagging and the dimples and the fact that I look like I've tucked this body into trousers and bras and under clothes for years, without considering it or caring for it or even looking at it properly for a decade. I am thirty-one years old with the figure of a woman twice her age. My mother has a better body than me. And I begin to sob my heart out then, but not just because of this body. In another time in my life, say, in those few elated days after I had Zac and I was also big, I was only too happy to have an apron hanging over my jeans because of what it meant. But this, it means something different.

You see, even though I'd never admit this, I've always thought I was slightly better than the people on this estate; that this phase of my life was just that, a phase, and that I was destined for better things and belonged somewhere else, that Zac and I would find our way back. That I would even one day find my way back to college—do that teacher training course; be a role model for my son. I've always thought, **I love my boy so much and that's enough**, but it's not, is it? It's not enough just to love them; you have to guide them too, and be strong. And I'm not strong, I'm weak—that's what I see when I look in the mirror. I'm no better than lots of people on this estate. I'm in the same bloody mess as they are.

There's only so long you can emote, I suppose, before you're just exhausted, and I finally flop into bed about eleven, allowing the dark to cocoon me and the thoughts to flow.

Growing up, our lives revolved around food. We commiserated, celebrated, and, yes, comforted ourselves with food. Dad never went to sea on a Monday because it's considered bad luck (don't ask me why—fisherman folklore), which meant that sailing day was often a Tuesday, which in turn meant that on a Monday night there'd be a feast: toad-in-the-hole, Mum's meat loaf, egg and

bacon pie . . . There'd always be a fat pudding—
a trifle or a tiramisu. Mum even said it was to fat-
ten Dad up before he set off for his three weeks in
the deep waters of Iceland or Greenland, where he
sustained himself on rum and cigarettes—but it
was doubtless to comfort herself too, for the fact
that she'd be once again on her own, worried that
this time he might not come home.

Once he'd gone, the baking as a means of dis-
traction would start: pies and flans and cakes and
crumbles . . . Mum says my brother was never happier than when his hands were in a bowl of flour,
but I'd say the same of her. Mum would know
beforehand if it was to be a good landing, and, if
so, she could get a loan partway through from the
dock office and she'd inevitably bring home some
food-based treat to celebrate after our poverty the
week before. Then of course there was the home-
coming meal, for which Dad would invariably
turn up late, stinking of beer, bringing packages of
cod or scampi from the catch as a peace offering.
Money may have been tight, but food never was,
in the fishing community. If Dad was out of work
or had made a few bad trips, then other skippers
and deckhands, not to mention lumpers, filleters,
anyone who knew him, would leave anonymous
fishy packages on our doorstep: haddock, pollock,
even lobster.

So there was always food, and I was probably always a glutton waiting to happen; it's just that van-

ity saved me from getting too fat. That, and love. But when I feel sad or lonely and it's late at night, I decide I might as well be temporarily happy with half a packet of biscuits—a coping mechanism that started when Jamie died and Liam left. I did it to fill the empty, gaping hole in my heart, but of course it was never enough. Nothing could fill it, and instead it's like the more I eat, the more life eats me up.

Have I comfort-fed Zac? I've certainly wanted to comfort him. But mainly I've eaten to comfort myself and he's just come along for the ride.

This is the first time I've thought about it like that. And now, I commit it to paper. Zac's fat because I'm fat. And I realize I owe him, big time. I've not been the best mother. I've already disappointed him with the news I didn't love his father, after all. Don't I owe it to him to at least give him more to go on in terms of who his dad was? Aren't I, as his mother, the best and only person to do that for him?

11

Mick

It's Tuesday—a Zac day, a favorite day—and he and I are sitting watching telly together. We like nature programs the best: **The Blue Planet**, **The Life of Mammals**, **Planet Earth** ... And this is "Planet Zac and I." It's our thing we do. It has its rituals, our telly watching: We both have a cup of tea and usually a slice of cake that Zac bakes with Lynda when he gets home from school—and I always sit in my armchair. Zac sits on the side of the couch nearest to my chair, so it's almost like we're sitting together. Up until he was about seven, he used to sit on my knee, or wedge himself between my thigh and the arm of the chair, and twiddle my earlobe—his equivalent of a comfort blanket. Now he's much too big to sit on his grandad's lap, and I miss those times terribly—the physical closeness, his pudgy skin, my nose in his hair that's just like our Jamie's used to be: straw colored and coarse as a bog brush.

Still, sometimes he'll reach over—as he did just now—and just hold my hand. Often I'll get a hug for no reason. And it's in those moments that I think how nobody tells you, not just that you love your grandchildren as much as you loved your own, but that they love you back—**so much, so intensely**—at least mine does. And in those first, wonderful seconds of a hug, I think how this is the greatest pleasure, the loveliest surprise of my life. And then I remember all I've done, my reality, and it becomes the greatest pain. Always so bitter-sweet. So when I say, cheerfully, "Hey, what have I done to deserve this?" I'm really asking myself that question—and falling short.

WHEN YOU'RE A recovering alcoholic, you live your life according to two coexisting timelines. There's the one on the surface, the one most ordinary people (that is, nonaddicts) live their lives by: what I did today; what I'll do tomorrow; what I did last week . . . Then there's the other timeline. It's tucked behind your heart, deep, deep inside yourself, all coiled up in angst, and it's all about **right now**: right now I'm not drinking; right now I'm doing okay. If I can just put one foot right now in front of the other and go on like that, then I'll continue to be okay.

I'll be nine years sober this summer and still, I can't see a time when I won't need to live my life by that latter timeline. If you were to unwind it from its coil and stretch it out, it would be the tightrope that I walk every day, so easy to fall off, and yet so far to go. Will I ever have another drink? I believe that I won't. But I don't know I won't. And that, for me, is the scariest thing in the world—except losing Zac, and my family, but I should have thought of that before.

ZAC GASPS SUDDENLY and moves to the edge of his seat. "Oh my God, Grandad—look how big the baby elephant is! How can that have come out of . . ."

I'm chuckling. "What? The mum elephant?"

We're watching **Zoo Babies**—another of our favorites. Lynda rolls her eyes as she fusses around us, plumping cushions, tidying away plates. She's constantly busy. It's how she copes. "You two, honestly," she says. "I've never known a pair so soft."

"Well, it's only the same way you came out of your mum," I say. "We're all just mammals at the end of the day, Zac. We enter this world in the same way."

He looks at me—eyebrows raised—as if to say, **Too much information**, then goes back to the program, but I know what's coming.

"Grandad, tell me again. The story of when I was born."

"Oh no, not that again." (I'm only teasing; I like it as much as he does.)

"Yes! That again."

And so I tell him how I burst out crying when I first saw him (he loves that bit—the little egomaniac) and how the first day he was home from hospital, he started screaming blue murder and nobody could soothe him. But how I picked him up and he stopped, just like that.

"And what did Nan say?" he says, grinning, even though he knows the answer; he's heard it a hundred times before.

"She said, 'Honestly, will you look at that! Pity you weren't so good with your own kids.'" And Zac giggles, as he always does.

I don't tell him how Lynda had added, "I was going to say that'll be the brandy on your breath, but I can't even say that anymore." Zac knows nothing of my alcoholism. He doesn't know how five months prior to his birth, I'd gone cold turkey after a lifetime of drinking.

Things had reached a head that Christmas—2004, when after I'd been down the boozer for ten hours straight, Lynda dragged me out of there and delivered her final ultimatum: **It's the booze or us.** Juliet was about halfway through her pregnancy then, and I remember Christmas Day, as I sat sloshed at the table, watching her go to and from the kitchen, helping her mum, my little girl about to become a mum herself, and I thought, **Enough, I can't do this anymore.** Aside from initially coming off the booze (that first time around, I managed to do it without AA), which was torturous, I can't deny it, those few months that followed were probably the best of my life. I'd always believed so much happens in the pub, when you drink, but so much more happens when you stop. Everything was illuminated, as if a dimmer switch had been turned up on my world. Colors were brighter, smells more vivid; thoughts were so clear I could almost watch them. Small miracles, all of a sudden, turned up everywhere I went and the simple pleasures were mine for the taking again: the way the sun passed beneath the clouds, lighting up the old dilapidated buildings by the dock, restoring them to their former glory; the way it lay down on Blundell Park pitch, making Grimsby Town players look like megastars; the sea air; the cry of gulls. I'd missed it all for so long.

But now I was alive again. I felt like a new man. I had so much to look forward to. First and foremost, my beautiful grandson. I glance at him now, completely absorbed in **Zoo Babies**, his mouth hanging open—still seeming to me, with his chubbiness and his wide eyes, and his heartbreaking trust in me, like a baby himself. He has brought me untold joy.

And I can still pinpoint the exact moment, the second, I fell head over heels in love with him. He was four days old and it was just me, Jules, and Zac in the house. Juliet needed a nap, so I said I'd watch him. He woke up from his sleep unsettled— probably wondering where his mum had disappeared to—and so I took him outside, into our backyard, and I stood with him, his warm little body lolloped over my shoulder. I can still, if I try, remember exactly how that felt, the weight of him. Anyway, I just talked to him—told him my stories of being at sea; the fifty-foot waves, and the times we were so close to going overboard we thought we saw Jesus's face in the sea spray. Eventually he fell asleep again, his head flopped right back, his mouth open, like it is now. And I looked down at him then, the newborn soft top of his head pulsing with brand-new life, his eyes moving beneath his lids, and I felt nothing but pure, exhilarating love, and I thought, **I don't ever want to go to sea again, or drink again. I don't want to risk anything that could take me away from him.** I'd made mistakes as a father, but I was going to make sure I was the best grandad I could possibly be. That was probably the best moment of my life. But then came that night Jamie died and all the lights went out, and it felt like I'd just woken up to life, only to lose it all again.

12

Zac

Fact: Seventy percent of the earth's surface is covered with water.

"Right, you lot!" Aunty Laura was standing in the middle of Cleethorpes Beach wearing shiny leggings and a ninja headband, swinging her arms like an orangutan; it was making us all giggle. "We need to warm up first. If you don't warm up before you run, or do any exercise for that matter, you're asking for trouble, all right, people?" Me, Mum, and Teagan nodded. We all had our hands shielding our eyes, because the sun was sneaking up over the sea, lighting Aunty Laura from behind, like she was an angel. "So I want all three of you to copy me. As you bend your knees—and I want really good, deep bends—swing your arms like this, got it?" (Except she was acting more like a sergeant major. Mum said it felt like we were in the army.)

"One . . . two . . . You can do a deeper bend than that, Juliet, come on."

Aunty Laura was like a professional. When she bent her legs, her bum nearly touched the sand. I was trying to do it like her, but my arms kept getting stuck at the top and I couldn't get my legs to bend at the same time; they just wanted to do their own thing. It was really, really funny.

"Er . . . If we could concentrate, Zac?" Aunty Laura was shouting, but her voice still sounded quiet, because it had been swallowed up by the beach. Cleethorpes Beach is massive and magnificent—you'd be mad to go abroad when you've got this on your doorstep—and the sand is perfect for making sandcastles. You don't even have to go and get water from the sea all the time to make it stick and all your turrets stand up. It's just like that naturally.

Mum was on my right and Teagan on my left (I was monkey in the middle) and we couldn't let ourselves look at each other, in case we started laughing. Teagan's arms were going way faster than mine, though; I could see them going crazy out of the corner of my eye. "Er . . . Anyone else feel stupid?" she said suddenly and her voice sounded small too. She was still wearing her red flower in her hair. It was shaking in the wind and I was worried she might lose it, that it would float up into the air and land in the dazzling sea, never to be seen again.

"Just concentrate, please, Teagan," said Aunty Laura. "I don't want anyone pulling a muscle today, just because you were too busy messing around to warm up properly."

A LADY WALKING her dog had stopped behind Aunty Laura. She was just standing there, staring—she wasn't even pretending not to—while her dog did a poo on a bit of seaweed. I didn't blame her, because we must have looked quite silly, but Aunty Laura's face was deadly serious (and she had no idea a dog was doing a poo behind her). It was making keeping our giggles in a lot, lot harder.

"Arms right the way round, please!"

"What if I take off?" said Teagan.

"Speak for yourself," said Mum. "There's fat chance of these thighs taking off anywhere any-time soon."

That was it then—we all just cracked up. Aunty Laura went strict again and Mum did a salute be-hind her back. Then we were all laughing—Aunty Laura couldn't help joining in this time. She said we were all a nightmare—especially my mum.

"Still the class clown, I see, Juliet Hutchinson," she said. "Still the bloody class clown."

IT WAS SATURDAY morning. The weather was sunny but cold, which is normally my favor-ite weather of all time—but we were all there on Cleethorpes Beach to go running. (At least it wasn't boiling. That would have been much worse.) There were still a million things I would have rather been doing on a Saturday morning than going running, though. Here are my top three:

1. Watching **Saturday Kitchen**. My favorite bit is when they do food heaven and food hell. At the moment, my heaven would be cheesy mashed potato and my hell would be mushy peas from the fish and chip shop. I can't believe anyone would actually like mushy peas. They smell like farts even when you just open the tub.

2. Watching footie.

3. Looking up facts in my **Factblaster** book.

4. Eating my own earwax on toast.

The last one's a joke. It's just to show how much I hate running. I'm here partly because it was Aunty Laura and Mum's idea and I didn't want to hurt their feelings, but mainly I'm here because of mine and Mum's pact . . .

"**Zac**," Teagan hissed at me after we'd finished the warm-up. I was already tired and we hadn't even started the run yet. "Come over here, I want a word with you."

I went over. Teagan wasn't sweating one bit. You wouldn't have ever known she'd even done exercise apart from the fact that she was having a go on her puffer. Teagan's got asthma; she's been off school in Year 6 because of it, so now she has to take her puffer a lot more regularly—just to be on the safe side. "Now, I know it was quite funny doing that." She was talking quietly so as Mum and Aunty Laura couldn't hear. Not that they would have been able to because the seagulls were so loud; it's like they know for definite the beach is theirs and they can talk as loud as they want. "But I really think we need to concentrate now, yeah?"

"Yeah," I said, like I really meant it (because I did). "Yeah. Definitely."

"I don't want you to waste any energy on getting the giggles," she said, putting her hair high on top of her head in a ponytail (she can do it dead fast, it's very impressive). "And I don't want you to use all your energy up in the first five minutes."

"I won't, honest."

"Good."

"I'm going to pace myself."

"And I'm going to spur you on," said Teagan, putting the puffer in her zipper. She was so determined, you could tell. "I'll be there when you're finding it hard, like a cheerleader. Because remember, we can't miss this opportunity. Your mum might not offer again."

She was right. I couldn't mess this up. Mum had promised that for every five minutes that I ran, she'd tell me a fact about my dad. It was an unmissable opportunity. It meant that if I ran for half an hour then she would have to tell me six facts—if I ran for an hour, that would be twelve—and who knows, one of them might be the vital clue. It might be the breakthrough in our investigation. That was why Teagan had come too, so she could spur me on and remind me how many facts I could get, if I could just keep going. How it could be the one fact that would lead me to my dad.

AT FIRST, WHEN Mum told me she didn't love my dad anymore, I was gutted; I even cried. It felt like the whole of this mission to find him had been a waste of time: all the information we'd put in our folder, all our meetings. It felt like there was no point in anything. There didn't even seem like there was a point in my dad coming to my birthday party if my mum didn't love him—it would just be awkward.

I know that when I wrote the letter on New Year's Eve, I still thought Mum hated his guts, and I didn't care then. I just wanted him to come and help us. It was a bit like how, if you were drowning, you wouldn't say, "No, sorry, you can't save my life because my mum thinks you're a shithead." You wouldn't be able to be fussy. But then, Mum said what she said on the night of the Date from Hell and it changed everything. I can't really describe it, except that every morning I woke up after that,

I felt excited, and the excited feeling was stronger than any other feeling I had; stronger than being scared or worried, and even stronger than the Call of the Stomach when it gets really, really powerful. It had got bigger than all those feelings, and taken them over. So now it had been taken away, those old bad feelings had come back—but worse than before—and I didn't want to do anything, not even see Teagan.

But then, after about four days, it was mad, but I had an epiphany. An epiphany is when you have a big realization. It's also when you have to take your Christmas tree down. You can't believe that one word can mean something so exciting and something so disappointing all at the same time.

My epiphany came when I did something really simple—I wrote down all the facts I still had and realized none of them had actually changed. I even had some extra ones.

1. **Fact: Even though Mum said she doesn't love Dad anymore, she did love him once, so definitely could again.**

2. **Fact: What I wrote in my letter is still true: okay, my dad did abandon us, but how can he know he doesn't want to be my dad if he's never met me? And how could he and my mum stay in love if they never saw each other?**

3. **Fact: It is up to me to reunite them— because who else is going to do it?**

4. **Fact: Mum has always told me my dad never wanted to know—but it isn't like she did either, is it? Not really. She's never gone looking for him or given him a second chance.**

I rang Teagan up and said to meet me down the bars, so I could show her all the facts. She was glad I'd had an epiphany. We even said we'd missed each other because we'd never gone as long as four days without seeing each other before.

She sat on the lowest bar with our file and read my list. Suddenly she did a big dramatic gasp.

"Number four!" she said, jabbing the paper with her finger. "That's so true and exactly what my mum did too—or what she didn't do, more like."

"What do you mean?"

"I mean that when my dad left us to go and live with Gayle, my mum was so sad and so mad, but she didn't try and persuade him to come back, did she? Or give him a chance to explain. She didn't do anything, except go to bed. It was so weird."

I shrugged, but I didn't say anything. I didn't want to be horrible about Teagan's mum.

"Basically, I just think adults give in," she said, putting her hair behind her ears. "They give up too soon because they just don't have the energy. It's why they need us sometimes, to put a rocket up their bums."

I laughed. "What're you on about, 'a rocket up your bum'?"

"My dad used to say that to my sister," said Teagan. "It just meant that she needed to try much harder."

The way she looked away when she said that, she missed her dad, you could tell.

Basically, Grandad always says to me that you can't give up at the first hurdle and I'd realized that this was all this was—a hurdle, a blip. "It's all right, all major investigations have a blip," said Teagan, as we walked home that day in the sunshine. "Why do you think programs like **Silent Witness** are so long? It's because they need time to find the murderer. They never find him on day one, do they?"

She was right, but I was still confused. "But we're not looking for a murderer," I said. "We're looking for my dad."

AUNTY LAURA LINED us all up, ready for our run. The beach curved ahead of us, like it was a giant arm giving us a big hug, and I tried to imagine that, that the spirit of the beach was giving me a cuddle to say, **You can do this, Zac! It's gonna be fine.** At the same time, I was trying not to look too far into the distance, because that

can fry your mind. The beach is ginormous, basically, and this one covers loads of terrains: it's got
dunes and grassy bits and rocky bits and it goes
far farther than Cleethorpes; it goes right round
England, possibly the world, and if I'd started to
think like that, my belly would have turned inside
out, because no way was I going to be able to take
on the mighty beach—this was going to hurt!

"How long are we going to be running for,
then?" said Mum. She was nervous; I could tell by
the way her voice had gone grumpy and she was
pulling her T-shirt down, even though it didn't
need it because it was nearly down to her knees
anyway.

"Don't worry, we're going to take it nice and
easy," said Aunty Laura, setting off (she'd tricked
us into starting when we weren't expecting it; it
was very sneaky). "Just start off walking if you
want, and build up to a jog if you feel you can
manage it, okay?"

I looked over at Teagan. There was no way I was
starting off walking. I had to run as long as possible to get my facts. So I started straightaway (well,
jogging; it definitely wasn't walking) and for the
first-ever run of my life (not counting the running
you have to do in PE), I didn't even think it was
that bad, and anyway, I was putting how much I
hated running out of my head and just concentrating on keeping going, keeping looking at the
pointy tip of the sand hug in front of us. Yesterday,

Teagan gave me a pep talk down the Find Dad mission HQ, and it was helping me focus. Teagan is brilliant at pep talks. If she doesn't make it as a gymnast, I reckon she should be a professional pep-talker. This was how hers went:

Teagan: "Think about those people in the jungle in **I'm a Celebrity, Get Me Out of Here**. Do you think they like drinking whale wee or eating mashed-up bull's penis?"

Me: "No."

Teagan: "No, they don't. They're just doing it because they want to win the stars, so that they and the other people in their team can have a three-course banquet instead of gruel."

It was the same for me and my run, except I was doing it for facts not stars, and it didn't matter how much I hated running, because I was doing it for Mum and Dad (and myself and Teagan)—and finding my dad was way more important than getting a fancy three-course dinner. If I had to choose between a year's supply of three-course dinners or just one day with my dad, I swear to God, I'd choose my dad.

My legs were hurting quite soon, so to distract myself, I looked out at the sea. The sun had laid sparkles all over it—if you looked at them, they flickered like the sparklers you get on Bonfire Night. Normally the sea fries my mind, though, the same as the beach, because you can't see where it starts and where it ends—it's probably the definition of infinity. Seventy-one percent of the world is water, after all, and almost all of that is the oceans. You'd think we'd all be swimming and paddling, having to wear our wellies all the time, but we're not. It's crazy.

Mum's arm was suddenly around me. "Well done, Zacster!" she said, as she overtook me (it's okay, her legs are longer than mine). "You're doing great, I'm already proud of you." Teagan was up front with Aunty Laura for now, but I didn't mind, I didn't need a cheerleader at the moment, and she was going so fast! With her ponytail swishing behind her and her pale skinny arms and legs, she looked like the spirit of the beach.

We were still on the pebbly bit, so it wasn't too hard, but my shorts were all scrunched up near my privates and rubbing like mad. I wished I was wearing shiny leggings like Aunty Laura—they looked a lot more comfy.

"How long have we been running for?" I said, just as the ground started to go up, so that it got harder. Mum looked at her watch and kept back a bit so that she was next to me. "Three minutes, but it feels a lot longer, doesn't it?"

I smiled, but I didn't speak again. I couldn't believe it had only been three minutes either, but was saving all my breath for keeping going. You've got to keep your mouth shut when you're trying to survive in the desert. It's one of the main tips.

Aunty Laura turned around. "All right, you two?"

"No, I'm bloody not!" shouted Mum.

"Come on, Jules. You can do this!"

"Yeah, come on, **you can definitely do this**!" shouted Teagan, so loud that she beat the seagulls. "Zac, are you all right?"

I nodded, but I still didn't talk. Teagan can afford to waste energy shouting because she's got so much, but I can't. I have to be careful.

The thing with running, I was finding out, is that it's not the same hardness all the way through like table tennis, or even football; it gets harder depending on what you're running **on**. Like I said, the stony bit was okay, but then you go uphill or, worse, up a hilly, sandy bit like we were on now, and doosh! It's like changing gear on your bike because it suddenly gets miles harder. My feet didn't spring off the sand; they didn't even go on top. My feet sank **into** the sand and I wondered if this was what it was like trying to walk on the moon and that was why astronauts have to be so fit before they can go into space.

"God, this is a killer." Mum was panting like a dog, but she was keeping going; I felt proud of her. I wanted badly to stop, or just walk for a bit, but I was no way going to do that if she was trying so hard, never mind getting my facts.

"Okay, that's six minutes now," said Teagan,

like she was reading my mind. "That's one minute more than five minutes and you know what that means, Juliet." (Teagan gets cheeky when she really wants something. She doesn't care. She just says it.)

"All right, Teagan, thank you! But yes, you're right, that's one fact in the bag."

I was happy we had a fact but worried it was only one and the running was already really hard. There was no way I was going to be running thirty—or even ten—minutes at this rate.

"Come on, Zac, you're doing amazing." Teagan was next to me now, giving me some encouragement. But my legs felt like two tree trunks, and my face was so hot that I reckon if you just touched my cheek it would have burned your finger.

People think running is easy, because the people who are good at it make it look that way. And I'm not just talking about professionals like Mo Farah; I'm talking about people at school. Take Connor, for example. People think he's weird because he says "mango" all the time and sometimes makes a noise like a horse, but Connor is a brilliant runner and that is an amazing skill. When you watch him, he makes it look so easy. It even tricks you into thinking that when you try it, it will be easy too. But it's not. I'm telling you, running is rock hard. You feel okay for about two minutes, then you feel like you're going to be sick.

We got to ten minutes, though—one more fact!

But Mum was worried. She kept asking if I wanted to stop.

Mum (peering at me, doing the worried Mum face as I just carried on looking in front): "I think he should stop, Laura. He looks like he's going to keel over."

Aunty Laura: "Do you want to stop, Zac? Shall we just have a pause?"

Teagan (whispering): "Do you want to stop? Because it's fine if you do."

But I was imagining the facts like stepping-stones leading to my dad; I couldn't stop now, I only had two. "No." I hardly opened my mouth, because it wasted energy. "No, I'm fine, I'm going to keep going."

I'll tell you a secret: I started to play the dad film—it was my secret plan to help me keep going. The dad film is just in my head; it's me imagining doing stuff with my dad. I like playing it when I'm trying to get to sleep or to take my mind off tough times—like running. There are a lot of different versions, but this one was the beach one: I was imagining my dad pushing me on a dinghy in the sea, or jumping over the waves or playing Frisbee. My mum's cool, because she doesn't mind doing stuff like that, but when I see other kids doing those things with their dads, I can't help wondering what it would feel like.

"Twelve minutes!" Teagan said. Playing the dad film definitely helped, but I still had three minutes to get to fifteen and another fact and it was getting really hard now. "Come on, Zac, you're doing amazing. You can definitely make it to fifteen minutes and beyond!"

But I wasn't sure I believed her anymore. It felt like I might puke.

"I know what he needs!" Teagan said suddenly. "He needs a fact, but a really good one."

"All right." Mum was almost walking now and flapping her T-shirt dress to get air in her. "Or we could just stop, you know? It might be easier."

"No, a fact," said Teagan. "One you can tell him now. And make it a goodie!"

Mum didn't say anything—nobody did for a bit. All you could hear were the seagulls crying out and all of us panting our heads off.

Then Teagan called, "Julie-e-et!" (Literally, she does not give up.)

Mum did a great big sigh—you didn't know whether it was because she was finding it hard to talk and walk or whether she didn't want to give me any facts. "Okay, he's got blue eyes. Beautiful light blue eyes like yours, Zac, with gold around the middle," she said.

I smiled at Teagan—I thought it was a pretty good fact. (And she'd called his eyes **beautiful**! This was a good sign.) It was epic to think there was someone walking around with the same eyes as me too, but Teagan was pulling a face.

"Mmm, have you got another one? Because I

like that, but there are a million people with light blue eyes in the world and I can't see how . . ."

I flashed her daggers. I thought she was going to blurt out that we wanted the facts because we were looking for him!

Thankfully, she stopped just in time. "Okay, what's his middle name then?" she said instead.

It was Vaughan. (Teagan said later it sounded like "porn." Aidan Turner's always going on about porn. He says it's where two lesbians get their bras and knickers off and kiss each other.) It just seemed like a really weird name to me, but it was an extra-good fact because it was **so** weird, nobody else in the whole of England could be called Liam Vaughan Jones. Plus, Teagan's plan was working: the more facts I got, the more determined I was to keep running.

I learned that my dad had half his thumb missing, because **his** dad had accidentally shut it in a door when he was really drunk, and also that his hair was really dark like Teagan's (not light brown like mine and Mum's), but Teagan wasn't satisfied. She wanted more. She wanted "the Dad Fact of the Century." Everyone, including Laura, laughed at that. And that was when Mum told me that my dad's dream was to be a chef—just like me. I couldn't believe it. It was one of the best things I'd ever heard in my life. I'd inherited loving cooking not just from Uncle Jamie but from my own dad, and I wanted to stop running then, I wanted to ask Mum more about everything—more facts about the facts!

I'd run for half an hour. It was more than I'd run in my whole entire life and when I finished, I didn't even sit down, I just bent over like you see the athletes do on the Olympics. And even though it didn't seem like I could get enough air in my lungs for ages, and even though my whole body killed and I had a big rash where my legs had rubbed, I'd done it, and it felt brilliant. I didn't know you could have pain that felt nice, but you definitely can.

AUNTY LAURA TOOK us to a café to celebrate. It was one with a stand with loads of different ice cream flavors at the front (paradise, basically). There was even mint-choc-chip, which is my all-time favorite, but guess what? I didn't even have an ice cream—I had a sorbet. (Mum didn't even have that—she just had a coffee!) "Have an ice cream if you want, Zac," Aunty Laura said as we all stood in front of the stand, our mouths watering like mad. "But I'm just saying that a sorbet has far fewer calories in it and that maybe it would be a shame to undo your good work."

It took all my willpower. You can't understand unless you're me what a big deal it was. But I did it, I resisted the call of the ice cream and got a mango sorbet instead (in honor of Connor). Nobody could believe it, least of all me.

13

Juliet

For reasons I don't want to think about too much, Zac started, the day after our run, to refer to it as the "Dad Beach Run" or, even more worryingly, "**My** Dad's Beach Run." He first said it just as I was downing a glass of orange juice, and I did that thing that you assume only ever happens in sitcoms: I nearly choked to death on it; spat it out all over the floor.

"Mum!" Zac walloped me on the back, concerned, as I coughed and spluttered.

"It's all right," I said, my face puce, when I could finally speak. "It just went down the wrong way." You could say that again.

I didn't understand at first why him saying this had alarmed me so much, but when I thought about it, I supposed it was because I was suddenly feeling like his name, **that** word, that concept—**dad** (such a beautifully simple and taken-for-granted concept in most people's lives, but like a bloody loaded gun in ours)—had suddenly shifted from the safe realms of the hypothetical to something living among us, something real and present.

It dawned on me that by me choosing to tell Zac information about his dad, I was uncovering him, excavating truths about him, like one of those dig-your-own-fossil toys Zac loves to buy from Pound-stretcher with the pocket money he gets from my parents. You get a plaster-of-Paris egg and a little hammer and you have to chip away at the egg to reveal the ammonite or dinosaur fossil inside. I think it's the discovering something that gives him so much satisfaction. All the "fossils" are lined up on his bedroom shelf.

As much as it alarmed me, though, I have to admit that I find it touching that it only took a few facts, a few scraps of information, and Zac is throwing the word "Dad" around like he's known one all his life. It's so typically forgiving of him. The stupid git doesn't want to know his son (more fool him), makes zero effort to be in his life, and yet a few sniffs of him and Zac's referring to "Dad this" and "Dad that."

Why did I even agree to tell Zac the facts in the first place? Because I'd already broken his heart, that's why. The expression on his face when I told him I didn't love his dad after all—I couldn't get it out of my head. I was meant to be running a Get Zac Happy campaign and suddenly he was as miserable as sin, so the least I could do was to give him something to go on, to motivate him on the run that was probably the last thing he felt like doing after such a major disappointment. (Let's face it, running is the last thing he feels like doing when he's perfectly okay.)

I didn't **want** to tell him anything, though. It felt like breaking the seal on the protective barrier I'd kept around Liam all these years. But in the end, I suppose I needed to see him smile again more than I wanted to keep a lid on all things Liam—only I got carried away. Somehow, Teagan wheedled far more out of me than I intended to give.

Things got worse after the run. I think the lack of oxygen paired with the giddiness of seeing Zac's whole being light up went to my head, because I was waxing lyrical, telling them about all sorts of things—our first kiss, the first time he told me he loved me—and the unsettling thing was that I enjoyed it. It was like there'd been this locked attic room in my soul for years, and suddenly the door had been opened, only for the fresh spring air to blow right in. We **did** have good times. We **did**.

However, in the way life has of giving with one hand and taking away with the other, my act of kindness backfires, when about a week follow-ing the run Mum and Dad turn up at my work. I'm outside at the time, writing a new lunchtime deal on the billboard that now stands outside the shop. Sandwich King is struggling. Never one to

pass up an opportunity to whip everyone into a
frenzy, Gino called a "crisis meeting" yesterday,
summoning me, Laura, and Raymond (even the
deliveryman is not to shirk responsibility) to the
backroom, where he broke the news that Sandwich King has already fallen in rank to "Sandwich
Prince" (his words, I point out) and that it could
very soon become Sandwich-No-More if we don't
do something, fast. Gino's dramatics aside, it **is** a
colossal worry. My God, the last thing I need is to
be out of a job. The problem, as we all suspected,
is a new café across the road, which with its "fancy
salad bar plus soup" approach is luring even your
die-hard sausage-sarnie-on-white types away from
us. Perhaps cosmopolitan café culture has finally
reached Grimsby . . .

Anyway, we all had to have a bright idea for
today and mine is a shameless rip-off of the Boots
Meal Deal: one sandwich and a pastry plus hot
drink for four quid. It's been given the go-ahead
by Gino and I'm therefore writing this in chalk on
the board when I spot a familiar twosome striding
toward me in the sunshine. I say a striding "twosome"; Mum's striding—I'd know that bust-first
walk anywhere—but Dad is trailing behind, as he
always seems to these days, as if he's an appendage
of Mum that has come loose.

It's unheard of for them to come into town, or
even get up, before nine a.m. (a by-product of grief,
and of Dad suddenly going teetotal), and my first

thought—with a jolt of the heart—is that something has happened to Zac. When you've been woken in the small hours to be told your brother is fighting for his life in hospital, your brain never behaves again. You're always, in some way, on high alert.

I slowly, nervously, stand up from my crouching position as they approach.

"What's happened?" I say, chalk hovering, pulse already quickening.

"See, you're worrying her now," I hear Dad mumble.

"Good, maybe she needs to be worried," Mum mumbles back, to which I pull a confused-annoyed face. At least it can't be Zac: "good" would never feature in a worrying situation about her only darling grandchild.

"Yes, sorry to just turn up like this." Mum sighs, not sounding sorry at all. "We are actually here to do some shopping too, but your dad and I need a word with you."

"O-kay." I'm still confused-annoyed. "Well, I can't just drop everything now, Mum, I'm working. Can't it wait?"

Mum smooths her hair down, as if she means business; Dad, I notice, is jangling a bit of change in his pocket and watching passersby as if this has nothing to do with him. "Well, what about your break?" she says. "Do you not get a break at all?"

"In an hour," I say. "But only a short one. I have to be back for the lunchtime rush."

"Okay," says Mum. "We've got to get a few bits in town anyway, so how about Bobbin's at ten forty-five?"

Reading my expression, she adds, "We'll pay, don't worry."

For the next hour, Laura and I try to work out what the pressing issue might be. Mum looked angsty rather than particularly angry—might it be that she and Dad can't look after Zac on their days anymore? They're packing up and moving to Spain? Panic briefly grips me—how would I cope without them? What if Sandwich King shut down? I'd be screwed. But then we figure they'd not be too fussed about leaving me, but Dad, in particular, would never leave Zac, the light of his life, and Mum would never leave my brother at his final resting place up at Grimsby's burial ground. Unless Dad has finally snapped and said they need to move on, start afresh, somewhere without the ghosts of the past whispering in their ears, Jamie's mates on every corner you turn—with their wives and kids; with their lives.

They're already there, standing in the queue, when I turn up at Bobbin's. Dad makes an attempt at small talk, whereas Mum is obviously eager to get going. I order a coffee and a piece of millionaire's shortbread, which I don't need, having nibbled earlier on half a dozen cheese straws that came fresh from the oven, in an anxiety-ridden trance.

Mum chooses a table in the corner and pours the tea.

"So what's up?" I start, looking from Mum to Dad. Mum then looks at Dad, who has his palms pressed together, the tips of his fingers at his lips, staring into the middle distance, and I suddenly think they're about to tell me they're getting divorced. I wouldn't be that surprised, I think; but I would—and this **is** a surprise—be sad.

It's not that.

"We're just a bit concerned," she says, putting down the teapot. "Well, no, very concerned actually, about things that Zac is saying." She's looking straight at me now, with her steely blue eyes that have never suffered fools, and I stop, midbite.

"About what?" I catch a shower of shortbread in my hand as she moves in, lowers her voice.

"About . . . you know who," she says. "About **Liam**."

She's barely uttered his name once, in ten years, and now she has, I'm taken aback to note a not unpleasant and totally involuntary flip of the stomach. "Yesterday, when he was at ours and we were baking, he said something about how he knew his dad had always wanted to be a chef . . . like him."

"Oh, that." I freeze. "Right."

"And when he was in the lounge with your dad, thinking I couldn't hear, he said something that actually made me gasp—didn't I, Michael? I actually gasped."

Dad nods wearily, almost reluctantly.

"Because he said he also knew that his dad's middle name was Vaughan and that he had light blue eyes like his, with the yellow around the middle. It was a lot of detail to be just a . . . coincidence."

"Oh God."

"Yes, **oh God**," Mum says, quite audibly, but my Oh God is more about Zac, my poor baby, innocently, excitably, unable to stop these words from toppling from his mouth, but having no clue about the weight of them. I feel a pang of motherly guilt at what I've expected from him.

"Well, he must have got this information from someone, Juliet," Mum continues when neither I nor Dad says anything. "And it sure as hell wasn't us."

I sigh, feeling suddenly exhausted. "Look, Mum." I feel torn. I don't want to upset my parents **or** Zac. "He's ten now; he's only going to get older. You can't palm him off anymore with one-word answers or expect him not to ask any questions."

"Yes," Mum says, almost triumphantly, tapping the saucer with her teaspoon for emphasis, "but I **can** expect you not to answer them, Juliet."

I roll my eyes toward the window before I even know I'm doing it because I realize, probably for the first time, how deluded and irrational Mum has become about this, how mad she sounds. I don't blame her. My brother's death ruined her, altered her chemistry somehow, so that she **is** irrational—but she's been so desperate to keep the truth from Zac, she's expected the impossible from him.

Mum does a quick scan of the room before she says the next bit. (When Jamie died, it was the talk of Grimsby for months, and even though much of the town has long forgotten Jamie Hutchinson, Mum still behaves as if he were headline news, which sort of breaks my heart.)

"I just thought we'd agreed," she continues, "that we were sticking to our story: he never wanted to know, he's not worth knowing."

"Yes, but Zac's not going to settle for that forever!" It's exasperation, mixed in with panic. "Maybe that was fine when he was five, six, seven even, but children get far more curious as they get older. I live with him, you don't, so you've no idea what it's like." I stop then, because the fact is, Zac did live with my parents for a while—only for a month, in November. After the Morrisons incident; when I wasn't coping, when, well . . . things were really not good . . .

Mum sips her tea; Dad, biting his nails, continues to behave like this has nothing to do with him, like if he's quiet and still enough, he might make himself disappear.

"Look, he's started to ask questions, a lot more

of them and much bigger ones," I say, skipping over the trigger for this: how, apparently, I told him I loved Liam. (My God, if my mother ever heard me say that, I think it may be the end of her.) "So I agreed to tell him a few bits of information. We had an arrangement: for every five minutes that he ran in that run we did with Laura on the beach, I'd tell him one fact. It was meant to be a motivator and it really worked, Mum; he ran for half an hour!"

Mum eyes me over her cup.

"Also I felt that if he was going to start wanting to know information, then at least, like this, I could be in control." I think back to that morning in the café after the run, where I'd waxed lyrical to a wide-eyed Zac and Teagan about how Liam and I met. It was possibly the antithesis of control.

"Ah, but that is where you're wrong!" Mum says, her eyes glittering. "Because actually, the more he knows, the less in control you are." She puts the cup down and pauses, possibly for dramatic effect. "Don't humanize him, Juliet," she says, "because once you start, that's it—he becomes a fully rounded person, someone Zac can identify with, even develop feelings for. Imagine how much that's going to damage him when he finds out the truth: that his own father as good as killed his uncle."

I look away then, because I don't believe that. I don't. Liam was not the person I thought he was, but a killer? A monster for getting drunk and starting a fight? I don't think so. Yes, he laid into Chris Hynd—God knows what possessed him—and yes, if he hadn't, my brother would never have intervened and got caught in the firing line, the blow from Liam being so strong that it knocked Hynd back **into** Jamie. It was an accident, but how could I ever say that to Mum? Like she says, Jamie would still be here if Liam hadn't started a fight that night—that's a fact. And as Zac's always telling me, you can't argue with facts. Also, demonizing Liam is the only thing stoking the fire inside of her; without it, it would die.

I look to Dad.

"Dad," I say. He's been so quiet, I've hardly noticed him. "What do you think?"

He opens his mouth to speak, but Mum cuts in.

"Oh, don't bloody ask him," she says, throwing down her napkin. "He sits on the fence; always has, always will."

FOR THE REST of the afternoon at work, I think about what Mum said at Bobbin's, but even more, I think about what Dad **didn't** say. When I was young, I was very much a daddy's girl. He shared my gregariousness (difficult to imagine these days when I go months without socializing); he was outspoken and "bubbly" like me (even though I hated that word with a passion back then, synonymous as it was, I believed, with "fat"). Yet since Jamie died, he's not just a man changed but an entirely different person. Now it's like we only communicate through Zac, almost as if Dad is avoiding me. Put us in a room together without Zac and I'm not sure we'd know what to say to each other. It's sad. I miss him.

The day before the funeral, all three of us went to see Jamie in the chapel of rest. If you'd have asked me several years earlier how my parents would react should something unthinkable happen like my little brother dying, I'd have said it would be Mum who would become hysterical and Dad who'd be the tower of strength, love, and composure, but that wasn't what happened at all.

Instead, there was just this rage from him at first and, like I say, I never knew who it was directed at—Liam, himself, or the universe. It seemed so out of control and primal. But then he retreated into himself and cried, and I don't mean silent, dignified tears; I mean head-in-hands inconsolable wailing. It was alarming, even in the circumstances.

Dad had always crumpled at the first sniff of a drink, but in all other aspects, he was a loving father and husband, and it scared me that he seemed to be dissolving right in front of our eyes; unreachable just when we needed him the most. It was like this puddle of grief shifted and slithered after him everywhere he went and you'd find him surrounded by it, submerged in it. I once caught him, a month or so after Jamie died—he didn't know I'd seen—sobbing in the backyard very early one morning, banging his own head with his fist, as if he couldn't stand what was going on inside it. He cried when you hugged him, clinging on to you for dear life. But Mum? She was hugging nobody. She was in her glass tower of grief: you could see her, but you couldn't touch her. This was between her and Jamie only. Nobody else was invited.

The man at the chapel of rest was very young himself—I remember that—and he seemed almost apologetic for being alive as he walked us down a wood-paneled corridor with a thick, dark green carpet like moss. We went past one, two, three rooms, until he stopped and, gesturing with his hand to a closed mahogany door with a brass handle, said, "Take all the time you need."

Inside it was cold and smelled of pine and antiseptic. They weren't fooling me. This was really a mortuary, with wood panels and thick carpets; a mortuary made to look like a cozy house. The coffin, which was on top of a trolley (more mahogany), was against the wall on the right and, against the wall on the left, there was a small table with a vase of flowers on top and a picture of Jamie—the one the press had used. It was taken on a rare family walk over the dunes in Cleethorpes, and in it Jamie was ruddy, smiling, thickset, and dripping with life.

The way Jamie's body was laid out, he had his head nearest to the door, so when you walked in, all you could see were his feet. He was wearing his favorite battered black-suede Converse All Stars. Mum and I had even managed to have an argument about that. I said they epitomized Jamie and he'd be comfy in them. She said she was not having any son of hers being laid to rest with "two rats" on his feet. (Little bro, I won out!)

Like I said, I thought it would be Mum who'd throw herself over the coffin and wail, but it was Dad who broke down the minute we saw my brother. He stood, one arm wrapped around his chest, as if keeping his heart intact, lest it should tumble right out, and one hand over his eyes. I was crying too, silent tears running too fast for me to wipe them away with my cardigan sleeve, but Mum was dry-eyed. She was fussing over Jamie like he was a baby (and, of course, I understood once I became a mum myself that he **was** still her baby, and always would be).

I edged nervously toward him. He looked like Donald Trump. (When Grandad died and Jamie and I went in to see him, the makeup they'd put on him had made him look so orange that amid the tears, Jamie had said exactly that. And it had lifted things; we'd sniggered snottily through the tears. But there was nothing to laugh about now.)

Mum was fussing: "Why have they got him

lying like that? He doesn't look comfy, Michael.
I want to put his pillow under his head. Couldn't
they have put makeup on his hands? They're all
mottled." They were a horrible, sickly purple-
yellow color, but his face looked almost normal,
save for a swollen jaw that looked like he had a
bad toothache. Dad just stood back and cried;
he didn't get close to him, kiss his forehead, or
hold his hand as you'd expect of someone seeing
their child for the very last time. Mum shot a look
backward at him. "Michael, did you not hear me?
I want to put a pillow under his head. That's flat,
that is, there's no support."

Jamie, would you listen to them? I wanted
to say. **She's even snapping at him now you're
dead.** If he could have seen us, I knew he'd have
laughed.

"Okay, I'll go and get one," Dad managed, but
it was so quiet, so small, almost as if he felt he
didn't have the right to be there. Then he turned
and walked out, only coming back to hand the
pillow to Mum before saying he couldn't stand it
anymore and had to leave.

Later, Mum could silence whole rooms with her
story about seeing her son in the chapel of rest,
just as she could with her vitriol against Liam and
"What He Did"—like spreading the gospel, only
in the reverse. She'd tell the hairdresser, Laura,
anyone who'd listen how handsome Jamie had

looked, how perfect; how Michael couldn't even touch him for the last time. She wasn't interested in the etiquette of death. She just wanted to talk about my brother, dead or alive. But Dad didn't talk about Jamie, Liam, or, come to think of it, much at all.

14

Mick

After a childhood listening to my old man and his mates regale me with their stories of being broadsided by monolithic waves, and witnessing the camaraderie in their near-death experiences, I wanted some of that too. I wanted the glory; to go to sea like some lads want to go to war: to be a hero in my own town. Ironic that now, with my boy lying dead in the ground.

It was June 1971, and I was sixteen when I finally got a job on the boats. Naturally, I got it from someone in the pub. It was where everything happened, after all, where everything started: relationships, lives (that summoning phone call from your mother, at the hospital), jobs, and big ideas. But it was also where those things ended too. And chances. I know all about chances . . .

Still, I'd got my dream gig as a galley boy, peeling spuds, rolling fags, and washing pots. But I was drinking with the big boys then; besides, you

had to drink to keep warm, keep awake, and simply deal with twenty hours straight in the freezing
wet and cold. Every day, twice a day, we'd get our
"issues" from the skipper: two mustard jars of rum
and three cans of beer. But right from the start I'd
be one of those who'd hide my issues in a drawer
and pretend I'd never got them, just so I could
get another. By the time I met Lynda in '76 I was
already a problem drinker, although neither of us
saw it like that. My party animal ways were one
of the things she loved about me the most; that
I rolled with the good times. And there were lots
of good times: whole summer days, when I wasn't
at sea, getting plastered and sunburned outside
the Fiddler. Our impromptu barbecues were the
talk of the town—Mick and Lynda Hutchinson,
always up for a laugh, a party—and people loved
that here because nobody (nobody we knew anyway) had much money. We couldn't afford to jet
off on holiday. What we had was each other (and
booze), and that felt, for a short while, like paradise.

The signs were already there, though. About
two years after we got married, before the kids
came along (so, around 1982), me and Vaughan
Jones (already infamous in Grimsby by then) got a
job on the **Jubilee Quest**. She was a five-hundred-
foot beauty that was to go fishing off Mauritania
for mackerel and herring, then take four days to
land on Gran Canaria, which was how long it took

to get the tons of fish off the boat. This meant a four-day party for crew with nobody back home, but a chance to fly home to see your wife and kids if you had them. But Vaughan convinced me we needed the party more than any wife, and so I told Lynda that because it was my first trip, I wasn't allowed to go home. My little scheme was only scuppered when Lynda bumped into my mate Tony Mackay, also a first-timer on the **Jubilee**, down Freemo Street with his wife, while I was probably propping up a poolside bar with Jones. "Hang on, Mick told me you weren't allowed to go home," Lynda said, to which Macca (everyone called him that) pissed himself laughing and she, not wanting to appear like the fishwife, the bore, laughed too, apparently: **Cheeky bugger, I'll kill him!** It was only twenty years later when I'd hit rock bottom and Lynda had given me that ultimatum—**It's the booze or us**—that she told me how gutted she really was that day she saw Macca in the street. And not just because I'd lied, but because I'd been weak enough to let Vaughan lead me astray, because (the way she saw it) I wanted to be drinking more with him than being at home with her. That was the day, she also told me, that it began to dawn on her that I may have a problem, although it would be a long time before she used the word "alcoholic."

The first time I ever used that word was when I stood up in a freezing-cold church hall at my first

AA meeting in January of 2006. **Hello, my name is Mick, and I am an alcoholic.** I thought they only said that in films, but you have to do it in real life, and the word felt like a terrifying relief to get out, like exorcizing a demon. It was six months since we'd lost Jamie, two years since my first attempt to give up, on my own, and I wasn't just serious about giving up then, I was desperate. Suicide was the only other option. Sounds dramatic, but that's the truth. Jamie had died. I'd failed him, my family, and my whole community—at least that was how it felt—and the only reason I had to live then was Zac, who I loved as much as Jamie. But nobody wants a drunk for a grandad, let's face it, and the way I saw it, if I failed at sobriety, the only thing I had left to give, then what was the point of me? I sobbed in front of seven strangers at the AA meeting that night. They said I'd done something so brave coming in the first place. I'd never felt like such a fraud in my life.

It took Lynda a long while to forgive me after the **Jubilee Quest** debacle. There were tears, apologies, empty promises—the staple diet of the alcoholic—but then obviously, because I was an alcoholic, I just carried on as before. And maybe that wasn't so bad when we could both go out, but then when the kids came along and it was a case of Lynda at home with the babies and me at sea or in the pub, then the fun ended—for her, anyway.

This was the eighties, though, when things were still comparably good in the fishing industry and Lynda—although furious for much of the time—was too occupied with the kids to bother trying to drag me home from the pub. By the time we got to the late nineties/early noughties, however, the jobs had really started to dry up and Lynda had to take on shifts at a care home to make ends meet. I felt like a failure, so I drank more and Lynda hated me more, and so I felt more of a failure and on it went. My drinking got messier, uglier. With fewer lads down the pub (they were out trying to get work, doing whatever it took to keep their families afloat when their fishing careers were sinking, which was what I should have been doing), I often found myself the only man at the bar; I was the sad, lonely alkie. But why? That's the question I ask myself still now. Yes, we were broke, but I had two gorgeous kids and a beautiful wife who could have fallen in love with me again, if I could have got a grip. And where did it come from, this addiction? I would have liked to blame it on an appalling childhood: I loathed myself, so I drank. But it was the opposite for me: I loved the drink, so I drank and drank, and **then** I loathed myself. It was all so avoidable, so unnecessary. But I'd fallen in love, seduced by the sweet release booze gave me, helplessly addicted to that moment—the tipping point, before which you still have a choice to carry on or not carry on. But then I always wanted to carry on, wanted the boat to tip so far that it couldn't then right itself, so that I could slide—like a slippery catch being returned to the sea—right out of that net and into the delicious, boundless deep.

The problem with that is that you have to come up for air eventually and face the truth about yourself.

15

Zac

Fact: The blue whale has the largest heart: it weighs approximately 1,500 pounds.

My other grandad's name is Vaughan Jones and he was a fisherman too—Mr. Singh told me. Mr. Singh is mega brainy. You don't think he is; you think he's half-asleep because he sits in his shop with one eye closed. But he's like an eagle: he watches everything from up on his stool, and he knows everyone in Grimsby because he's owned shops in every area of town.

I only found this out yesterday (if I'd have known sooner, I would have asked him ages ago about my dad). But I just asked him if he knew him by chance—I thought it was worth a try.

"Do you know Liam Jones?" I said while I was paying for the milk. (I also bought a Mars Bar, but it was the first chocolate I'd had that week. I definitely deserved it.)

"Who's asking?" said Mr. Singh.

"Me," I said and Mr. Singh laughed. "He likes cooking, like me, and he's got dark hair. He grew up in Grimsby."

"Why do you want to know?" said Mr. Singh. He looks so different when he smiles. You can tell he's kind deep down.

"It's for a school project," I said. It was the first thing that came into my head. "An investigation into local people."

Mr. Singh laughed again then and thought really hard for a long time. "Liam Jones . . ." he said, drumming his fingers on the counter. Mr. Singh's hands are so dry they look like they've been dipped in flour. "A Grimsby lad, you say? How old are we talking?"

"Dunno, thirty-two?" I said. It was a guess because my mum's going to be thirty-two in November and normally your boyfriend is the same age as you.

Mr. Singh shook his head slowly, but then it was like someone had reached inside his head and switched both his eyes on. "Liam Jones. I know Liam Jones! He's Vaughan Jones's lad."

"Who's Vaughan Jones?" I said. It felt really exciting.

"Vaughan Jones? He was a well-known skipper, was Vonny from the Rollo Estate. I bet your grandad knows him." (I was nodding and grinning even though I'd never heard of him.) "I haven't seen Vaughan for more than ten years," said Mr. Singh. "Since way before you were born. But Liam used to do a paper round for me when he was a teenager and I had Singh News up on the Rollo. Why you want to know about Liam Jones, any-way?" he said. "What's he got to do with your school project?"

But I was putting my shopping in my bag as quickly as I could, and then I was halfway out the door. "Thanks, Mr. Singh!" I shouted behind me. Then I ran home, fast as a peregrine falcon. I had to write everything down before I forgot.

IT WAS THE Thursday before we had a long weekend off for Easter and everyone (not just Connor) had ants in their pants and couldn't con-centrate. I couldn't, because this morning Tea-gan had said to meet her at Harrison's bench in the playground at break time because she'd had a brain wave about the Find Dad mission. Harri-son's bench is a bench dedicated to Harrison, who was a boy who died from a brain tumor when we were in Year 3. He came in to see us when he'd gone bald because of the cancer, then in the sum-mer holidays he just died. You couldn't believe it. Nobody wanted to fill his empty chair in the class-room, so we just left it, but every time you walked past, you could feel his ghost.

Teagan was already sitting on the bench when I got there, eating a bag of Frazzles.

"I've thought of the most important question to ask your mum," she said. Normally we have to say our code word, "mango," before we talk about the mission outside the roundabout HQ, but she just started talking.

"What is it then?" I said.

"We need to ask her where she was the last time she saw your dad. It's what they do in all investigations for missing people; I saw it on a documentary last night." Teagan watches loads of documentaries because her mum likes them so much. I watched one with her about a boy who had no arms or legs, just stumps; but he was still happy because his family still loved him. "They ask the searcher—the person looking for the missing person—when they last saw the person, what they were doing, and if they were acting weird."

"What, the searcher?"

"No, the missing person! Der! The searcher would know if they were acting weird themselves, wouldn't they?"

I nodded, but I wasn't sure. My dad did a runner ages ago now, so how would my mum remember anything? And was doing a runner even the same thing as being a missing person? It all felt confusing.

"It's basically just retracing your steps," said Teagan, when I didn't say anything for a bit. "But it's really effective. We need to ask your mum to go back in her tracks to that day she last saw him, because that will give us the most clues about where he might have gone after that. Trust me, it's what professional detectives do, except they interview people in a proper police station, whereas we'll just have to do it in your kitchen."

Teagan crushed the remaining bits of the Frazzles up in the bottom of the packet. If you do that, the crumbs are like "bacon bites"—the best part by miles of the Pizza Hut salad bar, only you don't have to go out to Pizza Hut. You get the Bacon Bites Experience for 56p. Me and Teagan discovered it.

I knew she was right about "retracing your steps" helping the investigation. Once I lost my **Factblaster** book, and was really panicking, then I retraced my steps and remembered I'd taken it to the chippy to read while I was waiting. I'd left it there two whole days earlier, but it was still there. People think there are loads of thieves on our estate, but they're just prejudiced.

The problem I had with Teagan's suggestion was that if we started asking Mum too many questions, she'd get suspicious that we were looking for my dad and then she might try and stop us because she wouldn't understand that it could be brilliant in the end.

I explained this to Teagan. She looked disappointed. "Oh," she said. I felt bad that I'd dissed her idea. "I hadn't thought of that. So we can't really ask her any more questions then?"

I thought about it for a minute. "We can," I said. "Just nothing too obvious." I told her not to worry, as secret investigations are a lot harder than normal, not-secret ones. Then I said we should go over the facts we already had from the Dad Beach Run and our mission so far. I wanted her to finish our meeting feeling excited again. It was the end of March—we only had until my birthday party at the end of May and we hadn't got the letter to my dad yet.

I didn't have the Find Dad mission folder with me, so I got out my spelling book and wrote in the back. We had to be careful because Miss Kendall was on break duty. Her bump is so big now she looks like Mr. Greedy.

Facts we already have about my dad:

- **His middle name is Vaughan.**

- **His dad's name is Vaughan Jones.**

- **His dad was a skipper and they lived on the Rollo Estate.**

- **Half his thumb is missing because his dad shut it in the door when he was drunk.**

- He's got really dark hair like Teagan.

- His dream was to be a chef like my uncle Jamie (even though when my mum knew him he was still a fisherman like my grandad used to be, but he might have gone to cheffing school like my uncle Jamie, you never know).

- He's got really light blue eyes like mine.

- The first time he kissed my mum was outside a pub called the Fiddler in Cleethorpes.

- On their third date, he cooked a ginormous three-course meal including Singapore crab (the best thing my mum's ever tasted) and my mum ate so much, she had to go for a walk around the block. My dad said that was the moment he fell in love with her.

"Hey, do you remember her face," I said to Teagan, when I'd finished writing the list, "when she was telling us that story about how he fell in love with her?"

Teagan did an impression of my mum with her gooey love eyes. It was very funny.

"And when she said about your eyes," Teagan said, sitting up, "she didn't just say they were 'blue,' she said they were '**beautiful** light blue eyes like yours' and she was batting her eyelashes. She looked a bit crazy!"

"See," I said. "So she can't deny she did love him once, can she? And even though she hates his guts now 'cause he left and never came back, our job is to find out why he did—so she might forgive him and they'll fall in love again."

By the time we had to go back in, after break, Teagan had cheered up.

SOMETIMES YOU CAN only really understand or realize something when the opposite happens to you. It's like when I was really hot, running on the beach, and I totally appreciated how nice ice-cold Fanta is. Grandad always says, "If you do everything the same, you'll get the same result." I never used to understand him. Me and Nan used to look at each other when he said it, because we didn't have the foggiest what he was going on about, but since the opposite has happened to me, I realize what he meant. Basically, after I (well, Mum) did one thing differently (go on a date), everything else that followed has been different too—it's been really good. So I've written a new saying: **If you change one thing, then everything after it will change too, probably for the best.**

I wrote my theory and how it worked down in the Find Dad mission folder. (Missions are like maths—it's good to show your working out.)

- If my mum hadn't gone on the Date from Hell, she'd never have got drunk and said she loved my dad.

- So, I'd never have decided to look for him.

- So, I'd never have agreed to do the Dad Beach Run, because I wouldn't have needed the facts about my dad (because believe me, that is the only reason I did it).

- But then, I'd never have tried running and realized that exercise is actually all right—it can even make you feel happy.

- I'd never then have agreed, with a good attitude (because it doesn't count if it's not with a good attitude), to go to the sessions with Jason and remembered how much I like him.

It's not even that I forgot; it's just that I hadn't seen him to remember.

I've got a confession, you see: before I started going on the exercise sessions three weeks ago now, I'd been avoiding him. I'd been praying on my **Factblaster** book that I didn't bump into him ever since seeing him outside the Your Fitness center the day Miss Kendall told us she was having a baby. It felt awkward, that's why, and I felt guilty. I felt like I was hiding a secret—the secret that I was looking for my dad—and I was worried that if Jason found out, he'd be sad, if he still loved my mum, and so it was best I didn't see him in case I blurted it out.

But then Mum said she'd set up these exercise sessions, and I freaked out, not just because of this but because I thought it might mean that he and my mum were trying to get back together again and it would ruin my idea to get Mum back with Dad. Once my mum had said she didn't love my dad anymore, that felt even more risky. (It's nothing against Jason. It's just all kids want their parents to be together; it's a fact.) I just couldn't resist in the end, though, because deep down I did want to see him.

Today's session was football (last week we did table tennis, which is much more energetic than it looks), and me and Jason were up at the playing fields behind the railway track like old times. We were about to start playing, but first of all Jason had to guess what I'd put in today's sandwich. It's part of the rule of our meetings: he sorts out the exercise bit, but I have to bring him a new sandwich I've invented. I make them at Mum's work. Raymond lets me in early on a Saturday morning to practice inventing new sandwiches; I help him unload his van then he lets me loose on the ingredients. I put on the plastic gloves and hat like my mum does and pretend I'm a professional sandwich maker; it's totally epic. I then go and make my new sandwich on the way to my session with Jason on Mondays. The extra bit that I've added to the rules is that Jason has to put on a blindfold while he tastes the sandwich then tell me what he thinks all the ingredients are. After the exercise we get to eat my sandwiches. They always taste extra nice by then because you're so starving.

Jason leaned against the goalpost and put the blindfold on. (We just use a football sock; it works really well.) Then I gave him my sandwich. I always wrap it up in the brown paper you can only get from Mum's work so that it looks professional.

"Right, what have you brought me today then?" said Jason, peeling back the paper and sniffing it. "Because whatever it is, it smells bloomin' good."

I smiled when he said that. It felt nice.

He took a bite and chewed **really** slowly. The way he did it, it was making me laugh. Jason can make you laugh when he's not even saying anything. Mum says it's because he's just got "one of those faces."

"Mmm, there's definitely chicken. Already better than that nonsense you brought me the first day: seven layers of lettuce and a lousy piece of ham—how's that supposed to sustain a growing lad?" And he's not just kind to you because you're a kid. It's like he hasn't even noticed you are one, but it's good, I like it.

He kept chewing. "I can detect tomato?"

"Yeah, but what **kind**?"

"Ah, sun-dried!" he said after a bit. "Very fancy, Zac, very gourmet, I like that." (I liked this game.)

"Yeah, but what **other** vegetables?"

"There are other vegetables?"

"Three different ones." I'd listened to what he'd said about how the more colors there are, the better it is for you, and I'd tried out different combinations at Mum's work to get a really good one.

"Okay, kale?"

"What?" I'd never even heard of it.

"Spinach then?"

"Yep."

"And red pepper."

"Actually, it's yellow," I said, glad I'd caught him out. "But I'll let you off, 'cause I'm nice like that."

This time it was Jason's turn to laugh because he knew I was doing an impression of him. "Well, Zac, you've surpassed yourself," he said after he'd eaten half of it. (He liked it so much he wasn't even saving it all for after.) "That, my friend, is the King of Sandwiches"—which I thought was cool, because I'd made it at Sandwich King.

Jason put the rest of the sandwich away and asked me what I wanted to do.

"Dunno. Go to McDonald's? Just kidding!"
You can kid all the time with Jason and he never
thinks you're naughty, but he doesn't laugh at all
your jokes either, so you know which ones are
really funny.

We did a warm-up—you always have to. Today's consisted of star jumps (a nine on my one-to-
ten scale of all-time worst exercises), a jog around
the pitch (only a six, because I'm getting more
used to jogging now), then some sit-ups, which are
definitely a ten. You have to be serious for days afterward, because if you laugh, your stomach feels
like you've been stabbed, but it's the only way to
get a six-pack.

"Right," Jason said when we'd finished the
warm-up and I was lying on the floor, dying from
the sit-ups, "shall we play some football then?" I
groaned, but I got up and walked over to stand
in goal. But Jason just stood there, stroking his
beard.

"What you doing?" he said.

"Going in goal."

"How come?"

"Because I always go in goal. I always went
in goal when I played footie with you, and Mr.
Grimshaw"—that's our PE teacher; Jason knows
him—"always puts me in goal as well. He says it's
the best place for me."

Jason nodded really slowly. He looked sort of
mad and sad at the same time. "Does he now?" he

said. "Well, I've got news for you, Mr. Hutchinson. Two bits, actually. The first is that I'm sorry if I've always put you in goal—that's crap and unfair of me and makes me a shoddy coach, not to mention a shoddy mate—and the second is that you're not going in goal anymore." He started to walk toward me then, all determined.

"What? Am I not?" My belly rolled like a wave. The only time I've been out of goal in PE (in Year 6, anyway) was once when we had a stand-in PE teacher who didn't know I always had to be goalie and everyone said I should get a bra because I had boobs that bounced when I ran.

"No, you're not," said Jason, putting his hand out. "Come on, out you come." I gave him my hand, but I still didn't move. "Come on," he said again, pulling me a bit this time. "We're going to get you moving."

"But I move in goal."

"I mean, really moving."

I didn't know what was wrong with me. I've always wanted to play football and not just be in goal. I've always wanted to run around, like everybody else, without worrying I'm getting sweat patches, or looking like I need a bra. I'd love to do all the tricks like "around the world" and "rainbow flicks" and dart in and out of all the players like a gecko. It looks like dancing when you see Jacob Wilmore do it. His feet move so fast, you can't believe it, and when he scores the goals, because it's only really him that does, everyone piles on him and loves him like a hero. Now I was being given the chance by Jason to try it all, with nobody else watching, and I didn't want to. It was stupid.

Jason let go of my hand. "What's up?"

"Dunno. I just want to stay in goal."

"Right, and what's going to happen next week?"

"I'll come out of goal."

"So what's the difference between this week and next week?"

I didn't say anything. I didn't know what to say. I was just starting to wish I'd not decided to come to these sessions now.

Nobody said anything for a bit. All you could hear were the trains whooshing by behind us.

Jason leaned on the goalpost and sighed—a really big one, like he was tired all of a sudden. "What are you scared of, Zac?"

"Nothing," I said, but it was a lie, because suddenly I felt scared of loads of things: looking stupid, going to school, being fat forever; Jason and Mum finding out I was looking for my dad; Mum and Jason getting back together. Most of all, I was worried about being crap at football (the running-around kind, not in goal). Of Jason being disappointed in me. I was thinking of what would happen when I met my dad too. Football is what sons and dads do together—it's a fact. Not one like in my **Factblaster** book, but it's still a fact. What if I met him and he wanted to do it, and I was still crap?

Jason put his hand on my shoulder.

"Is it that you might find it hard, if I make you run around?"

I shrugged. "Yeah, a bit. I mean, I can run; I did the run on the beach and it was all right"— even though I had the facts to keep me going— "but it's the football I'm worried about. Like, I love football and know loads about it, but . . . I can't do it, I can't do the skills and stuff. I can't even do a header. I'm too slow and get all out of breath really quick and—"

"Whoa, whoa! Steady on, Hutchinson." Jason pushed me away as he said it and put his hands on his head, all dramatic. But he was only joking; he did it to make me laugh and relax me. It kind of worked. "This isn't trials for Grimsby Town Youth Academy, you know. We're not trying to get into the SAS." A smile crept up—I couldn't help it. "We're meant to be having a **laugh**. Football, exercise, it's meant to be **fun**. That look on your face, you look like I just asked you to streak across Blundell Park."

"What's streak?"

"Running starkers, Zac; yer crown jewels flopping about in broad daylight, looking like chicken giblets, across a stadium full of people and, yes, you should be laughing because that's how funny your terrified face is."

"So you're not going to make it too hard then?"

"No! For one, your mum would kill me."

"And you won't be disappointed in me if I'm rubbish?"

"No. But I will be if you don't even have a go. Come on, you wally. Come and help me get these cones out."

I wasn't very good, but it was only my first go and I wasn't really bad either. The bonus was that it was loads more fun than I thought it was going to be. We practiced dribbling the ball between the cones. (A lot harder than it looks! You have to hold your muscles really tight.) I even headed the ball a couple of times! Jason said I was bound to be good at that, because my head was big, due to my mega brains, and anyway, he wanted to make my head even bigger. He said by the time he finished with me, I wouldn't be able to fit my head through the school classroom. I'd be a good goalie but a decent striker too. I'd be indispensable. ("Indispensable" means **so good or important that you cannot manage without it**—I looked it up in the dictionary.) All the time we were playing, Jason didn't tell me once to sit down when I didn't need to like Mr. Grimshaw, my PE teacher, does; we just played and I forgot about all my worries, but my mind was working stuff out too. Exercise is good for that. For example, I worked out why I thought Jason would be sad if he found out I was looking for my dad. When he was with my mum, I really wanted them to get married so he could be my stepdad, and now, since starting the Find Dad mission, I'd begun to wonder if Jason had felt that too, and wanted that too. But then Mum had dumped him and if I found my dad, I wouldn't be able to hang out with him, so it would be like I was dumping him too. It would feel horrible, like when your best friend chooses another best friend.

I try not to think about the day he and Mum broke up that much because it felt dead sad. One minute they were together—we were even supposed to be going on my first-ever holiday in Jason's mum's caravan in Skegness. The next, Mum said we probably wouldn't be seeing Jason because they weren't girlfriend and boyfriend anymore. When I went to bed that night, I cried for ages. I was sad that we wouldn't be seeing Jason much now, but most of all I was sad that Mum wouldn't have anyone being nice to her (I'm her son so it's not the same). Jason used to tell her she was pretty all the time. She always told him to get lost, but she liked it, you could tell.

AFTER WE'D FINISHED the football, we sat down to eat our sandwiches. They tasted like God had sent them down on a rope from heaven we were so hungry, and the sun was hot on our backs, which felt lovely, but then Jason started asking me questions.

Jason: "So what are you up to over Easter weekend, Zac?"

Me: "Nothing." (Actually thinking, **Looking for my dad!!!**)

Jason: "What, absolutely nothing? That's a poor show."

Me: (Silence.)

Jason: "Why've you gone all quiet? That's not like you."

Me: "What? I've not gone quiet."

Big silence.

Jason: "Well, maybe we could do a few extra of these sessions? Maybe your mum could come too . . . ?"

Me (my sandwich sticking in my throat so I couldn't even speak for ages): "No. No, we can't, unfortunately. We're actually really busy this Easter."

Jason (laughing): "I thought you just said you weren't doing anything."

Me: "I forgot."

Nobody said anything for ages. We were just there, leaning against the goalposts, eating our sarnies.

Then Jason said, "All right, Hutchinson, spill the beans. Is your mum getting married or something? Because it's really fine, you know."

"No!"

"Ah, well, it must be a secret mission you're on then; a special project. Don't worry, I get it."

My eyes nearly popped out of my head then. Did he already know that I was looking for my dad?

16

Juliet

It's my day off. Zac is at Connor's birthday party all afternoon—he was singing in the bath this morning, overjoyed to be one of only four people invited—and so I decide to go for a walk in People's Park. I say that like it happens all the time, when in actual fact it never has. I've never seen the point of "going for a walk." If you're walking **to** somewhere—a mate's house, the Chinese, the bus stop—then that's different, but just a walk for walking's sake? I've always thought that was a waste of time, a luxury; but I'm beginning to think that's just been a cover-up for my lazy-arse ways. I'm starting to get real with myself about this stuff and that's got to be progress.

I asked Laura recently, in fact, how she managed to lose all that weight years ago, expecting her to say, **Basic self-control, Juliet. You should try it sometime.** But she didn't. She said, "Being aware. You can't change anything unless you're aware of what you're doing now and what you want to change." It was a revelation and it stuck, which is saying something because another thing I've learned about myself recently is that not much does stick. I. Just. Don't. Learn. So I've stuck it to my fridge: **BE AWARE.** I may still choose to open said fridge and hack into a block of Cheddar with my bare teeth, but at least I'll have chosen to, rather than the cheese choosing me, which is basically how it's felt between me and food all these years.

I'm trying to be **aware** of being more active too. Zac's doing really well. I'm so proud of him. He's definitely lost weight, but it's not just that; it's that he seems so much happier. It's like he's got purpose suddenly. Whatever it is, my Get Zac Happy campaign might just be working and I want to support him by setting an example, but the truth is, I think I find it harder than him. I'll be virtuous for a couple of days then start worrying about everything—where were all these facts I was telling him leading us, and what the hell had I started?—and then fall spectacularly off the wagon.

RIGHT NOW, THOUGH, I stroll on through the park. It's a gorgeous spring day, the sky that powder blue that it only seems to be in early spring, and everything smells good and fresh. Things are going better for Zac; I feel tentatively at the beginning of an "up" curve, and yet, I also feel a sickly mix of something like déjà vu and foreboding because all spring days like this remind me of is the same time of year eleven years ago. Only then, I could truly enjoy it, having no idea how my life was about to derail.

I take the route around the lake, trying to feel again what it was like to be full of nothing but hope for the future. At this time—late March of that year (2005)—I was seven months pregnant, fat and joyful as a daffodil trumpet; madly in love and impatient to meet our son. I loved being pregnant, never more than when I was heavily so, and my flabby middle, normally a major obstacle to all things fashion, had swanned into this glorious, drum-tight beach ball that I could not stop looking at and that I showed off in the tightest Lycra at every opportunity. It was the first and last time in my life that I was proud of my body (and that I could go anywhere near tight Lycra for that matter) and I was in love with my new primal shape. I also loved the fact that when I walked down the street, I felt people were admiring, not judging me. **And,** I'd think wryly, **I've never been heavier! I've never eaten as much Edam in my life!** Liam always told me I was beautiful before I was pregnant, but I never believed him, always told him to shut up. But now, sometimes, I'd be standing just brushing my teeth or filling the kettle and I'd catch him looking at me with those ridiculous blue eyes, fist at his mouth as if stopping something, in case it overflowed . . .

"What?" I'd say coyly, knowing full well what, because he'd said it before, but also because for the first time in my life I felt it to be true.

"You're beautiful, that's what," he'd say.

I didn't know who was more excited about the baby—me or Liam. He wanted everything new for him. Hand-me-downs were turned down graciously, although in all honesty, we could have done with them, but I knew, even though he never said it, that Liam needed to prove that he could provide for his family. Most of all, I knew he wanted to prove (mostly to my mother) that he was nothing like his own father, which is why I'm so floored that things have turned out the way they have.

I KNOW EXACTLY what he was wearing that night, June 11, 2005, because I remember thinking how sexy he looked. "You won't want him anywhere near you when you're breastfeeding," women seemed to delight in telling me, but I must have been the exception to the rule, because although my body was battered from the birth, I could not get enough of him. My favorite thing to do was to study Liam's face, then Zac's, and count the similarities. I found new ones every day: the eyes, of course, but also the lips, the tiny earlobes, even right down to the strange X-shaped crease at the back of their necks. Looking at Zac was like discovering Liam afresh; falling for him all over again. I must have suspected my happy little world was about to be smashed to smithereens, however, because I can remember every last moment before Liam went out that evening in microscopic detail, almost as if I knew I'd better slow it right down so that it could be committed to memory: **I had it once, true happiness. It was real. It happened to me.**

So anyway, there we stood, that night, before he went out, in the front porch of the little two-up two-down we were renting, door open, the floral scent of early summer wafting in. He was wearing his black jeans and a red tartan shirt, with the top button undone, revealing just a small triangle of chest hair. Being so dark, he was always self-conscious of his hairiness, tried to cover it up, but I've always gone for manly men, I suppose, and I loved it, especially the way it smelled when I laid my face against it. And we'd stood there, me doing just that, Zac asleep over my shoulder, blissfully unaware this would be the last time he'd be in the presence of his father.

It must have been about seven thirty p.m., but it was still warm and sunny outside and I remember the way the shape of us then, our brand-new family, fell in elongated shadows against the beige carpet in the hallway. Outside, seagulls cried their mournful cry as if they knew something we didn't. Kids shouted. Skateboards rumbled up and down.

"Now, go and have a laugh," I said, stepping back from him and sweeping his black hair to the side, the way I fancied him the most. "Have some fun; you deserve it." I didn't have to say **and don't get too drunk** because I knew—at least I thought I did—that he wouldn't. If anything, he'd be doing my head in, calling every fifteen minutes to check on us, then coming home at half past nine . . .

He reached out and stroked Zac's head. "Sure you don't mind? I feel a bit guilty going out."

"Why? Don't!" I said, and I meant it. "**Your** nipples aren't attached to a baby twenty-four/ seven. I'd make a run for it, if I were you." And he rolled his eyes at my attempt at a joke. "Just don't let my brother go silly, will you? Because he thinks he can take his beer, but he can't, unfortunately. Look after him, won't you?" It seems darkly ironic to me now—if that isn't the understatement of the century—that it was my brother getting too drunk I was worried about, not Liam. If I had any concerns about Liam, it was that he wouldn't let his hair down; I felt like he'd been cooped up for months and needed a break.

The plan was that Liam would go over to my parents' house, collect Jamie, and then Dad would give them both a lift to the pub. To our amazement, not to mention pride, Dad hadn't touched a drop of alcohol for five months at this point, so was leaving the baby-head-wetting rituals to my brother and Liam. Mum—who was on a night shift at the care home—had instructed him to make them some stomach-lining pasta before-hand.

"I won't be late, all right?" Liam said, kissing first Zac on the forehead and then me on mine, laying his own forehead against it for a moment, so that our lips were nearly touching. What he said next will stay with me forever. "I'm really happy, Jules."

It slipped out, probably taking him by surprise as much as me, because he wasn't one for big emotional declarations, and I kissed him hard on his smiling mouth then, because I knew—or thought I did—how much he meant it. I thought it was a beautiful surprise to him that this was true, and that it had taken a baby, the ultimate commitment, to make that happen. Proof that he may have been Vaughan Jones's son genetically, but that was where the similarities ended.

But since everything happened, I've questioned that like I've questioned everything else; asked myself if when he said those words, he was not being genuine but trying to convince himself, having second thoughts about me, us, all of it, and that was why he went out and did what he did.

Zac was oddly unsettled that night and I'd just got him off to sleep and was drifting off myself when I was woken up by my mobile ringing—

Liam's name flashing up. I picked up. "Liam, seriously . . . For God's sake." I was irritated he'd called at such an inopportune time; little did I know I was about to have far bigger things to be mad about. I couldn't make out a word he was saying. He was sobbing, hyperventilating, and I bolted out of bed, shouting at him to tell me what had happened, which woke up Zac so that all three of us were screaming. He was obviously still drunk because he was slurring his words, making little sense, and all I could hear between sobs was **Jamie**, **fight**, **hospital**, **my fault**.

I was rifling in drawers for something to wear—all I wanted was to be with Jamie at this point—and Zac, who would have to come with me because there was no one else to look after him, was screaming blue murder in his Moses basket.

"How bad is he?" I was saying. "He **is** going to be all right, though, isn't he?"

But Liam wasn't talking, only sobbing, and the sobs stretched and stretched and then he said, or rather rambled, "There was a fight. I started it, Jules. I just saw red. I threw this punch . . . I never meant to. I was so pissed, Juliet. Shit. Shit. I was so drunk."

My neck went cold then, I remember that.

"Do Mum and Dad know?" I asked then, and, when he said they were there already, I said, "Tell them I'm coming." As I said it, I suddenly felt this icy screen descend—almost like a reflex—between the two of us.

Liam was still talking, but I hung up. That was it as far as I was concerned. I didn't want to hear any more from him. I didn't want to see him either—not then.

I bumped into him, though, as I was rushing through the doors of A&E, Zac strapped to my chest. "Juliet." He took hold of my shoulders, trying to make me stop. He was crying and breathing heavily, right in my face. "Please can I talk to you?" He reeked of booze and already didn't look like the same person to me. "Please, please . . ." But I couldn't, didn't even want to, look at him then.

"I can't, Liam," I said, trying to push him to one side so that I could get past. "Move, I've got to see my brother."

I walked away, down the long, overheated hospital corridors that seemed to be closing in on me, unaware, as yet, of the horrors I would find: my little brother, so unrecognizable because of all the tubes. I was only aware it was him because of my parents being there. Dad was sitting with his head in his hands—a pose he seems to have retained for the last ten years—my mother unable to look at me. She was mad with me—by association—I could tell, and I can't say I blame her. Sometimes I wonder if she's ever stopped being mad.

I didn't see Liam again after that. I only spoke to him, very briefly, early that next morning, after Jamie had died. His number flashed up and, not thinking straight, I picked up. He was silent at first, then he said, "I'm sorry. I'm so, so sorry. I love you and Zac so much. I know you don't want to talk or see me now, but can we talk? When you're ready?" I hung up. It wasn't even hate I felt so much as a sensation of being repelled, physically, by him; the opposite of the magnetism that had happened when we'd first kissed outside the Fiddler. The mooring rope had severed, and I was floating away. When those first few awful weeks were over and I found out the details of the fight, I began to see it all for the tragic, awful accident that it was. But right at that moment, on the phone, all I knew was that my brother was dead and my distraught parents held Liam accountable, and so there was no way I could have anything to do with him.

I've brought a flask of coffee and some miserable carrot sticks, and so I lay my cardigan down under a tree and sit. There's a children's play area opposite—or an adventure trail, I guess you'd call it—a big improvement on the rotting merry-go-round on our estate, anyway, and I wonder why on earth I didn't bring Zac here more often when he was little, when it was free and practically on our doorstep.

There are about six or so kids swinging from

various tires and wires on there, four out of that six (I know because I've counted) with their dads. I always notice dads. I've got a fetish for them like I imagine women who can't have kids, and long for them, must have about pregnant women. I like to punish myself by watching them with their children; how they chat and listen to them; how they're just there, pushing their kid on a boring swing, doing boring things, because they want to, because they love them. Because that's what being a dad is.

I munch noisily on my carrots from my people-watching hideout, the leaves fluttering above me. One minute, all is calm and there are two little girls on the seesaw; the next, there's only one, with the other one facedown on the floor. There's a big wail, followed—you know it's coming—by another, even bigger wail, and I stand up, like I always do when I hear a child crying like that, because my instinct is to go to them, but I don't have to, because her dad has already scooped her up in his arms and is holding her to his chest, comforting her. "It's all right," I can hear him say over her wails. "Come on, sweetheart, you're all right . . ." The way he's rubbing her back, swaying her gently in his arms to soothe her; the way he's talking to the concerned parents who've come to see if she's all right; it's so tender and natural that it brings tears to my eyes, and I don't know who I'm more upset for: the little girl, me, Zac, or even Liam.

The dad carries his daughter over to a bench to sit her down and inspect her injuries, which don't look more serious than grazed knees. He's wiry—not my type at all—but I watch him, wondering, not for the first time, could I have a relationship with a man based on how good a father he is, rather than how "right" he is for me? Does there really have to be the bloody fireworks? Last week I found something in Zac's room that I really wish I hadn't. I was dusting in there (that'll teach me) and I pulled out his toy box full of legless, headless plastic figures that he hasn't played with for years, when I found, slipped behind it, a blue ring-binder with a white sheet of paper taped to the front. **TOP TRUMPS FOR DADS,** it said, written in Zac's squidgy 3-D writing. **ZAC AND TEAGAN'S SECRET GAME!!** Obviously, there's nothing like the word "secret" to shoot your willpower dead, so I opened the file. There were several A4 sheets of paper, each headed with a different man's name. **KARL (Jacob Wilmore's dad), PHIL (Sam Bale's dad), MR. SINGH (Ravi's dad and Costcutter boss)** . . . Along the top of each page were different qualities—**Fun**. **Kind**. **Funny**. **Rich**. Then a score for each one.

That was it for me; I'd seen enough to confirm my fears. All these years I've convinced myself we're all right, just the two of us, that Zac doesn't feel he's missing out not having a dad, but I've just been fooling myself. He badly wants a dad.

What's more, he's obsessed with them—a dad fetishist, just like me. My son needs a father—isn't that more important than me needing the One? I don't have to have someone I can fall in love with; I just need someone who can love my son. I did the "soul mate"/passion thing with Liam, after all, and look where that got me. Maybe it's time to put my child before myself.

I FINALLY FINISH the carrot sticks—this is the thing about raw vegetables, I find, they take so long to eat—and stand up to go, but someone, just coming into my side vision, half catches my attention.

That someone ruffles my hair. "Hello, Jules."

"Jesus Christ!" It's Jason. I nearly have a heart attack.

"What are you doing here?" He's out of breath and sweating, obviously midrun. He looks sort of manly and vital, eyes shiny, face flushed.

"Oh," I say lamely, "I was just having a nice spring walk, actually. Getting some exercise, you know . . ."

"I approve. Hey, how did the big beach run go?"

"Oh, I was like a gazelle, naturally."

Jason surveys me, annoyingly amused.

"What?"

"Nothing, just your face," he says, chuckling to himself. "When you're talking about anything to do with exercise . . . you have a specific face."

"Thanks."

"Talking of exercise . . . Have you thought any more about what I said about coming to the sessions with Zac, or just on your own if you want? I think it would be really motivating for him, to know you were on board."

I have been thinking about it. I've thought about it a lot over the past week. I've thought about what Zac has put up with these last few years: a depressed, overeating, perennially poor mother; one who loves him with every cell in her body—but that doesn't change those facts. This was something I could do for him, for us, that would cost me nothing. And it would be with Jason—who I kind of miss, actually.

"Yes," I say, "I have been thinking about it, and I've decided I would love to. 'Bout time I got off my fat arse and did some exercise, eh?"

And he sniggers again. I wonder why momentarily, and then the penny drops.

"The face," we say, in unison this time. "The exercise face."

17

Mick

I want to go back now, to the moment Liam Jones first walked into our lives. I remember it like it was yesterday, which is a miracle in itself, since I remember so little about day-to-day life around that time, living as I was in a permanent boozy cloud. But I do remember that night with razor-sharp clarity: the doors of the TC's workingmen's club opening with a creak audible to all eight or nine of us sitting there at the bar in a pool of evening sun, and Vaughan Jones's lad, Liam, walking in, hand in hand with my daughter. I could almost hear Lynda's hackles as they went up.

It was an unusually warm Saturday in late October 2003, and my sister Kath and brother-in-law Brian were having a do for their twenty-fifth wedding anniversary. I say "do," it was really—as was always the case in our family—an excuse to go down the pub all day rather than for just a few hours, made legitimate by the fact that there were sausage rolls and a few sandwiches. I looked up from my fourth, fifth (I certainly wasn't counting), sixth pint, my eyes suddenly focusing on Liam's face.

It was as if my mind knew this man would become something so much bigger in my life—in all our lives—than just my daughter's boyfriend, and that knowledge somehow created a gap in those booze-filled clouds so that the sun could break through and I could see him clearly for what he was; so that I could decide whether or not my daughter needed protecting from him. That instinct to protect—so sharp when she was a newborn—kicking in even though it had been diluted over the years, in pints and pints of lager.

Our Kath's "do" had started some hours previously, so we were all well-oiled, but Juliet had been off doing something more interesting all day, saying she'd be bringing this new boyfriend down early evening to "meet the family." To be honest, neither Lynda nor I took much notice. She was nineteen and had had a few boyfriends by then, and anyway, we didn't really do "meeting the boyfriend" special dinners in our family (or in our community, I would argue). That was something that happened in films, or maybe the south, I don't know . . . But here, new squeezes, be they Jamie's or Juliet's, simply turned up to wherever they happened to meet us first and were expected to get on with it. We didn't ask them questions and they didn't ask us anything either. "Talking" in social situations—unless it was banter or ordering a round or arguing—just wasn't something we did. It was why I really struggled, at first, in AA. Telling people about myself, and listening to others do the same. Christ, it was so foreign to me.

But Juliet clearly wanted to "introduce" Liam formally; she obviously thought he was different—special—because she waited till we were all looking her way.

"Everyone, this is Liam," she said then, beaming (and I mean **beaming**; her eyes shone). "Liam, this is my family." She rested her head on his shoulder and pulled a face when she said the word "family," as if to say, **Yeah, sorry, but there we go, what can you do?**

"Hiya," he said, simply raising a hand, then putting his arm around Juliet. "Nice to meet you." He had incredible eyes; it was the first thing you noticed about him. You couldn't **not** notice; they were ice blue—exactly, I'd later realize, the same eyes as my grandson.

Nobody really said much, which was a bit embarrassing, so in the end I said, "I know you," and I lifted my pint up as a welcome, my equivalent of a handshake. "You're Vaughan's lad."

"I am," he said, relieved and encouraged no doubt that someone was actually talking to him, but also shifty, because he was aware of Vaughan's reputation about the town. "For my sins."

Juliet chattered on breathily, telling us in unnecessary detail about their day in that way she
used to, even as a little girl, before she had that
sparkle kicked out of her; but I was watching him.
He had lots of jet-black hair, like his dad did before it went gray, pale skin, and a tiny hoop ear-
ring in one ear. And I don't know if it was the way
he coughed, unnecessarily, into his closed fist as
Juliet was talking, or wafted his T-shirt, conscious
of the two patches of sweat that were blooming,
just under both nipples, but I saw he was nervous,
unconfident, almost apologetic. He was certainly
nothing like the lads Juliet had brought home from
sixth form: oozing with natural confidence. They
seemed to be either total poseurs or sporty jocks.

They went off to get a drink and immediately
Lynda nudged me. "Christ, Mick," she whispered.
"What is she doing? **Anyone**, anyone but him."

"Give him a chance," I said, mainly because
I was too pissed to really formulate a better argument, even though I too remember feeling
alarmed. Of all the blokes in Grimsby she chose
Vaughan Jones's son? The meathead, the trouble-
maker, the very person—in Lynda's eyes—who
had led me astray, even though I never needed
much encouragement. "And anyway, we can't be
sure it will last."

But I knew. I knew already. I could sense it in
the way he looked at her. There was nothing un-
sure about that.

18

Zac

**Fact: The term "Easter" comes from
Eastre, an Anglo-Saxon goddess who
symbolized the hare and the egg.**

Nan says Easter makes her emotional, she
doesn't even know why. She thinks it's partly
because Easter was my uncle Jamie's favorite time
of year for food and he always used to cook everyone a feast, so it makes her miss him more. On
Good Friday, two days before Easter Sunday, he
would cook a massive fish with one of his special
sauces. (You have to put up with fish instead of
meat on Good Friday to show respect to Jesus,
who had to put up with being on the cross with
rusty nails through his hands and feet.) Grandad
said that on Easter Sunday—which is the best day
of Easter for two reasons: one, you can eat your
Easter eggs and two, Jesus came alive again—
Uncle Jamie used to cook the best lamb you've ever
tasted in your life. It fell off the bone on its own.

The only way to get it to do that is to cook it for a really long time at the perfect temperature. Uncle Jamie was boss at cooking. I wish he was alive so he could show me his best skills. I daren't ask Nan because I don't want to upset her, but I bet she also gets sad at Easter because it's about a son (of God) dying, except Jesus rose from the dead and Uncle Jamie never did.

We're still going to celebrate it, though. Me and Mum are round at Nan and Grandad's today to have a special Easter tea.

"Okay, Zac." Nan cleaned her hands on her pinny, opened her purse, and gave me a ten-pound note. "Are you sure what you're getting? Say the list back to me."

"Mint sauce, some more butter, cream, and a bag of Mini Eggs."

"Good boy. Nothing else, okay? Don't be bringing any crisps or sweets back—I'll never hear the end of it from your mother. And don't be long, because we want to start eating as soon as possible. Your grandad's going to waste away."

The shop at my nan and grandad's is miles smaller than Costcutter. It hasn't got a sausage roll counter, but it's got a pick-a-mix and a cat called Mabel with only three legs, so if you add it all up, it comes out equal. It only takes five minutes to walk there and I tried not to step on the pavement lines to give a special good luck boost to our Find Dad mission. Yesterday, Mum told me she was going to start coming to the Jason sessions with me. It was definite evidence that she wants to go out with him again, which could ruin everything, but I couldn't show I was upset, because I didn't want her to get suspicious or to hurt her feelings. I just decided, right that second she told me, that we needed to "step up" the investigation (put a rocket up its bum, basically) so that we find my dad before my mum and Jason start falling in love.

This is what I've worked out about doing a secret mission: you can't avoid hurting people's feelings on the way to getting the big surprise at the end. It's a bit like when Aunty Laura's mum organized her a surprise birthday party for when she was thirty. Aunty Laura asked us all to go out to the pub that night, but we all had to pretend we couldn't—except her mum and dad. She thought nobody cared—it made you feel sick as anything inside—but it was all worth it in the end when she walked into the pub and we all shouted **surprise!**

Mabel was at the door when I got to the shop. It was like she'd seen me coming down the street.

Me (kneeling down and stroking her): "Hello, Mabel. It's your old friend Zac."

Mabel: **Purrrrrrr.**

Me (picking her up and giving her a cuddle): "Are you pleased to see me? I think you are, aren't you?"

Woman with a posh accent that was definitely not from Grimsby and should have been minding her own business: "I wouldn't pick that cat up if I were you; you don't know where she's been or what she's got."

People think Mabel's skanky because she's got three legs, but they're just prejudiced. I respect her more, because she's had to adapt to survive in a world of four-legged cats. It means she's braver, even if she can't jump as high as her friends. It's not even her fault she's got three legs. Her fourth leg got chopped off because it had cancer in it.

I found the mint sauce, butter, and cream dead quickly—I now wanted to get the Mini Eggs as fast as possible, then get home and put them on the Easter cake. Me and Nan made it this morning while Mum went shopping. It's Uncle Jamie's own recipe from his recipe book: a normal chocolate cake but with white chocolate buttercream inside and KitKat sticks all around the sides to make it look like a fence. It's even got an upside-down Easter rabbit that you make out of white icing and put in the middle. When we've put the Mini Eggs on the top, it'll look like the rabbit has done a dive bomb into them! If the cooked cake is as good as the cake mixture (Nan let me lick out the bowl **and** the food mixer, as Easter is a special occasion), it will have taken over lemon drizzle as my favorite of Uncle Jamie's cake recipes.

I looked for ages for the Mini Eggs but couldn't find them.

"Can I help?" said the lady behind the counter.

"Do you sell Mini Eggs, please?"

"I'm sorry, love, but I'm all sold out. Everyone's been wanting those this week."

I felt panicky—Uncle Jamie's recipe said "Mini Eggs"—but then the lady had a brain wave.

"Oh! I've just thought, though, we do have chocolate mini eggs in the pick-a-mix section—they're not quite the same as the normal ones, but will they do?"

"Definitely," I said. The relief felt lovely. The lady gave me a paper bag, then told me to help myself at the pick-a-mix counter, which was on the other side of the shop. I was just scooping out a load of mini eggs, challenging myself to get them to slide inside the paper bag without dropping even one, when **ooof!** someone slammed into the back of me so hard that the scooper flew out of my hand, and all the eggs went flying.

"Oops, sorry!" I turned around. It was Aidan Turner, with some other boys, not looking sorry one bit because he did it on purpose. "I just thought I'd do you a favor. You don't want to be eating all those, do you? If you're gonna lose some more of that belly?" He pushed his stomach out and rubbed it. Everyone killed themselves laughing (except me).

"They're not all for me," I said, trying to pick them up. "They're for my Easter cake."

"Fuck me," one of the other boys said—it was Kai Hardy. He used to be at our school but he was in Year 7 now, even though he looked fifteen, easy. "He's having a whole cake to himself as well as the shop's supply of mini eggs!"

"No, the cake's for everyone. I made it for my mum and my nan and grandad. We're having an Easter tea later . . ." Everyone just laughed harder.

Aidan Turner was picking up the eggs off the floor but then chucking some at me. They only hurt if they hit your face. One hit me right on the nose, making my eyes water, and I wanted, badly, just to run out of the shop then. I was worried they'd think I was crying when I totally wasn't, but I remembered what Teagan told me about them smelling fear, and also what Jason told me on our first-ever exercise session. "You're only doing this because you feel so crap about yourself," I said, dodging the egg missiles, while trying to rescue some from the floor and put them in my pockets. If I was going to have to make a sharp exit, it was better I had a few than none, even if they'd been on the floor. "You have to make someone else feel crap so you can feel better. You're all just tragic."

"Oooh, he's getting daring," said Aidan Turner. "He's giving us att-i-tude. He said 'crap'! You want to watch it, Jabba, because we'll rub the chocolate eggs onto your face like we did that chocolate cake if you don't fucking shut up."

"Yeah, you don't talk to us like that and get away with it, you little fat bastard," said Kai Hardy, and he pushed me then, but even harder than the first time, so that I went flying against a shelf, banging my back hard and making some packets of biscuits fall down. For a few seconds I couldn't breathe, and I thought I might faint, but then the shopkeeper came out from behind the till. Mabel was standing at the door, giving Aidan Turner her evil witch's cat eyes.

"What on earth is going on?" said the shop lady, and Kai, Aidan, and the others bent down and started picking up the packets of biscuits like they'd never done anything bad in their lives. "What have you been doing to this boy? Because he looks in pain to me."

That was when I made a decision.

I could have snitched on them, but then they would have got barred and probably done worse to me when we got back to school, or even during the Easter holidays, and I needed all my energy for the Find Dad mission; I couldn't afford to get beat up. We'd already started to go out and interview local people. Me and Teagan had a list of all the cafés to go in and check if my dad was working there and we were ticking them off—what if I got too scared to go out? I couldn't risk it. So I just stood up straight and made myself breathe again. "Nothing," I said. "I'm all right. I just tripped up and fell back and all the biscuits fell down. Sorry, I'll put them back." Aidan and his gang probably thought I was too scared to tell on them, but I was being strategic and there's a big difference.

It was only when I got out of the shop and was walking down the street that I realized what they'd said: **If you're going to lose some** more **of that belly**, which meant I'd definitely lost some.

I COULD ALREADY see Grandad smoking in the front yard as I was walking home. He gave up when I was born, at the same time he became teetotal, which doesn't mean you can only drink tea, it just means you don't drink alcohol, but Nan lets him have a cigarette on special occasions. He came out onto the pavement, opening up his arms. I wondered if he knew what had happened at the shop, but how could he?

"What've I done to deserve this?" I said, and Grandad smiled because it's what he always says when I go and cuddle him for no reason.

"Nothing," he said. "Can't a man just give his grandson a hug when he feels like it?"

He held on to me for what felt like a really long time. His jumper smelled of cigarettes, but the cuddle canceled it out.

Inside, Nan and Mum were setting the table. "Got the mint sauce, Zac? Good lad. Put that straight on the table, please." Nan had got her fluffy yellow chicks out that she gets out every Easter, and put one for each person—including Uncle Jamie—in a row in the middle of the table. One of them has only got one eye now, but I don't mind saying that one's mine. I put the mint sauce out, then went into the kitchen; Nan followed me and shut the door.

"Did you get the Mini Eggs?" she whispered.

"Yeah," I whispered back, holding up the pick-a-mix bag. I didn't know why I was whispering too; whispering is like yawning—it's completely catching.

"Good, well, finish decorating this then," she said, opening the tin and getting our cake out. "Put all the eggs on top and Mr. Easter Bunny in the middle."

"Why are we whispering?"

"Are we? Sorry, I'll stop," said Nan.

I started to arrange the eggs, trying to spread the colors out so that you didn't get loads of yellow or blue ones together. Nan was smiling at me, but her eyes were watery. "That used to be our Jamie's favorite bit, putting the eggs on, making sure there weren't lots of the same color too close to each other just like you're doing now. Mind you, it was a case of one on the cake, three in his mouth." She laughed. "He'd have eaten half of them by now."

"Does that mean I can eat some?"

"A **few**. And I mean a few," said Nan. "But, Zac?" I already had too many mini eggs in my mouth to actually speak. "Don't tell your mum. In fact, don't tell her you baked the cake with me, will you? And definitely not that I let you eat so much cake mixture. My God . . . you won't be allowed round here again."

At tea, we even had a starter because it was a special occasion. It was a fishy one—probably because fish was Uncle Jamie's specialty but also just because we eat a lot of fish in Grimsby. It's the fishy capital of England, probably the world. The starter was crayfish with a special sauce made with horseradish, which if you eat it on its own can really make your eyes water because it's dead spicy, but Nan mixed it with crème fraiche so it wasn't too bad.

"This is delicious, Nan."

"It is, it's bloody gorgeous," said Grandad.

"I love the sauce," said Mum. "It's like prawn cocktail but better."

"Well, thank your brother, not me," said Nan, tucking in. "He used to make us this quite often, didn't he, Mick?"

"He did."

"He'd do the most amazing fish suppers—do you remember, Juliet?" Mum nodded. "We'd have this for starter, then either haddock with his home-made batter, or a bit of halibut. What was that beautiful dish he did with mackerel, Michael?"

"Oh, with the beetroot and oranges?"

"Yes," said Nan. "So light, but so tasty and hardly cost anything."

The starter was delicious, then came the lamb. It was unbelievable. It just fell off the bone. And it had this crusty bit all over it that was made from apricots and bread crumbs. You'd never think of putting apricots on lamb, but it's delicious, believe me. Everyone should try it.

"This is definitely the best meat recipe from Uncle Jamie's recipe book," I said. "This and then the fried chicken that's like KFC but better."

Everyone smiled.

"Yes, he had the most amazing talent," said Nan. "For just knowing what flavors went together. You've got that talent from him, Zac."

"And also from my dad," I said. "'Cause he liked cooking too." But then Mum kicked me under the table; it proper hurt as well. "Ow!" I rubbed my leg. "I'm just saying, because I know Uncle Jamie was a brilliant chef, but I have got half my dad's genes, whereas from your uncle you probably only get a quarter, so it's much more likely that I inherited my cooking skills from my dad. It's like I got his blue eyes too."

"Zac," Mum said. Nobody was talking—the whole room had gone silent. "Can you just not—"

"What?"

"Please?" She was eyeballing me.

There was an even longer silence. I knew it was probably because I was talking about my dad and Nan doesn't like it, but I was getting a bit annoyed by that. I am half my dad, even though he left me, so to keep saying he's a completely horrible person is offensive. Also, Mum told me stuff about him, stuff that was nice—he couldn't have been **all** horrible.

Still nobody was talking. I didn't like it. The only sound was of our knives and forks on the plates. If Teagan had been here, she would have said, **Awkward**.

Nan was looking at her plate, eating very slowly. It was so quiet you could hear her breathing in and out of her nose. "See, I told you this would happen," she said then, putting her knife and fork down, and Mum sighed and Grandad said, "Oh Lynda, don't start."

"You start telling him things and he forms an idea in his head. He starts thinking about him and imagining him . . . Children are like sponges, that's just what they do." Nan was talking gently, but she was angry, you could tell by the way she was looking really hard at her plate and clasping her fingers together so hard that they had gone white.

More quiet. I hated this.

"I don't know what you want me to say, Mum," said Mum after a bit.

I heard Nan swallow. "I don't want you to say anything—about **him**, to **him**," she said, nodding her head toward me. "That's what. Because **he** does not need to know anything. It's not good for him."

"But I want to know!" I blurted out. I didn't want to join in, but they were talking like I wasn't even there. "I want to know, because he is my dad whether you like it or not. And I want to know that he wasn't that bad, because if he was, then some of the badness will have seeped into me. It just will. You don't just get the good genes, you know, like being good at cooking; you get the bad ones too."

Mum gasped. "Zac! Please don't talk like that. You haven't got a bad bone in your body, darling." She turned back to Nan. "See what you've started?" she said then. "Great, so he now thinks he's somehow rotten inside because you've demonized Liam so much. Because that's **also** what children do, Mum."

"Juliet," growled Grandad, putting his head in his hands.

Nan looked like she was definitely going to cry. When she spoke next, her voice was all wobbly. "How can you say that? How can you say I demonize him? You know why I think the way I do. You know why I can't have his name spoken in my house." She gives me a look that I know means she doesn't want to say anything more in front of me.

"Yes, but"—Mum was holding her hands up, she was so frustrated—"that's not Zac's fault, is it? Look, I'm cross with Liam too."

"Cross!" said Nan. "I think that's the bloody understatement of the century, isn't it?"

"Okay, I'm really, really sad—for Zac too; and so disappointed. But what happened happened and all this bitterness and hatred doesn't bring my brother back—and I don't think Jamie would have wanted—"

"Jamie?" I said. "Uncle Jamie? What's Dad got to do with Uncle Jamie? Did my dad know him?"

Nan flung her napkin down hard and got up from the table then, so quickly that everything shook like an earthquake was starting.

We all sat in silence, then Grandad stood up to go after her. "It's not your fault, Zac," he said, touching my arm. "Okay? None of this is your fault."

It didn't feel like that, though.

19

Juliet

After Mum storms off into the kitchen, followed by Dad, who shuts the door, Zac and I sit opposite each other, listening to them argue.

Mum: "I am sick to death of you sitting on the frigging fence, Michael."

Zac (gasping): "Did Nan just say 'frigging'?"

Me: "Yes, but that doesn't mean you can."

Dad: "I just think it's not fair to shut Zac down like that—whatever's happened. He's only—"

Mum: "What do you mean, whatever's happened? You know what happened! I can't believe you would say that, like it's nothing, like you think I've gone doolally and I'm totally unreasonable."

Dad (long silence, then sounding spent, a broken man): "I don't think you're being unreasonable, it's just, it's not his fault, is it?"

Mum: "No, which is why I'm trying to protect him—from **him**! From knowing anything about **him**!" (Mum's stage whisper went up an octave with every sentence. There wasn't much further to go.) "It'll only be pain from here, Michael. That is all."

Zac looks across the table at me with his big, sad eyes. I reach out and put my hand on his. "It **is** my fault, isn't it?" he says.

"What's your fault, Zac?"

"That everyone's arguing and the Easter tea's a dead loss." (That's Mum's phrase—I have to stop myself from smiling.) "It's my fault for asking questions about my dad."

"No, Zac, you didn't do anything wrong," I say, even though, to be honest, he did. Not wrong in the normal outside world, but wrong in this house, this life, this . . . cult. That's what it's felt like all these years, a cult where Liam is the Devil and **thou shalt not entertain the Devil under this roof**. Why has he suddenly started asking them questions about his father anyway? I'm flabbergasted at that. I could kick myself for not sitting down with him after Mum and Dad gave me the lecture in Bobbin's and telling him never to mention anything about his dad in front of them again. It's just, after a decade of brainwashing—from all of us, I might add, not just Mum, although she's always been Chief Brainwasher—I didn't think it would even enter his head, let alone that he'd have the nerve. Part of me was a little bit proud of him.

There are more hushed whispers from the kitchen. I am just about to suggest we go somewhere else when Zac says, "Mum, can I go and call for Teagan?"

"What, now?" I look at the clock. It's three twenty p.m.

"Yeah, I told her I couldn't meet today for . . ." He puts his fingers to his lips as if he was about to say something he wasn't supposed to, but then carries on. "I just want to see her. It's not a very nice atmosphere here, you know."

"I know." I can't argue with that. Mum won't come back from this—not today—and there's no point in the two of us staying here, treading on eggshells. "Off you go then. Just pop your head in and say 'bye before you go. They won't mind."

Zac leaves and I take the three Easter eggs I have (it isn't Easter Sunday until tomorrow; Jesus may not have risen, but my mother's hackles have, and it's ugly, and I need chocolate) and carry them, clutched to my chest, to my bedroom. I lie on my childhood bed and feel a horrible sense of déjà vu wash over me. I've been here before, both literally—lying here with my bootleg chocolate—and in the wider sense, in terms of how I feel. This bed is the same bed I used to lie on talking to my brother through the paper-thin walls—often in the early hours of the morning when we were underage drunk and giddy. Then, when Jamie died and Liam left and Zac and I moved in here for a short while, I spent hours in this room. Back then, I'd lie on this bed, listening to my mother's crying, the sobs that seemed to wrack this whole house, in the middle of the night.

In the day, she was often silent. It was Dad's river of tears that came then. She had a shrine to Jamie set up in his bedroom—the clothes he'd been wearing the night he'd gone out with Liam (unwashed, never to be washed), his framed catering certificates, the revolting bit of old baby blanket he nuzzled and sucked on till he was at least eight—and she often retreated to that room for most of the day to immerse herself in Jamie-ness.

Jamie was always far more babied than me when we were little and that was fine, because I was naturally more self-sufficient, but then when he died and everything happened, I needed Mum more than ever. But there was to be no mothering in this House of Tears now, and there was to be no sadness except my mother's, which was bigger than anyone could possibly imagine or understand. Mum had no business with life and would tick off every day on the calendar as one day closer to being reunited with Jamie at the pearly gates. It was like we'd all died.

And then there was the vitriol. Because, in her eyes, it turned out she'd been right all along after all: at his core, Liam was Vaughan Jones's son. I hated him for it too for a while. I even joined in, feeling so betrayed he'd managed to keep that side hidden from me; livid he'd proved my mother right when I'd spent years defending him. But as the years went by, and he never came back for Zac and me, the hatred turned to confusion, because it just didn't add up. He'd never got into a fight before, least of all instigated one—why then, if this **was** to be the start of his fighting and prison career, following in the footsteps of his father, had he waited this long? People don't just flip a switch overnight. I began to see that that fateful punch he threw at Hynd was basically a mistake, and everyone can make mistakes, can't they? And normally they get away with it. If Jamie had lived, then Liam would have got away with his.

I've been lying on this bed for almost an hour; I can't stay here any longer. I get up, stuff the last Easter egg into my bag to take home, and go downstairs. Mum's sitting on her own at the table, picking at some lamb on her plate with her fingers, when I go back into the dining room. Dad has gone for another smoke.

"I'm going to go, I think," I say, putting my bag over my shoulder.

"You as well?" She doesn't look up, just pushes a bit of meat around her plate, like nothing's happened, like it's everyone else who overreacted. This is always her way after an episode like this.

"Yeah, I'm sure you probably just want a bit of time on your own and I'd best be at home for when Zac gets back."

"All right, love." She sighs, rubbing her face. She is still tearful and I hover, considering giving her a hug and apologizing, promising I'll talk to Zac and ask him never to bring up Liam again. But I don't because I am torn, torn between my mother and my son. I hate to see what this has all done to Mum, but I have to think of Zac too—how frustrated he must feel, how confused.

I ALWAYS KNOW when it's going to happen and I know, as I close my parents' front door behind me, that it's going to happen now. The air is cool and damp; it's drizzling, just ever so slightly. It's a relief after the claustrophobia of my parents' house and I lift my face to the rain as I walk and feel freer, even though I am being pulled, as if by a magnet, to the shop at the end of the road and in my head I am talking to myself: **Just stop it. Just walk past. Just think of your son. Your time is surely up with this, kiddo.** But deep inside me there is a hollow pit, and it needs filling, otherwise it aches, it niggles, it nags and mithers. Something other than what is happening inside my head right now needs to happen and so I find myself drifting through the door as if my body has taken leave of my mind. That's how it feels. Like I'm in a trance. And then there is the dizzying surge of adrenaline coursing through me, a sense of elation reaching fever pitch with a ringing in my ears, and then I am walking down the road again, with a stolen Victoria sandwich, a Toffee Crisp, and a magazine in my bag, slightly breathless.

Then my phone rings. I leap out of my skin.

"Hello?"

"Juliet?" The voice is familiar and not, both at the same time; I can't place it. And it sounds distant, like the person is standing somewhere exposed but noisy—like an airport. "It's Uncle Paul here. I hope you don't mind me calling you, it's just, Zac is down the docks with his friend, he's asking after Liam Jones—I thought you'd want to know."

I freeze, feeling the weight of the bag in my hand. Liam. Why the hell has my son gone down there to ask about his dad? It's completely out of character for Zac to go somewhere as far as the docks without telling me first; he would never want to worry me. Uncle Paul must have got it wrong. Then the panic sets in. He was upset when he left Mum and Dad's, guilty that he'd somehow ruined things, and Zac's got such a conscience on him. Mum must have scared him with her reaction—he was probably already speculating, thinking there must be more to it than Liam just leaving. What if he's decided to run away, to **stow away**? What if he's aboard a boat right now, destined for Scotland? Or he's fallen over the harbor wall; got caught up in some machinery—the docks are no place for kids.

"I'm coming down," I say, already on my way. "Tell him to stay there." Then I hang up, my hands shaking, and start to walk toward Wellington Street, then, breaking into a run, toward Freeman Street, down toward the steel gates and the concrete, the harbor and the cranes, the boat masts, the edge of Grimsby—and, after that, only the deep, endless sea.

All I care about is getting to my boy, but I can hear my breath and the soles of my shoes slapping the pavement and I am vaguely aware of the seagulls lacing the sky above me, as if taking me there, guiding me toward him. It's amazing the reserves of energy you find in a crisis because I am flying, it feels like I've never run as fast in my life. My loot jostles in my bag and I feel a terrible guilt twist my insides: there I was just minutes earlier, indulging my shameful habit, my twisted craving—and my son, he needs me. He's in emotional turmoil.

Anger has seeped in with the worry by the time I get down the docks, however—anger born of fear, but anger all the same. It's been years since I've been down here and I am hit by a wave of nostalgia as the briny, fishy, industrial smell hits my nostrils: the smell of my dad and of my childhood.

It doesn't take me long to spot Zac and Teagan idly wandering along the harbor wall and I scream at their backs: "Zac!" They turn around immediately. "What the hell do you think you're doing? I've been so worried!" **It's okay,** I tell myself. **He's here, he's alive.** I walk toward him. "What are you doing here? Why would you **do** that?"

"I'm sorry." Zac's voice is faint, swallowed up by the space, the sea.

"Sorry is not good enough! You never, ever go anywhere like this without telling me first."

I am nearly standing in front of him now and he is blinking at me, shocked at quite how angry I am. "I'm sorry, Mum," he says, "I really am. I just wanted . . ." He pauses, takes a breath. "I just want to find my dad."

A strong breeze is coming in from the water, blowing our hair sideways, and the rain, delicate as cobwebs, is settling on our faces.

"Teagan," I say then, still breathless from running. She looks a mixture of sheepish and defiant. "Can you give us a moment?"

"Yep." She nods but doesn't move.

"On our own?"

She still dithers, at which point I realize a ten-year-old doesn't know what to do with herself left to her own devices somewhere like this, so I open my bag and take out a Cadbury's Flake Easter egg—the only one of the three I have left. "Here," I say. "Go and sit over there and have this; we'll only be five minutes."

She holds it, looking at it as if I've given her the golden Wonka ticket. "What, all of it?"

"Yes," I say, then: "Actually, on second thoughts, maybe save me a **tiny** bit?"

She looks at Zac, then grins at me before walking toward the wall I gestured to. "Okay, if you

play your cards right," I hear her say. Zac is looking at the floor, but I see a smile curl at his lips.

We stand looking at each other for a moment,
my breathing only just returning to something
even approaching normal. "Let's sit down," I
say, making my way over to the wall of the fish
market. "Underneath here, come on, out of the
rain."

I sit down next to my son. He's hugging his
knees, back against the harbor wall, face like a
jellyfish in a string bag, as my dad would say.

"What's going on, Zac?" I say, after a bit. "Come
on, you can tell me."

The drizzle continues—the weather's equivalent of a constant, white background noise—and
the breeze is strong but not cold and when you
look out, the boats, the water, and everything beyond is one big, amorphous smudge of mist.

"See that trawler over there?" I say when still
Zac doesn't say anything. "That's what your grandad would call 'a big ol' rust bucket.'" I think I
detect a smile, so I carry on. "It's the sort of trawler
he'd have gone to sea on too."

"It's a seiner," says Zac.

"So it is. Get your facts right, Mum."

Zac looks at me and smiles. I am making
progress.

"When I was little," I carry on, "Dad—your
grandad—used to occasionally take me on one
of his boats and show me around, show me what

everything was for and what everything did. Did you know that fish are attracted to a wreckage? If there's a wreckage, all the lights show on the GPS screen and the fishermen know there'll be a shoal of fish there, and so they're able to sail toward it."

"Seeing pound signs," says Zac and I smile because that's what Dad always used to say: "Whenever we saw fish, we just saw pound signs."

"That's right," I say, "and then they get all excited. They message the other fishermen out on their trawlers and tell them where the fish are too. They help each other out."

"Why has Grandad never taken me on a boat?" says Zac suddenly.

"I don't know, darling. Maybe you should ask him. He's not a fisherman anymore, though, is he?"

"My dad was, though."

"Yeah." I sigh. "Your dad was."

"I want to find him, Mum," Zac says, looking up at me, and when I see his eyes, I can tell how much. "I want to find him and find out the truth—why he did a runner, why, when he loved you and you loved him . . ."

I tip my head back and close my eyes. "Zac, darling, we've talked about this."

"I know, but you must have been in love at one point to have had me, and if you loved him once, then he couldn't have been that bad."

"Zac, he was never bad."

"But Nan says he was. And I need to know he wasn't, because otherwise that means I am, because I'm his son, and I've got his genes. It's not just eye color and hair color you get from your parents, you know."

I turn my body around then to face him. "Zac," I say. "Please, you must understand. Firstly, your dad was not all bad; nobody is. But also, even if he was—and he wasn't—isn't—even if he was a hundred percent bad, it does not mean that you have inherited any of that. You are the kindest, most considerate, most beautiful person I know—and I'm not just saying that because you're mine."

He searches my face as if for clues as to what to say next. "I need to know why he did a runner. Why he didn't want us." There's a moment's silence. "But you never went looking for him either, did you?" he says eventually. "You never gave him a chance to explain. Maybe there was a reason he left. But he never got to say why."

"No," I say, feeling my insides tense. He doesn't understand—how could he? But even though he knows nothing about the circumstances of his father's disappearance from our lives, there's a truth to his words. I didn't give Liam the chance to explain. And I didn't go looking for him. "No, I didn't. But I didn't need to, Zac, because actions speak louder than words and, like I've always told you, he left before I even had you." I've said this so many times, it **almost** feels true. "He never wanted to know. He just . . . he went. Really, it was a lucky escape."

Zac sighs and looks out at the gray sea, the gray sky, but I know there's more to come. I'm not expecting what Zac says next, though.

"Me and Teagan are looking for him," he says. "I want to find him, Mum. I have to find him. Will you help me?"

My heart is beating so fast it's making me breathless. I've dreaded this day, this moment, his whole life. I've only ever wanted to make him happy, or at the very least to not make him sad, but I realize he **is** sad; he's yearning and unfulfilled inside.

"Darling, I've got a secret," I say. I have to try something. "Since we got the letter—you know, about your weight—and you've been getting bullied at school and having a bit of a rough time of it all in general . . . I decided that all I wanted in the world was for you to be happier, to make you happy. So that's why I asked Jason to help, that's why I've been mean and put all the nice food in a secret cupboard. I wanted you to get fitter and happier. It's not about being thinner; I just wanted you to feel better about yourself, and—you have to trust me on this one—looking for your dad isn't going to make you happier. And what if it actually makes you sadder? What if we found him and then for some reason he still didn't want to know? I couldn't bear that, Zac. It would make me so sad to see you sad."

Zac fiddles with his jumper and doesn't say anything for what feels like ages, then he looks at me. "What will make me sad is not trying. I just want to know, Mum, I just want to know what he's like."

And I realize then that whether I like it or not, we've come too far. **He's** come too far. Zac's going to look for his dad—if not now, then when he's fifteen, sixteen. And it will be the biggest, most important, scariest thing he'll probably ever do in his life. Don't I—as his mother—need to be by his side?

I put my arms around him. "Okay," I say, cuddling him close. "Okay, my little big man. If you're absolutely sure you want to do this, then I will help you."

20

Zac

**Fact: Harp seals only feed and look
after their babies for twelve days.
Then they leave them to fend for
themselves.**

And then things really kicked off.

When we'd got home from the docks on
Easter Saturday—after Mum had agreed she'd
help us find my dad—me, Mum, and Teagan had
a special meeting. It was like a normal Find Dad
mission club meeting, except we didn't need to
have it at the roundabout; we could all just talk
about it in our kitchen, because it wasn't a secret
anymore. Mum said she had some conditions, if
she was going to help us—we had to do certain
things or she wouldn't do it. She said she wanted
to see our file of facts so far about my dad and
know why we'd gone down the docks without
telling her in the first place, and why we thought
that was ever a good idea. (When adults say that,

they're not interested in the answer, they just want to talk about why they think it was a bad idea. They just want to tell you off, basically.) We told her about me going to see Mr. Singh at Costcutter, anyway, and how he'd told me about my grandad Jones being a famous fisherman too and how this had given me the idea to go down to the docks— because loads of people would have heard of him and his son (my dad).

This is what we told Mum:

When I met Teagan after the Easter tea (that I ruined), we went down to the fish market at the docks. Grandad once told me that the fish market was the most important place at the docks, possibly in Grimsby, so we thought it was a good place to start.

There was a lady when you went in and her job was to answer the phone. You could tell she was good at her job, because there were loads of phones going off all at the same time, and she wasn't even getting stressed. We told her we were doing some research for a project on fishing for school and she told us we could go and talk to a man called Shanky, who was the manager of the market. When we got to his office, though, Shanky wasn't there. It was just his assistant, Barrel. Shanky and Barrel aren't their real names; they're just nicknames. Barrel is really called Mark Cross, but everyone calls him Barrel because he drinks too much beer and so his belly is like a barrel. He's not bothered. Having a nickname is a sign of affection. He gave us both a Jaffa Cake, then we asked if he knew Liam and Vaughan Jones and he started to tell us he did, that he'd even been on a trip with my dad once, that he was a "good bloke," but that he hadn't seen him for ages.

Teagan was writing everything down in our file. It was proper exciting (especially the bit where he said my dad was a good bloke!). But then Shanky came in—he was really called Paul Cruickshank; we knew that because it said it on his name badge. Cruickshank is the surname my nan used to have before she was married to Grandad, but I wasn't suspicious. I didn't even know Shanky was related to my nan, but it turns out he's her brother; he's my great-uncle! He went mad at Barrel for telling us anything. Then he called my mum.

"Right." Mum was covering her eyes with her fingers (she was still stressed about it even though we were fine, but it was what might have happened that was the worst thing). "So you decided that because you might find people who knew"— she didn't want to say "Grandad Jones," you could tell—"Vaughan Jones, then that was a good enough reason to go down the docks on your own without telling me?"

I looked at Teagan. It's embarrassing when someone else's mum is telling them off and it can make you laugh, so she was staring at the wall to be on the safe side. "Um, yeah, basically," I said.

"Do you know how dangerous and irresponsible that was?" Mum said, looking at me, then at Teagan. I felt bad for making her worried. She's got loads of things to worry about already, like not having enough money and missing Uncle Jamie. "Anything could have happened. You could have slipped and fallen into the water, got caught up in some machinery, been electrocuted—you could have died."

"I know and I'm sorry, but I told you," I said, "I was really mad and upset after what happened at Nan and Grandad's."

"Which is exactly why you should never have done something as rash as go to the docks, Zac. You should never do things like that while you're all het up and emotional—that's when accidents happen."

It felt proper scary when Mum said that. My neck even tingled. I started picturing all the ways we could have died, like getting mangled in a fish-cleaning machine, getting tangled up in a massive net, or falling into the water and getting sucked under a boat, joining all the sailors in their watery graves. It made me stop breathing for a second. I had to take a deep breath to start me breathing again. We didn't know then, what would happen to Teagan a few days later.

THERE ARE LOADS of different kinds of love, you can't even believe how many.

I thought love was just one feeling, but it's not. The way you love your dog is totally different from the way you love your nan and grandad, and the way you love your boyfriend or girlfriend is different from the way you love your child. Mum explained it to me on Easter Sunday—the day after she said she'd help us find my dad down at the docks—and I've been thinking about it ever since.

We were on our way to an exercise session with Jason at the time (Mum had ended up organizing a session, even though it was Easter Sunday; thank God Jason didn't mention how weird I'd been when he'd asked me about my plans for the weekend!) and I was on my favorite subject, saying how she loved my dad once, so she would definitely love him again—it was just she hadn't seen him in ages. She'd probably not stopped loving him, I said, she was just mad at him and also he wasn't here for her to practice the love feelings on. Mum said she was proud of my optimism but she needed to manage my expectations. "Also, it doesn't work like that, Zac," she said. "It just isn't that simple."

"But you wouldn't stop loving me just because you didn't see me for ten years," I said, which was when she explained about the different loves.

"The love you have for your children is completely different. It's unconditional." We were holding hands and swinging our arms dead high as we walked; we've done it since I was little—it's really relaxing.

"What's 'unconditional' mean?"

"It means you love them without conditions. You love them whatever they do and whoever they are."

"Would you love me even if I'd been born with no arms or legs?" I said, thinking about the boy in the documentary I'd watched with Teagan.

"Of course," Mum said. "Life would be very hard, much harder than it is now, but you'd still be my son, and I'd still love you."

"Would you love me if I was born with no brain?"

She laughed then. She looked pretty, because the sunset had made everything glow pink, including her face. "Zac, you wouldn't be able to survive with no brain, you wally," she said, and she was right. How would you know how to breathe and pump blood round if you had no brain? Plus, I wouldn't be anyone **to** love if I didn't have a brain. Your brain is where all of your personality is; the rest of you is just bones and skin. It doesn't even count.

We walked along to Your Fitness. Jason had opened it especially for us, even though it was Easter Sunday.

"Would you still love me if I killed someone?" I said and Mum had to think about it for ages, and then she said, "Yes, I think so. I would hate what you'd done, but I don't think I'd be able to stop myself from loving you. It would just be a feeling inside me that happened, even if I didn't want it to—like being scared or jealous." I knew what she meant because I still feel scared loads and I wish I could stop it. She told me then too, how she loved me the second I was born. She said it was like she knew me, even though it was the first time she'd ever seen me. She said I looked really wise and clever when I came out, like I'd been on earth before and could teach her stuff—it sounded mad. But mainly she just wanted to cuddle and look after me. She said meeting me was the happiest moment of her life.

Mum-love is a fact like that—it just happens, whatever you do; you can't do anything about it, like rain. It's not the same for dads, though (or earwigs—earwig mums only look after the strong babies, they just leave the others to die; it's well harsh). Dads only love you when they're sure that you're theirs—I read it in my **Factblaster** book. The reason they know you're theirs is that you look like them. It's why babies are always the spits of their dads; it's true as well—me and Teagan tested it in town. Nature made it happen so that more dads wouldn't run off. It's probably why my dad did, because he never met me so the magic nature bond didn't work. If he met me, he'd see I looked like him, then he'd change his mind. What I wrote in my letter still stands.

I WAS IN bed when it happened. I even heard the ambulance siren. I looked outside my window and saw it in the middle of the estate with its blue whirly lights. I thought it was for someone old that I'd never heard of and I was so tired, because I'd stayed up late making my nan and grandad a cheese and onion pie (to say sorry), that I went straight back to sleep.

Then this morning, I went round to call for Teagan because my mum was taking us to Skegness on the coach. We were going to go on the beach, in the arcades, get fish and chips, and not even come home till it was dark. It was going to be the most epic day ever, but then Tia, Teagan's sister, answered the door.

"Teagan's in hospital," she said. "My mum's there too. She had a bad asthma attack last night. She couldn't breathe and we called 999." That was when I realized about the ambulance in the night.

When I got home, I burst out crying. Mum said I couldn't have known that the ambulance was for Teagan, but I should have, because I'm her best friend, and best friends are meant to know facts that other people don't.

MUM AND ME still went to Skeggy. Mum thought we should go anyway, and that the change of scenery would do us both good, but even though it was nice, I missed Teagan loads.

We went to the beach, but it wasn't as much fun without her. Together, we would have made a boss sandcastle, with the deepest moats you've ever seen. (The secret is, you have to use your hands, not a bucket and spade, to make the strongest sand. Scientists have proven it—we looked it up on YouTube—it's not even a joke.)

Teagan has never even been to Skeggy—this would have been her first time—and I was mad at the council, because if they'd come to sort out the green fur on her bedroom curtains, she probably wouldn't have even had the asthma attack and she would have been here. It's why I decided to take a picture of me on my own and send it to them as a protest, so they knew the consequences of their behavior. Mum says people listen to kids more than adults, but I'm not sure that's true.

I walked along the beach with my shoes off. The sand was cold—it felt dead nice. I could see Mum waving across the road, with the fish and chips in her hand that she'd gone to get to cheer me up. I waved back, then carried on looking for my special shell for Teagan. We were going to visit her in hospital later on, and I wanted to take it to her. It needed to be a really nice one that would make her feel better about not being able to come to the beach today, a kind of good luck shell, that when she held it, it would help her get better. Finding a really special shell, though, was much harder than it looked. Loads of them were broken or a boring gray color that wouldn't suit Teagan. Most of them weren't special enough.

I walked for ages along the beach, looking at the ground all the time, waiting for my shell to call out to me, **Here I am! Choose me!** I picked up a silver one. I thought it might be it. I liked how it was shiny and looked like it might be precious, like money or jewels. It was proper silky inside and I nearly put it in my pocket, I nearly chose it. But then I saw another and I did a big gasp to myself, because I knew this was definitely the one. It was shiny white and pearly, but it was the shape that I liked the best: twisty and long with a point at the end, and grooves carved into it. I liked how it reminded me of loads of different things: a Flump sweet, a helter-skelter slide, or the tall pointy bit on a castle like they have in the Disneyland pictures . . . But it was when I realized what it really looked like that I knew it was my shell for Teagan. It looked like a rocket!

What this investigation needs, I could hear her saying, **is a rocket up its bum!** When I put my ear to it, you could even hear it roaring. People always say it's the sound of the sea, but I think it's more like a rocket taking off.

21

Mick

Not yet eleven and already the "your dad did a runner" story isn't holding like it was. It's like sinking sand beneath his feet, and it won't be long before it gives way altogether, because with every question Zac asks about Liam—like he did on Easter Saturday while I sat, frozen to the spot, wondering if that was going to be the moment the lid finally came off—with every piece of information he gathers, he is one step closer to knowing the truth.

The truth is so close. I can see it in the distance, gathering force, like I used to be able to see a storm approaching at that point between the sea and the sky. You know you're in for it then, but there's nowhere to go and you just have to sit it out. But this is different. I'm not just at the mercy of the storm; I'm an orchestrator of it. I'm like God, but all I can create is destruction. I look at my grandson—my beautiful grandson, the most precious person in my life—and I wonder what this will do to him, what pain and havoc it will wreak on his life. I'm caught between a rock and a hard place: I don't tell him the truth, and I can't live with myself; I tell him the truth, and he's devastated.

And this is the person who gave me a second chance at life; if it wasn't for Zac, I'd probably have drunk myself to death by now. But he was there and he needed me, needed me to airlift him from the wreckage—the wreckage that I played a big part in—and keep him safe and loved. If he was to be denied his father, then I owed him that. So that is one—the only—good thing to come out of this: I got sober, because I owed it to Zac. I got sober and I made damn sure I was the best grandad I could possibly be.

22

Juliet

"So, how was that?" says Jason, sitting down and sliding a coffee across the table to me.

We're in the canteen at Your Fitness. Jason has just tried to kill me with I don't know how many laps of the playing fields. (He said not knowing how many would be good for me. It would teach me to accept it, to "be with" the discomfort. I didn't accept anything. I just swore a lot.)

"Hard," I say, mortified I'm still sweating like a pig and we've been finished almost an hour, showered and everything. I can feel my thighs sticking to the plastic seat.

"On a scale of one to ten? One being the easiest?"

"About a seven."

Jason nods slowly.

"Oh God, a nine then. It was really bloody hard, Jase!"

He pulls a face, somewhere between apologetic and amused (although he's trying to hide the amused bit, which touches me). "The thing is, I haven't done much exercise this week. I just haven't had any time, so my fitness level has probably gone down"—**What, from your Olympic athlete level the week before?** I imagine him thinking— "and I've been really stressed, so you know . . ." I fan my face with a leaflet. The steam from the coffee is doing nothing for my excessive sweating. "The eating's gone a bit sideways too. I've been bad. Really bad. God, sorry."

A bit sideways is an understatement. On Easter Saturday, after everything that happened at Mum and Dad's, I scoffed two of the three Easter eggs I had on top of my crayfish and lamb—and that was already on top of, I realized, easily a day's calories in baguettes and "testing" the roast potatoes before we even sat down. Then, after the stress of Zac running off to the docks, his confession about the Find Dad mission, and, most importantly, me announcing I was going to help him, I didn't have a hope in hell of walking straight past the Chinese on the way home, did I? This was partly why I arranged the session with Jason on Easter Sunday—not that I told him that at the time—as an emergency attempt to work off some of those excesses. Except afterward I just carried on.

When I relay this to Jason—the reason I've fallen off the diet bandwagon—I leave out any "looking for Dad" bits, even though that's the main reason my eating's gone so pear-shaped. I don't even know why I don't tell him; I just feel he doesn't need or, more likely, want to know. He's given up so much of his time for us recently that telling him we're looking for another man in our lives feels kind of disingenuous.

"Jules." Jason smiles his cute smile and leans forward on his elbows. If ever you needed an arm model, I think, he would be your man. "You don't need to justify or explain yourself to me, you know."

"I don't?" I'm a bit disappointed. Where's the **Fame** speech, the **this journey is gonna take blood, sweat, and tears**? Isn't he meant to be all pumped up, bossing me around?

"No, I'm not the food or the fitness police, am I? I just want to help Zac so he's a bit happier in himself, more confident." He lowers his voice. "And I want to show him some karate moves to floor those little runts at school, if I'm honest."

I smile.

"That's what you want, isn't it? Plus"—he grins, leaning back, slapping the table with his hands—"he brings me amazing sarnies."

"He loves making those for you, you know."

"And I love eating them. They're so much nicer and better for you than the crap they sell here—and they call themselves a health center!"

I'm looking at his hands. He has nice hands

too—at the ends of those nice arms: slender fingered, big, tanned. I reach out and touch his right one.

"Thank you so much for helping Zac like this. I think it's boosted his confidence loads." I want to say it's helped me too since Jason suggested I come (and it was him who suggested it, I keep reminding myself of that), but feel that might be a bit much.

"No worries. I enjoy it. He's a lovely kid; more fun than a lot of people my own age in this place."

"What do you mean?"

"Oh, there's some massive egos; some top-notch knob-ends here, Jules, honestly. PTs who've lost sight of the fact that exercise is meant to make you feel good and be fun, who aren't happy unless their client is barfing in the bin at the end of their session, who think it's meant to be some sort of exercise in sadomasochism."

I cough, for effect.

"Oh, mate." **Mate? Since when did he call me mate?** "I'm sorry if I went too hard on you today. I didn't realize—"

"How fat and unfit I was?"

He rolls his eyes.

"Sorry," I say.

"Look, I'm having no part in the stories you tell yourself," he says simply. "Except to challenge them." He crushes his polystyrene cup. "Anyway, you know what I think." He gets up to go put it in the bin.

What does that mean? I wonder. Jason used to say I was gorgeous, and I never believed him, but God, I miss hearing that. Did he still think it?

"Can I ask you something?" I say, as he sits down again. I'm aware the way I'm sitting means my cleavage is all out, and I make no attempt to change the situation.

"Ask away."

"Well, what about me?"

He looks blank. "What about you?"

"Well, how come you asked me to come along to these sessions too? How come you've taken the time to give me an exercise plan and an eating plan and you're giving me this private session today?" Zac's at Mum and Dad's, and for once I wasn't working, so I took full advantage of the situation and booked a session. "You've gone to so much effort, just for **me**." Eek, cringe. That's too much. Not so much fishing for compliments as drawing them out of him like a leech and I don't really know why I'm doing it.

He goes to answer, but then something or someone distracts him. I follow his gaze. Dom is standing at reception. There is no warning, no time to run or hide.

"Oh shit." Jason stands up. "I forgot Dom was coming in to talk to me about something—just a client training thing. Do you mind? I won't be a sec."

"No." My already-hot cheeks blaze and I'm fighting a scene involving snow and handbags and some crazy woman screaming like a fishwife, but I know I just have to sit this out. "No, it's fine, I'll just sit here."

Thankfully, the way they are standing means only Jason is facing my way. I watch how warm and open his body language is, compared to Dom's, which, even from the back, is much stiffer and more aware of itself: hands on hips, chest puffed out. **I'm a guy who works out.** The other thing I've noticed since I've become a "gym-goer" (pigs will fly and all that, even this one) is how robotic these gym instructors both look and behave, like they've forgotten what it is to be human and are only interested in being superhuman. Jason isn't like that. He enjoys the people more than the exercise. In fact, if he had his way, he'd do half an hour lifting weights, then have a good old natter with a cup of tea—preferably with the over-fifties aqua aerobics class. Or Zac. He loves his sessions with Zac. He's so good with Zac. So good **for** him too.

I've been thinking a lot about Jason recently. Finding Zac's Top Trumps for Dads folder with its descriptions of the ideal dad, and realizing just how much he needs one, I'm kind of struggling to see why Jason is not that person; why I passed him up when he told me I was beautiful, when he was amazing with my son and laid-back to a fault. Laid-backness (bordering on laziness when not at work, Jason likes a good Xbox-and-pizza session just as much as Zac) may not be a quality you'd normally associate with a fitness instructor. You'd think they'd be all about personal bests and protein powders; weighing up your body fat percentage when they looked at you. But Jason isn't like that. He hates the "Egg White Brigade," as he calls them. "I challenge you to find a more mind-numbingly dull person," he says, "than one who utters the words 'an egg-white omelet, please.'" There's never been any denying that at a size eighteen (on an average day; I've been known to fit in a size sixteen after the norovirus, but also go up to a twenty and even higher if I don't watch it) I am overweight, but Jason, for some reason that I was—and still am—extremely suspicious of, always paid me compliments, always said I was sexier than the girls he trained, who, he told me, wanted to look like plucked rotisserie chickens and talk about glycemic index. He did it for work, gave the clients what they wanted—but he liked to come over to mine afterward, help me polish off a pot of spaghetti big enough to feed half the estate, and watch **The Apprentice** on demand. I used to be so paranoid about why he was with me, about what his other PT colleagues thought: **Why is he going**

**out with a fat bird when he could have the pick
of so many size-eight gym bunnies?**

It's begun to dawn on me, though, since doing
exercise with him—joining him in his working
environment—that exercise isn't about the scales
or the dress size for Jason; it's about being healthy
and, actually, happy. (I'm still struggling with that
concept but making progress. Zac worked out that
exercise made him happy back when we did the
beach run. The question now is yes, but does pep-
peroni pizza do the same job? The jury's still out
on that one.)

When Jase was little, he had leukemia. As a result he has a higher chance of developing heart
and lung problems and, weirdly, obesity. Exercise
then is not a way of him becoming superhuman;
it's just a way for him to stay a healthy human—
and, ultimately, alive.

IT'S OVER A week since I told Zac I was going
to help him. I knew it was the right thing to do. I
couldn't see I had an option since he was going to
do it anyway, and I wanted to be there, to catch
him if he fell—like he's always been there for me.
I wanted to be there for the emotional fallout. Because the way I see it, there will be fallout, whatever happens. I've decided there are four main
possible outcomes. I've written them down in the
notebook I bought, all guns blazing at the beginning of my Get Zac Happy mission, when, unbe-

knownst to me, he was already on a whole other mission of his own.

Possible outcomes:

1. **Find him but he rejects Zac.**

2. **Find him, the truth comes out, and he rejects Zac.**

3. **Find him, the truth comes out, and Zac rejects him.**

4. **Find him, the truth comes out, nobody rejects anyone, but I have to work out what to say to my parents.**

Writing everything down made the whole thing appear scarier than ever, but Jason feels like a rock I can swim to in these treacherous waters. I can rely on him—and this seems all of a sudden of the utmost importance. It's more than I can say for Liam, after all.

Jason comes back from talking to Dom and sits down. "All right?"

"Yep."

There is a long pause, while I pray for my cheeks to calm down.

"It's all right, you know, Dom didn't mention—"

"I don't want to talk about it—ever again."

"He probably even liked it, you know, being hit over the head, a bit of slap and tickle. Some blokes find that a huge turn-on."

I kick him under the table.

"Sorry," he mouths, smiling (the cheek! I thought he was meant to be pissed off about me going on a date with Dom, not taking the piss), and opens up the newspaper on the table while I sip my coffee, both of us content to sit in silence.

Eventually, he can feel me looking at him. "What?" he says.

"Nothing—just the beard. It really suits you, you know."

ONE THING I'VE discovered: joining a missing-person search costs money. After he'd learned that his dad wanted to be a chef, like him, Zac and Teagan took it upon themselves to go round cafés and restaurants looking for him. They did it once or twice in Grimsby; they would have done it more that day in Skeggy had Teagan been with us. I don't mind in principle, but I don't want Zac or Teagan loitering around cafés, staring at people to see if they have light blue eyes, or half a thumb missing—they'll get themselves arrested. So now I either go with them, and that means buying everyone a drink, or I give Zac (and Teagan—because Nicky, Teagan's mum, has even less money than us) a bit of money to get one. I'm also worried Zac is building his dad up in his head as this Jamie Oliver character, when the truth is, he could be an alcoholic, even in prison, by now, gone completely the same way as his dad. He could be anything and anywhere. I battle daily with my decision to help Zac find him and I can't talk to my parents about it, so that leaves Laura.

"So let me get this straight." It's Tuesday—when I usually work a late shift, but she and I have got a booking for "a cold platter" for a local business's client meeting, so we're on our own at the shop early in the morning. "Zac's decided to find his dad and you're going to help him?"

"Um, yeah." It sounds mad when she says it like that. Like the plot from a film, not something that happens in my boring life, that's for sure. By the look on Laura's face, she thinks so too.

"Correct me if I'm wrong, but I thought you never wanted to see him again, that you'd always told Zac he was better off without him, and, more importantly, that you felt you were **all** better off without him after what he did. I mean, what about your mum and dad? Do they know about these plans?"

"All right, Laurs . . ." I didn't expect her to be quite so alarmed. "Don't say that, I'm worried enough as it is, without bringing them into it."

I carry on chopping the feta for the salad, trying to calm the anxiety with the rhythmic action. In the face of failing business, Gino's taken the decision to go slightly more exotic with the cold platter—so it's not just egg and cheese sandwiches and a bit of lousy ham, it's Greek salad too. (**But go easy on the olives, please, girls, and the**

feta and the tomato . . . we have to keep costs down . . .) How am I going to explain this monumental life decision to my best friend when I've never been truthful to her about my real feelings? Laura saw it all play out when my brother died. She was round at my parents' house an awful lot that summer, and saw the Cult of Blame flourish. She heard the vitriol from my mother firsthand, because my mother tried to recruit Laura into her anti-Liam cult too. And all that time, Laura only ever saw me nod along and agree. She wasn't to know I was too numbskulled with grief and shock to formulate opinions of my own; too worried about upsetting my already fragile mother further.

Once out of the fog of those early weeks, however, I did formulate my own opinion. Liam let me down catastrophically; he was not the man I fell in love with—but he was no murderer, and he didn't deserve to be shunned from his son's life forever. (No, but he let himself be; he made that choice.)

I didn't tell Laura about my changing feelings, though, and what I really thought—why not? Out of loyalty to Mum? Yes. But also pride. Because the man I'd gushed about to her for so long had just fucked off, basically, hadn't he? He didn't love me enough to fight—and I felt ashamed about admitting that, even to her.

I look up. Laura is standing over me looking as threatening as it's possible to look in a plastic cap, waiting, I realize, for an explanation. "Look." I sigh, putting the knife down. "I've kind of changed my thinking on that." No, all wrong, too flippant. My true feelings have existed only in my head for so long that I've no idea how to voice them. The early-morning sun is flooding through the shop window, glinting off the knife and onto my face, so I feel even more in the spotlight.

"Go on," says Laura emphatically.

"Well, I'm still furious with Liam. I'll never forgive him. But it's not for what happened to Jamie. I can see that that was an accident now, just a horrible, tragic accident."

Laura still stares at me, listening intently.

"Well, he wouldn't have bloody meant to get in a fight that killed Jamie, would he? He didn't plan that, before he went out; he'd never done it before. It was completely out of character."

She continues to nod, and I continue to fill the space, damn her.

"I'm so mad because he never tried to get in touch, or tried to see Zac—who he was smitten with. He loved him, from the minute he saw him."

And I thought he loved me.

Seeing me get emotional, Laura moves in then and puts her arm around me.

"But he didn't. He didn't fight for us, and now we're trying to find him and I'm worried he's going to break Zac's heart all over again and I'll really never forgive him then."

Laura is rubbing my back maternally. "But can

I point something out?" she says. "And promise you won't shout at me? You never fought for him either, Jules." This is so much like what Zac said to me that day down at the docks that I feel stunned all over again. "I know your brother died, but you just let him leave and you never contacted him again. It takes two to fight for a relationship, darling, and no matter what happened to Jamie, you can't just fire all the blame at Liam."

So, two people—the two who are arguably, apart from my parents, the most important people in my life—have said that to me now: that I didn't fight either.

23

Zac

Fact: Nine out of ten shells are "dextral," which means they open to the right.

Guess Who is my favorite game to play with Brenda. Sometimes we play Connect 4, or armies with the little plastic figures in the sandpit, but Guess Who is my favorite, because I always beat her.

Brenda (giving me the funny look she gives me when she knows I've whupped her again): "Has yours got a bald head then?"

Me: "Nope!"

(Brenda puts all the bald heads down.)

Me: "Has yours got a beard?"

Brenda (sighing): "Yesss."

Brenda: "Has yours got a hat?"

Me: "Nope!"

Me: "Is yours Gerald?"

Brenda: "Oh, Zac. Honestly. You're far too good at this game for me."

It's proper funny when I keep winning. It's because I always choose the people who don't have anything different about them: no hats or glasses or funny mustaches. You only stand out if you're different, basically. It's why Brenda can't ever guess who my person is, because they just fade into the background. I've been seeing Brenda since November—it's April now—and in that time, she's only beaten me twice.

"So how were the Easter holidays, Zac?" asked Brenda when we'd put Guess Who away and were messing around in the sand. (I like making trenches, then putting the plastic soldiers on either side, ready for a battle.)

"Good."

"Did you do anything fun?"

"Me and my mum went to Skeggy on the bus. Teagan was meant to come, but she couldn't because she had an asthma attack and had to go to hospital."

"Oh, dear, I am sorry to hear that. I know you and Teagan are best friends, aren't you?"

"Yeah, but it's all right, because she's better now. It just meant we couldn't do as much of our Find Dad mission as we wanted."

Just like that, it happened. I didn't mean to tell Brenda I was looking for my dad—it just came out. Once it had, I wasn't that bothered, though.

The fact that my mum was helping us now made it not feel like a big secret anymore. It was definitely not a big secret anyway, because as well as my mum knowing—and now Brenda—there was also Jason. I'd told him while we were eating the Grimsby Fish Legend (it's the latest sandwich I've invented for him: tuna, anchovies, gherkins, and eggs) after we'd finished playing football last week. Out of the blue, he'd brought up how I'd sounded cagey when he'd asked me what I was going to do in the Easter holidays (he must have been feeling suspicious about it!). "Cagey" means reluctant to give information—I looked it up in the dictionary. Normally people are cagey when they've done something wrong, but looking for my dad didn't feel like a naughty thing anymore (except where Nan and Grandad were concerned, but I just don't talk about it anymore in front of them) so I told him. I wanted to anyway, because him and Mum are spending more time together—it's looking more likely that they're going to become boyfriend and girlfriend again, and it's going to end in tears when we find my dad, so I thought it would be good if I could kind of warn him a bit. I thought he'd be mad at me, but he wasn't, he just carried on munching the Fish Legend, then he said, "Well, I'm proud of you, mate, because that's a massive thing to do and you are leading it."

I didn't know what he really felt about it. You couldn't tell because he was hiding it.

Like Jason, Brenda already knew that my dad did a runner. I told her when I first started going to see her back in November, after the Halloween where Mum got done by the police in Morrisons and I was getting upset all the time at school. Now, though, she was asking what the Find Dad mission was. She said I didn't have to tell her, but I wanted to. I like talking about it. I didn't tell her everything (like my mum saying she loved my dad—because that's top secret), but this is what I told her:

- I wanted to know who my dad was and what he was like so we were looking for him (and that's what the FDMC was about).

- My mum knew and was helping us.

- We had meetings and a proper file, and I already knew loads of facts about him and that he was nice, because Barrel told me down the docks.

"Wow, Zac, I can see you're really excited about it," said Brenda. "That's quite big news." She was quiet for a second and then, "What's that you're doing in the sand?" she said. Brenda's funny. She always asks me loads of questions about what I'm doing in the sand, when all I'm doing is messing about.

"I'm just preparing them for battle."

"Ah!" she said. "Well, it's a very good idea to prepare for things, Zac. That's very wise. And have you thought about how you might prepare for looking for your dad? What your strategy might be?"

I was concentrating on preparing my army.

"Because it's a very brave thing you've set out to do and, of course, there's every chance you'll find him, but you might not too—or he may not want to be found. Shall we have a chat about the different things that could happen?"

I said I didn't mind, I just wanted **something** to happen.

You could tell Brenda was worried about me, just like Teagan and Mum are worried about me. They're worried what it will be like if my Find Dad mission goes wrong. I know it's 'cause everyone cares about my feelings, but it's not that helpful thinking bad stuff's going to happen all the time.

WE'D ONLY BEEN back at school a week after the Easter holidays, but it felt miles longer. Teagan was better now. She had to stay in hospital for four days. They gave her some medicine that made her asthma better but her face fat. She said she didn't care, though, because it was too thin anyway. It wasn't nice visiting her in the hospital, even though it **was** nice to see her. She was in a weird bed and kept having to put an oxygen mask on to help her get enough breath in her lungs when she got too tired. Her dad was meant to come too the night I was visiting—Teagan kept looking at the door in case he turned up. She really wanted him to come, you could tell, but it got right to the end of visiting time and he hadn't. I asked her if she was all right, and she said she was. I was glad I'd brought her the shell to cheer her up, though.

"Why do you think I chose this one?" I said, when I gave it to her.

"Dunno, but I like it! Is it because it's thin and spiky like me?"

"You're not spiky," I said, because she's not, she's nice and kind. "No, I chose it because it looks like a rocket and what do you think is your favorite saying?"

She laughed then. "You need a rocket up yer bum."

I felt loads better then, because she was smiling. She was back to normal.

I haven't even told Mum this, but I felt a bit guilty when Teagan had her asthma attack. I worried it was because we'd been down the docks when it was rainy and cold, which can be really bad for you if you've got asthma. She'd also forgotten her puffer that day and neither of those things would have happened if she wasn't helping me to look for my dad. When Teagan was all better and back at school, I told her I'd been thinking this, but she just pulled a face. She even looked a bit mad with me. "Me having an asthma attack has got nothing to do with you," she said. We were in the dinner queue so we just had to keep moving as we talked. "You feel bad about everything, you do. I've just got stupid asthma—it's nobody's fault. Except maybe the council's." I haven't told her I sent the photo of myself without her on Skegness Beach with an angry letter to the Housing Department. Only Mum knows.

I gave Teagan the chance to pull out of the mission, but she didn't want to; she said her life would be dead boring again if she wasn't doing it.

"Yeah, but we might not find him," I said while we were eating our dinner, thinking of what Brenda had said. (I don't have chips anymore and neither does Teagan.) "What will we do then?"

"We **will** find him," said Teagan.

"I thought you said we might not, though. I thought you said I should prepare myself."

"Yeah, well, I've decided thinking that is rubbish and it's more fun to think it will work out. If it does go wrong, then it will be rubbish anyway, so there's no point feeling rubbish while we don't even know what's going to happen."

I thought it was good she said that—especially when her own dad didn't even come to the hospital. If Teagan's dad didn't want to know, then who says mine will? Maybe Teagan was right, that night after we'd called up Finder Genie and I'd walked her back to her block and she'd warned me that my dad might not want to know either. I didn't want to have that thought, though, so I tried to think of something nice; something that would squash it and make it go away.

ONE OF THE good things about having Mum helping us find my dad was that we didn't have to wait till a special, secret FDMC meeting anymore. We could just ask Mum questions whenever we liked, and it didn't matter if the questions made her suspicious, because she knew what we were doing anyway.

On the Saturday after our first week back at school, Teagan came to Sandwich King with me while I made Jason's special sandwich for that day's session. Mum came too, as usual, and Raymond let us in. You could tell Teagan was properly better, because she was being stupid, like she normally is, trying on the plastic hats that Mum and Aunty Laura have to wear to make the sandwiches, then running outside in the street. It was a good job it was so early and nobody was in town yet—we were all laughing our heads off.

"She's a wee firecracker, isn't she?" Raymond said. Raymond is Scottish, so he says "wee" when he means "little"; it's nothing to do with going for a wee. He thought she was mad, but he liked her too, you could tell. Teagan liked him back. We decided he came sixth in our Top Trumps for Dads.

If he was younger, he'd come higher, but he might not live long enough to be the perfect dad. Teagan was asking him loads of personal questions like whether he was married (he is) and if he had any children (he's got four). Then she asked him how much money he earned (Mum said that was a step too far), because we've decided that when we're older, if Teagan doesn't make it as a gymnast, we could open a café like Sandwich King and Teagan could be like Raymond. She could drive the van and be the deliverywoman and we could unpack everything together and chat while we do it, every day.

After I'd made the sandwich (the Roast Dinner: pork with applesauce and grated carrot and sweet corn—it sounds bad, but it's really nice), me and Teagan asked Mum if we could ask her some more questions.

"About your dad, I'm guessing?"

"Yes."

"Go on then." Mum sat down with a cup of tea at the table at the window of the café and so we sat down with her. "Hit me with it, Private Detectives Hutchinson and O'Brien."

Teagan got out our notebook and found a clean page. It was a very important question, after all. We hadn't had a chance to ask it in Skegness, so we were asking it now.

24

Juliet

It was the most obvious question in the world: **What were you doing the last time you saw him?** So why had I given no thought whatsoever to what I would say? How could I have not seen that one coming? Lying was horrible, but God, I was good at it. Who knew I was such a natural storyteller? I was wasted making sandwiches; I should be writing books.

The story went like this:

I was seven and a half months pregnant and I'd been to town, getting a few bits for you. I loved buying baby stuff. I was so excited. I'd been in Superdrug that day, stocking up on talc and baby wipes and nappies, blissfully unaware that back at home, your father was packing his bags.

Teagan bored holes into me with her dark, serious eyes, twiddling her pen, like some Rottweiler journalist. "Yeah, but that wasn't the last time you actually **saw** him, was it? Not if you were in town and he was packing. The last time you actually saw him must have been before you went into town," she said. "So . . ." She paused, almost as if she was doing it for effect; I half imagined myself in a police interview room. "What happened the last time you **actually saw him**?"

And so in desperation I squeezed out another inspired story where I was still seven and a half months pregnant, but in this one, the night before I went to town to buy baby stuff, Liam and I had gone for a lovely walk along Cleethorpes Beach—beautiful sunset (the Devil's in the detail, after all)—then we'd got up the next day, nothing out of the ordinary, and he'd gone off to work around eight a.m. and later I'd gone into town, and that was it. Literally never heard from him again.

"How come you never mentioned the last walk you had on Cleethorpes Beach when we went running on Cleethorpes Beach, then? That is quite an important fact."

Teagan again. The staff at Thornby Academy who had written her off were going to get the shock of their lives when she turned up as an interviewer on **Newsnight**.

"Yeah, and also, I thought he was a fisherman," Zac joined in. "So why was he not on a trip? Or was it the first day of a new one? Did you not go and wave him off, like you did for Grandad? That's a bit tight, Mum."

Come to think of it, I'd have had an easier time on **Newsnight** with Jeremy Paxman.

"Well, you see, he was doing decorating at that point," I lied, digging a deeper and deeper hole. "When he was between fishing jobs, he used to do decorating and odd jobs around town."

"Write that down," Zac said and Teagan dutifully snapped the top off a new color pen. "Because that could be his job in the town where he lives now."

There were more questions: what was Liam wearing that last time you saw him (I did point out I hoped he would have changed since then); what kind of mood was he in; did he say he had plans for the day?

"Where do you get this stuff?" I asked, amazed.

"The Internet," Teagan said casually. "We just looked up 'things to ask when looking for a missing person,' didn't we, Zac?"

"Yep," Zac said, leaning back, clicking his pen on and off. Who **was** this ten-year-old before me? When had my son got so . . . **confident**? Then came the killer question. I'd have been proud of him, had it not been me who had to answer it. "What was the last thing you said to each other?"

I knew I shouldn't, but, perhaps like my penchant for nicking things, once it entered my head I somehow couldn't resist. I wanted—too much—to see Zac's face light up. And light up it did. "We said we loved each other," I replied. "We gave each other a kiss and said we loved each other."

"I'm definitely writing that down!" said Teagan excitedly.

I was so convincing, I almost believed it myself.

It must have been quite the day for making progress with the mission because after the interrogation at the café, Zac came up with one of his brain waves: "I know, Mum, we could try and find Dad's relatives! They'd know where he is. Did he have any brothers and sisters? If we could find out where they lived, we could go and see them."

I'm amazed, actually, that he hasn't asked me this before. Being an only child, Zac is always looking for ways to make his family bigger: "Does Aunty Kath and Uncle Brian's dog, Branston, count as a family member?" "There's a boy called Charlie Hutchinson who's just joined in reception—could he be my long-lost cousin?" So you can imagine his joy when I told him, in answer to his question, about Liam's half sister, Kelly—the result of Liam's mum's relationship with another man before she went for bad-boy Vaughan.

"So I've got a half aunty?" He was delighted.

"I suppose so, yes."

"Does she live in Grimsby? We could go and see her!"

"No, no, Zac," I said, my stomach turning over. "She doesn't live in Grimsby."

I did know where she lived, though. I just wasn't telling him that—yet.

IT'S THE MONDAY evening after Zac's Saturday interrogation at Sandwich King, and I call up Jase to see if he'll meet me for an exercise session down the playing fields. I feel awful for barefacedly lying to my son. It's a good job Zac is old enough now, on the cusp of eleven, to be left on his own while I go for a jog, because I'm finding it hard to look him in the eye. Perhaps the only good thing is that rather than doing what I used to do in the face of emotional turmoil (crack out the cheese on toast), I've started, gradually, to admit that exercise is more helpful. Also, I now have extra motivation. In the unlikely event that we do find Liam, I don't want him to think, **She's let herself go**. I want him to see that we've coped—more than that, that we've thrived—without him. I want to look better than I looked when we were together. And I'm getting there—that is one good thing about all this. It's not like the pounds are dropping off, but I can see the difference. I've toned up. I feel better.

When I spot Jason, a tall figure in an Adidas tracksuit, the three white stripes shiny in the setting sun as he stretches against a tree, I'm glad I called him. There's just something soothing about the sight of him and I'm transported back to the days when we'd sit watching **The Apprentice**, his arm around me on the sofa. It was never perfect, certainly not very romantic, but compared to how I feel now, the ground felt solid beneath my feet. And I'd be lying if I said I don't occasionally (quite often) think of us getting back together again, how it could be so much easier than all this. I'd have a boyfriend, Zac would have a father figure, and maybe he wouldn't feel the need, then, to find his dad—with all the risks that involves.

I wave at Jason and he waves back. "Come on, Hutch," he shouts. "Get a wriggle on. I haven't got all day, you know." "Hutch" is a new thing. I kind of like it and I kind of don't. A bit like "mate." No, I definitely hate "mate."

"I'm coming," I shout back. "Calm down. We haven't started the running bit yet, you know."

I've chosen a gorgeous evening for a run. It's been raining—April showers in full swing—but the sky is clearing now and the sinking sun is backlighting the clouds, making them look like molten lava and coloring the grass the most vivid green.

Jason takes me through a few lunges and stretches, but then rather than the presession flirty chat I realize I was hoping for, he's eager to get jogging straightaway. I get the feeling he isn't joking, that he doesn't have all night; that he's doing this more as a favor than because he really wanted to see me. The idea irks me somewhat.

We set off around the field, Jason zigzagging along the middle now and again to make it longer.

"How was your week?" he asks.

"Great."

"How's Zac and his 'finding dad' mission?"

"Oh, fine." I'm not sure how Jason feels about it so I don't get into it. "All good. You know Teagan was in hospital, though?" I say, changing the subject.

"Yeah, he told me. Is she okay?"

"She is now, but it was serious—they had to call an ambulance in the night."

"Oh God. You should ask her to come along to some of these sessions—exercise is great for asthma and controlling symptoms."

"Good idea," I say, thinking not a cat in hell's chance is she coming to these too. It's going to turn into a class, not a private lesson, if we aren't careful; and I like it as it is—just the three of us. (Well, ideally, the two of us.)

A full circuit done, and it's time for sit-ups—the absolute worst.

"So, have you managed to do much exercise this week?" Jason holds his hand out to indicate where my head needs to touch if I'm doing the exercise correctly. "Are you keeping your step rate up?"

Step rate? What sort of question is that to ask your ex-girlfriend?

"Yes," I groan. "How many more of these bastards?"

"Eight."

"I hate you."

"Eight's nothing, you can do that. Have you been practicing?"

"Yes!" I say, because I have. Perhaps not to the extent Jason would wish, but it has been known these past few weeks for me to do sit-ups and squats while watching **This Morning**, instead of just eating toast, and that is something I never thought I'd be able to say.

"Well, you can tell. You've definitely got more shape around the waist."

"Do you think so?" I say, delighted, lying down and stretching out at last.

"Definitely."

We do two more laps of the field, Jason doing that thing of galloping at the side of me, because if he goes as slow as I do, then he'll trip over his own feet.

"You don't have to make it that obvious."

"What obvious?"

"That I'm so slow."

"You're not that slow. Think what you were like when we first started these sessions, think how far you've come," he says. And he's right, I think, I have come far. To imagine I'd ever suggest running around a park of an evening instead of watching telly and eating crisps—and not only that but enjoy it. Well, a tiny bit. It's astounding, frankly.

IT'S ALMOST DARK by the time we finish. The air smells of spring and the recent rain, the birds are singing, and I'm aware of not wanting to go home, not yet.

"Do you mind if I just sit down for a bit?" I say, still breathless, hoping to delay the point at which we go our separate ways a little bit longer. "I'm totally spent."

I lie down on the damp grass, hoping Jason might be admiring my new shapely waist and my skin, which I hope is glowing in the lilac dusk like his. But I obviously look up at him for a moment more than is comfortable—for him at least—because he laughs nervously and steps back.

"What are you doing? Looking at my nose hair?"

"No," I say, smiling. "Just looking at you."

He holds out his hand. "Come on, up you get," he says. "We should do some stretches before you go."

"Is there a rush?" I say, as he helps me to my feet. "Because we could, you know, go for a walk, have a chat?" I flutter my eyelashes flirtatiously, jokingly—clearly not joking at all.

Another nervous laugh. He seems confused and we stand looking at each other for a moment or two before . . . I don't know what comes over me—a rare moment of decisiveness, I suppose, of deciding life doesn't have to be this complicated and maybe all my answers are standing right in front of me—but I step forward and go to kiss him.

But he turns his head.

"Jules . . ."

"Oh God." I stare at the ground, my face blazing. "Oh God. Well, that was embarrassing."

"Look, I—"

"No, it's okay." My eyes are smarting.

"Well, it's obviously not. You're obviously upset."

"I just thought . . ." What **was** I thinking? "I think I got carried away; thinking a few weeks' exercise had completely transformed me! That I must be irresistible! But I'm not, I'm not." Jason stands there looking utterly awkward. **This** is utterly awkward. "I'm still . . ." I blow my cheeks out—a lame attempt to make a joke of it, but Jason knows me better than to be joking about my weight so I guess I think I may as well go the whole way then: a no-holds-barred pity party. "Look, I'm not stupid, you know. I know it's why you—men— don't go for me." He's shaking his head and looking away, but I steam ahead. "It's why I haven't got a boyfriend, let's face it. It's why Zac's big too and unhappy and gets bullied—why I'm not enough and he . . ." I stop myself just in time. "It's why Dom didn't want to go anywhere near me . . . It's why you didn't want to go out with me. Probably." I know I've gone too far with that one and I inwardly wince, but it's out there now.

"Er, hold on, that is enough," says Jason crossly. Jason rarely raises his voice and it shuts me up. "First of all, I did not say I didn't want to go out

with you; it was **you** who said you were in no state
for a relationship, making it impossible—which is
an entirely different thing—and second, the reason I did that, and also why Dom didn't want to
go anywhere near you, as you put it, is nothing to
do with your size."

I raise an eyebrow.

"It's because you're unhappy, Juliet."

I look away like a moody teenager.

"And full of self-loathing. Nobody wants to go
out with someone with such low self-esteem."

"Low self-esteem," I mumble. Did I have low
self-esteem? I knew, full well, the answer to that,
but was it really that obvious?

"Look," he says eventually, when I don't say anything, "I just think you need to work a few things
out before you start trying to have a relationship—
work out what you really want—because, well, I
don't think it's me."

I sigh. I guess I already know that he's right.
"Well, look on the bright side," I say, mustering everything I can to try and make this less awkward
for us both, even though it still stings. "At least I
didn't hit you over the head with my handbag."

25

Mick

I can see Liam even now, Zac in the crook of his arm in the maternity ward, that look of love and terror in his eyes. I recognized that look so well from when my two were born, and after I'd kissed my daughter and met my first grandchild, who I was daft about—everyone said it from the off—I ruffled Liam's hair and joked, "Our Jules seems fine. You're the one who looks like you've been hit by a train." He looked up from Zac, half laughing, half dazed, with that thought I also knew well written across his face: **How the hell could anything so beautiful, so perfect, have anything to do with me?**

That was what Liam and I always had in common: low self-esteem, I suppose; this belief that we had to prove ourselves, that anything good that happened to us was a fluke. That was why I stuck up for him where Lynda was concerned, because I saw so much of myself in him. But it was also the reason I knew how to hit him where it hurt the most too; how to destroy him. When he looked at Juliet like he thought he was the luckiest man alive, it was the same way I'd looked at Lynda thirty years before and continued to do until grief and bitterness ate her up. I was relieved, if I'm honest, to see Liam looking so smitten with his son, because he'd gone AWOL for a while when Juliet first announced she was pregnant and I'd worried then, in case he actually was a dead loss like Lynda said he was; in case he was his father's son after all. Vaughan may have been a mate (just a drinking mate, it turned out; unsurprisingly, he buggered off the minute I ditched the booze), but I didn't want that for our daughter any more than Lynda did, even though she said I didn't care, that I didn't have high enough standards for our kids. That's always been Lynda's beef with me, that I have low standards.

Lynda was devastated when Juliet told us she was expecting. She was livid too, mostly with Liam. Juliet was only twenty, after all, and more academic, if she chose to put her mind to it, than our Jamie, who was always more practical, and Lynda had big ideas she might be the first of our family to go to university. She'd already messed up her A levels by that point, anyway, **because of Liam,** Lynda said, although I knew my daughter (because she is so like me) and I knew that she let that happen all on her own, ruled by her heart, not her head; far too swept up in love to give a toss about exams. But she was retaking a couple of them that year, and although I can't see she'd ever have left Grimsby and Liam to go to university, Lynda held out hope. That was until one evening in November, when she came home, leaned against the kitchen sink, and made her announcement that was to be the beginning of the wheels coming off our lives. "There's no easy way to tell you this, so I'm just going to say it," she said. "I'm pregnant."

Lynda, like I said, went ballistic. I, apparently, didn't go ballistic enough. (I was pissed. 'Course I was.) But what was the point, anyway? Where was ranting and raving going to get us? It had happened. She was over three months gone. Lynda told Juliet she'd ruined her life, that so many opportunities wouldn't be hers for the taking anymore—a statement I know she regrets, despite everything, because she couldn't love Zac more than she does. My only question, when things had calmed down, was, "And what does Liam say? Is he going to stick by you? Is he going to go to college and get a decent job?" Because I knew more than anyone that being a fisherman in 2005 was no path to a secure life.

Juliet was very defensive, emotional. "Of course he's standing by me!" she was shouting at the top of her voice. "He's not just going to run off, is he?" But then he did. A week later, he just disap-

peared. Juliet told us that it had been a shock and
he just needed some space, but I was worried then.
I sobered right up. I thought, **You fucking dare,
Liam. You fucking dare leave my daughter in
the lurch.** I'd have been ready to take it up with
him and Vaughan if he had; I'd have gone ballistic
enough then. Lynda, of course, was all "I told you
so" in that defeatist, fatalistic manner that has always been her way, but which masks the fact that
she's as scared as anyone else.

But then, after a week or two, he came back. It
turned out Juliet was right. He just needed to get
his head together. Of course, we worried he would
do it again, but I can honestly say that from that
moment on, you couldn't have asked for a more
devoted and committed partner for your daughter,
a better father for your grandson. It was like he'd
been waiting for this chance to shine all his life.
And shine he did. Even Lynda changed her tune.

"I don't get many people wrong, but I got him
wrong," she said out of the blue to me one night
and I dared to smile smugly—her response to
which was to whip me around the earhole with a
tea towel. But it was true. You couldn't have wished
for better. He was shaping up to be a great son-in-
law, father, and mate for Jamie. Because, this was
the thing—it wasn't just Juliet he got on with; he
and Jamie hit it off. Liam benefited from Jamie's
bolshy confidence and social ease, and Jamie loved
how laid-back and good-tempered Liam was. How

he never expected anything from anyone. That's the Liam I remember. That's the Liam I knew. But then what happened happened, and we were back to square one. "I told you so," Lynda was saying again, but with real venom now our son was dead, and those words, Jesus Christ, they still cut like a knife.

26

Zac

**Fact: The building of Manchester was
started in AD 79, when the Romans
constructed a wooden fort.**

Life is full of peaks and troughs. The peaks are
the up, good bits, and the troughs are the bad,
down ones. It's like when you go out on your bike
and you go down a dip, there's always a hill after
it. You can't have one without the other, it's just a
fact of nature. And that's what life is. It's like rhubarb and custard days, but bigger, because it's not
just what a typical day is like, but your whole life.

The best thing is when a peak happens when
you're not expecting it. They don't happen that
much; you're really lucky if you get one a year. I
thought I'd had mine when Mum said she'd help
with the Find Dad mission, but then something
even better happened . . . Mum said we could go
to Manchester! We could go to find my aunty
Kelly's house and ask her where my dad is.

Mum came to meet us from school on Thursday especially to tell us. We walked home and she waited till we were just turning the corner, near the Casablanca Club, to drop the surprise. I think the Casablanca Club has got good karma, because only good things ever happen there.

"So, I've got a bit of news for you both. As part of the Find Dad mission—our mission—I'm going to take you both to Manchester on Saturday."

"What?!" Me and Teagan both said it at the same time, it was funny.

"I've found out that that's where Kelly lives—and we're just going to take the plunge and go there. We're going to put a rocket up this investigation's bum, as you would say, Teagan."

"Yes!!" I did a punch in the air.

"Teagan, I've asked your mum, and she says it's fine. As long as—**as long as**"—she had to say it again to make sure Teagan was listening, because she was already doing gymnastics on the pavement, she was so excited—"you take your inhalers **and** a spare one and wear a cardigan all the time."

"I am not wearing a cardigan. Joking! I'll wear my Minions onesie. I'll go naked as long as I get to go," she said, doing a cartwheel.

Kelly is Dad's half sister. She's only a half sister because they've got the same mum, but Kelly's dad isn't Vaughan Jones, it's another man we don't know the name of. My mum has even met Kelly, because when she was pregnant with me, before my dad just disappeared, her and my dad went to visit her. Then a few days ago, she looked Kelly up on Facebook. She found out she still lives in the same area in Manchester that she used to. Mum has her address, so we're going to go to her house, to see if she knows where my dad is. Mum's already sent her a message on Facebook to say we're coming. I'm dead proud of her for her dedication to our mission.

"Now, I don't want you to get your hopes up, you two, though, because even though she's said we can go, she might not want to tell us much information."

"Why not?"

"Oh, people, life . . . It's just complicated, Zac."

You thought you couldn't get a bigger peak, but then Mum told us the next bit: that before we go to Kelly's house, we're going to go to the Sea Life Center, which is a massive aquarium. Mum's saved up the tokens on the side of our Cheerios packet so that it's miles cheaper. (The last time we went to an aquarium was three and a half years ago when I was seven and I touched a stingray. It's in my top ten best things that have ever happened in my life—and now I'm probably going to get to do it again.)

"What's an aquarium?" Teagan said, which was dead funny because she'd squealed when Mum said it, but she didn't even know what Mum was talking about.

"It's like this amazing big place with loads of fish in it," I said.

"Eh? But Grimsby's got the most fish in it of anywhere else in the world."

Me and Mum laughed when she said that. She's not going to be able to believe her eyes when she sees the aquarium. It was fate she had her asthma attack and couldn't come to Skegness, because there was a much bigger peak, just around the corner. That's what I mean about life—you just never know.

IT'S A HUNDRED and sixteen miles from Grimsby to Manchester. After London, which is a hundred and ninety, it would be the farthest I'd ever been in my life. You could get food on the train, but it was daylight robbery. So I'd made my special sandwiches for everyone. I just took Jason's favorite two, and did those. We had Aero chocolate mousse too. (They were only 30p in the six o'clock fridge.)

Mum let me and Teagan sit next to the window after we'd eaten our sandwiches (we ate them as soon as we got on; it was only nine a.m. but we couldn't wait), then we did a challenge. The challenge was to see how long we could look at one thing out of the window, and how much we could remember about what we'd seen as we went past. I wanted to remember everything, but your eyes couldn't beat how fast the train was. You could try, but you could never do it, so you just had to give in because it was too frustrating.

"Penny for your thoughts," said Mum. It's just a saying—you say it when someone looks like they're thinking. I was thinking about Nan and Grandad, hoping they wouldn't find out we were going to find my dad. I knew they'd (especially Nan) be mad if they knew, like they were mad on Easter Saturday, but Mum says I'm not to worry about it anymore. She says Nan is just upset with Dad for leaving us and she's being protective. I know that's nice, but I don't understand how you can be the same angry with someone ten years after they've done the bad thing. It's impossible. Sometimes, if me and Connor or even me and my mum have a row, I promise myself I won't talk to them for ages, but I only ever last an hour, max. It's just boring and lonely, basically, being in a mood with people. You end up missing them, so you can't keep it up.

"Your eyes look mad," Teagan said.

"Do they? What do you mean?"

"They're going like this." She made her eyes go dead fast from side to side. She looked like Mr. Dabrowski, who lives on our estate. He's blind, but his eyes move all the time.

ME AND TEAGAN decided we needed to go and explore. We had to find a place for an urgent FDMC meeting, to discuss what we were going to ask Kelly when we got to her house. Mum wasn't going to come inside with us, you see. She said it was for the same reason she thought it was a good idea that I sent the letter to the council instead of her—adults are more likely to listen to children than grown-ups.

There were loads of weird people on the train. You could have a good time just looking at them. There was a woman with loads of black makeup on and tattoos all over her arms—she was definitely a vampire—and there was a man snoring. It was the funniest thing ever. He was just snorting like a pig with his mouth open and didn't even know.

We got to a door that said **First Class**. You could tell it was first class already, because even the glass of the door and the sign were posh. There was nobody stopping us going in, so we just sat down for a bit. I was scared in case there was a secret camera and we'd get charged loads of money, but Teagan didn't care.

"Let's have our meeting in here."

"But what if we get done?"

"Don't worry, Zac, honestly. First class is where all people hold important meetings. You can't have it in the normal bit where there are loads of little kids crying because they've dropped their felt-tips."

I could see what she meant.

"When I'm a professional gymnast," she said, getting out the file, "I'll only ever go in first class—especially if I've won a medal in the Olympics. You never go in normal seats if you've won a medal for your country, you know. You get in everywhere free. You don't even have to pay to go in the toilet at the station. You just have to show your medal."

I decided then that if I couldn't be a medal winner, I would be a chef for people who were. I could work in the first-class bit of a train. "I'll cook you lobster thermidor every day if you want."

"What's lobster thermidor?"

"The poshest dinner you can ever have. Rich people literally have it once a week; it's as normal for them as spaghetti hoops."

MANCHESTER PICCADILLY STATION was the maddest place you've ever been to in your life. Everyone was late for their trains. There was a woman talking over a speaker all the time; you couldn't even understand what she was on about, she just kept on talking. Everyone was talking. The only person who wasn't was Teagan—it was the first time me and Mum had seen her quiet. She literally didn't speak for ten minutes; we were a bit worried! She just followed me and Mum.

The aquarium was sick. Teagan couldn't believe her eyes—she was just running from one thing to the next like she was crazy, and Mum had to tell her nicely to stop hogging the windows, where you could see in to the sharks and the jellyfish and the stingrays just gliding around, like they were totally the boss of you. Our favorite bit was when you walked down the corridor in the dark, but above you were glass ceilings and you could see the fish. It was like being underwater and in space at the same time, and when you reached out your hand, you could pretend like you were tickling the dolphins' bellies. We touched a stingray too, but I think that the dolphin-belly tickling in underwater space where everything was lit up beat that in the best things that have happened in my life so far.

After the Sea Life Center, we had to get the bus to a place called Chorlton, which is where my aunty Kelly lives. We found her road on Google Maps, then asked the bus driver what stop it was. We had to do loads of detective work just to get there.

We stood on the street corner for a bit while Mum fussed with my top. (I was wearing my favorite shirt with the palm trees all over it. It's like what people wear in the Caribbean.) "Now, don't be nervous," she said. "Or you, Teagan. I told Kelly you were popping in, and she's fine with that." Mum kissed me on the cheek, then Teagan, on the top of her head. "And anyway, you two are so cute, I'm sure you'll charm the pants off her in no time." The idea of Kelly with no pants on made me and Teagan both laugh.

Mum gave us the box of Celebrations we'd got for Kelly (even though it wasn't a celebration, not yet), wished us luck, told us what number it was,

then she went for a walk. She said if she didn't hear
from us beforehand, then she'd see us outside the
newsagent's at the bottom of the road in an hour.

Kelly must be loaded, because her house was
massive. It was on its own—not in a block like
mine—and it had four big windows at the front,
instead of two like Nan and Grandad's. It even
had grass and flowers and a garden at the front,
not just concrete, with a big tree that shook blos-
soms all over you when you walked past. I rang
the doorbell. I knew Teagan would think I was
going to expect her to do it, so I wanted to surprise her. It wasn't a buzz one like at my house, it
was a proper "ding-dong" one like you get on the
telly. We waited, but nobody came, then just as I
was about to ring it again, you could see a person
through the glass.

The person opened it, but it wasn't Kelly. It was a
girl. She was chubby like me with long brown hair
and she looked a bit younger than us. I guessed
she was nine.

"Um, hi, we've come to—"

"Mum!" the girl shouted, before I had chance
to finish what I was saying. "There's some people
at the door."

Just then, a lady ran down the stairs. She had
blond hair in a bob like Miss Kendall and she was
thin—you could see her bones through her jeans.
She had a top that showed off her belly button. It
had a diamond stuck in it. "Libby, just go upstairs

for a bit, will you?" The girl (Libby) stared at us for a moment, then went off. But she kept looking back. She wanted to stay and talk to us, you could tell. I smiled at her, so she knew I knew.

Kelly was holding the door open but not that far. She looked a bit nervous, just like us. "All right? I'm Kelly and you must be Zac?" she said, holding her hand out. I nodded and shook it. She stared right at me then. "Bloody hell," she said and I felt my cheeks burn. She'd only just met me and she was swearing. If I did that, my mum would kill me.

"And you are?" she said to Teagan, as Teagan just walked straight past her and into the house.

"Teagan," said Teagan. I didn't know what to do, so I just followed her in.

"Right, well, hello, Teagan," Kelly said, closing the door. "Come in, why don't you?"

You could tell they were rich because everything matched. We got taken to a room at the back of the house that was all glass. It had a big settee in it, even though we'd just passed the front room where there was another massive settee made out of leather, and you could see the garden through all the glass, which was ginormous compared to my nan and grandad's and had a trampoline. I really wanted a go; it looked totally boss.

"In case you're wondering who I am," said Teagan, looking around, "I'm Zac's deputy."

Kelly laughed. "Sorry?"

"I'm helping him."

"Helping me find my dad," I said. It was the first time I'd ever said it to anyone who didn't live in Grimsby, and it felt scary and exciting at the same time. I felt like we were the police on a proper investigation.

I gave Kelly the box of Celebrations we'd brought, which she said Libby would be very pleased about, and then Kelly told us to make ourselves at home and went to get us a drink. We both sat down on the settee. It was spongy—you sank into it like my beanbag—and the sun was coming through the glass roof, making it warm as anything too.

Teagan nudged me. "If this is his sister," she whispered, "then I bet your dad's rich too."

"I don't think he is."

"I do."

"I wouldn't really care if he was, either."

"I would. I'd love to have a rich dad—he'd have to be nice too—but if he was rich, you'd get to go to loads more places. You'd get to go to an aquarium every week if you wanted."

Just then, Kelly came in with the drinks. "Right, it's just Ribena, I hope that's okay." She'd put ice in them, like you get in the pub. She passed mine to me. "I'm sorry I swore at you the first second I saw you, Zac," she said, "but you've got exactly the same eyes as Liam. I couldn't believe it."

Me and Teagan looked at each other. I didn't know what to say. I just knew that her saying that

couldn't understand what she was saying. It just felt totally crazy.

"When you were two weeks old, your mum and dad brought you to visit me in Manchester." She was talking, but it sounded like gobbledygook. "I told your dad not to bother, that it was a trek with a newborn baby and that I'd go and visit him soon instead, but he was so proud of you, he couldn't wait to show you off."

I didn't know what to say. My brain felt like it had forgotten how to talk and I just felt dizzy, like I might fall over. And over and over again, the thought going round and round in my head: **My dad met me. He held me. My dad knew me . . .**

When I looked up at Teagan, she was frowning. Her brain was just working it out, you could tell. **My dad met me . . .** I had the achy feeling in my throat when you know you're going to cry and I just wanted to get out of there. **He knew what I felt like and smelled like. He probably even changed my nappy and fed me. Someone took a picture of him holding me, looking like he actually loved me. But he still left.**

I gave Kelly the photo back so quickly, it was like I'd thrown it at her. Her hands weren't ready.

"We've got to go now," I said, kind of just blurting it out because I still couldn't really talk properly, and Kelly looked surprised.

"But what about the trampoline?" said Libby. "I wanted to go on the trampoline with you."

"I'm sorry," I said. I felt bad; she looked disappointed. "But we've got to go and meet my mum now." I just wanted to get out of there. **My dad met me . . .** That was all I could think. **He met me and he still left.**

27

Juliet

Zac sits on the bench outside the newsagent's and stares straight ahead, his face blotchy from crying. Teagan is sitting beside him, her arm looking minute around his shoulder.

"Zac, speak to me, you're scaring me," I say again, standing over them; but still, nothing.

"Teagan, will you tell me what happened, then?" She shrugs apologetically but is also mute. "Please? Someone?"

I need some water; my mouth has gone completely dry. I don't know what was said at Kelly's house. I just know that as he walked back to meet me, my son was giving me evils for the first time in his life and I hated it; it was awful.

When I contacted Kelly on Facebook I had no idea how she felt about me, or Zac, or my parents; whether she was on Liam's side in all of this, because he was her brother, or whether she even cared. I just knew she was a direct link to Liam and that it was worth a shot, for Zac. After all, the worst that could happen (I thought) was that she'd say no. But she didn't; she (somewhat reluctantly, I admit) said it was all right if Zac went round for a chat about his dad. And I'd specifically said when I'd messaged her: Please don't tell him about the night Jamie died and Liam's part in it. I may well have to tell him, but it needs to be me that does, or his grandparents—nobody else. He's not ready yet. It would devastate him. He knows Liam left, but he doesn't have to know why. He just wants to know where he might be now, and also some general information about his father—I'd hesitated, my fingers hovering above the keyboard before writing the next bit, but I'd done it in the end—about the person who is, after all, the other half of him.

She'd sent a message back an hour later saying simply You can trust me with a thumbs-up emoji, and I'd thought to myself, **I hope to God I can**. But now, looking at Zac's face, I wonder if I should have trusted her, if she'd told him anyway. I knew, when I contacted her, that this was risky; that if she said yes to meeting Zac, that we could be one step closer to finding Liam but also to the whole sorry story emerging. However, I knew that I'd made a promise to Zac. And so I pushed any concerns to the back of my mind and got in touch. But now I wish—God, I wish—that I hadn't.

Teagan is lightly—almost maternally—patting

Zac on the back now. Zac is glowering into the middle distance, his eyes still full of tears. I've never seen him like this.

I sit down next to him and put my hand on his knee, but he jerks his leg away so I remove my hand, put them both between my knees, and try to distract myself with the comings and goings of the bus stop over the road.

Suddenly Zac speaks. "Mum, you lied to me," he says, and it feels like my bowels have turned, instantly, to liquid. "You've lied to me forever— why did you **do** that?" He shouts that bit, and then he's in tears again. Not just little, trickling tears either, but heartbroken tears. He's doing that awful, awful, utterly defeated sobbing that he's not done since he was six or seven.

I've dreaded this moment since he was born, and now it's here, and it's **so** bad, it's like some pitying greater power has decided to airlift me out of my own body to save me from myself so that I don't have to live through it, because for a few seconds, I feel completely absent. Is this what they call an out-of-body experience?

Zac, though, is still looking at me, sobbing, and waiting for an answer. Teagan is swinging her legs and looking at the floor, probably appalled with me too.

I stare up at the low, gray Manchester sky, which seems to be lowering itself down on me, like a tomb, and close my eyes. "Oh, Zac."

Everything then is in sharp focus: how he's always put Jamie up on a pedestal; how much he loves his grandparents and how it would destroy him to know his own father was the orchestrator of their misery—no matter how accidental; how his own ideas about who his dad is, or might be, will now be smashed to smithereens. This is catastrophic. Zac is taking breaths, trying to calm himself down now, and blinking back tears, fighting them with all he has. He hates crying in front of me—but, more so, in front of other children. Even Teagan.

Teagan leans forward slightly, so she's looking at his face, and touches him lightly on the arm. "Should I go?" she says softly. "Do you want me to go, Zac?" A ten-year-old dealing so maturely with this fallout, it puts me to shame. I send her off to look in WHSmith for a bit and I turn to him, but he won't look at me.

"Darlin', what did Kelly tell you?" It feels like I've never dreaded an answer more. "What did she say?"

Zac looks at me and blinks; a tear trembles, then runs down his chubby cheek. Whatever it was, I know he wants me to say that it isn't true, but I can't. He doesn't speak. And neither do I.

I never wanted him to find out at all, ideally, but I certainly didn't want him to find out like this. I choose my words carefully; I tread ever so gently. "Look, I know you must be so shocked right now. You must have so many questions, Zac, but I want you to know that any feelings you have—whether you feel angry or sad or both or none . . . whether you even feel ashamed. They're perfectly okay, okay?"

He frowns, confused. "Why would I feel ashamed?"

Oh. I didn't expect that response. "Well . . . you wouldn't, you shouldn't, but just in case . . ." I'm stuttering, stumbling over my words. "Sometimes, if someone else does something bad that hurts someone else—especially someone else we love—then we, because we're related to them . . ." Where am I going with this? This is all wrong. I feel ashamed, that's what I'm really saying.

Suddenly his face kind of curdles. "I don't get it. Why would I feel ashamed when it's you who's told me all my life that he never even met me? You told me my dad did a runner before I was even born, but he didn't. I know he didn't, because Kelly showed me a picture of him holding me on the day that my dad and you brought me to visit her when I was two weeks old. She said that Dad didn't leave till I was nearly three weeks." He pulls the cuff of his shirt down and wipes away a tear.

I think back to the Facebook message. I was so adamant that Kelly not tell him about the fight and Liam being instrumental in Jamie's death that I forgot to tell her the other story I've always maintained: that Liam never met Zac. I forgot to tell her there was **that** secret too. I can't believe how stupid I was, not to think of that.

Zac's face is crumpling. "She said he was dead proud of me, that he couldn't wait to show me off. She said he loved me."

"And he did, Zac! He loved you so, **so** much."

He looks at me for a long time then, searching my face, then he looks straight ahead. "No, he didn't," he says flatly. "He didn't really love me. Why, if he loved me so much, if he was my dad for nearly three weeks, did he still leave me, then?"

THE TRAIN JOURNEY home is much quieter than the journey there. Zac falls asleep almost immediately, exhausted from all the emotion; and Teagan, after playing on my phone and fighting it for half an hour, follows, her head intermittently lolling onto Zac's shoulder and back up again.

I try to nod off too, but sleep won't come, so I watch the world whiz by outside the window for a while, trying to calm my thoughts with the trees and the fields and the cows, then I watch Zac and Teagan, the two of them completely dead to the world: Zac with his forehead against the glass, mouth open; Teagan with her head flung in the opposite direction now, her dark hair, which could be beautiful if she'd only brush it occasionally, swept across her face. Perhaps if I'd been able to comfort Zac, I think, to have said with conviction, **I'm sorry I lied to you, but he did love**

you, he really did, I'd feel better, but the fact is, I couldn't, because I don't believe that to be true anymore.

In fact, if anything, him saying those words—"He didn't really love me"—only makes that more solid in my head because he's right. How could he have done? How could Liam have truly loved my son, if he can stay away like he has? Not at least **try** to seek forgiveness from my parents, to make them see that even Jamie wouldn't have wanted this: for Zac to lose his father and Liam to lose his son.

But Liam **has** stayed away. He's never tried to seek forgiveness. And I feel an awful leaden feeling like wet concrete settle at the pit of my stomach at the thought that Zac is right and therefore this whole mission to find him is futile and will only hurt Zac more.

I'd like to stop it, now. All of it. It's too late for that, though. It's already hurt Zac; and the awful part is, I know there is worse to come.

28

Mick

For the first couple of years after Jamie died—
and still occasionally now—Lynda said that
she didn't want any new photographs of the family
in our house, because all she saw when she looked
at them was the space where our Jamie should be.
I used to agree, just so she felt understood. But it
wasn't the photographs without him that bothered
me, so much as the ones **with** him, since every
time I looked at those, I saw him die, over and
over and over again.

It would seem as though his face was coming
closer to me—that lovely, big Jamie grin that I'd
give my right arm to see one more time. And then,
just at the moment I felt it was safe to reach out
and touch it, it would morph into another face—a
face being thrown backward, or his face with all
the tubes taken out because he didn't need them
anymore, lifeless on a hospital bed. It lasted for
six months after he died. If I'd have told anyone,

they would have told me to go and get help. But I didn't talk to anyone about my suffering; never have, never felt I deserved it. And anyway the visions left me, until now.

Now they're back with a vengeance. It's like my mind is trying to test me—**How much can you take until you snap? How close do you have to get to the edge to finally confess?** The first one came a week ago when I was down here writing in this journal. I felt something sort of give in my head like a fuse being blown, and when I looked up from the page, there he was, my boy, his face coming toward me. It was glorious, and then, just at that point that I reached out to touch it—pow! It was being pounded from the side like a boxer in a ring; thrown back. A day or two later, the next vision came. In this one, I am in the pub, knocking back drink after drink. My face is getting ruddier, my eyes wilder, the edges more blurred. And all the time, Jamie is sitting at the other side of the bar, shouting, "Dad, Dad!" But his voice sounds like it's underwater, it's muffled and I can't hear it very well, and anyway, I'm too busy getting drunk. I'm too lost in the booze and sweet oblivion to take any notice of my son.

29

Zac

**Fact: Usain Bolt is the
fastest man on earth.**

I don't even know how it happened. All I know
is that I was staring into the plastic box, and
that there were only three fairy cakes left.

"Well, where did the others go, Zac?" It was
just my luck that Mr. Grimshaw (PE teacher) was
the one running the after-school cake sale today.
He's got it in for me anyway—this morning he
made me take my jumper off to do PE and told
me that his mum who is seventy-eight could run
faster than me. I don't care, I wasn't even trying.
"Did you eat them? That's pretty good going for
before the cake sale has even started."

I stared into the box, with the sick/starving feeling. I knew my face would be bright red, because
I could feel it and it was mega hot. It was as hot as
it was after dancing at Jason's mum's fiftieth birth-

day party, but without the dancing. I knew it was me who had eaten them too (and Teagan—she ate two of them), but I couldn't believe it. I couldn't even remember doing it. I just know that I came in this morning with ten chocolate fairy cakes (they were the best I'd ever made too—not too dry, with just the right amount of buttercream; I made them with Nan) and now there were only three. I'd have got away without anyone noticing, but just before going-home time, we all had to line up in the playground with the cakes we'd brought in and help Mr. Grimshaw put them out, ready for the sale at the end of the day. The cake sales are to raise money for the school; it's a different class's turn to do them every month and this month it's Dory class (my class—all the classes are named after fish). You have to lay all the cakes out on tables that we put out in the playground, so everyone can buy them after school.

I was still looking in the box, but only because I didn't want to look up at Mr. Grimshaw's face.

"I gave some to Teagan too," I said, but Mr. Grimshaw was helping Courtney get hers out now—he wasn't interested in my excuses.

"And Connor." That was a white lie, but I knew Connor wouldn't let me down if I asked him to be my alibi. (We're good friends now—even more so after I went to his party.) I just stood there. I wasn't sure if I was meant to get them out anyway, or just take my three cakes home. Neither seemed like the right thing to do.

Mr. Grimshaw finished helping Teagan get hers out (she'd brought a Swiss roll; it was from a shop and you had to cut it up, but it didn't matter), then leaned over the table and looked at me. He was shaking his head and smiling. "All right, Zac, get out what you've got then. It's better than nothing. Just, you know, try and hang on till the sale actually starts next time, won't you?" I put the three cakes out as quickly as I could, took my plastic box, and left. I didn't stay for the sale, even though Nan had given me a pound to spend—I was too angry.

I've been feeling angry a lot since we went to Manchester. I was mad with Mum for lying to me (and I hate being mad with my mum; if you're mad, you can't relax and have fun) and I was mad with myself. I wasn't mad with Teagan, but we were having a break from the Find Dad mission club. I wasn't saying I definitely didn't want to do it, but I wasn't feeling very excited about it anymore, and I didn't know what the point was. My dad spent nearly three weeks of his life with me and still didn't want to be my dad, so obviously the magic bond hadn't worked for us. Or maybe he just didn't like the look of me.

It made me think about the facts in my **Factblaster** book—maybe they weren't all a hundred percent true. How did they test them anyway and how could you be sure? Who says that babies look like their dads so that their dads stay around? I didn't know what to believe anymore.

It felt like loads of troughs had come at once— and not just for me. Teagan heard last week that her dad is moving away to Sheffield. He didn't even ask her if she minded, he just said he was going because Gayle from Ladbrokes' son lives there and she wants to be near him. It's totally unfair, though, because Teagan is her dad's daughter— doesn't he want to be near her? Teagan says she's all right about it and that she never wants to see him again anyway, but I can tell she's upset. I don't even know if she wants to help me find my dad now. I just know that, probably, the FDM is off.

Never mind, it was good while it lasted. We did a lot of cool stuff. If we hadn't done the mission, we'd never have gone down the docks and met Barrel, or called up Finder Genie; we wouldn't have got to go to the Sea Life Center, or Manchester, or done loads of stuff.

I started to walk back home. I didn't want to get on the bus with Aidan Turner and Luke Shallcross and everyone on it. I just wanted to be on my own and not think about anything for a bit. I wanted to get back home, have my tea, and watch telly. I decided to go a different route through the park. There was no reason, I just fancied a change of scenery, but God must have been against me, or I must have done something to make him angry at me, because then something bad happened.

I'd got halfway across the park—I was even feeling a bit better—when someone shouted, "Oi, Jabba," from behind me. My heart kicked in my chest, but I didn't turn around, I just ignored them. But then they said, much louder this time, "Oi, Jabba, can we have one of your cakes? Oh no, we can't, because you ate them all, you fat lardy git!"

I didn't know what to do. I couldn't run, because then they'd just run after me, and I didn't want to turn around and give them the satisfaction. So I just carried on, looking straight ahead. I wasn't thinking anything. I was using all my brainpower to keep walking, to get closer to the other end of the park and to the street, where there would be people so they couldn't start on me.

"Fat Mango!" someone called then, but it wasn't Connor, I could tell—they weren't saying it like an affectionate nickname. "Fat Man-gooo, yes, we're talking to you." I started walking faster then; there was an alleyway not far away that I knew came out onto the street, and I thought if I could just get to that and run through it, then I could get to the street a lot faster, and if they were still picking on me, I could just shout out dead loud. But I could hear footsteps getting faster behind me; I could hear them laughing.

"I don't know why you're so scared." It was Luke Shallcross, I could tell, because his voice is all croaky (it's because it's breaking—he's going through puberty early). "You're so fat after all them cakes, if we punched you, you wouldn't feel it anyway."

"Yeah, there's about three meters of flab to get through first," said another voice—Aidan Turner. "There are some advantages to being as fat as you, you know. There'd have to be, otherwise you'd probably feel like killing yourself." They started laughing even louder then, but I started crying, I couldn't help it, and I looked around just to check how close they were, but it was the worst thing I could have done, because Aidan Turner saw my face. "Aw, don't cry!" He was laughing his head off; it sounded like a donkey. "We've got something to help with the flab. We've got something to help with those moobs, Jabba. You'll be glad you bumped into us."

I just started running then. There was no point trying not to anymore. I was nearly at the edge of the alleyway. My MO was I'd peg it as fast as I could up there and I'd be safe, I'd be in public. But it was no good. They were after me. There was nothing I could do. It was like the rain—there's just nothing you can do about that either. Some things are out of your control.

Suddenly it was like when you're in the sea and a massive wave comes that you're not expecting and it knocks you right over, because I was on the floor with I don't know how many people on top of me, and my face was against the stones and it hurt like mad. "Get off me! Fuck off!" But they were just laughing and laughing and mimicking me: **Get off, fuck off.**

"Get it out," said one of them. "Quick, get the bra out!" I was kicking my legs and butting my head back, but there were three of them—it was Luke Shallcross, Aidan Turner, and Daniel Lancaster from the other class—and only one of me, and I couldn't get them off me. Then one of them dangled something in my face while one took my jumper off, pulling the arm so it ripped.

"This is just to give you some support," he said. "It's a G cup, so just your size."

It was a white lacy bra. I knew what was coming and I closed my eyes. I did a silent prayer to Jesus for it to be over quickly. I told him I would try harder to lose weight, try harder in PE, not get biscuits out of the secret cupboard, not be mad with my mum anymore, if he could just make it stop.

My belly was now on the gravel and the stones were sticking into my skin. I was trying so hard to get off the ground, but when I lifted my body up, they put the bra around me. "You should wear this in PE, so your boobs don't wobble around, Jabba."

"Video it!"

"I am, hang on!"

"This is fucking hilarious!"

I did one last massive kick of my legs, and it must have got whoever was on top of me right in his Jacobs because he shouted, "Ow! Shit! You little fucker," but I could breathe again, which was a start! I managed to get to my knees. I reached my hands behind me, but I couldn't undo the bra, there wasn't time.

"He can't get it off," they were all saying, laughing. Luke was laughing so much he was crying. Tears were rolling down his face like a baby. "If you're gonna start wearing a bra, then you need to know how to undo it, Jabba!"

I didn't run then, not then. I just picked up my stuff and held the jumper in front of me so you couldn't see the bra. My face and my stomach stung like crazy from all the little stones digging in and the bra was digging into my side too—the hard wires at the front were all twisted—but I was determined not to cry. "You're just all tragic," I said and they copied me: **You're just all tragic.**

"Good luck getting your bra off!" Aidan shouted. "It looks nice, though, and we've got it on video."

And **then** I ran, faster than I've ever run. To the light, and the street. To home.

30

Juliet

With just the two of us in the house, the dynamic can be intense. There's nowhere to hide if there's tension or an argument; no other parent or sibling to turn to, or moan at, to share the emotional load of just being someone's parent, someone's son. I've never felt that more than this week when, since Manchester and finding out that I lied to him, Zac has been so angry with me. He's not said anything. It's not Zac's style to lash out, but he's shown me in his defiant buying of sweets on the way home from school, not bothering to hide the empty wrappers in the pockets of his school trousers; his refusal to get up in good time for the bus, so that I'm rushing him and nagging him to get dressed and out the door. I know he's hurting, but there's no easy way out of this. If we were going to venture down this road, there was always going to be pain.

It's like the weather knows about the turbulence

in our house and in our lives, because it doesn't know what to do. One minute, it's the brightest spring sunshine, the sky china blue, making even our estate look like a place where good things can happen; the next, there's a downpour—as heavy as if a rugby team were busy emptying buckets of the stuff from the sky. But the sunshine won't stop; it just carries on blazing straight through that rain, as if competing as to who will win out.

It's during one of these bizarre blazing-sunshine-cum-torrential-downpours, a few days after we got back from Manchester, that I am looking in the cupboards above the wardrobe for some spare lightbulbs, of all things, and I find the shoe box. I'd completely forgotten about it. I never really go in this cupboard anymore, but rummaging among Zac's old board games and boxes containing everything from his old school-books to an Ikea toolkit (and yes! lightbulbs), I find an old Dolcis shoe box with **Me, Pregnant** scrawled across it in black marker pen. My heart jolts with the sudden collision of my past and my present. Zac won't be home for twenty minutes or so, so I take it out, sit on the bed, and open it. It contains, among other things, the little hospital wristband Zac wore when he was born: **male baby of Juliet Hutchinson,** it says in blue pen. When the midwife handed me this gorgeous ten-pound bundle, she asked me what we were going to call him, but at that time we couldn't decide between Zachary and Elijah—"Since when were you bloody religious?" Dad had said—and so the midwife wrote **baby of . . .** until our baby became Zachary James, which, of course, now seems like some sort of premonition.

Also in the box is the tiger sleepsuit that my brother gave to him and that we brought him home in, and Foxy, his first-ever toy. I hold it close and sniff it. It still smells of baby, of my baby—or that could be my imagination—but either way, I find it so hard to believe that that baby is going to be eleven in three weeks, that he starts secondary school in September, that very soon, my little big man will be an actual man and it's all going so fast.

Far. Too. Fast.

Looking for his dad, finding out what he's found out in the past few weeks, has, I fear, forced him to grow up faster than he's ready to, forced the "little" out of "little big man"—a name I've always called him, in my mind at least. I don't know what I thought I was protecting him from by telling him that his dad left before he was even born. I wonder—no, I **know**—that it wasn't just him I was protecting; it was myself too.

There's something else in the box: a small brown envelope with a set of Polaroids inside. They're pictures that Liam took of me every four weeks or so in my bra and knickers as my bump grew. I look so happy in them, so comfortable with my body, pointing down at my belly, grinning in the one where I'm just beginning to show. And there's another photo taken in Mum and Dad's back garden. It's of Liam bending down and kissing my bump, a starburst of sunlight bouncing off his black, glossy hair, like a crown of light, like something religious, and he's looking at the camera with a surprised, delighted look on his face and I'm looking down, giggling at him. I thought I'd be relieved when Zac said the search for his dad was off: **Thank God, I've got away with it for a little while longer.** But here's the thing: I don't feel relieved, I feel disappointed, because I realize it's not just Zac who wants answers—it's me. I need to know why he never came back. I need to know why he never fought for us or wanted to see his son at least. Most of all, I need to know what really happened that night, because I realize I never actually asked him the details. I just took what Mum said as fact.

The doorbell rings, making me jump. **That's weird**, I think. **Who would be ringing the doorbell at this time?** Zac has a key to get in. I quickly put the top back on the shoe box and hurry down the stairs toward the front door. The sun is blazing through the glass, as if there hadn't been even a drop of rain just ten minutes ago. The air feels still, and I can see a shape—there are two people—but it's what I hear that turns my stomach to ice: this animal cry. My baby.

I fling open the door.

"I just found him like this, on the corner of Guildford Street, so I walked him home . . ." There's a woman—I'd say she's in her sixties—standing on my doorstep with her arm around Zac.

"Oh God." My baby, what have they done to my baby? "Thank you, thank you so much . . ."

"Let your mum look after you now, pet," she says, rubbing Zac's arm and smiling a sad, regretful smile.

The woman leaves and I take Zac inside. He's sobbing so much he can't speak, not even to tell me what happened. His face is grazed down one side, and there are spots of blood and particles of grit almost pushed into the soft plumpness of his cheek. He's wearing his jumper—which is covered in dirt and ripped—but holding his shirt for some reason, and he's doing that hiccupping crying again, just like he did in Manchester, and I hate it. I can't bear the sound. I sit him down on the bottom step of the stairs, pull him into me, and hold him like that, rocking him and stroking his hair, until finally the hiccups subside and he's calm.

I don't realize about the bra until much later, when I have to help him get it off and I see the deep welts it's left on his skin. I clean the grazes on his stomach and face with cotton wool, ever so gently picking out the bits of grit, and put Sudocrem on them, then I put him in his pajamas and settle him on the settee with some toast. He doesn't want to talk about it, he says. He just wants to eat his toast and for me not to ask any questions—not now.

We watch telly for a while, him lost in a program about the feeding habits of sharks and me in my thoughts about how on earth anyone could be so evil to my son, who has never knowingly done anything to hurt anyone else in his whole life. Then I ask him what he wants for tea—I say he can have anything he likes. He says chicken Kiev and oven chips, so I go to Costcutter. It's four forty-five p.m. and just beginning to rain again. I didn't think to put on a coat when I left—my head's all over the place—so I run across the estate to the shop, covering my head with a plastic bag—and it's there, already, like it always is, the little voice, the craving; anything to ease the horrible, empty churning in my stomach, to have some feeling other than this one.

Mr. Singh is busy serving a man with his child, making small talk about the "schizophrenic" weather, and I make a beeline for the freezer. I'm hoping he hasn't even seen me come into the shop, so I open the freezer, take out the chips and the chicken Kiev, which, I tell myself, I can't really afford anyway, as I don't get paid until next week, and it's for Zac, to help him, to cheer him up after the world has been so cruel to him—surely the world can forgive me this? I wait until I can hear the shop bell indicating the man and his child have left, and I quickly stuff the food into the plastic bag and then under my fleece, freezing cold against my T-shirt, and walk briskly to the door.

"Hang on a minute!"

I stop dead. Everything seems to stop: the rain, the world, my heart.

"I wasn't born yesterday!"

I am frozen, glued to the spot, out of ideas as to what to do, and so, like a slow surrender, I simply let the bag with the food inside fall from underneath my fleece onto the floor and I burst into tears. "I'm sorry!" I cover my face with my hands with the shame, like a child who's hiding: **I can't see you, so you can't see me.** "I'm so sorry! I was going to pay for it," I say, which is both patently untrue and completely pathetic in the circumstances.

Mr. Singh picks up the food from the floor, quickly and flustered, as if he is as shocked as me with this turn of events.

"I'll have to call the police, Juliet," he says, his voice steady and calm. "You give me no choice. I shall have to call the police and bar you from this shop."

The horror and seriousness of the situation piles on top of me in an awful avalanche of fear and self-loathing: What have I done? What have I done to my life? Mine and Zac's life? I'm his mother—he already feels let down by his father, by me for lying to him. He only **has** me; what will this do to him if he finds out?

"No, please!" I've still got my hands clamped over my face like a child. "Please, please don't call the police, Mr. Singh. I will pay for it, and give you more. I will do anything, anything at all. I will never do it again. Just please don't call the police. I've had a terrible day, I'm sorry, I'm so sorry." And then I sob, because there's nothing else for it. It feels like my life has just come crashing down around my feet, along with the oven chips and the chicken Kiev, and there is nothing, nothing to be done.

Mr. Singh stands in silence, the food in his hands, looking at me as I sob like a baby, like Zac did just half an hour earlier. Finally, I dare to uncover my face for a second, and wipe my eyes and then my nose with my fleece sleeve. "Zac came home today," I say between sobs, "and he'd been bullied so badly. Some boys had put a bra on him, Mr. Singh. They pinned him down, scraping his face into the concrete, and made him put on a bra, can you believe it? Who would do that to my beautiful child? And he was so devastated, so humiliated. I just wanted to cheer him up. And so I asked him what he wanted for his tea—I told him he could have anything he wanted—and he said oven chips and chicken Kiev, but I couldn't

really afford it and I wasn't thinking straight, I
don't know why I did it . . . I wish, God, I wish I
hadn't . . ."

Mr. Singh puts the food on the counter. I think
he's going to say, **I'm sorry, Juliet, I really am,
but you leave me no choice**, then go to call the
police. But he doesn't. Instead, he puts an arm
around me, then, when I don't stop crying, puts
both arms around me and holds me while I sob
onto his shoulder. "If you promise," he says, very
slowly, whispering into my hair, "if you swear on
your life never, ever to do this again, then I won't
call the police—and you can have the food. But
if I ever catch you doing it again, I shall call them
with no hesitation, okay?"

I nod quickly, stepping back and uncovering my
eyes. "Definitely. Definitely. I swear on my life."

"This shall just be our secret, okay? We'll put it
down to a very bad day."

I tell Mr. Singh I'll give him the money anyway, when I get paid, and then I walk—slowly,
still shaking, trying to give my face time to look
normal again—across the estate to home and to
Zac. The rain is falling heavily now, the sunshine
gone again, and the sky is the kind of purple-gray
that tells you it's not going to stop anytime soon.
And I think of him sitting there, at home; how
sad, how let down he must feel; how out of control his life must seem. And I know I can't go on
like this anymore; **we** can't go on like this—this

family. I can't let another day go by where my son believes his dad left simply because he didn't want him. I have to tell him the whole truth.

I let myself in with my key. "I'm back," I call out. "I got your chicken and chips. I'll just put them in the oven."

"Okay." Zac's voice is still small, still buried in trauma. "Thanks, Mum."

I pass the lounge—the door is ajar—and I can just see the soles of Zac's feet and his red, Man U pajama-clad legs sprawled across the settee, hear the soothing, familiar burble of kids' TV. He's only just recovering, I think, and now I'm about to blow his world apart good and proper, but I don't have a choice. He has to know and I, as his mum, have to be the person to tell him. I want to be that person—I realize that now.

I turn on the oven, then spend far too long arranging Zac's tea on a baking tray, trying to get each chip equidistant apart, putting off the inevitable. I close the oven door, eventually, and lean with my fists on the kitchen worktop, my knuckles white through my skin. I look out at the drab estate—the shrunken and only world that Zac has ever known. Then after a deep breath, I walk into the front room in three decisive strides. Zac, still with white Sudocrem smears on his face, looks up at me with his father's eyes. "Zac? Can you switch off the TV?" I say. "There's something I need to tell you."

31

Zac

**Fact: The first English cookery book
was written in 1390 and it was called
The Forme of Cury.**

I knelt down in front of Uncle Jamie's grave. I
know they say you're not meant to sit on people's
graves, but I knew Uncle Jamie wouldn't mind this
one time. I can't explain why, I just did. What I
had to say to him was too important.

I got out the recipe I'd written down—I'd put
it in a plastic cover specially, because my Marmite
pasta one hadn't lasted two minutes; it got rained
on and all the ink splodged everywhere—and I
slipped it under the stone angel, so it wouldn't
blow away.

It's spiced cod and scallop linguine, I said
(not out loud, just in my head, even though I was
actually talking to Uncle Jamie in heaven). **It was
one of my dad's favorite recipes and would definitely have been on the menu if you'd ever got**

your ambition of opening a seafood restaurant together.

You might think my uncle Jamie wouldn't want anything from my dad, that he'd hate his guts because it was his fault he's dead, but it's not like that, I know. It's why I've come here—to explain. I closed my eyes like I was doing a prayer, but I said it all in my head so that the other people wandering around the graveyard wouldn't think I was a crazy beast.

Uncle Jamie, I know how you died now. I know you didn't fall off a bridge, breaking your spinal cord. Everyone just told me that because they thought I'd be too upset by the truth, which is that you died because of a fight—a fight that my dad started and that meant your brain got too injured to survive.

Uncle Jamie, you have to listen to me. I know my dad might have started the fight (because he was really drunk) and that he did a stupid thing, especially because you were younger than him and he'd promised my mum and nan that he'd look after you, but it was just a terrible accident, you have to believe me, and I know my dad will be so, so, so sorry that you ended up dead, that he will have missed you, that he even probably loved you, because you were his top friend.

I started to tell him stories to remind him of stuff; stories my mum told me about him and my dad. I told him about the time he and my dad drove to Sheffield in my dad's Škoda and how it broke down, but how they ended up getting on so well with the tow truck man who picked them up that they went to his party that night and kept in touch after that. I reminded him of when they went on a three-day fishing trip to Scotland together on the trawler my dad worked on, just them two and the seagulls, for three whole days! I told him about the dream they had of opening a seafood restaurant; how my dad was dead jealous but proud of him going to catering college, but how my uncle Jamie would tell him some of the recipes he'd learned and how they'd play **MasterChef**. My dad and Uncle Jamie would cook the same dinner and Mum, Nan, and Grandad would give them both marks out of ten (they weren't allowed to know who cooked what), but my uncle Jamie was always best at puddings and baking and my dad was best at seafood. (It's because he worked at sea. He had the sea in his veins, like me.)

I told my uncle Jamie all this, because I wanted him to remember what good friends they were and how there was no way my dad would have meant to get drunk and into the fight where my uncle ended up dead; how he would have missed him, I knew it, probably still did—like I would miss Teagan till the end of my life if she died. I told him how I knew Nan blames Liam, but she only hates him so much because she loved Jamie so much.

(Mum explained it to me—the hating makes the loving when he's not here a bit easier, because it's something else to think about. It's like when I'm scared of getting bullied at school, I play the dad film in my head and it helps, it really does. It's just a shame my nan does hating instead of playing a nice film in her head, but maybe that could change.)

I stopped talking to my uncle Jamie then, and I stood up to go. I thought I wouldn't be surprised if my uncle Jamie knew all this anyway. 'Cause God knows all the truths in the world. He can see right into your head and your heart, so I bet the people up in heaven with him can do the same.

A FEW DAYS after the bra thing (just saying the word "bra" makes my face go hot now), and Mum telling me the truth about my dad, all of Year 6 went on a school trip to Bolingbroke Castle. Except Aidan Turner and Luke Shallcross; they got suspended for what happened. My mum made me tell on them. Actually, she didn't make me; I decided I had to. Teagan said the only thing bullies are scared of is being told on, because they think you never will. So I did and they got a massive bollocking, and I realized then that that was what I was most scared about—but it's happened and so far it's all right, they haven't murdered me! And life doesn't feel as scary as it did before it happened, so maybe telling was a good idea.

It's a shame the video they took had already got shown around a few people—including Aidan's brother and his friends, who are in Year 8—so now I'm known as "bra boy." It's embarrassing, but it's not ruined my life. I've got Teagan and I've got Connor, and I've got all the truth about my dad now and even though I'd never have chosen to have Aidan and his mates do what they did, and even though I'd never say it out loud to anyone, not even Mum, it was sort of worth it, because if they hadn't, then maybe she wouldn't have told me the truth. I still want to find him. I've still got my mission. He might turn out to not want to know me, but at least I'll know.

"Right," said Mrs. Bond. She was in her normal, nonteacher clothes because she was coming on the school trip with us; she didn't look like a head teacher anymore, she just looked like a mum. "Can everyone find a partner, please, that you don't mind sitting next to on a coach for the next hour?"

I was already standing next to Teagan; she's the only person I'd ever want to sit next to. And anyway, she's so little, it's not a squeeze. If I sit next to anyone else, I have to clench my bum cheeks in and worry all the time that my arm's touching theirs and annoying them. Then I can't relax for the whole time I'm there, which is really annoying for me.

We all put our bags in the special drawer under

the bus, then we had to stand behind our coach partner so we were all in a line and get onto the bus. Teagan was in front of me and Connor was behind.

"You might regret sitting next to me today, I've got a really bad cold," said Teagan, as we got on the bus. You could tell as well; she was coughing a lot.

"Have you got your puffers?"

"Yeah."

"Wasn't your mum worried about you coming to school if you're poorly?"

"Yeah, but I didn't want to miss the trip. I already missed Skegness—I'm bored of it."

"Oh, right. Well, don't worry about sitting next to me. I don't catch colds; it's 'cause I eat loads of tangerines, my mum says."

"No, it's because you eat loads of everything," Connor said behind me, but I just told him to shut up. I didn't mind. It was even quite funny.

Bolingbroke Castle is just ruins now—I looked it up. It was built by Ranulf de Blondeville—his name is very funny. You can't believe how old the castle is or that there were real people living in it, doing normal stuff like eating their breakfast and brushing their teeth eight hundred years ago— even though they didn't have toothbrushes in 1220; they just had sticks to poke the bits of food out. We were going to look at the old walls of the castle, then go walking around the gardens and the woods. I sat down next to Teagan. Connor poked his head between our seats and stuck his tongue out so we turned around. "I've got a good idea," he said in one of his silly voices (he's got loads), pulling a silly face. "Let's go an hour away to look at a **wall**, shall we? Even though I've got one in front of my house." I laughed but in secret. I was excited. It was going to be more fun than normal school anyway.

It took about an hour and a half to get there—it would have taken only an hour but Emily Macdonald was travel-sick and so we had to stop. She tried to get it all in the paper bag, but it overflowed and went on Miss Farrell's lap and she had to pretend she didn't mind. Teagan didn't feel well either, but it was because of her cold, not feeling sick. She had to keep telling Connor to shut up behind us, so she could lean her head on the window and close her eyes. It felt weird not to talk about the dad mission when that's all we've talked about for ages, but I didn't feel like Teagan was in the mood, not just because she was poorly but because she thinks I should leave looking for my dad for a bit. She thinks I've got enough to worry about and that if my dad did get drunk and do fighting, that he might not be a good dad after all. I think another reason she's not in a good mood about it is because of her own dad. She's dead upset about him. She's not showing it, but I know.

The castle was pretty epic even though there

wasn't any castle there anymore, just walls. But we stood where the courtyard would have been and imagined all the rooms that went off it, then we went to where the main big hall would have been, while a lady with a really quiet voice gave us a talk about the history of the castle.

"And Ranulf de Blondeville built this castle when he came back from the Crusades in the 1220s . . ."

Next to me, you could hear Teagan's breathing. It sounded like she was whistling. I could even hear it over the lady's talking.

". . . and eventually, John O'Gaunt, Duke of Lancaster, inherited the castle and he became the guardian of Richard II when he became king at just ten years old."

"Gosh, can you imagine that, children?" said Mrs. Bond. "The responsibility of being king at your age?"

None of us could.

We saw the remains of the kitchen tower, where they would have prepared all the meals, and even the room where King Henry IV would probably have been born. It didn't look that comfy.

After the talk, we went for a walk in some woods and fields around the house. We had to go in our pairs, so I went with Teagan, but she couldn't walk that fast because her cold meant her asthma was bad and she was getting out of breath. She didn't want anyone to notice, though, so we walked a bit away from everyone, even though Mrs. Bond kept saying, "Zac and Teagan, keep with the group, please."

The walk was quite good. We had to do a nature trail, ticking off different names of trees and flowers, and I did a competition in my own head as to how many different ones I saw, but I couldn't really concentrate, because Teagan wasn't well. "I'm all right," she kept saying, but she was coughing loads and had to keep stopping to take her puffer—only it didn't seem to be working. And you could hear her making the whistling noise when she breathed, which was happening when she breathed out and when she breathed in. I tried to chat to her to take her mind off it and at first she was joining in, but then I realized she'd gone quiet. You need to worry when Teagan goes quiet.

"I think I should go and get the teacher," I said, looking to see if I could see our group because we were getting farther and farther behind. "You don't seem well at all."

"No, Zac, it's all right, I'm all right." Teagan can be stubborn as anything, she never wants to give up, but sometimes it's not sensible. "Just stop looking at me. Just ignore me," she said. But how can you ignore someone who can't breathe?

We carried on walking, but Teagan was coughing almost all the time now and kept having to stop. Then she started crying.

"Right, I'm getting Mrs. Bond," I said. I didn't

care that Teagan might be angry with me anymore, I just wanted to get someone to help. "You
stay here." My heart was pounding then—what if
she died? What if she died right here and I couldn't
save her life? I was probably more scared than I'd
ever been in my life, but I couldn't show it because
it wouldn't help Teagan if she knew I was panicking. Then Teagan sat down on the floor, but
not like she meant to, more like she couldn't even
stand anymore, and I had to try really hard not to
cry too then, because she couldn't breathe, she just
couldn't. She was trying to take in oxygen—you
could see her ribs through her T-shirt going up
and down—but the more she tried, the less she
could do it.

"Don't cry, Teagan." I crouched down next to
her. "You'll make it worse." I didn't want to leave
her now, so I looked around for if I could see anyone. I could see a group that looked like ours, but
they were ages away. "You're going to be okay,
okay?" I knew what I had to do then. "I'm going
to carry you."

I put my hands under her bum and I lifted her
up. She was so light, it was easy as anything, and I
carried her through the bushes and trees and down
the track toward the others, who I could see in the
distance. The time seemed to stretch. You could
just hear my footsteps and Teagan's horrible whistling and the breeze blowing through the trees,
like it was trying to breathe for her. And I was

trying to talk to her, to say anything to make her calm down. "Think about our mission, Teagan." I was walking as quick as I could with her in my arms, her legs banging against my side, but it was okay, it didn't even hurt. "You have to get better because we've still not found my dad, have we? We still have to do the mission. I need you." And then Mrs. Bond was there—I could see her standing with some of the other children—and I was so relieved, I nearly burst out crying. They were just standing, watching me carry her all the way up the track with their mouths open. They couldn't believe this was happening, you could tell. Then Mrs. Bond was walking quickly toward us, then she was running. "Miss!" I stopped and, using my knee, bumped Teagan back up in my arms because she was slipping. "You have to call an ambulance, she's having an asthma attack."

IT WAS LIKE the ambulance knew we were going to call because it arrived in literally five minutes. A lady and a man in green suits got out; they didn't take Teagan in the ambulance straightaway, though, they just came and knelt down next to her. One put a blanket round her and one a mask on her face, and they were talking so nice to her: "All right, sweetheart, just keep calm, my love, we're going to get you breathing easier in no time at all . . ." It made me feel better.

Mrs. Bond told everyone to stand back and give

Teagan and the ambulance people some space. Everyone was silent, we were just watching, even though it was scary as hell, and the muscles in Teagan's neck and stomach were sucking in, trying to get some air, and there was nothing you could do. It was the worst moment of my life. Then Connor started shouting: "She's fucking dying, you mangoes!" and Miss Huxley had to take him away. It's not his fault and he doesn't mean it; his Tourette's gets worse when he's stressed. But right then, I wanted to gag him. I put my hands over my ears. I just wanted him to shut up.

They normally only let one person in the ambulance with the patient, and Mrs. Bond had to go, but then Joe Hilditch said, "Zac saved her life, he should definitely be allowed to go," and then other people joined in, saying that I'd saved her life because I'd carried her to Mrs. Bond so they could call an ambulance.

I'd always wanted to go in an ambulance with the siren going, until it happened to me; then I realized that the siren only goes if it's an emergency and emergencies are only terrifying, not exciting.

They had the mask over Teagan's face still. It was making a noise like Darth Vader and steam was coming out of some holes in the side of it.

"I know it looks scary," said the lady paramedic, "but it's really going to help her breathe. It's called a nebulizer." I just nodded my head—I couldn't speak—and I tried to make Teagan's eyes over

her mask look at mine, and I tried, really hard, to
smile.

We got to the hospital, but the medicine in the
mask hadn't worked as much as they'd hoped and
so they had to give her another one, then move her
to another part of the hospital where they could
look after her better. And all the time that this was
going on, I was just concentrating on not showing I was upset, because it's really important to be
calm if someone's having an asthma attack, but
it was getting harder and harder not to, because I
seriously thought she was going to die.

Then, after they'd given her an injection and
the second Darth Vader mask, she started to get
better—it was a miracle. Her ribs weren't going up
and down so much, she was doing **so** well! And I
was doing a secret prayer in my head to God for
saving her life. Then, her mum turned up.

She was crying her eyes out already and I don't
blame her, she must have been really worried
about her child—but it was annoying because
Teagan was calm and now her mum was here, getting all emotional, and trying to hug her with her
cigarette-scented coat on. Hugs and cigarettes are
both bad for asthma.

"Hello, baby girl!" She was stroking Teagan's
hair with one hand and wiping away her tears with
another. "Oh, baby, I was so worried. I thought I
was going to lose you. I knew I shouldn't have let
you go on that trip, I knew . . ." Then her mum

turned and smiled at me, even though she was crying. "And you, Zac. You saved Teagan's life."

"Oh no, no, I didn't."

"I think you did," said Teagan, through the mask. I was so happy she could talk again, but then she started asking after her dad.

"Did you tell him?" she said to her mum. "That I was in hospital? Is he coming?"

Her mum looked sort of embarrassed and sad at the same time then. "I did ring him, baby," she said. "And I told him you were in the hospital. I told him to get down here, to see you . . . to be a father for once in his life, but what can I do? What can I do, Teagan?" She stopped talking. I was pleased. I didn't want Teagan getting all upset.

"And? So what did he say?" said Teagan. She could take her mask off now, but she was really tired after the asthma attack, and she needed to be as relaxed as possible.

"He said to tell you that he loves you," her mum said, after a long pause. "And that he's **thinking** of you." The way she said it, the expression on her face, she was dead mad at Teagan's dad, you could tell.

After a bit, Teagan's mum went to find the doctor to talk to. That was when Teagan burst into tears, because she's like me, she doesn't like crying in front of her mum, she doesn't like upsetting her or worrying her. She was looking away from me, trying not to cry in front of me too, because she always wants to be brave, does Teagan. But I knew why she was upset.

"You wish . . . you want your dad to be here, don't you?" I said after a bit and she nodded.

"I miss him," she said. "I really miss him, Zac. I just wish I didn't miss him so much, because it really hurts."

"I know," I said, because I missed my dad and I'd never even met him, so I couldn't even imagine how Teagan must feel.

"But . . ." I knew what I had to do now. It came to me in a brain wave. "Don't be sad, because when we find my dad—and we will find him, I promise—I'll share him. Like, maybe he can be sort of your dad too?"

She laughed then, even though she was still crying. "Okay," she said. And I was laughing a bit too. I think it was because I was nervous and happy, and relieved she wasn't going to die, all in one. "All right, that would be good."

I had to do it now, I had to find my dad. Not just for me and Mum, but for Teagan too.

32

Juliet

"Dad? It's me, Jules."

"Hello, love." There's a pause. "Everything all right?"

"Yeah, everything's fine."

"Good. I'll just get your mum, shall I?"

I'm lying on my bed and I hit the mattress in frustration as I hear him draw breath, about to yell down the hall. "No, Dad," I say.

"Oh, what?"

"Actually, it was you I wanted to speak to."

I thought I'd be able to handle everything on my own. For a short while after I told Zac everything I felt so light, so unburdened. I felt like this was the beginning of a new life for us; one without this secret weighing down on me, waiting for me in the small hours of the night and at the end of Zac's questions; hovering over us all at Christmas and birthdays and, yes, especially at Easter. He went instantly pale when I first began to explain everything. He was quiet for a very long time. And then came the questions.

Zac: "Was my dad a murderer then?"

Me: "No, Zac, absolutely not!"

Zac: "Do you blame him for Uncle Jamie dying?"

Me: "No, not anymore. I think he was stupid for getting so drunk and fighting, but I don't blame him, no. It was just a tragic accident and Uncle Jamie was just terribly unlucky. You know, things like that happening are very, very rare."

Zac: "But Nan and Grandad blame him, don't they?"

Me: "Yes, they did—and I did too at first—but that's why he left, darling, not because he didn't want you, but because it was so hard for him to stay in Grimsby."

And just because Nan and Grandad (Nan in particular) still blamed him, it didn't make him necessarily guilty, I said—of anything other than being reckless—and it was like this conversation wasn't as difficult as I'd feared; what had I been worried about for ten years? But then it was Zac, later that evening when he'd mulled it all over, who delivered the killer question, reminding me of exactly **what** I'd been worried about.

"But if Nan still hates him and maybe Grandad too, then even if we do find him, how is he going to be able to be my dad? How is he going to be able to come to Grimsby and come round to Nan and Grandad's for Sunday dinner and see me, and maybe live with us, and be in our family?"

And, of course, I didn't have an answer to that, and so just like that I fell apart, I couldn't handle it anymore: the responsibility, the feeling that it was just me and Zac and this humongous secret like a wild animal unleashed. Teagan being in hospital made everything feel even more fragile, more precarious, even though I have never been prouder of my son for doing what he did that day. But I needed somebody else to know the secret was out there, and Dad seemed to be the only person to tell. I was fully prepared for him to go ballistic: **How could you do this to your mother, Juliet? After everything she's been through?** But I felt I'd reached the edge and there was nowhere else to go. At the end of the day, Mum and Dad weren't the ones living with Zac every day, feeling his sadness and rejection. They weren't the ones alone with him on this journey, this quest to find Liam and to get answers to all the questions that had no doubt already done untold damage over the years, eating away at him and eroding his confidence. Ten years of not knowing who your dad is, or where he is, or if he loves you—I'd like to see my parents deal with that as well as Zac has. In fact, I'd like to see myself deal with that as well as Zac has.

So this is my chance to do this for him, to stand up to my parents and face whatever wrath comes my way, because I **am** a good mother. And I **do** know what's good for my child.

I tell Dad we need to meet. "Somewhere private, somewhere that Mum won't find out, or turn up to."

"I see," Dad says after a pause and I can hear him swallow. "I know . . . I know a good place." It's like he knows what's coming.

DAD IS ALREADY there when I get to the Jubilee Café that afternoon. Having not been down the docks in ten years, this is my second time in the past couple of months, and everywhere pulses with nostalgia; I have that disorientating sense of everything being different, and yet nothing having changed at all. This place certainly hasn't. Not one bit in ten years: same blue plastic seats stuck to the bare-tiled floor, same checked plastic tablecloths and naff paintings of seascapes and men with lobster pots on the walls. Dad is sitting in his old place too, at the back on the right—and yet where is the man I knew and loved from that time? My hero daddy who went to sea, with the wild black curly hair and whiskers stiff with sea salt that I loved to bury my face into, as he scooped me up, fresh off the boat. This one has gray hair, short back and sides; tired, sad eyes. Like a man defeated by life. I suddenly have a fierce sensation of missing the old dad.

"I got you a tea," he says, as I take off my

jacket and put it over the chair. Outside the two chalet-style windows that face us is a still, steel-gray sea, a murky horizon, broken only by a few brightly painted boats. "And took the liberty of getting you a toasted teacake too. You're not on a diet, are you?"

"What do you think?"

"I think yes, but you'll have it anyway, just not eat for the rest of the day," he says and I laugh—we both do—and that moment of being known, that small, father-daughter intimacy, feels so incredibly precious. It's been so long.

"So this is nice." Dad speaks first, but his eyes—the only part of his face I can see over his mug of tea—look scared. I want to get this over with.

"Dad, you know when we came on Easter Saturday and Zac was asking questions about Liam and it all went a bit wrong and you and Mum both got upset?"

"Mum got upset," he corrects with a firmness that surprises me but encourages me to go on.

"Yes, well, that's what I wanted to talk to you about. It's about Liam." Over his cup of tea, his eyebrows rise; an alarm is raised. "Dad, Zac wants to find him," I say. "More than that, he's started looking for him." He puts the tea down. I force the last words out. "And I've said I'll help him."

For I don't know how long (but long enough for the bloke in the overalls at the counter—the only other person in here—to order his tea and

sit down), Dad is silent. There's no going ballistic about Mum, no recriminations or **what have
you done**s. And it's strange, but in that moment,
I suddenly see what I've always known: that Dad
wouldn't be angry with me because, apart from in
those first few weeks after Jamie died, there hasn't
been any anger from him. He's never supported
Mum on her blame crusade (although to be fair,
he's never challenged her either); he's merely gone
along with it. For him, instead of anger, there is
just that deep, deep sea of sadness that I can never
seem to reach across. I've always sensed he's on
a different plane of grief to Mum, but he's never
come out and said which one.

"He's desperate for answers, Dad; and for the
facts—you know what he's like with his facts. It
was getting harder and harder to keep information
from him and I just didn't want to do it anymore.
I couldn't. It felt like too much of a responsibility to keep it up. And he's desperate for a father
figure." I'm rambling, the words are coming in a
torrent, but it's such a relief to get them out—even
if I'm not being a hundred percent honest about
how far I've already gone down the road to finding
Liam. "Not just a father, but a dad. It's heartbreaking. Do you know what I found?" Dad is cupping
his mug, his head bowed, but I can see the tension
in his face. "I found this file that he and Teagan
made, listing all the dad-aged men they knew,
and how they'd rate as dads; who would make the

best one . . . There are dads of kids from school in there . . . Mr. Singh, who owns bloody Costcutter on our estate!"

"How far's he got?"

"What?"

"How far has he—you and Zac—got, you know, in finding him?" says Dad, not meeting my eyes.

"Not very far." I'm still tentative, not knowing what Dad is thinking, how far I can go with this. "You'll know, since that awful Easter lunch, that I've told him some stuff—that he's got the same eyes as him, that Liam was a deckhand but that what he really wanted to be was a chef. Zac loved that," I say, remembering how his face lit up. "He loved the fact that they shared the same ambition."

The same ambition as Jamie too, I can see Dad thinking.

"Anyway . . ." I stop. Maybe I've already said too much. "I just need you to know, but to hold off telling Mum for now. I'm not saying you need to help us find him, just please don't tell Mum, okay?" But he's not saying anything. "Dad, say something. Are you angry with me?"

He shakes his head but as if he still isn't taking this in; he's lost in his own thoughts, and the worst of it is that I still haven't told him everything. What was the point of coming here today and not telling him everything? I won't get this chance again.

Dad is rubbing his face with his hands now; he looks like he might cry. There I was thinking he'd go mad at me, and he's just going to cry. I lean forward and speak as quietly as I can, even though there are only us and one other person here, because I am still frightened there is about to be an almighty explosion. I can't believe he is just going to sit here, looking so lost.

"Dad, he knows everything," I say then. "Because I told him. He knows that Liam didn't leave until he was nearly three weeks old, he knows what happened that night with his dad and Jamie . . . He knows everything."

And then Dad does it—he puts his face in his hands and his shoulders shudder as he starts to cry.

He mumbles something, but so quietly that I don't hear it. Then he draws breath in through his teeth like it takes all his mental power to say the next bit.

"It's my fault."

"No, no, Dad, it's not your fault."

"Yes, it is," he says again, looking at me, tears trembling in his eyes. "It is my fault."

"But, Dad, you couldn't have known what Liam was going to do that night," I say. "You couldn't have stopped what went on, any more than I could have—you weren't even there. It was a tragic accident. But that's all it was: an accident. A tragic accident."

But Dad is shaking his head vehemently. "No, it's my fault. It is. It's mine."

And I understand then why he's behaved so oddly all this time. Just as I blame myself for not being there for Zac, for not being able to protect him from the bullies, he blames himself for not protecting Jamie from Liam or what happened; he blames himself for not being there that night.

33

Mick

One morning, in late July after the June that Jamie died and Liam left Grimsby, Lynda came into the kitchen, holding a letter. She handed it to me over the breakfast table with a shaking hand. "How dare he? How has he the audacity?" She was seething, the words spitting from between her teeth. "He knew there was every reason we'd see it before Juliet—and he expects us to **give** it to her?"

I looked at it. There was no mistaking that sloping, left-hand scrawl, and anyway, since Jamie died, I'd been expecting this; I always knew we'd hear from him again. I presumed, sooner or later, that he'd call Juliet. But clearly, even if that was the case, she hadn't responded, so this was his only remaining method of communication.

"Perhaps he didn't think we'd recognize his writing," I said. I felt sick and hot.

I was in the middle of my breakfast. I put my

spoon down and turned the envelope over in my hands, looking up at Lynda as if for some idea as to what to do with it. She looked back at me, incredulous.

"Well, rip it up then," she said, appalled. "Because I don't know about you, but I'm not interested in one word that man has to say—he makes me sick—and if he thinks Juliet is going to know he even sent it, he's got another think coming."

She stared at me for a moment or two longer, and when she realized I wasn't going to do any such thing, she marched out of the kitchen in disgust, calling me spineless—which, of course, I knew was true.

I didn't read it that day—I couldn't bear to, for reasons that were different from Lynda's—but, obviously, she didn't know that. Two days later, however, and I couldn't resist. It was like an act of self-harm. I wanted to take that letter and metaphorically beat myself over the head with it. I can remember unfolding the piece of A4, my fingers sliding with sweat as his writing revealed itself: black ink, tall, thin. It was a piece of him, a reminder that this wasn't going away; the truth of it all, what I'd done, what I'd not done, not said. The utter and total weakness in me.

The letter was two sides long, but I only made it through the first page, which was one apology after another, him saying he understood that what he'd done was unforgivable, but that he loved them; he only wanted a chance to be heard, if not forgiven. He just wanted a chance, that was all. **It's the not being able to hold you and Zac, not being able to touch you that's the worst,** he wrote. **I've got a constant pain in my chest with the longing.** That did it for me; I couldn't carry on. The thing was, he didn't even need to say it; I could feel the longing for both of them in every millimeter of that pen stroke. There was no address, but there was his mobile number written in the top right-hand corner. Obviously he knew Juliet had it, didn't need reminding of it. But then it wasn't meant as a reminder. It was a desperate appeal for her to get in touch—but she never would, because she'd never know he'd written a letter at all.

Me folding that letter and putting it back in its envelope was the moment at which I think I loathed myself the most—the most I've **ever** loathed myself. Because this letter meant another secret to add to the secrets I was already keeping about what really happened that night. He'd reached out, with all the risks of rejection that entailed, laid himself open, pretty much begged for a chance to be part of Juliet's and Zac's lives, and because of me, they'd never know about it.

Oddly, I didn't feel that guilty about Zac at that time. He was too little to know any different; to miss what he'd never had. But Juliet—she was different. You could see her mourning the life she thought she'd have every day. Losing that spark she'd always had—certainly any dreams she ever had of going to university, becoming a teacher. She'd make a fantastic teacher.

Me and Lynda had lost our son and, God knows, that was hard enough. But our Juliet, she'd lost her brother **and** the father of her child—the man she loved. I could have done something about that—but in order to save my own back, I didn't. You couldn't get much lower and I knew it. I felt it every time I looked at her.

Five more letters arrived in the following year or so, each of them harder to open, harder to read. It felt like Liam's yearning for Zac in those letters grew at the same rate as my love for him—for this child who lived in my house for the first year of his life, who I saw smile and walk and laugh properly for the first time, when his own father was missing it all. My guilt grew too; but my resolve to do the right thing, to tell the whole truth—since I knew if and when I did, it could mean me losing everyone, including Zac—waned. I couldn't, I couldn't. I couldn't bear to look my daughter in the eye either, knowing what I did about that night; those letters; what I'd done.

The more time passed, the less I could imagine ever telling—that possibility was floating away from me like an iceberg on the sea and the farther away it got, the more I hung on to Lynda's words: **He was always no good. Just like his father, he was—it would have come out in the end. The**

whole family is better off without him. I never believed those words before Jamie died; I didn't even believe them when I said them, to Liam's face in the hospital corridor. I regretted them the instant they left my mouth because I knew why I'd said them, and it wasn't because they were true.

There were no letters for a couple of years. Zac turned two, three, and then suddenly, at the beginning of 2009, a letter arrived with the postmark **Northallerton Barracks, West Yorkshire** on it. Liam had joined the army. He'd been posted to Afghanistan as an army chef.

> **I wanted to do something drastic to prove to you and Zac that I was a man, I suppose, that I wasn't like my dad, that I was made of different stuff. Most of all, though, I needed to prove it to myself. When Zac was born and I fell in love with him instantly, I'd never felt more confident. My love for him and for you was so huge and real that I knew I'd never let you down. I knew it. I trusted it one hundred percent and it was the best feeling in the world. But then what happened happened that night and your dad let me know in no uncertain terms that I was my father's son and that I'd already turned out like him, and I believed him. I felt like, who was**

I kidding? I was my dad, through and through; I'd let you all down and you were better off without me. But that fight I started was the first and last fight I have ever started. I know my regret about the consequences of it won't change a thing, but I need to tell you this. I need you to know I've never thrown a punch since. It's taken me a long time and a lot of soul-searching, but I believe with all my heart now that four years is enough to prove I never will. I believe I am a good person, Juliet, that I could be a good father too—but do you? That's the question. Can you believe me?

I forced myself to read on. He explained that he was on his first tour of Afghanistan; that it gave him great satisfaction to be boosting the soldiers' morale, but that he'd lost friends already, he'd seen horrors, had to cook on the front line too—had to be a soldier, in short. After that, I didn't dare open any letters. What if he got injured or even killed on the front line (it seemed unthinkable, but then I'd already lost my son, and unthinkable things happen to people every day) and I'd never owned up to my part in that night? Then there was what I'd said to him in the heat of the moment in that hospital corridor; how it had destroyed him and driven him away. How could I live with myself, after that, if he died thinking I really believed that of him? Especially when, actually, I only said it because it was easier to tell him **he** was just like **his** father than admit the truth: it's **me** who's the chip off the old block.

After that, three more letters came, and I opened none of them. Until today . . .

Because I need clues—clues as to where Liam is now. If I can't do anything to change the past, then I need to change the future. I need to use all the power I have to reunite Zac with his dad, and my daughter with the only man she's ever loved. She's never said that, of course. But some things don't need to be said.

Lynda is out. The house is quiet except for the TV on very low—something about neighborhood wars; I couldn't tell you, because I haven't been watching it, I just always have the telly on low to drown out the voices in my head. My demons, which are there day and night.

I've kept the letters all this time, at the bottom of an old golfing bag. I took up golf when I got sober. It was something that could take me out of the house for long periods of time and keep me occupied, and the bag was somewhere I could guarantee Lynda would never go. There are three letters here—I've no idea if there will be anything in them that will help, but it's worth a try. I pray to God he hasn't emigrated to Australia or, perhaps worse, that he has written to say that if I should ever be man enough to come clean, he no longer wants to know.

The dates of the letters vary from 2010 to the most recent—2013. I start with that one—that surely will give me the most up-to-date information, potential clues as to where he might be now, if and when he left the army. I thumb the envelope open and slide out the folded paper, but something loose flutters to the floor. It's a check, made out to Juliet, signed by Liam, and the blood rushes to my face with emotions I can't fully identify: a toxic mix of shame and regret. How many more checks are hiding in the letters I was too much of a coward to ever open? How many did he send, before he realized they weren't being cashed? I open the letter: that tall, thin writing, and with it, his voice. It fills the bedroom; it fills my head. It fills me up with regret.

I am writing because I thought you'd want to know that as of this week, I fulfilled mine and Jamie's dream . . .

34

Zac

Fact: Maggots can be used to heal people's wounds. It's called "maggot therapy."

"Grandad, do you want to know one good fact about maggots?"

Grandad smiled, his eyes crinkling up in the sun. "Are there **any** good facts about maggots, Zac?" he said, opening up the Tupperware box to see them all wriggling around. (Maggots smell disgusting, like wet, stinky dog. When you open the box on the first fishing trip of the summer—like this one—they can make you nearly puke.) He put one on the end of the hook, then chucked some in the canal for extra bait. "Having said that, if there are, I know that you of all people will know one."

"I do," I said, as Grandad cast my rod for me. (I'm only good at pole fishing. I still can't really do the reel that well.) "I know a really good one. Maggots can be used to heal people's wounds. Say, like, if someone is diabetic and their skin doesn't heal very quickly, the doctors can give them 'maggot therapy.'" (I looked it up under "maggot facts.") "It's where they put maggots on the wound so that the maggots clean it and it heals up quicker."

"Really? I didn't know that."

"See, I told you I had a good fact about maggots."

"I'm not sure I would classify it as good," Grandad said, casting his rod next. "I mean, it's good in that it's a fact I never knew, but I wouldn't fancy those horrible little grubs on my skin, would you, Zac? Urgh."

Grandad threw a few more maggots in and we waited. It was very quiet again.

"Grandad?"

"Shh." He put his finger to his lips and smiled at me, but longer than usual. "Let's just be quiet for a second, shall we? Just sit and enjoy the peace and each other's company. We can talk in a minute; we just don't want to scare off the fish at the beginning."

Normally I love the quiet when we go fishing; it's dead relaxing, especially if I've had a bad day at school. You might think fishing's boring, but it's not because even when you're doing nothing, you're excited that something might happen—and anyway, it's not quiet, there are loads of noises when you're silent and can notice them. Birds do crazy singing, for one thing—it's not a nice gentle tune like you think it is; their voices go up and down like mad, especially now, in the evening, like they're scrapping to be the loudest or the highest— and the fish blow bubbles that make a noise like if you do a fart in the bath, just a little one. Me and Grandad decided it. It made us laugh. I even like the midges that make the sky look like summer's starting, telling me there's loads of days like this coming, out fishing with Grandad. Today, though, I was nervous. I didn't like the quiet. I was trying to think of anything to say so we wouldn't have to be in it. I wished I could think of another fact.

You see, I knew Grandad knew that I knew about what really happened with my dad, but neither of us was saying anything about it and I couldn't relax. My mum told me she'd told him; she said there were going to be no more secrets, not anymore. To be honest, I'm still a bit mad with everyone for keeping such a big secret from me in the first place, but I know they did it to protect me. They didn't want me to know that they blamed my dad for Uncle Jamie dying and that that was why they really hated him—not just 'cause he abandoned us—or to know that my dad was someone who got into fights and got drunk. I **am** disappointed a bit. He didn't score well on Top Trumps for all that. But I still want to find him. I still need to meet him and know who he is; I still need to ask him in person why he never came back. It's like Teagan said in the hospital: while I don't know for sure, there's still hope that he could be a good dad, whereas Teagan knows for sure that hers isn't good. It feels really unfair. The thing I was worrying about now, though, was what Nan and Grandad were going to say about the fact that I was still going to look for him.

"Now, you mustn't worry about Grandad," Mum had said to me, after Grandad had called to ask if I wanted to go fishing. "He probably does want to go fishing so he can talk to you, but he's not angry with you—he understands why you need to find your dad, Zac. And he says he'll deal with Nan; you're not to worry."

But I **was** worrying. If Grandad wanted to talk to me (and we did usually have our best chats when we went fishing), then how come he was now telling me to be quiet? I couldn't relax. And you need to relax for fishing. It's a bit like a detective mission. You have to be patient, but you have to keep the faith. The minute you lose the faith that you'll catch a fish, you won't catch one—it's like the fish can tell.

It was as if the heron that comes to visit us all the time on this canal could tell too—that I didn't like the silence—because he suddenly flew down and sat down opposite us. "Hello, Mr. Heron!" It stretched out its wings like a massive cloak. "What have you been up to today, then? Catching more fish than us, I reckon. Maybe you can give us some tips? Let us know where those fish are hiding. Mr. Heron! I'm talking to—"

"Zac," Grandad said suddenly.

"Yeah?"

"It is all right, you know."

"What is?" I said, my belly turning over because I'd worked it out.

"Look, I can tell you're worried, and there's no need. I know you're looking for your dad and I know you know I know, because your mum told me."

He looked at me and I smiled. But my heart was still banging really, really fast, because I didn't know what he was thinking. Was he upset with me?

"I . . . I just wanna meet him," I said, when Grandad went back to looking at the water because I wasn't saying anything. "It's not because I think he'll be better than you, or Mum and Nan—'cause you've always been like my dad, anyway, and you've always done dad stuff with me like watching football and stuff like this, like fishing. It's not even because I don't feel bad about my uncle Jamie, 'cause I do . . ."

"Zac." Grandad put the fishing rod down and leaned forward. "Seriously, Zac, you have to listen to me. What happened to Uncle Jamie that night and whatever your dad's involvement in it was or wasn't, it's got nothing to do with you, do you hear me? Absolutely nothing."

There was a big flock of birds then. They were sticking together, moving across the sky, which was all fluffy and pink like marshmallows. We watched them as they did their show, as they changed patterns in the sky for us.

"I know," I said, "but I still feel bad 'cause Nan does blame my dad. You blame my dad. And so me going to look for him still feels bad or wrong . . . Like it's going against you." I was trying to talk quiet, so we didn't scare the fish, but I was glad we were talking about it because I just needed to get it out.

"Look, Zac," Grandad said and Mr. Heron flew off then, like he knew we needed our privacy. "And don't worry about scaring the fish or the birds, for that matter, this is really important. Do you remember that day we went fishing and we talked about how Uncle Jamie died?"

"The day we caught the trout?"

"Yes." Grandad smiled. "That day we caught a trout. Do you remember how I told you that he'd died falling off a bridge?"

"Yeah, but I know that's not true now."

"It's not, but what I said about it being an accident is. Do you remember that bit? I said it was a terrible accident but that you should never tell Nan I said that."

I was nodding. I did remember. "Because the truth is different for different people and she wouldn't see it like that?"

"Exactly," said Grandad. "And that's still the situation. But sometimes being so sad—as sad as your nan is—is too hard, and so you get angry instead. It was an accident and your dad didn't behave as he should have that night, but he's not a bad person, Zac, he really isn't a bad person—he's a very good one, I can tell you that for a fact."

It felt dead nice when he said that, but I was still confused.

We sat in silence for a bit. It didn't feel as awkward now we'd talked, and I could concentrate on the fishing, waiting for the pull on the rod, or the little bath-fart bubbles at the surface that would prove there were fish underneath, waiting to be caught. Then suddenly, there were the mad up-and-down voices of the birds again, like they were all having a scrap. Then, it was weird, but the birds stopped and it was silent again. I had one question I was dying to ask.

"He still never came back, though, did he?" I said, but Grandad carried on looking at the water. "My dad," I said, "he never came back."

When Grandad spoke then, it was just one big sigh. "No, Zac, he never came back." And he was swallowing so hard, I could see his Adam's apple going up and down. "But I can help you if you still want. I can help you find him. I've got some clue as to where he might be."

I couldn't believe he was saying this to me. I thought he'd be angry, not help me!

"But what about Nan?"

"Leave Nan to me," said Grandad. Then, "I do love you, you know. You do know that, don't you?"

"Yeah," I said, because I did. I knew it. Like I knew Mum loved me, and Nan, and maybe even Teagan.

"I love you as well," I said. It didn't even feel that embarrassing.

"Good," said Grandad. "Good. At least we're clear on that then."

We sat there till it was nearly dark and the sun was this massive red gobstopper that sank bit by bit into the canal. And that was when my grandad told me some of the stories of my dad's life. That was when he gave me the clues that would crack my investigation.

"WE CAUGHT A perch—this big!" I said, bursting into Nan and Grandad's house after fishing, showing how big it was with my hands. I was in a good mood, because of the fish, but also because of what Grandad had told me—I couldn't wait to tell Teagan. Everything felt exciting, and back on . . . But there was something wrong.

Nan was sitting in the dark and Mum was there, which was weird, but she wasn't sitting down on the settee having a cup of tea, like she normally would when she picked me up; she was standing there as if she'd been waiting for us.

"I said we caught a perch and it was this big!"

I said, again to the dark room. I just wanted everyone to be normal, to go, "Well done, Zac! How much did it weigh?" like they normally did. But they weren't doing that, and they weren't interested in my perch. They were just sitting, saying nothing, in the dark. It was too weird.

Then Mum said, "Zac, darling, can you just pop upstairs for a bit while me, Nan, and Grandad have a chat?"

Then Nan was giving mega evils to Grandad—it was horrible, I hated it—and Grandad swore under his breath and walked off into the kitchen and Nan shouted after him, "Er, no!" and got up from her chair, but Mum made her sit down again. "Don't you **dare**, Michael, don't you dare walk off." I didn't know what was happening, I just knew it felt horrible, like everyone hated each other. I could see Grandad in the kitchen. He was standing in front of the window, his hands on his head, looking out at the backyard, and you could see the moon, which had finally taken over the gobstopper sun. Then suddenly, like he'd decided on something, he just walked back into the front room, all determined. "Zac," he said, "I think your mum's right, I think you should go upstairs for a bit. Everything's all right, we won't be long."

"Well, I don't see why he shouldn't be here," Nan said. "Where he can hear everything. Then he might hear it from **my** point of view and consider **me**, because let's face it, nobody else seems to have done."

"Zac, upstairs now!" Mum shouted then, and I bolted. I went up those stairs two or three steps at a time, even though I'd had enough of everyone talking about things without me there, keeping things—important things, like about my dad—secret from me. "Please stop dragging him into it," I heard her say as I went. "He's ten years old."

I went into my room and shut the door. It used to be my mum's room, but when I stay over at Nan and Grandad's it's mine—Nan just puts on my Manchester United duvet cover. I stood with my ear to the door. I didn't want to listen, but I couldn't help it. It was like the feeling when you know you shouldn't eat another bag of crisps but you do, then you end up feeling sick. I could hear everything.

Nan: "How could you? Just tell me that? How could you—both of you?"

Mum: "But, Mum, however did you think we could have gone on like that for the rest of our lives? Keeping all that from him?" (I knew she meant me.) "We couldn't. It was going to come out sometime."

Nan: "That does not mean you have to go looking for him! It's like you're doing it deliberately to upset me."

Oh my God, she knows about the Find Dad mission, I thought. **How does she know?!**

Grandad: "Lynda, please—oh fuck." (Grandad said the F-word! It was unbelievable.) "We need to talk. I can explain."

(Big silence then.)

Nan: "What do you mean, 'I can explain'?" (Another big silence.) "Jesus Christ, Michael, don't tell me you're helping look for him too?"

I turned around with my back to the door. The man in the moon was there, hanging outside my bedroom window with his sad, kind face again. It was like it had come especially, so I wasn't on my own.

Nan (again): "How do you think I will ever be able to look at his face and not see Jamie's, eh? Answer me that. How will we ever be able to welcome him back into the family, spend Christmases with him and have him come into **our** home, the home where my son is not because of **him**! Don't you think I've been through enough? That I've suffered enough?"

Grandad: "Lynda, please. Stop. You have to stop putting all the blame on Liam."

Nan: "Why should I? Why would I? All I know is that you drove two young men to the pub that night, both sober, both very much alive—and only one survived. And it wasn't my son. I don't have my son. I miss him so much . . ."

I could hear nothing but Nan crying then; it was awful. Then there were footsteps stomping up the stairs and Mum flung open the door before I had a chance to move, so I went flying.

"Oh God, Zac, you didn't hear all that, did you?"

"No," I lied.

"Anyway, we're going," she said. "Come on, we're going home."

I already had an idea for what I was going to do next.

35

Juliet

Nothing compares to the heart-stopping moment you realize your child is missing. They say everything slows down, but I would argue it speeds up—your heart, your fear, your love, the whole point of your life. It all collides then combusts within you in that split second. A siren goes off.

The morning after Mum's announcement that she knew about the Find Dad mission (Uncle Paul told her Zac had been down the docks asking after Liam, and that he'd seen me there too; and Mum, knowing I'd started to tell Zac stuff about his dad, had put two and two together), I go into Zac's room to find he isn't in his bed. The bed is made, as if he's never even slept in it. There's no sign of a rush to get dressed, no window open (I discover later this is because he simply slipped out the front door when I was asleep—so much for security).

I stand in his empty room, which is red and

warm as a heart due to the sun blaring through his closed Manchester United curtains, with my own heart firing bullets in my chest. Last night, he was so upset: upset about the possibility that he'd hurt his nan; distraught that news of his mission—the mission he'd started—had devastated her. But he still felt he had to carry on with it, that was the thing. Ten years old and feeling that torn inside? I know, as his mum, that it's a recipe for disaster for a kid like Zac, whose conscience belies his years; he can be emotional and impulsive. There's no telling where he might be or what he might have done.

I get dressed quickly and go over to Teagan's—if anyone will know where he is, she will. It's a beautiful day: clear blue sky, sun winking across the tops of the high-rises, as if mocking me and my panic. We're almost in mid May now—three weeks from the anniversary of Jamie's death—and it strikes me: is this the precursor to another life-altering trauma?

I hurry across the estate toward Teagan's block, feeling sweat prickling between my shoulder blades, and see a woman running toward me. At first I think it can't be her, because she never leaves the house. But as she comes closer, I realize from the greasy hair and strange gait that it is unmistakably Nicky, Teagan's mum. She's already hysterical, as if running from a natural disaster.

"Juliet! She's not in her bed! Oh God, oh Jesus . . ."

She falls into my arms; she reeks of fried food and sadness and cigarettes. I hug her. "It's all right, Nicky. Zac's not in his bed either, so they're bound to be together. I'm sure they're fine. They'll have just gone on some little adventure." I keep my tone light, try to be positive despite my own panic. She needs it more than me, that much is clear. If I were drunk, she would have sobered me up by now.

"What if she hasn't got her inhalers with her? She's not that well at the moment. She could die, Juliet, she could die. My baby! Oh God . . ." She sobs onto my shoulder.

"They'll be together, Nicky, looking after each other. Honest, don't worry. They won't have gone very far."

I take Nicky back to hers and make her a cup of tea—she's no use to anyone in this state. Then I check Teagan has taken her inhalers (she has), beg Nicky not to call the police (not yet), and phone my parents.

"Mum?"

I am met with silence, then a very stony, "Yes?"

"Mum, I need you to help me." (There's no time even to say that I have no time for arguments.) "Listen, don't panic"—she's already panicking, though, I know it; having lost a son, she panics if she loses her car keys—"but Zac wasn't in his bed this morning and neither was Teagan. We don't know where they are at the moment. Can you put Dad on, please?"

"What do you mean, he wasn't in his bed? Where is he then?"

"We don't know—I don't know. But I'm not worried, not yet," I lie. "Please can I just speak to Dad?"

A pause, then: "Your dad's not here." I am watching Nicky sip her tea, slowly, shakily, like a sick patient. "I kicked him out."

"Mum!"

"You better call him on his mobile—he can explain. But it's Zac you need to be worrying about now. Zac . . ." She pauses. A long pause. "And finding Liam."

"WHITBY?"

Dad is apparently already heading toward Nicky's flat, where I still am, from wherever he crashed last night (of course he would end up on the Harlequin; **of course** he would . . .) as he imparts this piece of wisdom as to Zac's whereabouts. **"Whitby?"** I say again. "Why the hell would he have gone to Whitby?"

"You've just got to trust me on this one, Jules." His voice is gruff from lack of sleep and trying to walk quickly at the same time as talk. "I can explain—I will explain—but first we've just got to get there as quickly as we can. Do you know any-

one with a car?" (Dad stopped driving soon after
Jamie died. He said being on the road just felt too
risky, and he couldn't risk anything else bad happening to our family.)

"No!"

"Not Jason?"

"Nope, he runs everywhere."

"Laura?"

"No. Oh, hang on, though, maybe her boy-
friend has one we could borrow." I try to picture
Dave and whether I've ever seen him in a car. Then
I call Laura.

"He does have a car, but it's in the garage.
Clutch went last week," she says, "so he can't help."
I'm about to despair when she says, "But I know a
man who can."

SHE'S WRIST-DEEP IN Hawaiian chicken mix
when Dad and I arrive at Sandwich King. Raymond is unpacking supplies, and both of them
look panic-stricken on our behalf.

Out of the corner of my eye, I see Laura take
the sandwich van keys off the fob, which hangs
next to the microwave. She dangles them in
the air.

"Oh God, Laurs, no," I say when I clock what's
going through her mind. "Gino would never forgive me."

"I can drive, I'm fully comp. Raymond, you

could man the shop for the day, couldn't you? I'd pay you for it, obviously, time and a half?"

"Laura, seriously, I'll lose my job," I say.

"But it's to get Zac."

"Exactly!" I'm thinking of the time he came in with chocolate all over his trousers and I had to leave early; how Gino found out we'd been making sandwiches for Jason; how he said my son was taking over **his** life, never mind mine . . .

"Jesus, Jules." Laura grabs her coat and makes for the door. "He may be a bit of a dick sometimes, but he's not a complete ogre—so much for your faith in human nature. He's not even in Grimsby so he need never know, and anyway, I'll deal with him if he's got a problem. I'll refund the petrol. We'll do a **Ferris Bueller** and rewind the mileage."

Dad and I have no choice but to follow her outside to the van.

"But it never worked!"

"What didn't?"

"In the film, when Cameron tries to rewind the mileage of his dad's sports car, it doesn't work."

She unlocks the van and opens the door. "Just shut up, will you? And get in."

There's only space for one next to the driver at the front of the van, so Dad and I sit in the back, among the empty crates and the boxes of supplies. There are no seat belts and it's definitely illegal, but that's the least of my concerns. All I care about now is getting to Zac.

The first half hour of the journey consists of us leaning through to the front of the van helping Laura get on the right road, because it turns out that although she can drive, she hasn't actually done so for a year and she's certainly not driven a van. We finally get her on the road, however, and all goes quiet, save for the low hum of the radio. I suppose I'm conscious that Dad isn't saying anything, but it's partly that I'm used to it, and partly that I'm preoccupied, too busy frantically scrolling through my phone, praying for news from Teagan's mum or Zac himself. Suddenly I glance up, though, and Dad is looking at me. I hold his gaze for a moment, expecting him to look away, but he doesn't, which unnerves me.

"Dad?"

He doesn't speak.

"Dad, you all right? It's going to be okay, you know. We will find him."

"I've got things I've got to talk to you about, Juliet," he says.

"Yes, I know." I remember what Mum said about kicking him out. "But they can wait till we get there, can't they?"

"No, they're things I need to tell you now."

36

Zac

Fact: Octopuses have three hearts.

Whitby is the best place I've ever been in my life. I couldn't believe that of all the places in England, my own dad lived there. There was a massive beach—better even than Cleethorpes—and cliffs and boats and slot machines (miles more than Cleethorpes) and a massive hill with a big crumbly castle on top. It was sick. It looked like the burned-out skeleton of a dinosaur.

"What's that?" I said to Teagan, over the seagulls—they were even louder than they are in Grimsby.

"It's Whitby Abbey."

"How do you know?"

"Because my aunty Sheila's been there, it's dead famous. Dracula even lived there."

"What?" I said, looking up at the abbey, imagining Dracula perching on the edge in his black cloak, blood dripping from his lips. "What do you mean, Dracula lived there?"

"Zac, stop asking questions," said Teagan, crossing the road. "We've only been to three restaurants so far, we've loads to do yet."

She was right. The Find Dad mission was the reason we were here—the only reason—it was just we were so close now that I was getting nervous. It was going to happen; I was going to meet my dad. What if he didn't want to know me? What if he didn't like the look of me, like he didn't when I was a baby (even though Mum had said it hadn't been like that at all; it was all because of Jamie that he left, not me)? It felt too big for my head. I wanted it more than anything I'd ever wanted in my life, but also I kept looking at people walking around with ice creams, or going up the steps to the abbey, and wishing I was one of them—just a random person on holiday, instead of Zac Hutchinson on the most important day of his life.

When my grandad told me my dad lived in Whitby and owned a seafood restaurant, I couldn't believe it. It was the biggest clue ever and he'd never told me; but that was because he never knew I was looking for him and also because he was worried about me finding him because of everything that had happened. He was worried it might upset me. But once he understood I **needed** to find him, he wanted to help, so that was when he told me the information about Dad living here and owning a seafood restaurant like he and Uncle Jamie dreamed of doing. He'd done it, in Uncle Jamie's memory. It was more proof that he missed him.

Then I overheard the horrible row at Nan's, and I know it was bad, but me and Teagan decided we needed to do something drastic—we had to finish our investigation once and for all. It seemed like everyone was upset with everyone anyway, so if I found my dad and it turned out bad, then nothing would be worse than it already was—but I had a very strong feeling it would turn out good. It was an unmissable opportunity, especially now we had our vital clue.

So me and Teagan gathered all the money we had from both our piggy banks (it was £49.76) and we got on the bus at Grimsby. It was just me and her and it was still so early that the bin men trucks were in the streets and the sun was still on its way up, at its most glowing, making everything feel new. It felt like the scariest, most exciting thing I'd ever done. I felt bad for Mum because I knew she'd be worried, but I also knew it would be worth it. I had a voice in my head that I couldn't ignore—and, also, one main rule of missions is that you have to finish them; they're not worth anything unless you do.

Our MO when we got here was to go in every seafood restaurant and ask if Liam Jones worked there. We'd know him when we saw him, anyway, because we had some vital facts. We knew he had really light blue eyes like mine, black hair, and half his thumb missing. I'd seen the picture of him at Aunty Kelly's anyway. I'd know my dad anywhere.

We found another restaurant. It was called Mario's and it had a board outside with **The Finest Seafood in Whitby** written on it. It looked posher than the one we'd just been into, which mainly served fish and chips, and there were fish tanks around the tables—I hoped nobody ate the goldfish that were in there. I hoped they were just there to look at while you had your lobster thermidor.

Teagan marched straight to the back to ask if this was my dad's restaurant, but I stayed in the restaurant bit. I'm shyer than Teagan, but that's okay. If you're detectives working in a pair, it's always good to have one confident one and one who's more shy—because they can do the looking around while the other one goes straight in. It was true as well, because just then, a man came down the restaurant stairs. He did it two at a time, whistling as he went, so you knew he did it all the time, and that he worked here, and he was wearing a white shirt like a waiter.

"Excuse me, is this a seafood restaurant?"

He smiled like he thought I was funny.

"It is, yes, can't you see food?"

The man started laughing then and I laughed to be polite, even though I didn't know what was funny, then the man said, "So how can I help you, young man? Are you looking for someone?"

That was when I asked if Liam Jones worked here and the man knew his name; he knew my dad was a chef. "Ah, yes," he said, "Liam Jones. He doesn't work here, but I know where he does."

MY DAD'S RESTAURANT was called the Oyster—I liked the name—and it was on a cliff. The man told us how to get there. You had to walk back over the bridge where we were, down toward the sea, then up loads of steps again. It sounded like hard work, but I would have done it ten times to meet my dad. Whitby is a really busy place and there were loads of cars and people coming over the bridge, but both could only come slowly because there were so many of them; nobody could rush, because there wasn't room. Suddenly, when we were halfway over, Teagan stopped. "Zac." She turned around, her eyes wide as anything. "That was your nan!"

"What? No, it wasn't." It couldn't be.

"It was, it was your nan," she said, and she had to shout above the seagulls and the cars. "I swear on my life, she was in that taxi just gone over the bridge!"

"Don't be stupid, why would my nan come to Whitby?" I said, jogging to try to catch her up. "How would she even know I was here?" But then it felt like ants were crawling over my skin, because Teagan would never say she swore on her life unless she was a hundred percent certain—at least ninety-five percent anyway. And what if Grandad had told Nan what he'd told me about my dad living here? What if she was so mad that she'd come to stop me, or have a fight with my dad over Uncle Jamie?

"What did she look like?"

"Your nan!" said Teagan. "Her mouth looked all sad—it was definitely her."

I hadn't thought of Nan having a sad mouth before, but when Teagan did an impression, I realized she was right. I felt sick (but mostly starving, because I'd only had a Double Decker for my breakfast, as we'd had to save our money for the bus and my dad's restaurant). But I couldn't think of Nan now; I had to finish the mission. If I started to worry about my nan coming to Whitby to stop me, then I might get too scared and give up.

YOU COULDN'T BELIEVE the view from my dad's restaurant. It was even better than the one of Grimsby from Teagan's bedroom. The whole building was basically windows, so that if you looked through the front one (we were still standing outside, trying to get up the courage to go in) you could see all the way through the restaurant to the windows at the other end and to the view. It was of the sea, of course, which was so blue it didn't look real, and so sparkly with sun it made you feel happy just looking at it. I wondered if my dad had ever looked at it and thought about me (probably not, because the view was so nice, you couldn't think about anything else). But even if he hadn't, just knowing what he looked at every day felt nice—like I knew him better already.

"Zac." Teagan was nudging me. "Aren't we going to go in, then?" I nodded, but my stomach hurt. I didn't know if it was because I was so nervous or because I was hungry—but it was the same sort of feeling.

"HELLO." THERE WAS a lady at the front behind a desk, like the lady behind the desk at the fish market, except (I checked) this one only had one phone to answer. The woman looked behind us, as if she was expecting someone else. Then when no one else came, she turned back to us. "Can I help you?"

I looked at Teagan. I didn't know what to say.

But Teagan was amazing. "We'd like a table, please. We've come all the way from Grimsby."

The woman frowned and looked behind us again. "On your own?"

"Yes," said Teagan. "We had to get the bus this morning and since then he's only had a Double Decker and me a bag of Frazzles so we're absolutely starving."

"Right," said the lady, her mouth twisting.

She looked sad like she was going to have to turn us away because we were on our own, but then Teagan said, "We **came** on our own, but my parents are coming too. They're just a bit held up at the moment." She paused and looked at me. My heart was banging in case this all went wrong. "They're still at the abbey, you see, learning about Dracula. We were a bit scared so we came here first to get us a table."

The lady looked from Teagan to me, to over the other side of the restaurant, and I said a little prayer: **Please, Jesus, we're at the end of our mission now. Please can you make it that she lets us in.**

"You can phone my mum if you want," said Teagan. And even though it was probably the most serious moment of my life so far, a giggle bubbled up. I had to try really hard to push it back down again. I couldn't believe what a risk taker she was! She didn't even have a phone!

There was a long pause. It seemed to go on forever, but then the lady said, "Nope, I believe you. You look like a very honest young lady to me. Now, let me find you all a nice table. What will it be? Four of you?"

THERE WERE LOADS of people having their dinner already and everybody's voices were echoing—it was a nice sound, of people having a good time—and there were big, fancy lights in the ceiling, which was really high up, and the tablecloths were so white they hurt your eyes, and the sun was glinting off all the knives and forks, probably because they were real silver. It was the poshest restaurant I'd ever been in in my life—posher than Toby Carvery, although I bet they didn't do all-you-can-eat vegetables here or giant Yorkshire puddings—and all the time the lady was taking us to our table, I was looking out for my dad. My heart was going mad at the thought he could just come out from the kitchen anytime; that maybe he was already in the room, breathing the same air as me. And it was the scariest, maddest feeling I'd ever had. I felt dizzy, like I might even faint.

"Is this table okay?" said the lady. It was more than okay because it was right next to the window, so you could look down at the sea and watch the seagulls that flew across to say hello, and I was facing the kitchen, so if my dad came out, I would see him first. The lady handed us a menu each. They were heavy and blue leather with gold letters—I bet they cost a bomb. "Someone will come and take your order when your parents arrive and you're all ready, but why don't you be looking through these while you're waiting?"

Me and Teagan just looked at each other and smiled. "Oh my God, that was close," said Teagan over her menu once the lady had gone. "I thought she was never going to let us in."

"You were a genius!"

"Shall I go into the kitchen?" she said. "Go and see if I can see him?"

"No, I'm not ready," I said. "I'm so nervous, I feel sick. I don't think I'll even be able to eat anything."

"Oh my God, you **are** nervous," said Teagan, and I laughed. I even felt a bit better.

"I would be nervous if I were you, but we're here now, we're so close, Zac! And just think how you'll feel when you meet him; when we've accomplished our mission."

"But what if he doesn't like me?"

"What're you on about?" said Teagan. "Why would he not like you?"

"I dunno." It was the first time I'd said it out loud and I was suddenly scared it might come true. "Just maybe he won't. You can't like everyone, can you? And maybe he won't be expecting me to be so . . . you know."

"What?"

I had to look out of the window when I said it, because it felt embarrassing, even in front of Teagan. "Big," I said. "I'm big, aren't I? I'm bigger than most ten-year-olds."

Teagan just looked confused. "So? You're also nicer and funnier and better than most ten-year-olds, and anyway, I'm smaller than most ten-year-olds. I wear clothes that are for seven-year-olds!"

It was true, but I'd sort of forgotten that Teagan was really small. Maybe after a bit of knowing someone, you just forget stuff like that.

We decided to order some food, quick while the

lady at the front was busy with everyone coming into the restaurant. One o'clock must have been when everyone had their dinner in Whitby, because suddenly it was packed. We decided my dad was bound to come out at some point. Maybe if we ordered something fancy, then he'd be the one to serve it to us, to explain what was in it like he used to do when he played **MasterChef** with Uncle Jamie—my mum told me all about it.

The only problem was, you couldn't understand the menu, because most of it was in a foreign language, with words we'd never heard of, like "bouillabaisse." (How did you even say that? It was the most stupid word ever.) But a waitress came in no time. She didn't look very old. We decided she was probably Year 10 at the most and we ordered some prawns because we knew that word and what they'd taste like and then some mussels with chips on the side. It was all delicious and I was watching the kitchen doors, but he still didn't come out, so then we ordered some scallops and a fish called a turbot and then . . .

"We'll have the Singapore crab," said Teagan, when the waitress came for the third time and we'd finished the prawns and mussels (we still had our chips and the scallops and half the turbot fish left). The waitress frowned. She looked very surprised.

"Are you sure?"

"Yes," we both said.

"Because it's a big main course—**another** main course." She wanted to say, **And you've already got loads of food** and **You're being extremely greedy**, you could tell, but she knew it was bad manners. But we said we were sure and we ordered it anyway and it was only then that I looked at our table and realized how much food we'd ordered and wondered how we would eat it all—or, even worse, pay for it all.

Teagan wasn't worried. "Zac, it's your dad's restaurant," she said, scooping a mussel out with her fork (she'd never tried them before, but she wasn't scared to; it was typical of her). "You won't have to pay." As she said it, she checked with her eagle eyes over at the front bit again, to make sure the lady hadn't noticed our parents hadn't arrived, hadn't clocked that Teagan had told her a massive fib. Then Teagan said something funny, which was that mussels are the food opposite of broccoli, which looks nice but tastes disgusting, whereas mussels are the other way round. We were trying to think of other food opposites (it's harder than you think), but then I stopped talking, and my stomach did this massive flip-flop, because the kitchen door swung open and out walked my dad. I knew it was my dad because he was wearing chef whites like those my uncle Jamie is wearing in the picture I have of him in my room, and he had black hair and looked like the picture I'd seen, and he was not thin or fat, he was just perfect normal sized. And then he was almost at our table, and I saw his eyes. They were exactly like mine.

"Hi, guys." He crossed one foot over the other and leaned on the table with his hands—half his thumb was missing! I looked at Teagan. She'd seen it too. "I understand you've ordered the Singapore crab?"

We nodded, but neither of us could speak, we were too busy looking at his thumb and his eyes and then at each other. "Great choice, by the way. It's probably my favorite dish and is absolutely"—he blew a little kiss with his hand, which made us smile, even if we couldn't talk—"gorgeous, with garlic and chili; it's just the right balance of spicy and fragrant . . ." He was dead passionate about cooking, just like me. "But I just wanted to make sure you were aware it was thirty-six pounds, and it **is** the whole crab and I see you've already ordered a lot of food, some of which you've not eaten yet, and I just wanted to make sure"—he leaned in close, so that nobody else could hear, so that he was looking with his light blue eyes with the yellow around the middle into my light blue eyes with the yellow around the middle and my heart was banging so loudly, he must have been able to hear it—"you have means to pay for it all and aren't going to find yourself panicking when the bill comes, as I notice you're not with your mum or dad."

It all felt too big for my head again and my

throat closed up, like I was going to cry. **Do not cry,** I was saying to myself, **whatever you do, you** can't **cry.** And I was looking at my dad—my own dad, with my dad's arms and hands and face and half a thumb, and blood pumping around his body right now, that was half the same as my blood, my genes—and I said, "I can't pay for it all." I made the words push themselves out. "I'm really sorry. I'm sorry we ordered all this food, our eyes were too big for our bellies . . . I just . . . I wanted to meet you."

Liam smiled. "Meet **me**?" he said. "Why?"

"Because you're my dad."

HE WASN'T TALKING. I just wanted him to talk. And he wasn't moving. He just carried on leaning on the table staring at me, but he wasn't even smiling now, he looked deadly serious. Then he turned around, so he was facing the other direction, and he bent over and put his hands over his face. I looked at Teagan. My throat ached. What was wrong? Why had he turned around? Was he mad with me? Not pleased to see me? Was the Find Dad mission the worst idea we'd ever had? And then I did exactly the thing I was dreading I would do; I started crying. I couldn't keep it in.

Teagan leaned forward. "It's all right, Zac," she said, but she was worried too, you could tell. She looked scared and she never looks scared and my dad still wasn't turning around. "It's all right, honest, don't cry."

But then my dad did turn around and he was crying too. He sat down next to me. I was scared for what he was going to do, what he was going to say, but then he did the one thing I wasn't expecting him to do: he put his arms around me and pulled me close, so that my face was right next to his, and he smelled of fish (but really nice, fishy cooking smells) and deodorant, and my dad; because all dads have their own smells like mums, and even nans and grandads.

"Why're you crying?" I said, even though it was hard to hear me, 'cause my mouth was buried in his chef whites. "Are you upset? Are you disappointed?"

"No, I'm happy," he said. "Why are you crying? Are **you** upset?"

"No, I'm happy too," I said, and my dad just stayed like that for ages, hugging me, and Teagan reached across and finished off my chips, and mine and my dad's cheeks were so close, our faces were touching, so that I could feel his prickly stubble, and I accidentally tasted the saltiness of his tears.

Me and my dad couldn't stop looking at each other for ages. We just kept looking, then laughing, and my dad told the people on the table next to us that I was his son. And me and Teagan told him how we'd launched the mission to find him, and how we'd never given up. (He had tears running down his cheeks—it turns out my dad isn't one bit embarrassed by crying.) And my dad said he had so many questions and wanted to ask all about my mum and how she was, but that he was going to sort the Singapore crab for us first and then he was going to see if someone could take over so he could take the afternoon off. And it was the best day, the best moment of my life so far— better than catching a trout, better than touching a stingray and even tickling dolphin bellies—and I thought about my uncle Jamie and the heaven game and how this would definitely, definitely be the first door I'd go to when I died and got to heaven, to knock on it and experience it again. Teagan and I went a bit crazy when my dad went into the kitchen. We couldn't believe we'd found him; we couldn't believe it was mission accomplished!

But then, out of the corner of my eye, I saw the restaurant door open, and in walked my mum, and then my grandad.

My whole body went cold.

"Oh my God," said Teagan when she saw them coming toward us. "Oh shit."

And then—because we'd had **so** much custard, I suppose, finding and meeting my dad—just as my mum and grandad were walking toward our table, the door opened again and I nearly fainted because this time my nan walked in. It was the rhubarb bit happening but in the most extreme way it ever had.

It was so unfair. We'd got this far. I'd found my dad and he was glad, I knew he was. He was happy I'd looked for him and he was cooking a Singapore crab for me, for his son, right now, and we were going to spend the afternoon together. I was going to tell my mum and get them to meet and they could probably, maybe, fall in love again. But I wasn't ready to tell her just yet. I wanted to pick the perfect moment—not for her to arrive here, now, when I wasn't ready—and I just wanted to enjoy meeting my dad for a bit longer. I'd wished for this day all my life, definitely since we'd started the Find Dad mission in February, and now it was going to be ruined before it even got started, because Nan was going to stop us. And I felt bad—I really did—that my uncle Jamie had died and Nan was so sad, but it wasn't a good enough, big enough reason for my dad not to be able to be my dad. It wasn't a big enough reason for us not to be happy anymore.

But my mum was coming straight for us, followed by Grandad and then Nan, and the whole restaurant seemed to have gone quiet; everyone was looking at us. And just then, in the worst timing in the world, my dad came out of the kitchen with the Singapore crab. He was walking from one direction toward us, while my mum, nan, and grandad came from the other direction.

Mum hugged me really tight. "Zac, Christ. Teagan—thank God you're okay."

Then my dad was standing there with the Singapore crab and his eyes locked with Mum's and then Grandad's and then Nan's and my heart broke, because it was all over, I knew it, before it had even started, before I'd had even one day with my dad.

Grandad was looking at Dad. He was definitely going to kick off, start shouting at him about my uncle Jamie and about how sad my nan was, but then my dad said, "Not now, Mick. Shall we not talk about it now while Zac's here?"

My grandad looked at me for a long time; there were tears in his eyes. And then he nodded—it was like he was bowing to me—and he walked out. And I said, "Please, Nan," because she was also looking at my dad, and she looked ready for a fight. "Please don't shout at my dad."

Nan said, "I'm not going to shout at your dad, darling. If anything, he should be shouting at me, definitely at your grandad," which was so confusing and I had loads of questions. But anyway, I was too busy looking at my mum, who was looking at my dad, who was still standing there, holding the Singapore crab. She still loved him, you could tell. You could see it in her eyes.

37

Mick

So here I am—at the end. It feels like the end of the earth too, standing on this jetty in Whitby, nothing but the North Sea between me and Norway. The wind is strong despite the sunshine. I must look a sight, standing here while a gale nearly blows me into the sea, but I don't care. In fact, I prefer it this way. It seems right and just that I should be exposed to the elements, not warm and comfortable as I finally get it all straight in my head, admit it all to myself—all of it—while my son lies cold in the ground.

I need to understand how we got to this point, I remember saying to Carol back when I first started seeing her in January. **I need to understand how our son isn't here anymore and why I couldn't protect him.** And I do understand now: booze; addiction; weakness as a person, as a man. If I'd been stronger, more of a man, Jamie would still be here; Zac would have his dad; Juliet would have Liam. The drink has been the undoing of me and this family, so perhaps I can comfort myself with the fact that I, at the very least, succeeded in giving it up. The tragedy is that it took what happened to happen before I did.

I made the fatal error of the recovering alcoholic that night, June 11, 2005. **I've done so well, five months without a drink. Surely one won't hurt?** But hurt it did—me, and everyone I love.

I was giddy after becoming a grandad for the first time. But giddiness is a danger zone for the alcoholic—happiness, sadness, any extreme of emotion. "Surely a man can toast the arrival of his first grandchild?" That's what I said to Jamie as I stood at the bar that night, my pulse quickening at the mere sight of those optics. **Surely one won't hurt?** I'd driven both him and Liam there after making them stomach-lining pasta just as I'd promised Lynda. I'd even let them get out of the car and was turning around ready to go home. But then something switched in my head. I'd reached the limit of my self-discipline, or I genuinely felt I was in control, I don't know which, but **Surely one won't hurt?** slid into my head like a vision-altering lens, and before I knew it, I was on two, and three and four . . . That moment where the boat tips so far you can't right it anymore had been and gone and it was heaven for a while, oh God, it was bliss. But then, almost as soon as I'd got into the water, I was flailing about, out of my depth. And then it was, **Surely a man can have a shot on the birth of his first grandchild? Surely a man can buy his future son-in-law and his son a shot to celebrate something as momentous as this?** And another, and another. After all, I felt proud and jubilant ('course I did, I was wasted). I loved Jamie, I loved Liam, I loved Zac and everyone in that pub. But then one pint too many, one shot too many, and things turned very quickly from loved-up to stoked-up, to fighting talk.

I went to the gents'. Chris Hynd was next to me at the urinals. He's always been a wind-up merchant and he started going on about this and that, something and nothing, but I could feel myself getting riled. As we left the toilets, Liam happened to be coming in. He was already oiled—not as far gone as me, but getting there on the pints of Foster's with tequila chasers I'd basically thrust upon him. And so, seeing him drunk and an easy target, Hynd started to wind him up too. He had the two of us tucked into a corner between the gents' door and the door to the bar, taking the piss—like I say, something and nothing. But then things got serious; he chose to say the wrong thing to the wrong man. "Seen your girl around, Mick—she's a big lass these days, isn't she? Let herself go a bit?"

I looked at Liam. He was frowning, trying to compute what he'd just heard, hoping he hadn't heard right.

"She was fucking pregnant until a fortnight ago, you imbecile," I said. I just saw red.

Hynd laughed then, and it was that, that sly smirk of his . . . I felt my blood boil. I went for him like an animal. I had him up against the wall opposite the gents', clutching his hair and holding his head back, spitting into his stupid face, "You fucking ever, **ever** bad-mouth my family again and I'll fucking kill you." That was four pints and God knows what else talking all right, because I may have been a drunk, but I've never been a violent man. But I'd had five months off the booze and it had me now, firmer than ever, in its grip. He said something else and I went for him again and it was then that Liam tried to stop the fight, pulling us apart, and me to the side. "Mick, maybe it's time you went home," he said. "Don't waste your energies on this waste of space—think what Lynda would say if she knew you were out. Think of how well you've done."

But it was Hynd that walked off then, flicking my shoulder as he went. "I've not fucking finished with you, mate. I'll see you later." And it was like the lights going on at a party in that moment; I came to my senses. **It's either me or the drink, Mick.** I could hear Lynda's words in my head, see her at her wits' end, delivering her ultimatum. **It's the booze or us.** And something obviously clicked because once we were back in the bar, I put one foot in front of the other and, without saying good-bye to either Jamie or Liam, I walked off, leaving them both with Hynd, got in the car, and drove, well over the limit, back home.

It wasn't even nine p.m. then. If I went straight home, I could be sober for when Lynda came in from her night shift at six a.m. and she'd be none the wiser—that was my thinking.

But I'd already started the fight, hadn't I? I'd already fueled the boys with alcohol and set up the domino effect that would end with my boy dead and this family in ruins. I wasn't thinking of that then, though. I was thinking only of myself and of Lynda's wrath, and what I could lose should she find out I'd fallen spectacularly off the wagon, and not looked after the boys—our boy.

Then it was two a.m. and Jamie was lying in a hospital bed, clinging on to life, and I wasn't thinking about what I'd done or even what Liam had done. I was thinking only of Jamie and willing him to live. I still had every hope—stupid bastard that I was—that everything would be okay. But then Jamie died. The impossible happened, and I fell apart. That was when I spat those words out: "You're just like your father." In the heat of the moment, I believed them too. For a month, maybe two, I told myself it was true, and that this family was better off without him. Zac—and Juliet— had had a lucky escape. I even joined in gladly with Lynda's blame crusade and her vitriol. But as time marched on, and the letters arrived—as I always knew they would—that conviction became harder and harder to hold on to. But of course, I'd fallen head over heels in love with my grandson by then; I loved him more than I knew it was possible to love another human being—and I couldn't give him up. Couldn't tell the truth about that night. Couldn't—wouldn't—take my share of the blame.

Until now.

I looked up—the sea stretching out in front of me, miles and miles of blue—and I thought of Jamie falling to the ground that night, felled by Hynd, in a fight started by Liam, in a train of events put into motion by me, and of the last moments I saw him alive. And I walked straight back to the restaurant and I walked inside. I saw my daughter, my grandson, my wife—and knew I was very possibly about to lose them all.

"Juliet," I said, and I looked at Liam as I said it. I made myself look him straight in the eye. "Can we go somewhere, please? I have to talk to you. I have to tell you the truth."

38

Juliet

Zac dances like his dad, or Liam dances like his son, I'm not sure which way round it is. I'm watching them both now, dancing to Justin Timberlake (Liam was head of the playlist for the eleventh birthday party) amid the swirl of disco lights, and they do, they dance the same way: their feet don't move much, but there's a lot of "upper body" action; lots of arms and knees and hips—a **lot** of hips. They yawn the same way too, unnecessarily loudly and always saying "sorry" afterward. The first time Liam did it, Zac and I looked at each other in disbelief. They're both scared of wasps, though Zac is allergic to stings—I don't know what Liam's excuse is for flapping about like a pantomime dame—and they think Marmite with pasta is an actual bona fide meal, and get in a bad mood if they don't eat for longer than three hours. Mind you, so do I. That's not a son-and-father thing, that's just a family thing, maybe even a human thing.

What else have I discovered in the past two and a half weeks since Liam came back into Zac's life? Into ours? I know that I didn't know stuff before, I just guessed and presumed. But Zac, he knew; he seemed to know the truth from the outset, or at least that everything would be okay. Or perhaps he just had faith—which is different to knowing; it's trusting. And even though sometimes in this mission to find his dad, it's felt like he's had faith in the Second bloody Coming, he's still had it in bucketloads, and when he's felt it slipping, he's hunted it down—like he has his dad—and brought it to me, to this family. I'm so proud of him for that. I am watching him now, dancing at the same time as chatting to Connor and Teagan, like an ordinary eleven-year-old, thinking how he is anything but ordinary to me—my extraordinary son.

Something catches my eye at the other side of the Casablanca Club—a door opens, there's a glimpse of pink evening sky, and I realize it's my dad leaving. He doesn't say good-bye, he just slips out, an hour before the end of the party. I watch him go, then five minutes later I watch Mum follow, but they won't be going to the same house tonight, not for a long while, perhaps not ever again. But at least they're talking, and I've got a feeling this is where the real recovery starts for both of them, for our family; after all, how can you begin to heal when you don't know the truth? When you don't even know what sort of wounds you're dealing with?

It was Zac who still wanted his grandad to come to his party despite everything, but that's not to say he hasn't battled with his emotions.

"But I'd be grounded forever if I told a lie for ten years," he said the other day. "Even if it was a lie of omission." After Dad confessed everything about what really happened that night, Zac and I had a chat about lies and, Zac being Zac, he Googled "types of lies." It was there that he found this term "lie of omission" and he's been throwing it around ever since. I don't mind. I think it makes him feel better. He finds it easier to forgive his grandad a lie of omission than the truly deceitful sort. He knows my dad had his reasons, and many of those were about him. Dad's fear of losing him.

Forgiveness—as a concept—has been a new thing for Zac, though, and I can tell he's thinking about it all the time. This morning when we were in Poundstretcher of all places, buying decorations for this party, party bags and balloons, he suddenly said, "How come Grandad doesn't get punished?"

And I put whatever I was holding down and looked at him. "Oh, he is being punished; he has been punished," I said. "He's let you and all of us down, for one thing, and I'm sure he feels guilty. That's his punishment."

Zac was quiet for a while, then as we were walking home, laden with bags, he said, "But I'm confused, Mum. Because I'm really mad at Grandad, but I still love him too."

And I said, "Me too, Zac. Me too," because it was true. Love, I've learned, has a mind of its own, and just because someone does something bad, something unthinkable, you don't stop loving them. You can't just turn it off. I tried to. I tried to turn off my love for Liam for ten years, but now when I look at him dancing with our son, I realize that all that time I thought I was angry and full of blame, I never was; when it was easier to believe Mum that Liam was just like his dad, I never did. All I ever was was heartbroken. All I ever felt was abandoned. I yearned, longed, crawled the walls for him—and he never came.

I decide to go outside for a breather, while everyone's still busy dancing, before I have to begin the cleanup effort in earnest, the going round with a bin liner to collect paper plates and leftover pizza. The air is cool and refreshing outside the Casablanca Club and I lean against the wall— also cool after I've been inside with the heat of the disco lights and several sweaty eleven-year-olds— and I sip my Tango from a plastic cup. The sky's been Tangoed too, I think—that's how Zac might describe it; it's streaked with orange and pink and even purple, and the sun, an ever-decreasing fiery smudge, is about to lose its battle any moment.

Zac decided he wanted his party here instead of at the Toby Carvery because he believes this place to have good karma, to be a place where only good times happen. And he's right, I think. Good things do, and have, happened here—and they happen to this family as much as any other. That's the thing about unhappiness, I've discovered—and by that I don't mean depression as such but deep, chronic unhappiness. It stops you thinking that good things can happen, but that doesn't mean that good things don't.

There's the squeak of the club door as it opens, the crunch of footsteps on gravel. Jason appears.

"'Ello, 'ello. Mum thought she'd have a crafty minute to herself, did she?"

"Is that allowed?"

He comes to stand next to me. "I think so," he says, folding his arms and leaning against the wall too. "Although to be fair, Zac and I did make all the sandwiches and Liam moved the tables, did the music—what did you do anyway?"

"Piss off," I say, elbowing him, even though I know he's teasing. "Only eleven years' worth of parenting **on my own**!"

There's a long silence, broken only by the cry

of seagulls—so ever-present I hardly notice them anymore—and "Dancing on the Ceiling," just audible from inside the Casablanca Club.

"What do you think of him, then?" I say, turning to Jason.

"Who? Zac?"

"No, Liam, you daft thing—now you've met him."

Jason looks away, then at the floor, and smiles to himself and I smile too. I don't really know why.

"He seems like a lovely bloke, but I don't think it matters what I think of him. It's what you think that matters."

"What's that supposed to mean?" I say, and Jason gives a big—I can't help but think—deliberately dramatic sigh.

"Well, it's always been him, let's face it," he says, crossing one foot over the other, looking at me, even more cheekiness in his smile than normal. "Hasn't it? Let's be honest, Jules. It's always only ever been him that you wanted, that you loved, that I think . . . no, I **know**—and Zac knows too, by the way"—he lifts a finger, so bloody smug that he has this on me—"that you still love."

I don't know what I'm meant to say to that, what he thinks my reaction will be, what he's thinking or feeling, and I search his face, looking for clues, but he doesn't give anything away.

"Look, I'm sorry about . . . when we went for a run in the park, you know."

"It's all right. I am pretty irresistible after all."

I tut and roll my eyes. "Yeah, well, I'm just sorry in general," I say and Jason shrugs.

"Don't be. I've still got you in my life, haven't I? And anyway, it was Zac I really missed."

"Ha!" I say. "Charming."

"It was—I'm just being honest. We laugh at the same things, we really get on. I love hanging out with him."

"And him with you," I say.

Just then, "Happy" by Pharrell Williams comes on—Zac's favorite—and Liam appears. I can only just make him out in silhouette, the sun having dipped now behind the Casablanca Club. "I'll leave you two to it," says Jason and he pats Liam on the shoulder. "Loving the playlist, mate," he says and he goes back inside.

Liam leans against the wall next to me too, so close I can almost feel the warmth of his arm, feel the fine black hairs on them, that I seemed to know and love individually once, and I focus on them, inwardly pinching myself to check it's true: he's here, right now, this is real; his arm millimeters from mine, our hands almost touching.

"I hope I didn't interrupt anything," he says.

"No, no, I was just getting some fresh air."

"I brought you this—still your favorite?" He hands me a bottle of ice-cold Bud.

"You beauty. Where have you been all my life?" I say, and there's awkward laughter when we realize what I've said. I sit on the ground then and Liam joins me. The words hang between the seagulls' cries.

"Seriously, though, where have you been?" I say when I can't bear it any longer. "Where were you, the past eleven years? 'Cause it's been awful"—I just come out with it (what have I got to lose now?)—"bloody awful without you."

"I wrote letters to you, Juliet." His voice is gravelly, tired; it strikes me as . . . full of regret.

"I know, but I didn't get them."

"I called even, but by the time I did, you must have already changed your number."

We've been over this already in the past three weeks. I've read the letters now (seen the checks he sent—of course he did, that's Liam all over). Some of the ink is smudged with my tears. Of all the secrets this family has kept over the past ten years, those letters are the one that hurts the most and I'm not sure if I can ever forgive Dad for that. Only time will tell.

This is all so bittersweet, I think. Hardly a centimeter between Liam and me right now, and yet oceans and oceans of wasted time. And if it weren't for Zac, we wouldn't be sitting here at all.

It's as if Liam has read my mind. "You know, it's not just me who wrote letters," he says suddenly and I look across at him questioningly. Those startling blue eyes look back at me, and I think I've missed them, you, so much; and my God, it's like looking at my son. **Our** son. "Zac wrote me one too. He gave it to Kelly and she sent it to me. It was asking me to come to his eleventh birthday party," he says, when my surprised silence indicates he should go on. "It said that everyone was mad with me for leaving, but that he thought I'd change my mind if I met him."

I smile. My boy!

"He's got confidence, self-belief, our son, you know," says Liam. **Maybe that's true,** I dare to think, **maybe that's true.**

"And I think that's going to grow now," I say.

And then it's just us and the music and the gulls and, without saying anything, we both stand up and look inside the club's window—disco lights shifting across it—so we can watch our son at his birthday party. He's dancing, his head bobbing up and down, a great grin plastered on his face and his hair stuck to his head with sweat.

"He's an amazing kid, he really is. You've done a totally brilliant job," says Liam.

"I know," I say, meaning the bit about Zac. "I'm so proud of him. He's so loving and funny and bright and giving, Liam, you'll see—I think so, anyway."

Silence before Liam, still watching Zac, moves his hand slowly along the windowsill and puts it gently on mine. "Of course he is," he says, eyes still on Zac. "Because so are you."

Epilogue

Zac

Definition of fact: "something which can be proved as true."

August 2016

"I can't believe you've still got those sweets from October," I said, looking at the Halloween bucket in the middle of Teagan's bedroom floor. It was the only thing left—everything else was in boxes, being carried by my mum, dad, or Jason down the stairs to the removal van, or in the removal van already.

"There's only licorice laces in there," said Teagan. "They're disgusting." She stuck her tongue right out and made a stupid face. I was going to miss knowing that face was just on the other side of the estate from me. "You can have them, though, if you want. They can be my leaving present to you."

"Nah," I said. "I think I'll give them a miss."

We just stood looking around Teagan's empty room. It looked so depressing with no furniture, just boxes and the lonely Halloween bucket in there. You couldn't believe how bad the damp was when you could see it properly: like black clouds all over the ceiling. Most of all, you couldn't believe what a good time we'd had in such a disgusting room. How many funny times I'm going to remember for the rest of my life.

Teagan's new house on Orchard Avenue is proper nice. It's on a brand-new street with baby trees planted and has even got a shiny black front door. But I'm still going to miss this bedroom. Even though Teagan's not moving far, and we can still hang out together, it won't be the same as knowing that, when I look out of my window, across to hers, she's asleep in her bed, probably with her red flower in her hair.

Teagan did a big sigh. "It's such a dump, isn't it?" she said, looking around. "You got me out of here, Zac. It was your letter that did it."

"I don't think it was just my letter. But maybe it helped."

"Yeah, your mum was right, grown-ups do listen to kids in the end."

"Yeah," I said. "In the end."

Suddenly someone screeched—me and Teagan looked at each other, then ran to the window. I knew it was probably the last time we would. It felt like the last time we'd do loads of things. You couldn't believe it, because the scream was coming from my mum!

"Oh God," said Teagan.

"Oh no," I joined in. "Not again."

Mum and Dad were meant to be carrying Teagan's boxes to the removal van, but instead it looked like they were having a scrap in the sun!

But then I realized that Mum's scream was actually a laugh, and that they weren't scrapping— Dad was just trying to put her over his shoulder and carry her across the estate! She was kicking her legs and screeching and Dad was laughing too. But then Dad put her down, straightened down her dress ('cause you could nearly see her knickers), and kissed her instead. It was a proper snog. It went on for ages and ages! And Dad was holding Mum's face and Mum had her arms wrapped tightly around him and even though their mouths were pressed together, they were smiling, you could tell.

We watched them.

"Now **that**," said Teagan, after what felt like ages, "is what you call true love."

I thought about what Grandad said to me that day we caught a trout—about how the truth is different for different people. But **this** truth, I decided, it was the same for all of us.

Acknowledgments

This book has been a long time in the writing. So long, in fact, that my own little big man—my son, Fergus—was nine when I started and is now nearly a teenager. I want to thank him for reminding me of the wonderful faith and optimism that children possess and for being my first port of call when it came to making Zac's voice authentic. (**Nobody really says "sick" when they mean "good" anymore, Mum . . .**)

This is my first book for Berkley and my first outing as an author in America, and I can honestly say this has been the most exciting and fulfilling few months of my working life. You would think that bagging one incredible agent in the UK would be luck enough, but Grainne Fox, my agent in America, has proved herself to be equally genius. Grainne (and Lizzy), I can't thank you enough for believing in and "getting" **Little Big Love** and for doing such a smart and passionate pitch. It's no overestimation to say that your agenting has changed my life.

None of this would have happened, however, if Amanda Bergeron at Berkley had not loved it enough to buy it! Amanda—it's every writer's dream to be shown the enthusiasm and sheer love you and all the team at Berkley have shown for this book from the start. You're such a sensitive and intelligent editor, and it has been a total joy to work with you.

I also want to express my heartfelt gratitude to all the team behind this book at Berkley, including in no particular order (and I really hope I haven't left anyone out!) Jen Monroe, Claire Zion, Jeanne-Marie Hudson, Jin Yu, Craig Burke, Lauren Burnstein, and Roxanne Jones. Receiving an e-mail containing all your quotes about how much you enjoyed **Little Big Love** was a career highlight and I'm so grateful.

There are certain specific people outside of publishing who helped me with the research and writing of this book, and I want to thank them for their time and generosity: number one has to be Paul le Shone—or "Shonney"—without whom this book would definitely not be the book it became. In 2014, all I knew when I set off on a research trip to Grimsby in Lincolnshire, England, was that I wanted to write about an ex-fisherman character. I was hoping to find inspiration in Grimsby—it is the "fishing capital of Europe," after all—but thanks to Shonney, an ex-fisherman himself, I went home with a lot more than that: countless remarkable stories, almost all of which found their way into these pages, and a packet of the finest Grimsby haddock to boot!

I'm very lucky to have so many supportive friends (author and nonauthor), but I want to particularly thank Rosie Walsh, who has so generously championed this book from the start. (The way you've made me feel about it, Rosie, has been like a special, writerly gift—thank you.) Also, for research help, appreciation goes to Clare Mackintosh, Dorothy Maudson and Weelsby Academy, Jimmy Rice, Alistair Scott, Jason Murgatroyd, and Dr. Nonni Reed. Love and thanks as always to Louis, who is my first reader and general champion. And to my family—thank **you**!